MIDNIGHT LIES

A gripping detective mystery full of twists and turns

CHRIS COLLETT

DI Tom Mariner Book 9

Joffe Books, London
www.joffebooks.com

First published in Great Britain in 2022

This paperback edition was first published
in Great Britain in 2022

Cover art by Nick Castle

ISBN: 978-1-80405-192-4

PROLOGUE

It came on suddenly. One moment she was in her element, being dazzlingly witty with these sophisticated people twice her age and more, making them laugh, holding them rapt. In that moment she held the power and it was exhilarating. Until it wasn't. Those same faces, fixed on her with amusement and interest, began to ripple around the edges, their features becoming blurred and indistinct, and she felt a lurch as the muscles below her diaphragm constricted. The loud rock music that had seemed so cool started pounding uncomfortably in her ears.

'Oh God, I'm going to—' She turned away to find a bathroom, fast, but the floor suddenly sloped and furniture that had looked solid bent away from her as she stumbled forward. Panic welled up inside her, but just as she was about to go arse-over-elbow he was there at her side, a firm support, murmuring gently in her ear and guiding her away from her audience, along a hallway and into a shockingly bright bathroom. And while he held her hair out of her face, she threw up her guts.

'I'll take you home,' he soothed. And she didn't care that his gaze lingered on her breasts, or that his eyes were unnaturally bright. She just had to get away from here.

But he had business to take care of first, so he left her for a moment, leaning against the wall, trying to remain upright and garnering

1

curious glances. Through the press of bodies, she thought she saw a face she knew, but it was gone again before she could be sure. Then he was back. Out in the cool air, they took a wide berth round the aquamarine swimming pool and down the manicured lawn, where the bright lights and music faded, the sudden silence leaving her ears ringing. Lower down, the ground became bumpy and uneven so that she had to lean on him. As the darkness closed in, a nagging voice in her ear said this was a bad idea, but he was kind and she felt so ill and desperate to go that she let it happen. Anyway, the reek of vomit would surely be enough to deter him. Once or twice she stumbled but each time he was there to catch her, and half-carried her through the gate at the foot of the garden and onto the path through the woods, where the canopy of trees blotted out any remaining light. His torch lit the way but it suddenly went out.

'Bugger,' he said. He didn't sound too upset. He turned towards her and the sweet smell of alcohol on his breath made her want to retch again. By now the night air had begun to clear her head, so that when he grabbed at her she was ready for him. Aiming a clumsy knee at somewhere around his midriff she surprised him enough to make him lose his grasp and overbalance.

'Bitch!'

Wrenching herself away, she scrambled into the trees, driven by fear. Brambles clawed at her dress and limbs as she shoved her way through, ignoring the nettle-stings and scratches, on and on until the pain of heaving in air was too much. She stopped, gasping, and listened. The blood pumped in her ears. Nothing. He must have given up.

He came from nowhere, knocking her off her feet. They sprawled into the bracken, his hands pawing her as she struggled to roll away. She staggered to her feet, but before she could move, something warm slithered around her neck, gripping her tightly, squeezing hard. She fought to draw breath. Amid her terror she noticed the softness of his flesh.

* * *

DCI Ginny Reid loved her work. Cold cases weren't the sexiest in the service and she knew that many of her colleagues on the Norfolk force thought her job was tedious beyond belief and certainly not worth the resources invested. Most were of the opinion — though they never said it to her face — that the role should be restricted to retired officers or civilians. But Ginny loved the problem-solving, she loved the meticulous research, and she loved that she had the potential to answer questions that had gone unanswered for years, sometimes for decades. She didn't even mind that late one evening, when other people had their feet up in front of the TV, she was cooped up in a mortuary inspecting the sorry remains of a fellow human being. Because today looked like the rarest of days, when that potential was about to be fulfilled.

Most historic cases were not high priority in policing, so Ginny hadn't expected the consulting anthropologist's results so soon after the grisly find had been taken back to the lab, but Ted Whitehouse couldn't leave such a tantalising mystery unexplored, and he liked Ginny Reid.

Now, from the other side of the gurney where the meticulously cleaned bones had been arranged, Whitehouse confirmed what she'd suspected. 'These are the remains of a young woman, probably in her late teens.'

The atmosphere in the room thickened.

'It could be her, then?' said Ginny, her voice catching. This case had been on the books for so long, she couldn't quite believe they'd made a breakthrough at last.

Whitehouse held her gaze over his half-moon spectacles. 'It could,' he said eventually. 'The evidence from the site itself suggests the right approximate date. Of course, we will need to run more tests, DNA and so forth, but given the dating evidence, the proximity of the site to her disappearance, and the similarity in size, there's every reason to think that this is Robina Scanlon.'

'Any chance of a cause of death?' she asked.

'The fracture of the hyoid bone and the absence of any other obvious trauma, such as gunshot, would *suggest* strangulation — either manual or ligature, though we can't be one hundred per cent certain of that.'

Inside Reid seethed a maelstrom of emotions. Excitement was certainly there, triumph, even. A breakthrough like this was a rare thing. But both were tempered with a desperate sadness that this young woman's life had ended so abruptly, and almost certainly, with violence, and that she had lain too long in the ground undiscovered. Now all she, and what was laughably called her 'team', had to do was try to determine exactly how and why she had died, and at whose hand. It would really be something if she could give the surviving family members some closure.

On a bench to one side, bagged up, were the meagre exhibits recovered from Robina and the deposition site — one large and several smaller scraps of blackened and rotting fabric and a bag containing a pair of once-white block-heeled sandals.

'The dress is the most informative item of clothing,' said Whitehouse, drawing Reid's attention to the largest of the bags. 'It's flimsy so would be consistent with the date Robina disappeared, high summer, and it has been quite badly torn, just here, on the shoulder. It suggests a possible scenario.'

'Her underwear?' asked Reid, looking at the smaller bags.

'Intact, as far as I can ascertain,' said Whitehouse.

'Will we be able to get anything from it? Fibres, fluids, that kind of thing?'

'That will be for our friends at the forensic service. Given how long she's been in the ground, I'd temper your expectations. However,' Whitehouse went on, 'I have positive news about this.' He picked up a bag which contained a soil-encrusted silver bangle. 'This was still on her wrist. There's a clear fingerprint on the inside. It's made by a greasy substance, to which the soil had adhered. Sun cream, perhaps? The print may well turn out to be Robina's, but it might be worth running it through the database. If we're really lucky, there may be residual traces of DNA too.'

Ginny wasn't optimistic that the print would deliver up much, but if they did, by some miracle, identify a suspect or suspects, it might prove invaluable. Meanwhile, with this level of certainty, they could begin the laborious task of reviewing the old case material and tracing witnesses. It could be days — weeks, even — before they uncovered anything useful. But there she miscalculated. Less than twenty-four hours later, DC Scott Sinclair brought her a witness statement.

'Whoever wrote this, he was close to the victim. And it's possible he's one of us,' he said.

'What on earth makes you say that?'

'The name rang a bell. That course I did last November? I felt sure I saw it on the delegates list.'

'You remembered it?'

'Same name as one of our best ever centre forwards, so it stuck. Anyway, I checked last night, and I was right. I know it's a long shot but it's worth a punt, isn't it?'

'I suppose so,' said Reid. She smiled. 'Supporting Ipswich Town has some compensations, after all.'

CHAPTER ONE

DCI Tom Mariner began Sunday afternoon feeling virtuous and buoyant. He'd had a productive Saturday, fixing a broken cupboard door and clearing the sluggish shower drainage, before visiting his ward Jamie at the residential care home for adults with autism spectrum disorder. He'd even found time for a quick lunchtime pint with Tony Knox. Since his old sergeant had joined ROCU — the Regional Organised Crime Unit — they had to snatch the opportunities where they could, and lately these were few and far between.

And then this morning at 8 a.m., when he was barely awake, Suzy had called him from Beijing. As usual it was a frustratingly broken call thanks to her poor Wi-Fi, but the gist of it was that she would be returning to the country a little earlier than expected, in three weeks' time. For Mariner it was a tempered relief, after months of internal speculation. Suzy had loved being in her parents' homeland, and had found her research work stimulating, but she'd also talked with enthusiasm about a particular male colleague. Although her eighteen-month tenure at the university was coming to an end, Mariner thought for a while that she might stay on. But her mum wasn't in the best of health, and now she really wanted to come home, so she had booked her flight. She sounded happy about returning — perhaps he'd been reading too much into things.

It felt like a cause for celebration, so in the afternoon he strolled along the canal into Birmingham city centre to visit a couple of his favourite hostelries. As usual at the weekend, the runners and dog walkers were out in force. The sun had finally broken through after a bitterly cold few days of heavy frosts and freezing fog, which, in some parts of the country had failed to disperse. And in addition to the regular trains passing by, there seemed to be non-stop air traffic overhead: planes diverted to Birmingham International from the fog-bound capital.

Until recently Mariner would have walked home from the pub too, but he was starting to get those little reminders — in this case, from his knees — that he was no longer as fit as he used to be. Instead, he made his way to the nearest bus stop. He didn't have long to wait. He showed his warrant card in lieu of a travelcard, and climbed the stairs. The pleasure of a ride on the top deck had stayed with him since childhood — the perspective from up here often turned up the unexpected.

For the first few stops, he was on his own, until, at the indoor arena, a middle-aged man with a young child came up and took up one of the front seats. When Mariner next looked around, a handful of people had joined them, including a youth in his late teens, who threw his backpack unceremoniously onto the seat and flopped down next to it, all the time conducting a loud and expletive-peppered conversation on his phone. Blocking it out, Mariner returned to gazing out of the window. Raised voices interrupted his thoughts and he became aware of an altercation between the young man and the older one at the front of the bus. The older man was asking the other to quieten down. 'Or if you can't, at least tone down your language.'

In response the young man turned away and continued his expletive-ridden conversation even more loudly. The bus was approaching a stop and as it braked the older man rose from his seat and moved forward. 'I'm talking to you,' he said, grabbing the lad's arm and wrenching the phone away from his ear. 'There are other passengers on this bus and not all of them want to hear what comes out of your filthy mouth.'

The lad stood and squared up to him. 'Fuck off, Granddad. I got as much right to be on this bus as you.'

Mariner braced himself. The privilege of free travel on public transport for police officers carries the responsibility to intervene to enforce the law, if required. But before he could move, things escalated. As the bus jerked to a halt, the lad lunged towards the man, who clutched his side and fell to his knees as crimson fluid seeped through his fingers. Grabbing his bag, with a giant bound over his seat and into the central aisle, the young man swung on the stair post and careered down the stairs.

'Call an ambulance!' Mariner shouted to the other passengers and, leaping up, ran after the lad. Unaware of the drama unfolding above him, the driver had stopped the bus and opened the doors for new passengers to embark, giving the young man a clear exit. Shoving his way through, he jumped off the bus and went running along the road and into a side street, with Mariner in pursuit, swearing under his breath. *Christ,* he thought, *I'm too old for this.* The kid had ten or more metres on Mariner but lost time fumbling to try, unsuccessfully, to shoulder his backpack. As Mariner pounced, the lad swung round and swiped at him.

Mariner gave chase along one street and into another. A warren of flats and maisonettes surrounded them. He was gaining ground. Finally, his quarry ran into a garage bay at the back of a block of maisonettes. At the far end, a skip was set against a three-metre wall topped with shards of broken glass. He was cornered, backpack in one hand, knife in the other, keeping Mariner at bay. Their breath steamed in the frigid air. Then, without warning, the lad whipped round and ran at the skip, and with the agility of a free runner, vaulted up the side and launched himself onto the garage roofs towards freedom. Mariner sprang forward and made a last desperate grab for the boy's ankle, getting only a fist of fresh air.

Hurling his bag up ahead of him, the young man scrambled up the half-pitched roof of the garages, but as he did, the bag began to roll down the corrugated iron towards the skip. Twisting round, he tried to seize it before it fell and as he did so, his foot skidded down the slick metal grooves. He scrabbled for purchase on the guttering, but with a loud crack it sagged and broke away. His trajectory broken, he lost his balance, and flailed in mid-air.

The knife spun from his hand, narrowly missing Mariner, and clattered to the ground and — it seemed to Mariner, in painfully slow motion — the boy toppled backwards. His head struck the corner of the skip with a sickening *thunk* and he collapsed in a crumpled heap on the wet tarmac and lay still. The backpack thudded to the ground behind the skip.

'Jesus.' Mariner dropped to his knees, his heart going like a steam hammer from the exertion. The boy's breathing was shallow and his pulse weak, but they were there nonetheless and Mariner placed him in the recovery position as he wrangled his phone out of his pocket and called for help. As the boy's head lolled, he averted his eyes from the splinter of white bone poking through organic matter. The blank windows of the surrounding flats stared down at the dismal scene.

The ambulance and a squad car arrived simultaneously, ten minutes later, by which time Mariner's breathing and heart rate had returned to normal. He identified himself with his warrant card and talked the medics through what had happened, as they immediately set to work.

'I'm Stacey and this is Dan,' said the young woman, without taking her eyes off the casualty. She knelt down beside him, oblivious to the wet surface. 'Do you know his name?'

'Dean Clifford,' said Mariner. 'At least that's what his wallet says.' He'd found it sticking out of the lad's jeans pocket.

'That'll need attention too,' said Dan. It was only then that Mariner became aware of the warm blood trickling down his wrist from a gash on the back of his hand.

'Looks worse than it is,' said Mariner.

He left them to their work on Dean Clifford and went to talk to the uniformed constable who was waiting patiently beside a patrol car, making the occasional response into his radio, which crackled intermittently with conversations taking place elsewhere.

'You all right, sir?' the constable asked, as Mariner approached.

Mariner nodded. He didn't know if he'd been recognised or if the 'sir' was the usual member-of-the-public courtesy. He indicated Dean Clifford. 'He's not doing so well, though.'

They watched for a moment as the paramedics, talking all the time to the young man, checked his vital signs, attaching oxygen and intravenous drips. 'These were in his pockets,' said Mariner. 'I took the liberty . . .'

He held out the wallet and phone he'd carefully retrieved in his handkerchief. 'You know about the incident on the bus, on the Pershore Road, Constable . . . ?'

'Constable Briggs, sir. My colleagues are attending.' He tapped his radio.

'Do you know what's happening up there? I saw the old man collapse, but then I was chasing this one.'

Briggs nodded. 'Scene's a mess. A lot of blood, apparently. Still waiting to hear from the hospital about the victim. And this is the assailant?' He gestured towards the prone form now obscured by the two paramedics.

'Yes. Over there's the weapon.' Mariner pointed to where the knife lay. 'And somewhere in that corner, behind the skip, is the rucksack he was carrying.'

Briggs leaned into his vehicle, and emerged gloved and with evidence bags and a clear plastic tube. After bagging the phone and wallet, he picked up the knife and placed it in the tube, then walked to the skip. After several seconds of scuffling and grunting he re-emerged, manipulating the backpack into a big Keepsafe bag. Whether the man on the bus lived or died, all of these objects would be important evidence.

'And can I have your name and address, sir?'

Mariner gave his name, which the constable wrote down without any apparent recognition, and took out his warrant card for the third time that afternoon. 'And a number is all you'll need for now.' The constable's eyes widened and he seemed suddenly less sure of himself.

'Right, sir. I'll need you to make a more detailed statement later, but can you tell me exactly what happened?'

Mariner summarised the events as concisely and accurately as he could. Perhaps he had underestimated the extent of his own injury. He was feeling a bit lightheaded. Or maybe that was just the after-effects of the uncharacteristic sprint.

'And he just fell?' the constable clarified.

'He let go of his backpack and it rolled down the roof. He turned to grab it, lost his balance and fell. He hit his head on the corner of the skip there.'

The constable looked up, suddenly awkward. 'Have you been drinking, sir?'

'That's why I was on the bus,' said Mariner.

'How much?'

'Three pints, over the course of the afternoon.' Mariner held his gaze, challenging him to make something of it. 'And yes, when you get back to base, you're going to need to contact the IOPC.' Dean Clifford was in a serious condition. He might even die. The Independent Office for Police Conduct would have to ensure that nothing Mariner had done precipitated either eventuality.

By now, the unconscious Dean Clifford was being stretchered into the ambulance, his head heavily dressed and secured with a neck brace, and IV drips inserted into both arms. The crew's priority was to get him to hospital as quickly as possible, and they were preparing to leave. Stacey came over to tell them as much.

'You want a lift?' she asked Mariner, looking again at his hand. The bleeding had stopped now, and it looked little more than a scratch.

'It's nothing, really,' he said. 'I'll get myself up to A & E, but thanks.'

'Make sure you do,' she said, jumping in beside Dean Clifford. 'And if you haven't had one recently, get a tetanus shot.' Her colleague shut the doors and they left soon after, blue light flashing.

Briggs drove Mariner to Balsall Heath operational command unit where the first-aider dressed his hand and he gave his statement, in as much detail as he could. As an additional precaution he submitted his clothing for forensic examination. The officer who sat with him was sympathetic, making sure he was comfortable. He'd be thinking, *There but for the grace of God*... His verdict when he'd read through Mariner's statement seemed to be that it sounded like a nasty accident.

'Any news on how Dean Clifford's doing?' Mariner asked before he left.

The constable went to find out. 'Undergoing surgery,' he said, on his return. 'Touch-and-go at the moment.'

'And the man he attacked?'

'Nasty injuries but not life-threatening.'

Mariner hoped for Dean Clifford's sake that he would pull through — of course he did. But he couldn't help thinking that if the worst happened, it would make things a lot less straightforward for him too.

By the time a taxi dropped Mariner off at home later that evening, he had started to come down from the adrenalin surge. His hand was throbbing and his head was offering strong competition. He lasted until the middle of the evening, then took some painkillers and was out cold within minutes of his head hitting the pillow. Just a few hours later he was rudely awoken again, by the jangling of his mobile.

It was coming up to 3 a.m., the dark dead of night. The caller was Clive Berry, an officer from Traffic. Berry was outside somewhere, and barely audible at times, the wind rasping across his phone and with a backing track of unidentifiable noises, punctuated by the odd shout.

'Sorry to disturb you, Tom,' he said, almost yelling to make himself heard. 'I'm at a road traffic collision on the outbound A38 Rubery bypass. We've got a vehicle in the ditch at the side of the road.'

Mariner pinched the bridge of his nose in an effort to clear his head. It felt as if someone had taken a sledgehammer to it while he was sleeping. 'Fatalities?' he asked, wondering exactly how this concerned CID.

'The driver, an elderly man. No cause of death yet.'

'I'm sorry to hear that,' said Mariner.

'Thing is, Tom, there's a complication,' added Berry.

Another one? 'What kind of complication?'

'Can you get down here, smartish? I think you'll want to see for yourself, before we lock down the scene.'

Mariner felt like crap and seriously considered for a moment delegating to someone else, like DS Vicky Jesson, but she had family responsibilities. Time enough for her to get involved. And it might be nothing anyway, though Berry was an experienced officer.

Throwing on the first clothes that came to hand, and with a quick slug of orange juice, Mariner jumped in his car. The rain had subsided, leaving a fresh, breezy night with a clear star-speckled sky. Traffic was sparse and it took him a mere ten minutes at that hour to make the three-mile journey from his canal-side home to the outer suburb of Rubery — the last stop before the open countryside of Worcestershire. The road had been coned off and further blocked by a squad car parked at an angle across the road. The absence of any oncoming traffic told him that both sides of the carriageway were shut. This was the main access route from the south of the city to the motorway network — commuters would be thrilled when they tried to get into work later in the morning.

Once through the cordon Mariner drove on another mile before he rounded a bend and saw the mass of flickering blue lights: three police vehicles, two fire tenders and two ambulances. He parked some way back and walked down. The sharp atmosphere amplified sound and even at this hour Mariner could hear the background hum of traffic on the M5, half a mile away. It was hard to make out at first what had gone on here, and it was only when he had woven through the gaps between the vehicles that he finally saw the dark estate car, a VW Passat, off the road and on the verge, its nose crumpled against a tree and tailgate up in the air. Arc lights cast an eerie glow over everything, and to one side a tent was being prepared to protect the immediate scene from the elements until a thorough forensic search could be conducted at first light. With nothing more to do at the scene, the ambulance crew were preparing to leave, but the traffic officers were standing around waiting for something. Turned out it was for him. Clive Berry emerged from the huddle.

'Tom. Thanks for coming down.'

Once he was gloved and suited, they ducked under the inner cordon and Berry led Mariner to the front of the car. The driver, an older man with a full head of grey-white hair, sat back in the seat, his eyes closed, the only mark on him a dark circle on his forehead where a bruise had formed. The airbag had done its work and now hung deflated from the steering wheel, like an upside-down version of Munch's *The Scream*.

Berry held out a plastic evidence bag containing the VW logbook and a driving license. 'We recovered these from the glove compartment. He's a Viktor Paszek, address in Cofton Hackett.'

'And the complication?' asked Mariner.

'Round here.'

Mariner followed Berry to the rear of the Passat and the open boot. Inside, the rear passenger seat of the car had been folded forward to create a larger space, and when he shone his torch in, Mariner could see that much of it was taken up with what looked like a giant woven nylon bag, the sort builders used for moving sand or gravel. The impact had pushed it against the front seats. The smell of creosote was strong and when Mariner picked up one of the pellets that littered the floor around the bag, he found it was a bark chipping, of the kind used to prevent garden weeds growing through. To one side of the bag, a gallon-capacity plastic bottle had tipped over on impact but remained sealed.

'Antibacterial floor cleaner,' said Berry. 'And you don't notice it so much now, but there was another odd smell in the car, so I checked this out. I assumed — as was no doubt the intention — that it was a big sack of bark chippings. But then I shone my torch in.'

With the car sloping away from them, Berry had to reach in, and with his night stick, carefully eased down the side of the bag nearest to them, as far as it would go. More chippings dropped out, revealing that they'd been arranged to conceal something underneath. In the glare of the torchlight, it took Mariner a few seconds to work out what it was that he was looking at. To begin with it looked like black fur, but then he realised that the pale fleshy thing was an ear. He was looking at the side of a human head. He craned into the car as far as he could and saw that the ear was framed by jet black hair, some of it matted with blood, and below this was the curve of an almost translucent jawline.

'What the hell's going on here?' said Mariner, more to himself than anyone else.

'Your guess is as good as mine,' said Berry. 'If there's an innocent explanation for this, then I'm buggered if I can come up with it. I think we can safely assume that this one's coming your way.' He was right — this was no longer a simple RTC, it was a crime scene.

'Who phoned it in?' asked Mariner, straightening up.

'Lorry driver on his way down to Taunton, on a tight schedule so didn't want to hang about. Obviously, he hasn't been checked out yet, but he left full details. It's a puzzler.' Berry's assessment was spot on. 'The post-mortems and forensic examination of the car will turn up more information.'

'Given the circumstances, we're looking at two forensic PMs,' said Mariner. He took out his phone. 'The super will be delighted. I'll get the SOCOs down here. What time does it get light now? About six, half-six?'

'That's about it,' said Berry. 'We'll make sure the road closure's flagged up for the rest of the morning. It'll give our guys time to run a reconstruction to try to determine the cause of the accident.'

'Thanks,' said Mariner. 'I've got some phone calls to make.'

CHAPTER TWO

Vicky Jesson had retreated from the regular Monday morning chaos of trying to get two of her three kids ready for school and out of the door; had plumped instead for making herself look presentable enough to face the world. She was listening to Emily and Maisie bickering as usual and wondering if she should break it up when the doorbell rang.

'Can somebody get that?' she yelled from her bedroom. No one did and the bickering went on uninterrupted. Manipulating her hair into an elastic band, she hurried down the stairs.

'S'all right, Mum, I'll get it.' Emily had appeared from nowhere, miraculously wearing her coat, school bag slung over one shoulder. She opened the door just a crack, forcing Jesson to peer round her to see who it was. 'Mum!' Emily protested, blocking her view. But Jesson had seen enough to recognise Jayden.

'Hi, Mrs Jesson,' he called.

'Hello, Jayden.'

Emily rolled her eyes at her mum.

'Are you off, then?' Jesson asked.

'What about Maisie?' Jayden asked.

'Not ready,' said Emily, all set to close the door. 'Too bad.'

'Yes, I am!' Maisie appeared, struggling breathlessly into her coat. Jesson snatched a kiss as her younger daughter flashed past and with quick goodbyes, the three of them were on their way down the drive. And not yet eight-thirty. Wonders never ceased.

'I'll see you outside school at seven tonight,' Jesson called after Emily.

'I *know*!' came the exasperated response. Parents' evening was never something Emily wanted to be reminded of. But then Jesson wasn't exactly looking forward to it either.

Before closing the door, Jesson watched them for a few moments as they strolled off down the road, Jayden playfully teasing Maisie about something. He was so good with her.

In fact, thank the Lord for Jayden Starr. Emily continued to insist that he and she were 'friends, that's all', and just as well when she was only fourteen years old. There would be plenty of time for the friendship to blossom into something more — or not, as the case may be. Meanwhile, Jesson determined to make hay while the sun shone and enjoy the fact that her older daughter, in the last weeks at least, was a changed girl around her new friend.

While Aaron and Maisie caused her no trouble at all, it was always Emily who got into scrapes. When she was little, she'd fallen off swings, off her bike, into a duck pond. She had graduated to forgetting homework, talking back in class, losing her dinner card. The fact that her siblings seemed to manage without any such dramas only made it worse. While Jesson found it easy to lavish praise on the other two, it seemed that whenever she spoke to Emily, it was to tell her off — naturally, that didn't go unnoticed. And when she tried to redress the balance, Emily inevitably sabotaged her efforts. 'Middle-child syndrome,' one of Jesson's friends had told her, and when she had looked it up, she found an almost word-perfect description of her relationship with Emily.

But lately Emily was mellowing, and the reason was obvious. Jayden had become a regular visitor to their house, and, albeit based on fleeting exchanges as he was on his way out of the front door, Jesson had got the impression of a mature and polite young man.

Driving into work, Jesson wondered anew at the resilience of her kids. She'd felt guilty and selfish when she'd uprooted them to move to Kings Heath, to be nearer to their grandparents and allow her a shorter commute to work, and the move hadn't been without its challenges. Aaron had been fine — his easy-going nature meant he got on with anyone, and he soon made new friends. And Maisie would have been moving up to secondary anyway, and was still at an age when friendships ebbed and flowed from one day to the next, so she'd coped well. But fourteen was never a good age to swap schools and, playing exactly to type, Emily had protested all the way. In the end Jesson had succumbed to old-fashioned bribery and bought her the new iPhone she was so desperate to have, to help her stay in touch with the girls she'd left behind.

Truth be told, Jesson wasn't particularly sorry to see the back of Emily's friendship group from the old school. They hadn't always been the most supportive. And she was proud of Emily. After a rocky start, she had buckled down. Jayden appearing on the scene, another newbie not long after Emily had joined the class, was an added reward — for them both. His influence was a welcome addition at this crucial time in Emily's education. *And now,* Jesson thought, swinging into the compound at Granville Lane police station, *it takes me only fifteen minutes to get to work instead of fifty.*

Jesson's upbeat mood was short-lived. As she approached the main entrance, a man emerged from the building. He paused for a moment at the top of the steps, patted down his pockets until he found cigarettes and lighter, then bent his head to light up. And at that familiar gesture, Jesson's skin crawled.

She watched, mesmerised, as he descended the steps and walked away down the street without a glance in her direction. Was it him or had she been mistaken? A while back, when it was physically impossible, it seemed that she saw his face everywhere. But that hadn't happened in a very long time. So why now? Unless it really had been him.

But what would he have been doing here? She stopped off in reception to speak to the duty officer.

'That man who just left here?' she asked.

'Michael Corbett. Daily parole sign-in.'

Shit. 'Why here?'

'Now that Kingsmead's closed, we're his nearest station. He's been coming along since January.'

'Really?' And it wasn't until today that she'd seen him.

She wasn't usually this troubled by the criminals she'd arrested, but Corbett was particularly unpleasant — a computer hacker who had a thing for underage girls. It was a lethal combination, the appalling consequences of which had been narrowly averted more than two years ago, when Vicky and a colleague had arrested him. The oily toad would have no trouble fooling a parole board; she shouldn't be surprised to learn that he'd been released early. Still, the thought that he was coming to her station regularly filled her with unease.

* * *

Mariner leaned back in his chair and yawned, long and loud. It felt to him like the middle of the day. When no more could be learned at the scene of the accident, he'd gone home for a quick shower, a bite to eat and change of clothes, and was now at his desk in Granville Lane before the cleaners had finished their shift.

He called SOCO first and was pleased to get hold of Carina Woodward. With her at the helm, he could rely on the scene being processed quickly and efficiently, and she wouldn't want him breathing down her neck while she worked. When the SOCOs had done their work, the bodies could be bagged and tagged and sent to the specialist mortuary attached to the Queen Elizabeth hospital.

Until they had the identity of the second individual and knew more about how he or she had died, there was a limit on what could be done there, but a priority would be to locate and notify Viktor Paszek's next of kin. As soon as it was decent to do so, Mariner contacted the CPS to get the wheels in motion for a search warrant for Paszek's property. There was no certainty yet that a crime had been committed, or that Paszek was responsible, but why else would there be a concealed body in the boot of his car? And Mariner wanted no unnecessary delays.

Mariner then phoned the QE hospital where Dean Clifford had been taken, and learned that he remained in a critical condition.

He was finishing that call when Superintendent Davina Sharp knocked on his office door and came in. She was, as always, immaculately turned out in a navy business suit and crisp white blouse. She looked the polar opposite of how Mariner felt.

'You haven't slept well,' she observed.

'It was an eventful day yesterday,' said Mariner.

'So I hear. I've had the IOPC on the phone this morning.'

'That was quick. Did they give anything away?'

'Only that the family of the young man—'

'Dean Clifford.'

'Dean Clifford . . . The family have made a complaint.'

'Already? About what?' They'd have only learned of the incident a few hours ago.

'A matter of principle, perhaps. It means we won't be able to keep the inquiry in-house. It'll have to be independent, and I'm sure the IOPC will want to expedite it. There's been a lot of criticism of late that these investigations are taking too long. And if it's as straightforward as it sounds, this is one they can process quickly.'

'Suits me,' said Mariner. 'The sooner it's done, the better. I understand it's touch-and-go with Clifford.'

'Want to tell me what happened?'

Mariner went over it again, briefly. 'What do you want me to do?' he asked, knowing there was a chance that he could be suspended, pending the investigation.

'There's no question in my mind that this was an unfortunate accident,' Sharp said. 'The IOPC don't seem to think at this stage that there's any reason you can't continue to do your job. But I'd understand if you want to take a few days. God knows, you've got enough leave owing.'

'I'll think about that.'

'I'd suggest you contact your Fed rep, too,' said Sharp. 'Let him know what's coming down the line. And this RTC?'

'Is an interesting one. I'm expecting an update from Carina, any time.'

As he spoke the phone on his desk rang.

'I'll let you get on,' said Sharp.

And the day was yet to begin.

* * *

An hour later, Mariner faced his eager team, armed with a handful of images emailed through by SOCO, his hand still conspicuously bandaged.

'Cut myself shaving,' he said, in answer to the quizzical looks.

Over time they had gelled into a formidable crew, combining substantial expertise with youthful and — if he counted himself and Charlie Glover — not so youthful experience. DC Kevin Bingley was the newest recruit. Having joined them on loan from uniform, he'd shown an aptitude for the work and had chosen to make the full transfer soon afterwards. DC Charlie Glover and DS Vicky Jesson were old hands, with forty years' service between them, and DC Millie Khatoon sat somewhere in the middle — she was back to work full time now after maternity leave.

Mariner gave them the same brief summary of the previous afternoon as he'd given Sharp. 'Obviously I will cooperate fully with the IOPC. But life goes on,' he concluded. 'What's more important for us is what came up on our patch during the night.' He pinned a couple of photographs to the board.

Glover was the first to speak. 'What is it, boss?' Older than Mariner by several years, Glover was a traditionalist in every sense, from his haircut and clothing to his approach to policing.

'It's an odd one, to be honest,' Mariner said. 'On the face of it, a straightforward RTC. A VW Passat estate was found in a ditch off the Rubery bypass in the early hours of this morning. No other vehicles involved.' He described the scene as he'd seen it on arrival, drawing attention to the second photograph of the car.

'That's why it was a nightmare getting in this morning,' said Khatoon, with feeling.

'Vehicle documentation has identified the driver of the Passat as a white male—' Mariner tapped the blown-up driving license photo — 'Viktor Paszek, aged seventy-seven, with a local address at Briar Lane, Cofton Hackett, off the Barnt Green Road.'

'Sorry, why does this concern us?' asked Jesson.

'That was my first question too. This is why.' He added a photograph of the builders' bag, and talked them through what had been discovered in the boot. 'No cause of death for either of the fatalities as yet. There appeared to be blood in the hair of the hidden individual, and along with the fact that he or she had been deliberately concealed, I'd say we're looking at something sinister. I understand that both bodies have now been removed, and are on their way to the mortuary, and I'm sure Stuart Croghan will let us know when he's about to proceed with the examinations.'

'What's the connection between them?' asked Glover.

'That's what we'll have to establish,' said Mariner. 'The only thing we have at the moment is that they were both in Paszek's car. There is, of course, a slim possibility that there isn't a connection. Paszek's car could have been used as a dumping ground for the body without his knowledge. But as I say, it's remote. Our first tasks are to ascertain the identity of this second person, and find out as much about him or her and Paszek as we can. Traffic are working to determine

23

the cause of the accident, and have put out an appeal for witnesses.'

'Who called it in?' asked Jesson.

'HGV driver, so we need to contact him and get a statement. Control room will have his details. And we should request the audio file of the call. Charlie, both jobs for you, I think?'

'Right, boss.'

'To begin with we'll work from what we know,' said Mariner. 'So far, we have an address for Paszek but no next of kin, so that's a priority, along with getting a formal identification. Millie, you and Kevin go down to his address. We're on the lookout for relatives, neighbours, friends and anyone else who knew him. Start gathering intel to help us build a picture of the man. See if you can find out what these are for, too.' He held up a bunch of half a dozen keys of varying size and shape. 'I've applied for a search warrant, should we need it.'

'Do we mention his passenger?' asked Khatoon.

Mariner considered for a moment. 'It's enough to say that there was another person simply "in the car" with Paszek. No more detail at this point.' He turned to Glover. 'Charlie, can you be nominal on this and collate the evidence as it comes in? We'll see what turns up before appointing a separate doc reader. Vicky, I'd like you to take exhibits.' Mariner's mobile pinged. 'Stuart Croghan's ready to go,' he said to Jesson. 'We'll get down there.'

* * *

'Are you all right, boss? It was quite a day you had yesterday,' Jesson said, as she and Mariner drove in towards the city centre.

'I'm fine, really,' said Mariner, before deftly changing the subject. 'Have you thought any more about what I said?'

'I've thought about it, yes,' said Jesson, gazing fixedly out of the window, 'in the same way that I've thought about going blonde. I just haven't made up my mind yet.'

'OK . . .'

'I'm not sure if the time is right,' she went on. 'You think that the kids won't need you so much as they get older, but actually the reverse is true. I don't want to take my eye off the ball now that they're teenagers.'

'The pay rise would be useful though, wouldn't it?'

'I'm not going to argue with that, but . . .'

'But.' Mariner let it go. He was well aware of Jesson's commitment to her family. As a single mum she had little leeway. But he also knew that self-confidence wasn't her strong point and that sometimes she needed a bit of a nudge. 'Just for the record,' he added, unable to resist, 'the time is rarely right. It's always going to be daunting to take a step up. But you've done way more than your two years as a sergeant — you're practically taking on an inspector's responsibilities already. And you're not—'

'What? Getting any younger?'

'No! I wasn't going to say that. Well, all right, I suppose I was, in not so many words. But it's true. You're bloody good at this and you could go all the way, but you need to move on before you get too comfortably stuck in a rut, like Charlie.'

'Charlie likes his rut.'

'That's exactly my point. It's fine for Charlie. It suits him, and we'll always need workhorses like him. But we also need strategic thinkers, people who can be creative and take the initiative.' Mariner sighed. 'I'm only nagging you because Sharp keeps on at me.'

She wasn't expecting that. 'Sharp talks about me?'

'I think she sees you as a potential successor. If you stay on this patch. And,' he added, slyly, 'if you don't let the grass grow . . .'

'Wow.'

'You must have had some idea.'

'She's always been encouraging, but I thought that's how she was with everyone.'

'That's true. Her style is more carrot than stick, but she focuses her energies on a select few. And you're one of them.'

'Wow,' she said again. It gave her something to think about.

CHAPTER THREE

'I'll catch you up,' Khatoon told Bingley, as they headed out to Viktor Paszek's place. 'Just popping to the ladies'.'

'Okey-doke.'

By the time she got to the cubicles, the nausea had passed. She stood for a moment looking in the mirror, waiting to see if the feeling would come back, but it was gone.

Outside, she found Kev leaning against the passenger door of the car checking his phone, a picture of relaxation.

'Sorry,' she called. 'You all right to drive?'

'You sure?' said Bingley. 'It's your turn.'

'Yeah, it's OK, I'm feeling a bit iffy,' said Khatoon. 'Something I ate probably.'

'Right.' He gave her a lingering look.

As they pulled out of the car park, Khatoon said a silent prayer of thanks — not for the first time — that she'd landed such an easy-going partner. Kevin was always so affable. Sometimes it was hard to believe how tough he could be when the situation demanded it.

'It's a bugger for the boss,' he said, easing out into the traffic on the Bristol Road. 'That thing with Complaints.'

'He'll be all right,' Khatoon said confidently. 'Best thing we can do for him now is get on with our jobs.' She hoped that was true.

Viktor Paszek's house was in a row of three detached properties, tucked away a mile and a half along the narrow and winding Briar Lane, and surrounded by fields. They got to it by process of elimination, as Paszek's was the only house with no number displayed. His immediate neighbours had no fewer than three estate agents' boards planted next to the gates.

'They're keen to get away,' said Bingley, pulling up onto the narrow grass verge and hearing the light scratch of holly leaves on the bodywork. 'Think they know something?'

'We might need to go and ask,' said Khatoon. 'How's your move going?' Bingley and his partner Sasha had recently had an offer accepted on a house.

'Slowly,' said Bingley, as they got out of the car. 'We're still waiting for the couple at the top of the chain to find something that's to their liking. And they're fussy. Don't seem to appreciate that some of us might be in more of a hurry.'

'Your mum won't mind that, though, will she?' said Khatoon. When he said nothing, she turned to look at him. 'You have told her about all this?'

'I'm getting there,' said Bingley. 'We've touched on it a few times, sort of generally. But she must know it's coming. I spend practically every weekend at Sasha's flat now.'

'You have to tell her, Kev,' Khatoon admonished, 'or it'll come as such a shock for her. She likes Sasha, doesn't she?'

'She sees her as the daughter she never had.'

'Well, that's a start, but even so, it's going to be tough for her,' said Khatoon. 'She's got used to having you around these last few years.'

'She'll cope. We're not planning on moving that far away,' Bingley reminded her.

They passed through a pair of redundant gateposts and crunched onto the gravel drive, and into an illustration in a

Hans Christian Andersen story — the witch's house. Paszek's home burrowed down among tall, leafy evergreens that made it dark and sinister. The date stone above the front door said 1906 and it didn't look as if much maintenance had been done on it since. The paint on the wooden windowsills was blistered, and the roof, sporting clumps of green moss, gently sagged at one end and was missing a tile or four. A separate timber-clad garage stood at an angle to the house, and looked equally in need of attention. And that had to be an asbestos roof.

Khatoon rapped on the tarnished lion's head knocker in the centre of the front door, whose green paint was cracked and faded almost to grey. She tried twice more, but no one came. No light shone from behind the windows, and the greasy film made it difficult to pick out anything beyond.

'I'll have a look round the back,' Bingley called, as he disappeared from sight.

* * *

Bingley had to fight his way through rampant laurel bushes to get there, and as he rounded the corner of the house, a flock of birds at a well-stocked feeding station flew away, tweeting in alarm. He emerged into a wide garden, perhaps as much as half an acre. Down the centre was a lush green lawn, bordered by a proliferation of leafy shrubs in all shades of green and red, the new growth coming through bright and vibrant. Where the lawn ended there was a regimentally laid out vegetable patch, with sections of freshly turned soil and a row of canes, bound at the top to form pyramids waiting for runner beans to creep their way up. Bingley went down to the shed, which was unlocked, but all that was inside were shelves cluttered with gardening detritus.

Just above the line of poplars that marked the foot of the garden, thirty metres away, there were views south-west towards Droitwich, with the Malverns beyond.

'Hello!' called Bingley. 'Anyone here? Mrs Paszek?' But the peace was shattered by the sudden roar of a train, which passed along the line running by the bottom of the garden. As the sound faded, he became aware of another noise: the distant growl of farm machinery.

* * *

'Anything?' called Khatoon, coming round to join him and peering into the downstairs windows.

'Only a well-kept garden.'

'Let's try the neighbours. Only three places out here, and isolated, they must know each other.'

Khatoon took the middle house, leaving Bingley to carry on to the third. This house looked in much better condition than Paszek's, but was similarly uninhabited. Not unusual in the middle of a weekday morning. As she walked back to the lane, she heard Bingley talking to someone and seconds later he caught her up. 'Any luck?' she asked.

'Not exactly,' said Bingley. 'Young mother. She and her husband are renting, and only moved in about a month ago. They've said hello to Paszek, and he's taken it upon himself to put their bins back after the rubbish collection, but that's all.' He gestured up towards Paszek's house. 'Are we going in?'

'Yeah, let's get kitted out,' said Khatoon. 'We'll start with the garage. The sack had bark chippings in it, and you wouldn't keep them in the house.'

'Sounds like a plan,' said Bingley.

Wearing protective gloves, Khatoon tried each of the keys in turn and eventually found the right one. The garage door was swollen with damp, and dragged on the concrete base and across the gravel as Bingley pulled it back, rotten splinters breaking off as it moved.

The air inside was damp and earthy with undertones of engine oil and creosote. The only light came from an opaque and grimy side window, so Bingley got out his torch, and while Khatoon lingered in the doorway, he made a careful circuit of the space, sweeping for anything that stood out as unusual or concerning. An oil patch on the floor suggested that Paszek was in the habit of parking the VW in here, and the beam of light picked out an additional space at the back, which had been used as a workshop. The workbench and vice had a thick layer of old sawdust and wood-shavings, amongst which lay half-buried a spirit level and two screwdrivers. An untidy jumble of gardening and DIY tools were stacked against the walls, all liberally covered with dust and thick cobwebs, which didn't look as if they'd been disturbed in a long time. Bingley began lifting the corner of a tarpaulin that covered a sit-on lawn mower, but when a quantity of dirt and debris, and then a huge spider dropped off it and scuttled lightly across his hand, he dropped it again.

'Nothing in here looks overtly suspicious,' he called to Khatoon.

'Hm, let's see what turns up in the house,' she replied. 'If it comes to it, we can get some lighting in and do a proper search.'

'Hello, what's this?' Bingley stooped to pick up a crumpled ball of white polythene, its edges curly, where it had been ripped in two. He flattened it out. 'A bark chippings sack,' he said, pulling out an evidence bag.

Finding nothing else in the garage, they closed it up and went back to the house. Khatoon unlocked the door, but let Bingley go in ahead of her.

'Jeez,' he said, stepping over the threshold. 'It's colder in here than it is outside. Hello?' he called out. 'Anyone home?'

The surrounding trees let little light in, and the frigid air smelled of stale food. Khatoon flicked on the light and their hearts sank in unison. They'd stepped into a narrow reception hall with a quarry-tiled floor, which was piled thigh-high down one side with untidy stacks of plastic-wrapped magazines, topped by layers of junk mail. Bingley pulled a magazine from the pile. '*Sewing and Embroidery*, June 2015,' he read. He took a few steps forward and peered into the two downstairs rooms. 'Bloody Nora,' he said. 'It doesn't get much better. Viktor Paszek was a bit of a hoarder.'

Khatoon followed him in. The presence, underneath everything, of a sofa and TV seemed to designate the first room off the hall as a lounge, but it would be impossible to relax in this room. Almost all the floor space was crammed with solid, old-fashioned furniture, including an ancient cube-shaped TV, and every available surface overflowed with a miscellany of artefacts and papers. Stacks of newspapers and more magazines spoke of interests ranging from model trains to antique furniture. Almost everything bore a dense patina of dust. The only exception was a small card table, on which chess pieces were set up, apparently mid-game. Around the board were littered scraps of paper with scribbled columns of letters and numbers. The same notes appeared elsewhere, on windowsills, shelves and the mantelpiece.

'This is going to be a job and a half,' said Bingley, coming to join her. 'Are we thinking bachelor?'

'With an interest in needlework? Widower or divorcee seems more likely,' said Khatoon, stepping forward. She'd spied a number of framed photographs on one of the shelves. Most were black-and-white shots, faded by time, but two were in colour: one was of a wedding, though not the traditional white wedding. It had been taken outside a registry office, of a younger Viktor Paszek and a woman wearing clothes fashionable in the seventies. Another was a portrait of the woman alone, in a formal pose, and taken on a different occasion. Khatoon picked her way through the clutter, rescued it and passed it to Bingley. 'She looks like the wife. No recent pictures though, so I'm thinking ex or late.'

'Shall we check out the rest of the house?' said Bingley. 'It might not be so bad.'

It was wishful thinking. The adjacent room that looked out over the back garden was much the same. They moved towards the kitchen, but Khatoon hesitated on the threshold.

'What is it?' said Bingley, almost bumping into her.

'Nothing. It's just . . . Do you mind doing in here? I'll go and have a poke around upstairs.'

'Sure. That bad, is it? You all right? You look a bit peaky.'

'Kevin, enough!'

'All right, all right,' Bingley raised his hands defensively, and turned back to his search.

Climbing the stairs, Khatoon was angry with herself for taking it out on him. She was behaving strangely, she knew that, but she just couldn't help it. Everything about this place made her feel on edge.

* * *

The kitchen was confirmation for Bingley that Paszek was a man living alone, and though marginally cleaner than the living rooms, it was an equally chaotic mess. The remains of congealing food were on a plate by the sink, along with three stubby beer bottles, and a check of the full pedal-bin turned up packaging for a number of ready meals for two, which in Bingley's book simply meant that Paszek had a normal appetite.

Crumbs crackled underfoot as he walked across the floor to inspect the kitchen cupboards. In the first, he found the shelves filled to the top with neat stacks of baked beans and pilchards. Another contained the same arrangement of jars of sauerkraut. The cooker was spattered with cooking oil and more crumbs, but the fridge was clean, with only milk, cheese, butter, some jars of various pickled commodities and some withered vegetables.

The drawers held the usual: cutlery; tea towels; spare bulbs; and one was a repository for miscellaneous items. But then he found what he was looking for: one half-filled with mail. Some of it was of the unsolicited kind — pizza delivery leaflets, Indian restaurants, charity appeals, local election pamphlets and such. But in between he found the occasional legitimate piece of correspondence: a couple of bills; a pension statement; and an MOT and servicing certificate for the Passat. This was more like it. He bagged them up to take away. To one side was a tray of old keys. Mostly they were unlabelled, but one had a crumpled tag attached by a piece of string with a faded 'G' printed on it. It would be tedious but they'd have to go through them all. Bingley could see nothing else in here that would help them, so he went upstairs to give Khatoon a hand.

* * *

Where the downstairs rooms were crammed to bursting, upstairs the main bedroom was more restrained, spartan even, with just a double bed, a wide standalone wardrobe and two chests of drawers.

'He was on his own,' said Khatoon, opening doors and drawers. 'No hairbrushes or make-up, and just his pyjamas under the pillow. But he kept her clothes.' She opened one of the wardrobe doors, to reveal a row of women's dresses and blouses. Heeled shoes in a variety of colours and styles were lined up underneath. But when she looked up, Bingley wasn't there.

'Hey, look at this!' he called from across the landing. Khatoon found him just outside the second bedroom. They could go no further as the whole of the room was taken up with a tabletop train layout. Even the door had been removed from its hinges and propped up on the landing to create more space. 'It's fantastic!'

It was impressive. Whole miniature communities had been created, complete with roads, parks and shops, with tiny people milling about, and all threaded through with multiple railway tracks, tunnels and stations. Before she could stop him, Bingley had ducked under one side and popped up in the middle of the board beside a control panel.

'Can I have a go?'

Khatoon rolled her eyes. Sometimes he was more of a toddler than her eighteen-month-old son. 'No! This is not what we're here for.' But he couldn't tear himself away from it yet, so she left him to it.

The bathroom presented further proof that no woman currently lived in the house, but the third and smallest bedroom had been preserved as a sewing room, with an old-fashioned treadle sewing machine, an ironing board and two shabby easy chairs, all of which had a dusty abandoned feel.

'Have you noticed a computer anywhere?' she asked when Bingley finally appeared again.

'I haven't even seen a flatscreen TV,' said Bingley. 'Maybe he didn't do technology.' It was a reasonable conclusion. 'So what now?'

'I need some air,' said Khatoon. 'Let's get outside for a minute and I'll phone the boss and let him know the state of play. Then I suppose we'd better get stuck in.'

CHAPTER FOUR

Mariner and Jesson's first port of call was the forensic service facility to the north of the city, where the VW Passat was being processed. It had been stripped down and the components moved to different areas of the workshop for closer examination. The lead technician took them round to show them what had been discovered so far.

'We've found a couple of external areas of damage not caused by the final impact that may be of interest.' He walked them over to one of the benches. 'This offside wing light cluster has got some old damage, which is spread down on to the bumper. As you can see, we've got a cracked headlight and smears of what we think is blood, which have gone for testing. Then the rear bumper, over here, is smashed along this section, with scuff marks and traces of something that looks like wood stain; what you'd use to treat fencing. He might have hit a fence at some point. The inside edges of the fractures in the composite are clean.'

'What about the interior?'

'Nothing out of the ordinary yet. Only the sort of traces we'd expect to find in any car, but we'll keep looking. The exhibits are all bagged up and ready for you to take. The most interesting are probably these.' He picked up a large evidence bag. 'A set of overalls that were in the boot under the bag. There's some staining on them — could be blood.'

Other bags contained documentation from the glove compartment, a miscellany of pens, old chewing-gum packs and tissues, along with larger items; a stained sheet of heavy-duty polythene and the bottle of cleaning fluid along with some new-looking cleaning cloths.

Mariner's phone pinged.

'Stuart Croghan's ready for us,' he said to Jesson.

But the journey to the south of the city was a frustrating one. A breakdown on the inner ring road had brought cross-city traffic to a standstill and it was an hour and a half before they pulled into the hospital campus. As they finally approached the entrance to the mortuary, Mariner's phone rang. 'I'll pick it up afterwards,' he said, switching it off and pocketing it.

Inside they put on protective clothing and went straight to the examination room, where Viktor Paszek lay on a steel gurney under the bright lights. Croghan had already begun the dissection.

'You look how I feel,' he said to Mariner, glancing up as they entered the room.

'It's these all-nighters,' said Mariner. 'I'm getting too old for it.'

'You and me both,' said Croghan, even though he was a good ten years younger. 'Busy weekend?'

'You could say that. What can you tell us?'

'First off, I can tell you that Mr Paszek died of myocardial infarction.'

'Heart attack?' said Jesson.

'Yes, and not at all surprising,' said Croghan. 'His arteries are in quite a state. Either that or a stroke were going to do for him sooner or later. We'll run the usual toxicology tests, but it's the kind of event that could have occurred at any time for any number of reasons. My guess is that, apart from the initial painful jolt, he wouldn't have known much about it.'

'So, the chances are that he lost control of the car, and skidded off the road,' said Mariner.

'That's a fair assumption, yes. Estimated time of death between midnight and 4 a.m.'

'It was called in just before three — and he was certainly dead by then.'

'Makes sense. Apart from the heart, he's not in bad shape and led a pretty active life. I would say he was a keen gardener. There's soil under his fingernails and ingrained in the fingertips. I've taken scrapings, so we'll find out if there's anything else in there.' He picked up Paszek's right hand to show them. 'Also, you can see some cuts and abrasions here, and he's scraped the knuckle of his thumb.'

'Anything else?'

'At some point in the past, it looks as if he might have broken his left femur.' Croghan pointed out a faint red scar running the length of the man's thigh. 'These are Mr Paszek's effects.' Each item was sealed in an evidence bag, and most appeared to contain items of clothing, and Paszek's shoes. 'Nothing remarkable that I could see.'

One bag contained a cheap old-style mobile phone. Mariner pressed the power button through the polythene and the screen came to life. 'Max might get something off this,' he said. 'And our second casualty?'

'Come with me.' Croghan led them through to an adjacent and almost identical room. In the centre was a broader steel table but the shape covered with a sheet did not resemble a human form.

'This chap is going to be trickier,' said Croghan. He removed the sheet to reveal the builders' bag, its four corner seams carefully cut, with the sides folded flat onto the table and covered with a sprinkling of bark chippings. In the centre of these was a human body in a kneeling position, face pressed to his knees and clothed in a thin, navy blue jacket and jeans. The side of the face that Mariner could see was lacerated and swollen, shades of black and purple.

'As you can see, we have a problem,' said Croghan.

'Rigor?' said Mariner.

'Unfortunately, we missed the window,' said Croghan. 'He must have been manipulated and placed in the bag before it set in, which would have been less than about four hours after he died. But now it has, so we have to wait until it passes to unfold him.'

'When will that be?' asked Mariner.

'Hard to tell. It can last up to seventy-two hours.'

'And it's definitely a *him*?'

'Oh yes. Due to the size of the body, I initially thought he was an adolescent,' said Croghan. 'But if you look under here, on the jawline, there's what looks like some well-established beard growth.' Mariner and Jesson leaned in and caught the metallic whiff of damaged flesh. 'From the hair texture, I'm thinking he may be of Southeast Asian ethnicity,' said Croghan. 'And as you can see, he's suffered some significant injuries.'

'Where's the other shoe?' asked Mariner, noticing the stockinged left foot. He turned and scanned the exhibits bench.

'Haven't found it yet,' said Croghan. 'It could be underneath him, of course. But if it isn't . . . It wasn't found in the car?'

'No. There's something not quite right about his position,' said Mariner, stepping around to the front of the gurney and crouching low for a different perspective. The man's right leg was at an odd angle and his right side seemed to have collapsed. 'He looks lopsided.'

'He is,' said Croghan. 'Together with the blood staining on the clothing it suggests some pretty serious damage, as if he's been struck multiple times with force.' He stepped back to allow Mariner and Jesson to see for themselves.

'He's taken a beating?' said Jesson.

'Something like that.'

'Delivered by Paszek?' asked Mariner. 'Given the relative sizes of the two men, it would have been savage.'

'Not necessarily. Apart from the abrasions I pointed out on Paszek's hands, his knuckles are clean. It doesn't look as if he's been in a punch-up recently. But Paszek would certainly have had little problem lifting and manipulating the body into the bag.'

Mariner surveyed the body thoughtfully. 'Is there any chance of a photo for ID purposes?'

'Not one that would be any good,' said Croghan. 'His face is a mess, even if I could get the correct angle. I'll get a better idea of his age when I do a full examination, which should confirm it. We've got his fingerprints and a blood sample has gone off to the lab for DNA profiling. Results should come through to you in the next day or two. But I won't be sending you away completely empty-handed. This was in his back pocket.' Croghan went over to the exhibits bench and picked up a small bag. It contained a soft cigarette pack, with two cigarettes remaining. The pack was branded *Sapa* and bore the bold black-and-white legend: *hút thuốc có thể làm hại sức khỏe của bạn.*

'Smoking can damage your health?' Mariner hazarded. 'Any idea what language that is?'

'Google Translate will tell us,' said Jesson. She took out her phone and typed in the words. 'Vietnamese. And you were right about the meaning. Cigarettes are bad news the world over.'

* * *

Khatoon and Bingley were taking a systematic approach to the deeper examination of Paszek's home, but it was going to be a long job. They'd found nothing useful upstairs, and Bingley had even looked in the loft, which was thankfully unboarded and empty. Which brought them back to the two downstairs living rooms. They'd begun by quartering them, identifying locations for other potential information sources and then began clearing spaces to get at them. The most likely locations for meaningful material were an old-style bureau-cum-writing desk, a chest of drawers and a dresser, along with numerous boxes simply stacked in the corners of the rooms. What was immediately obvious was that Viktor Paszek — and perhaps his wife before him — didn't believe in throwing much away. They'd already found bank statements and wage slips going back forty years.

'Lots of medical appointments for Mrs Irma Paszek here,' said Khatoon, starting on a new box. 'I wonder if she passed away after an illness. And opticians and doctors. God, some of this is ancient.'

'This is interesting,' said Bingley, suddenly.

'What is it?'

'I've got the buildings insurance bills here. These are for 2010. But some of the bills aren't for this place,' said Bingley. 'They're addressed here, but for a place on Hillfield Road.'

'It must be where they lived before they came here.'

'The ones for this place are here too, same dates. Perhaps he was a landlord. There'll be other evidence here somewhere if that's the case.' He took off his glasses and rubbed his eyes. The gesture made Khatoon feel suddenly weary.

'Let's knock it on the head for today,' she said. 'Start afresh in the morning.'

They gathered up the evidence they'd found. Before leaving, Khatoon tried next door again, but there was nothing doing. Driving away from the property, Khatoon suggested to Bingley that they take an alternative route to Granville Lane. They followed the lane under the railway bridge and found that on the other side, an expansive tract of land was being cleared and a giant board announced the creation of hundreds of new dwellings.

'This development must extend right up to the railway line behind Paszek's house,' said Khatoon. 'That's going to spoil the view.'

CHAPTER FIVE

As he and Jesson left the mortuary, Mariner turned his phone on again, and almost immediately it rang, though not before he'd noticed three more missed calls from Superintendent Sharp. The caller was Charlie Glover.

'How's it going, boss?' Glover sounded cheerful. 'Just wanted to give you the heads-up: the super is looking for you. She wants you back at Granville Lane pronto.'

'I've just seen the calls,' said Mariner. 'Any idea what's up?'

'Not a clue.'

Sharp had warned him that the IOPC would want to begin as soon as possible, but this was quick, even by their standards. Mariner hoped it wasn't budget problems either when they were embarking on a complex case potentially involving a foreign national.

'Well, we're on our way.'

* * *

Mariner walked along the corridor to Sharp's office half an hour later, to find the door closed, and when he knocked and entered, she wasn't alone. Not the budget, then. Seated in the two chairs in front of her desk were a man and a woman he'd never met before. No uniforms either, so the IOPC was still a possibility. The empty mugs on the desk were an indication of how long they'd been waiting for him.

'Tom, this is DCI Ginny Reid and DC Scott Sinclair,' said Sharp, without preamble. Both got to their feet to shake Mariner's hand. The woman was in her early fifties, Mariner thought. Her blonde hair was tied up, with a fringe that accentuated her inquiring blue eyes. Sinclair was younger and heavier, his receding hair grey at the temples.

'They've driven over from Norfolk and would like to talk to you.' Now it was Sharp's turn to stand. 'I'm going to leave you to it. Can I get you anything else?'

The visitors declined the offer, and as Sharp left, she signalled to Mariner to take her chair. Reid and Sinclair sat down again and Sinclair took out a notebook. The sun was shining in, making the room uncomfortably warm, despite the open window.

'What's this about?' asked Mariner. It had to be important for both officers to have travelled this far, and something that apparently couldn't be discussed on the phone or by video link.

'We're on Norfolk's case review team,' began Reid. She was softly spoken, her gaze open and keen. 'A property on the Norfolk border is being developed. While clearing the land to lay foundations for a new building, contractors uncovered human remains in a shallow grave. Yesterday it was confirmed that the skeleton is that of a young woman who disappeared more than forty years ago.'

'How can I help?' Mariner was still mystified.

'Her identity was confirmed a few days ago. Her name was Robina Scanlon.'

It took Mariner a second or two to place the name, and when he did, it came with a jolt of nostalgia that took his breath away.

'What's your name?'
'Robina.'

'Ribena? Like the drink?'

'Ha, a comedian, are you?'

'The name does mean something to you then,' said Reid.

It must be written all over his face. She was a skilled interviewer, Mariner thought, trying to regain mastery of his brain synapses.

'If it's the same one,' said Mariner, simultaneously realising what a ridiculous thing it was to say. It had to be. With that name and in that part of the country . . . it would be too much of a coincidence. 'I mean yes, I met her . . . knew her.'

'Perhaps you could tell us *how* you knew her.'

'We met on a camping holiday, when I was a kid, a teenager. I was camping, that is. She was staying in a caravan nearby with her family. We met at a country fair.' Mariner felt his skin flare a little, the heat in the office suddenly oppressive. 'We spent about a week together on and off, and then we — my mother and I — came home several days before Robina was reported missing.'

He could visualise Robina now, standing with the other kids in the field near the pale rectangle left behind by his tent, frantically waving goodbye as they bumped across the meadow, that mischievous smile on her face. He was astonished at how vivid the memory was.

'And home was where?' asked Reid.

'Leamington, just down the road from here. God, I haven't thought about Robina for years, but . . .' He looked up at Reid. 'I don't understand. You mean she's been a crime in action all this time?'

'You seem surprised by that.'

'I'm astonished that I've never picked up anything about the case while I've been in the job,' said Mariner. 'She crossed my mind from time to time, and I did try looking her up once. But it was years ago and I found nothing. I assumed she'd turned up again.'

'But you never saw her after that holiday?'

'No. I might have written to her once. In fact, I know I did.' Suddenly he could see, and even smell, the new

43

cream-coloured writing pad and matching envelopes, specially bought from WH Smith, and his own handwriting spelling out her name. 'She never wrote back.'

'It's likely that she died soon after she went missing,' said Reid.

The shock of it struck Mariner anew. Flashbacks crowded his mind; Robina funny, opinionated, carefree. Looking forward with relish to the rest of her life. But now, he learned, there had been no rest-of-her-life. Instead, it was brutally cut short. It was impossible to grasp. For a moment his emotions got the better of him and he had to avert his face from Reid's scrutiny for a few seconds.

'How did you track me down?' he asked, returning to safer ground.

'You and I were on the same training course last autumn,' said Sinclair. 'Can't have been that riveting because I remembered your name from the delegates list.'

'Really?'

'I had to check back on your first name, but to a lifelong Tractor Boys fan, yours is a distinctive surname.'

'Paul Mariner,' said Mariner. 'No relation, of course.'

'It was quite a break,' replied Reid.

She dipped into her briefcase and produced a few photocopied pages, which she passed to him. 'You might like to refresh your memory.'

Mariner began reading. He was in turn fascinated and alarmed by this sudden, surreal incursion back into his teenage life. The statement was alien and yet so familiar, like dozens he'd engineered and read himself, but this time in his own words. Looking at it now, it was clear to him that it was only part of what would be classed as an information-gathering exercise, confirming his residency in Leamington and his movements subsequent to that holiday. He even spoke about a bangle he'd bought Robina, flagging it up as something that might help identify her. He was thinking like a copper even then.

'Is the statement still true to the best of your knowledge?' asked Reid.

'It is,' said Mariner.

'You must have had your own ideas about what had happened to her?'

'I didn't dwell on it much,' said Mariner. 'On one level I found it hard to comprehend; this girl that I'd known suddenly in the news. The coverage focused on the fears for her safety, but with my limited knowledge, I couldn't quite believe it. She was strong and assertive, or at least she seemed that way to me as a naïve sixteen-year-old.'

'The consensus was that Robina had a rebellious streak, so the possibility of her having run away was the obvious line to follow in the first instance,' said Reid, 'But the family — in particular her mother — never believed it. The kind of girl she was — happy and from a close-knit family — it seemed unlikely that she wouldn't at least get in touch. And apart from a handful of false alarms, there were no credible sightings of her beyond the immediate vicinity.'

'You never went looking for her yourself?' said Sinclair. 'You say in your statement that you were "good friends". You bought her a present. Was it more than that?'

'A bit,' said Mariner, shifting in his seat. 'But we both knew it was only going to be a holiday thing. A pretty girl like her, it was obvious that it was only a question of time before she'd meet someone else. And she was older than me. I was still at school, though I hadn't told her that. I imagined there'd be dozens of people out searching for her. What would I have been able to do? I had no way of contacting her. No mobile phones back then. I was as mystified as anyone else.'

All the same, it wasn't like him to sit back and do nothing. He tried to remember how it had been, how he had felt at that time. He'd been concerned about her. That ache that had begun as they left the campsite had stayed with him for the entire endlessly tedious journey . . . And then another memory hit him like a steam train.

'I'm not sure that I was thinking about much more than myself,' said Mariner, feeling some shame in the words. 'Just a couple of weeks after we got home from that holiday, after Robina disappeared, I did my own vanishing act. I had a huge row with my mother — the last of many. The next day I went out as if I was going to school, but caught the train here, to Birmingham. I never went back.'

'Sounds dramatic,' said Reid.

'It had been brewing a long time,' said Mariner. 'I've never really put those two events together — the holiday and me walking out — but that was it. I had limited funds and nowhere to stay in Birmingham, so I ended up living in a squat. I was there for weeks, in my own turmoil, and completely lost touch with the outside world for a while. It's been suggested to me since, more than once, that I had a sort of breakdown.'

Reid gave him a measured look. 'Rough time.' She managed to sound less accusing than her colleague. They had a nicely honed and nuanced good-cop/bad-cop thing going on.

'It felt like it back then. It was some time before I contacted my mother. And then it was only a single, one-sided communication: a scribbled message on a postcard to let her know her that I was all right.' It was Jack Coleman — the man who'd gone on to be his boss — who had persuaded him into that. 'It was a good few years before I returned to the house.' Long after it had ceased to feel like his home. His relationship with his mother had never fully recovered.

'Where was your dad in all this?' asked Sinclair.

'Nowhere,' said Mariner. 'My mother was on her own. I didn't know who my father was until a few years ago. If that's at all relevant.'

'Did you ever discuss Robina's disappearance with your mother subsequent to that?' asked Reid.

Mariner exhaled. 'When I did resume contact, our relationship was difficult, to put it mildly.' By then she'd had her own missing person to contend with. A boy on the cusp of his seventeenth birthday disappearing after a family row wasn't exactly a police priority. 'And she had no idea of the extent of my friendship with Robina anyway. As far as she was concerned, Robina was only one of the group of kids I'd hung around with.'

'What was the row about?' Sinclair cut in.

'What?'

'With your mother?'

Again, Mariner wondered about the relevance of the question. 'I got my hair cut and got a few piercings. I fancied myself a punk.'

'You had a Mohican?' Reid was amused by that.

'Not quite,' Mariner said. 'But I was kicking against the week I'd just spent with a bunch of long-haired hippies.'

'And your mum didn't appreciate it.'

'On the contrary, she thought it was wonderful that I was "expressing myself". That was the problem. She was so bloody tolerant of everything I did. Her take on it was that I would get it out of my system ahead of the glittering career she had planned for me. My whole future was mapped out, a straitjacket ready and waiting for me to step into. It's why telling her about Robina and me would have been a red rag to a bull.' Even after all this time he struggled to keep the bitterness from his voice, and he was well aware of how self-pitying and pathetic it sounded. As an adult it was an episode he struggled with, and found it near impossible to accurately convey how desperate he was to escape his mother's suffocating attentions. 'It was by complete fluke that I discovered how to really rebel against my mother. I joined the police. She never forgave me.'

'Why did you join the police?' asked Reid.

'It felt like the right thing to do at the time. An attempt to find order in the chaos.'

'It had nothing to do with Robina.'

'No.' Or had it? 'Where exactly was she found?' he asked.

'In the grounds of a retirement home, close to where the caravan site was. They've been excavating to extend the property and fortunately for us the guy operating the JCB watches a lot of crime drama and keeps his eyes open.'

'Do you know how she died?' He had to ask though he hated to even contemplate it.

'Nothing is confirmed yet,' said Reid. In any event, she was under no obligation to tell him.

'I don't remember any retirement home around there,' Mariner said.

'Its designation has changed more than once,' said Reid. 'She wouldn't have been found at all but the land boundaries have been pretty fluid too, and this particular area was a recent acquisition. Trying to get a clear sense of the layout of everything back then is giving us real headaches, isn't it, Scott? While the caravan site is marked on the maps from that time, all they show of the area around the crime scene are woods and farmland.'

'I could tell you what was there at the time,' said Mariner. 'It's crystal clear in my mind. Bet I've still got my maps somewhere too.'

'Really?'

'I'm a bit of an anorak in that regard. I collect them, and I'd never throw one away. And I'll have annotated them too. I usually do.'

Reid and Sinclair exchanged a glance. 'Any chance you could dig them out?' said Reid. 'We really need to build an accurate picture of the geography of the area, as it was.'

'There might be photographs as well,' said Mariner. 'I've still got papers belonging to my mother at my place. She kept all sorts of random stuff and I've only looked at a fraction of what's there. But I can go through it, just in case there's something.'

'That would be great, thanks. We have to get back, but if you could scan anything . . .'

An idea was beginning to take root in Mariner's mind. 'Would it help if I came over there?'

'Definitely,' said Reid. 'Robina's family have asked to see the deposition site, but I'd prefer to keep their visit short and focused, to minimise any further distress. If you could walk us through the location, as it was then, we could spare them unnecessary trauma. You spent time with Robina too. You must have known what was in her mind as well as anyone.'

'Anything I can do to help,' said Mariner. 'But it goes without saying, we're talking about a very long time ago and stuff I haven't thought about for years.'

'That's the nature of historic crimes, isn't it?' said Reid. 'And you never know. The case has been revisited half-heartedly a couple of times over the years, but with no new evidence they've only been light-touch efforts. The discovery of Robina's remains changes things, but realistically the chance of a breakthrough is small. We're driving ourselves mad with "what ifs" and it would be great if we could at least answer some questions for the family and give them some sort of closure. There might be something useful you remember, even if it only corroborates what's already there.'

She was right. It was worth a try.

'I'm due some leave,' he said. The idea had only crystallised in his mind as they'd been talking, but he felt sure that Superintendent Sharp would sanction it. That side of Norfolk was a four-hour drive away, and would mean at least one overnight. 'It won't be for a day or two,' Mariner said. 'There's a lot going on here.' He wondered if Sharp had told them anything about yesterday's incident. (Was it really only yesterday?) 'And I'll need to clear it with my guvnor.' He felt a small qualm as he spoke. They'd just picked up a live one that was looking far from straightforward. But, he told himself, the team was more than capable. It would be a great opportunity to let Jesson stand on her own two feet.

'Of course.' Reid passed him her card. 'I appreciate any help you can give us. Naturally the nursing home want to resume building work as soon as possible, but we've negotiated a week's suspension in the first instance, so that's the deadline we're working to. Meanwhile we're ploughing through statements and tracing witnesses. Just let me know when you're coming, and we can book you a room at a local hotel.'

Their business concluded, Mariner showed them out.

CHAPTER SIX

Mariner took his time climbing the stairs, mulling things over in his mind. By the time he got back to CID, Sharp had returned to her office.

'Reid and Sinclair could do with some help,' he told her. 'And I've offered to go down there.'

'Why am I not surprised?' said Sharp, with a wry smile.

'I can take a bit of leave, go when the IOPC have finished with me. There's the Paszek inquiry, but that's still in the early stages, the spadework to be done. I wouldn't anticipate staying long.'

Sharp nodded in agreement. 'It might be good for you to get away from here for a couple of days,' she said. 'You'll need to appoint someone to cover for you as SIO while you're away. Any thoughts on who that might be?'

'It'll be between Charlie and Vicky.'

'Mm.' That much she'd surmised.

'My instinct is Vicky. I'm pretty sure she's considering taking her inspector's exams, so it would be good preparation for her,' said Mariner.

'I agree. Charlie's more experienced, though. How will he take it?'

'You know Charlie; he's pretty laid back. He'll be OK.'

'Decision made, then.'

* * *

A range of exhibits had come in, including those from the post-mortem and others from the SOCOs at the crash site and Mariner found Jesson and Glover working together, logging them in, ahead of sending off the relevant ones to the Forensic Science Service. He asked Glover to come and see him when the task was complete. When he appeared, Mariner broadly outlined the situation to him. 'So, given the demands on my time in the next week or so, I'm going to ask Vicky to act as SIO,' he said. He didn't want to get Glover's hopes up.

His sergeant shrugged. 'Sounds good to me.'

The same exchange won him a searching look from Vicky Jesson, following on so soon after that conversation they'd had earlier in the day, and with her it was more of a hard sell. Initially, she was rather less enthusiastic than he'd predicted.

'So soon?' she said. 'I don't know if I'm up to it.'

'Do you think I'd offer it to you if you weren't?' he said. 'I won't be away long, a matter of days at the most. In my absence, you're the best person to hold the fort. It's a great opportunity.'

'Yes, it is,' she conceded. 'Thank you. I won't let you down, boss.'

'I'll be around to get things started, but then you can take on the briefings from tomorrow.'

'Really?'

'Why not? You discuss cases with your colleagues all the time. It's just a question of getting feedback from everyone, adding yours into the mix, and guiding the discussion.'

'They'll be expecting me to come up with ideas.'

'No more than usual. We all chip in all the time,' he reminded her. 'I'd suggest that you try to be as prepared as possible, but that would *really* be teaching Granny to suck eggs. Charlie keeps a thorough policy log, so draw on that and pick his brains beforehand. You don't have to do it all single-handed. Include the others in your thought processes.'

'But they're my mates. What if they don't take me seriously, or resent my sudden authority?'

'They will and they won't,' said Mariner. 'You underestimate the respect they have for you. If you like, we can both go over tomorrow's actions before the end of play today.' He glanced at Khatoon's empty workstation. 'Where's Millie?'

'Loo, I think,' said Bingley, busy stretching an elastic band as far as it would go over the back of his chair.

'OK, we'll wait.'

The elastic band snapped. 'Ow!'

Mariner gave Jesson a see-what-I-mean look. Once Khatoon was back, he kicked off the briefing, reporting first what he and Jesson had learned during the morning.

'The post-mortem on Viktor Paszek has confirmed cause of death as a heart attack,' he said. 'The head injuries he sustained in the crash were post-mortem, so we are satisfied that there was nothing suspicious about his death. We're awaiting confirmation from Traffic, but it remains probable that the heart attack is what caused Paszek's car to leave the road.

'The bad news is that the PM for our unidentified male has been delayed,' he went on. 'We're waiting for rigor to pass, before he can be straightened out. It means we can't get a good look at him yet, and Stuart Croghan can't start the examination.'

'How long will we have to wait?' asked Glover.

'It should pass sometime today, so hopefully we'll get something in the morning. It means there's no photograph yet, and Croghan's not so sure we'll get a meaningful one, even when we can get to his face. He looks as if he's been knocked about a bit, and while it's been confirmed he's a fully grown man, he looks a little undersized for his age. Skin and hair texture suggest Southeast Asian heritage.'

'We have got this,' said Jesson, passing around a photograph of the cigarette packet, before sticking it to the board. 'It would be reasonable to assume that the writing gives us a clue to his nationality — Vietnamese — but obviously we can't take that for granted. Could just be a pack he's picked up on his travels, or that someone's given him.'

'And there's this,' said Mariner, showing the photograph of the remaining trainer. 'We only have one shoe, so somewhere along the line he lost the other one.'

'Doesn't look like any brand I've ever seen,' said Bingley.

'Which might again suggest that he's a foreign national — or that he buys cheap brands on Amazon. Finding the other of the pair is crucial. It might give us a substantial pointer to where and how he died. And at the moment it's all we've got.'

'How about a name, Charlie?' said Khatoon.

They'd been here before — last time it was a young woman who went unidentified for many months. Charlie Glover had assigned a name to the anonymous photograph pinned to the wall and it had helped to humanise her for them all, until her true identity was finally discovered.

'I'm not so up on Vietnamese names,' said Glover. 'But I'll see what I can do.'

'So, to Viktor Paszek,' said Mariner. 'We know now that he died of natural causes; a stroke of luck for us, because if he hadn't, whatever he was up to would have gone unnoticed. I understand we haven't yet found a next of kin?'

'We think he was widowed,' said Khatoon. She explained what had brought them to that conclusion. 'There's no evidence of any children. Only two lots of immediate neighbours. Next door were out all day, but Kev spoke to the people in the third house in the row. They're new, so didn't really know Viktor.'

'It goes without saying that we need someone to formally identify him too,' said Mariner. 'What else did you find?'

'The house is a nightmare,' said Khatoon, describing their first introduction to it. 'But there's nothing on the face of it to show that a violent death occurred there, or in the grounds. The only possible place it might have happened is the garage, so the SOCOs are going in tomorrow for a closer look. It'll take at least another day to finish the search, and we've barely scratched the surface of the paperwork.'

'We still don't know for sure that Paszek played any part in our John Doe's death,' said Mariner. 'But we've got a lot of material to pass on to forensics, so hopefully we'll get something from that. Vicky?'

'The useful stuff has come from the RTC,' she began. 'The builders' bag that contained the body was resting on a sheet of heavy-duty polythene, and there were items in the boot including a set of men's cotton overalls and a pair of heavy-duty rubberised gloves. They've gone to the FSS to check for traces.'

'The gloves might show us he was squeamish about handling the victim,' said Mariner. 'Or that he was seeking to distance himself from the cause of death. We might also find out if he had anyone helping him.'

'There was a one-gallon can containing industrial-strength cleaning fluid in the boot too,' said Jesson. 'Probably intended for giving the car a thorough clean after the body was removed.'

Mariner turned to his other sergeant. 'Charlie?'

'I've got the data from the speed cameras for the A38 for Sunday night. Unfortunately, there are no cameras out as far as Paszek's road, off the B4120, so I've looked at the nearest intersection of the B4120 with the A38, working back from the time of the accident. I was surprised to find Paszek coming at it from the city side.'

'He wasn't driving from his home?' said Mariner.

'No, so I tracked back some more, and finally picked him up at 20.06 heading away from home and in towards the city. Luckily for us, he stays on the A38, but we lose him just after the Orthopaedic Hospital. A number of junctions he could have taken from that point. So, I asked myself, where did he go and what was he doing between five past eight and just after two in the morning?'

'Did you get an answer?' asked Bingley facetiously.

'Of sorts,' said Glover, missing the levity. 'I widened the scope of the search and Paszek shows up on Linden Road heading towards Cotteridge at just after midnight. He continues on to the Pershore Road South, the A441, heading towards Kingsmead. But then he vanishes again. He reappears further down the A441 at 2 a.m., turning on to Longbridge Lane. From there he drives out of the city on the A38.'

'Where he had the accident,' said Mariner. 'Given what we haven't found at the house, it's reasonable to assume our John Doe was killed elsewhere, and Paszek was on his way to dispose of the body when he crashed. It could have happened at any point when Paszek's off the radar, or before that, meaning there's a crime scene out there somewhere.'

'I can try to fill in the blanks with CCTV from those areas,' said Glover. 'But a lot of it's residential, so we'll fall short in places.'

Mariner turned to Khatoon and Bingley. 'We need to find out more about Paszek, in particular, friends and acquaintances, where he might have disappeared to during that time.'

'We're heading back to Briar Lane first thing tomorrow,' said Khatoon. 'We'll try the next-door neighbours again, and something might turn up in his paperwork. There's plenty to go on. But we think he might have owned another place as well.'

'A house?'

'We don't know for sure,' said Bingley. He told them about the buildings insurance bills. 'They were addressed to Paszek on Briar Lane, but dated ten years ago. He could have been some sort of landlord.'

'That could open things up a bit,' said Mariner. 'What about his electronic footprint?'

'We haven't found one,' said Khatoon. 'There's no computer. I think he might have been a bit of a Luddite.'

'Anything back from his phone?'

'Not yet, boss,' said Glover. 'But shouldn't take long. There are only a handful of numbers and Max is looking into them. It might help to be able to do a background check of his finances.'

'We'd struggle to get a court order at this point,' said Mariner. 'We'd have to be clear about what we were looking for; demonstrate that it's more than a fishing expedition. There might come a time, but we need more background first. So, a lot to do, folks,' said Mariner. 'And as I won't be here for a couple of days, Vicky will be taking over as acting SIO.'

'Is everything all right, boss?' asked Khatoon tentatively. She was speaking for them all, he could tell from their faces.

'Fine,' Mariner reassured them. 'I'm just taking a couple of days' leave. Apart from the inquiry into Sunday's incident, which will be ongoing for a while, I've volunteered to assist with a cold case over in Norfolk.'

'That's a bit random, isn't it?'

Khatoon shot Bingley a look. 'You do know you said that out loud, Kev, don't you?'

'I only meant—'

'You're right,' said Mariner. 'It is. It just so happens that a case has resurfaced that I have links with, going back a number of years. That's all I can say for now.' He was hoping they'd assume the connection was a professional one. He'd enlighten them at a later date, if necessary. 'Now, bugger off home, the lot of you.'

Jesson stayed behind after everyone else had gone. 'You're going to be fine,' Mariner said. 'But you don't always have to make a point of being the last to leave.'

'I won't, it's just that I've got Emily's parents' evening at seven, so thought I may as well hang on and go straight there. If I go home first, I might not muster the courage to go out again, especially for that.'

'Oh, come on,' said Mariner. 'Emily's a good kid. Bright and knows her own mind — like her mum.' Mariner had spent a lot of time with Jesson's eldest daughter when she came in for a bring-your-daughter-to-work week.

'She made quite an impression on you, didn't she?'

'She was useful to have around. I see a potential recruit there, one day.' He looked at his watch. 'What time did you say it was?'

'Yeah, I should go,' said Jesson. 'Wish me luck.'

Mariner wasn't sure if she meant for the parents' evening or the investigation. He returned to his office to find a message from a Martin Nawaz, asking him to return the call as soon as possible. As he'd already guessed, Nawaz was IOPC.

'We'd like to interview you tomorrow morning, if that's convenient,' Nawaz said. 'While everything's still clear in your mind. We can be at Granville Lane at 11 a.m., if that's convenient for you.'

It was as good a time as any, now that Jesson was in place to pick up the slack. Mariner agreed, conditional on the availability of his Police Federation rep. He put through a call to DCI Simon Bell immediately after hanging up, apologising for the short notice. Fortunately, Bell could make it. In some ways Mariner felt this representation was unnecessary, he couldn't anticipate anything contentious arising. But he would have been a fool not to safeguard himself. On his way out he stopped by Superintendent Sharp's office to let her know.

'Are things in hand on the Paszek investigation?' she asked.

'All in hand.'

'Then don't come in tomorrow until you need to,' she said. 'Be fresh for the interview.'

* * *

At the last minute, Jesson found she was rushing. Was this how it would be if she was promoted to inspector — racing between work and home, making her children wait? Always at the back of her mind was the battle between committing to more responsibility — and by definition more hours — and being there for the kids. Although things were going smoothly at the moment, she knew that they were all at a tricky age. Jesson loved her family and she loved her job. The only problem was trying to reconcile the two, and she couldn't always expect her mum to be her safety net. She hoped Doris was up for a challenge over the next week while she was SIO.

With hundreds of parents converging on the school, the surrounding streets were jam-packed, cars vying for the insufficient parking spaces. It meant that she was the one who was late, a fact that Emily interestingly failed to capitalise on when they met just inside the entrance. In fact, Emily seemed subdued. It made Jesson even more anxious. *Whatever you do, stay calm*, she reminded herself. It was a lot to ask. Parents' evenings in the past had been gruelling; that weird kind of speed-dating coupled with less than glowing testimonials and an unresponsive daughter. The last such event at Emily's previous school had been awkward, to say the least, when Emily's form teacher had accused her of developing 'an attitude'. And not in a good way. Jesson primed herself to dole out encouragement and commiseration in equal measure.

'Have you got your list?' she asked.

Emily waved a sheet of paper in response. 'English first, Mrs O'Kane.' Emily flashed a wry smile. 'Buckle up, Mum.'

But tonight was an altogether different experience to the last. Yes, the endless queueing and time constraints were the same, and inevitably some teachers fell back on the generic and superficial, but the overwhelming message was that now Emily had settled into her new school, she was working 'consistently well' (though not 'hard', Jesson noticed) and was seeing some good results. The word 'diligent' was used by one teacher, for goodness' sake.

'Well, aren't you the dark horse,' Jesson said, as Emily linked arms with her on the way out, all the names on their list crossed off two exhausting hours later.

'Em!' Jayden was loping over.

Emily went to meet him. 'How'd it go?' she asked, and the two moved off to one side for a private post-mortem. Behind Jayden came a couple of about Jesson's age, who smiled and walked towards her, the man running his hand around the inside of his shirt collar, as if releasing steam.

'Glad that's over with,' he said. But he didn't seem unhappy and Jesson guessed they'd had similarly positive feedback.

'You're Jayden's mum and dad,' said Jesson, stating the obvious. 'It's nice to meet you at last. I'm Vicky.'

'You too,' said his mum. 'Carol and Jim.'

'Jayden's a lovely young man,' said Jesson, watching the two youngsters laugh at a shared joke.

'We're so glad he's met Emily,' said Carol. 'We weren't sure how well he'd settle into his new school, but she's been so kind to him. We're grateful for that. She's a lovely girl too, and a good influence.'

'First time for everything.' Jesson smiled, pleasantly surprised. The evening had been a revelation. Emily and rave reviews didn't often go together and tonight they were coming from all directions. 'I was going to say the same about Jayden. Long may it last.'

'Absolutely,' said Carol.

'We should go,' said Jim, glancing up at the wall clock. He flashed an apologetic smile. 'We've left the younger ones with a babysitter. Good to meet you.'

To reward Emily's hard work, Jesson promised a family meal out at the weekend to celebrate, and when they arrived home half an hour later, they found the house quiet, Doris and Maisie sitting watching TV together.

'You look happy,' said Doris. 'How did it go?'

'Very well,' said Jesson. 'I'm proud of her.'

'Well done you!' Doris beamed at her granddaughter, who already had her phone out, her attention elsewhere.

'Thanks, Gran. Just going up to talk to Jayden.'

Jesson couldn't help laughing. 'Of course you are,' she said. 'It's such a long time since you saw him.'

'And how about you?' asked Doris. 'Good day?'

'Not bad. The boss is off for a few days from tomorrow though, and I'll be covering. It's going to mean some long ones and more late nights.'

'Aaron's in his room,' said Doris. 'And we're all right, aren't we, sweetheart?' The question was directed at Jesson's youngest, Maisie, who nodded wordlessly, without looking up from the screen.

'Thanks, Mum,' said Jesson, for what felt like the thousandth time. 'But you must say if it gets too much.'

'I love it. You know I do. I'm lucky to be able to spend time with them.'

CHAPTER SEVEN

Driving home, Mariner reflected on what a strange couple of days it had been. Nothing that had happened could have been foreseen and just thinking about what he had on his plate right now set the adrenaline fizzing. Unless someone came forward to identify their John Doe, the Paszek case was going to be a challenge, and would take some untangling. But that was now — temporarily — out of his hands. The IOPC investigation would run its course, and until the interview tomorrow, he wouldn't know what he was up against.

And then there was Robina Scanlon. The sadness he felt was a physical pain in his abdomen. He didn't envy what Reid and Sinclair had ahead of them: locating witnesses from all those years ago; and relying on hazy memories that may well, with the passage of time, have constructed a set of different truths. What they'd be hoping for was one piece of irrefutable, tangible evidence that advances in forensic science might uncover, which, at the time, would have been out of reach. It was a tall order.

The evening was mild, so he took a bottle of beer and a notebook out into his tiny garden, overlooking the canal, and sat down to try to think himself back to that summer. One of the strengths that assisted Mariner daily in the workplace was his recall. He leaned against the wall and let the memories come. They were hazy to begin with, flashes of sound and vision. The heat and sun immediately came to the fore, then as the events of those weeks began to take shape in his mind, he started making notes, jotting things down as they'd occurred chronologically.

Having captured as much as he could inwardly, it was time to look for other evidence to verify what he remembered. He ran a few Google searches to see what was online. All he found was the odd paragraph on true crime sites, accompanied by the same image of a teenage girl looking prim in her school uniform, and bearing only a passing resemblance to the young woman he remembered. Then there were two newspaper articles from a number of years ago. The first was a poor scan of an anniversary piece from five years after Robina went missing. The second was a more recent digital article and reported on the 'tragic mother', Patricia Gray, who had died never knowing what had happened to her daughter. Gray? Mariner wondered if she had split from Robina's father and perhaps returned to her maiden name or married again. Mariner had witnessed first-hand the strain the disappearance of a child could place on a relationship.

The article included a quote from Robina's sister Dawn. Dawn, yes, he could picture her easily. Was she older or younger than Robina? Can't have been much in it. They were both a similar height, though Dawn was chunkier and less feminine.

Mariner drained his beer bottle. Time now to search out the less accessible materials. The cellar was a useful storage space, but it had become a lazy dumping ground; a halfway house between things outliving their usefulness and being disposed of.

Easiest to put his hand on was his map of the area. He still had the original Landranger Ordnance Survey series in their bright pink covers. The East Norfolk map was in good condition, having only been used that one time. And as he'd expected, he had doctored it, adding his own annotations.

The campsite, the stalls, the caravan park. A circle in pencil marked the place where he had pitched his tent. Not the only thing he'd done there.

The boxes from his mother's house were consigned to the furthest corner of the cellar, and he had to move away discarded camping equipment, an old vacuum cleaner and a couple of framed paintings, along with boxes of Suzy's books, before he could drag them out into open space.

The documents and mementoes brought from his childhood home had previously been disturbed only once. Then, he'd been hunting for the clues to his parentage. At that time, anything he'd deemed irrelevant had been unceremoniously chucked back into the boxes. But he did retain a vague memory of snapshots in their egg-yolk yellow Kodak packets, the sort that, back in the day, had to be collected from the chemist. It seemed absurd now, the idea of taking a film to a shop to be developed, not knowing for days how many frames — if any — would turn out to be any good. He sifted through the case where he thought he'd seen them, but the only photographic wallets he could find contained photos of him as a child, mostly alone but occasionally with his mother or his grandparents.

He worked his way through the manila envelopes, where he struck lucky, not as expected with the snapshots, but with some press clippings cut from national newspapers. POLICE HUNT MISSING TEEN; GIRL, 18, DISAPPEARS; RIVER DREDGED FOR MISSING ROBINA. Why on earth had his mother kept these? Was it for him? Had she imagined at the time that he was about to walk back through the door? When he eventually did, either she had genuinely forgotten the clippings, or she took some warped pleasure from withholding the information. Hard to tell with her which was more probable.

According to the newspaper reports, Robina was last seen on the afternoon of Thursday, 27 August 1976, walking across the campsite with an unknown man. Mariner and his mother had left the weekend before — they'd been at the campsite from Saturday 15 to Saturday 22. That made sense because at the time Rose Mariner was employed behind the counter at Woodward's department store, and would have had to work the following Monday.

And there, in amongst the cuttings, in a gold packet held together with a perished elastic band that immediately broke when he touched it, was a handful of faded images taken on his old instamatic camera. The fuzzy resolution was appalling by today's standards, and they had, without exception, faded to a bluish hue, but he'd made sure to take them. He could remember the urgency of wanting a snapshot of Robina. If there was no photograph, how would he remember what she looked like? No smartphones or Facebook back then. They'd made promises to keep in touch but, as he'd intimated to Reid and Sinclair, with no great expectation that it would last. It would mean writing letters and buying stamps or making expensive phone calls, which for him would also entail a walk down to the street corner to the payphone, and maybe joining a queue to use it. There were two pictures of Robina alone; despite the poor quality, there was no doubting it was her. The first was when he'd caught her unawares beside the shower block, on his last evening. The other was a more posed shot beside his tent. Even now, as an adult, he was struck by how beautiful she was, with dark eyes, thick shoulder-length hair and a dimpled smile.

Mariner checked through what was left in the cases, and satisfied that there was nothing else, took the envelope up from the cellar, closing the door firmly behind him. Then he sat with another bottle of Hobgoblin and spread out the photographs on the table. The remainder of the shots were group photos, an attempt to hide from the others what was probably obvious to all of them. He'd been behind the camera, so was in none of them. He'd always preferred that. Seeing those faces, it felt as if it had all been days or weeks ago, and he had no trouble remembering the names or what they had been doing at the time when the pictures were taken. His immediate and most vivid recollection was of the noise; the shouting, banter and laughter of six or seven youngsters having the time of their lives. He realised then that it was one of the few times when he'd truly felt part of a tribe.

There were photographs, too, of his mother's friends, which she must have taken. At most he counted eight people, sitting around in a group, on folding chairs beside the camper van. It had been a happy time for Rose too. Talking long into the evening with like-minded people and putting the world to rights. There had been laughter and music; folk and protest songs accompanied by guitars. One of the faces sprang out at him; someone he'd stayed in touch with and had seen relatively recently. Hers were the paintings he'd had to move to get to the boxes. Maggie Devlin had been there that summer, of course she had. In her seventies now, Maggie had always been as sharp as a pin. He should speak to her before going over to East Anglia. She'd undoubtedly have some insights to share.

In the bottom of the envelope Mariner found a leather wristband, with a stud fastening and embossed two-tone design. Robina had bought it for him, and at the same time he'd got her a silver bangle. But then he came across something he felt sure he'd never seen before. Mixed in with the photo wallets was a letter-postcard; the folding sort that had space for a longer message on the inside and lick-flaps around three of the edges, which were still sealed. On one side was a montage of photographs of Great Yarmouth, and on the other side was his name and Leamington address.

Mariner first attempted to ease open the narrow flaps, but each time all that came away was a wafer-thin shred of paper. Instead, he fetched a sharp knife from the kitchen, slid it into a tiny gap in the corner and slit the three sealed sides, before opening up the page, his heart thumping with anticipation. The paper had a distinctive smell and he wafted it under his nose to try to identify it. Cigarette smoke. The letter itself was disappointing; just a short note, covering less than half the available space, in writing that was clumsy in places and not readily legible. No address header or date.

He turned it over. The blurred postmark was also Yarmouth — was that date 29 August? He held it under the light but couldn't be sure. Posted two days *after* she disappeared, if that was right. Had she still been alive then, or had someone else found it and posted it on her behalf?

Dear Tommy, I hope you got home all right and it was OK with your mum. I already miss you such a lot I think my heart will burst. I think about us lying together in the sun, in the long grass where no one can see us, with all the bees buzzing all around. You put your arms around me and hold me tight. Then you kiss me and our tongues touch. We take off all our clothes and lay down and you can squeeze my breasts and I'll stroke your chest and touch your penis. I can't wait for us to be together again.

Lots of love and kisses, Robina xxx

It wasn't at all what he'd hoped for or expected. Though explicit, it was surprisingly formal and restrained, making no reference to the time they'd already spent together — especially that last night, in his tent. He tried to hear her reading it aloud but while he had no trouble conjuring her voice, he couldn't get it. Had she been worried that someone else might see it, or was it just Robina being Robina and taking the piss? She'd been good at that. Folding it up he replaced it in the envelope, with everything else and set it to one side to take with him to Norfolk. It wasn't too late, so he picked up the land line and dialled a Warwickshire number.

'Hello, Maggie? It's Tom Mariner.'

'Tom! How lovely to hear from you!'

'How are you?'

'I'm well, thank you.' But she sounded guarded, not quite her usual self.

'Are you sure?'

'In fine fettle. I'm guessing you've heard it on the news, too, then. Robina Scanlon.'

'Norfolk police have paid me a visit,' said Mariner. 'I'm driving over tomorrow to do what I can to help.'

'Really? How?'

'Only to give them some idea of the lie of the land back then.'

'Don't they have local people to do that?' asked Maggie, surprised.

'I expect so, but my name came up, and as I'm in the job . . .'

'That was a memorable summer, wasn't it?' she said. 'We made some good and enduring friends that year.'

'You and Rose, you mean?'

'Yes.' She reeled off some names, but while they rang vague bells, Mariner couldn't bring the faces to mind, and said as much.

'Yes, well you had other fish to fry, didn't you?' said Maggie. He could hear the mischief in her voice.

'You knew about that?' he said. 'Did Rose?'

A throaty chuckle from the other end of the line. 'Why do you imagine we all stayed so long at the pub that last evening?'

'She knew about *that*?'

'Rose was rather proud of you for taking the opportunity. She saw it as part of your education. She trusted that you would be sensible, and it was only ever going to be short-lived, wasn't it? No future in it,' she said, dismissively.

'What do you mean?' said Mariner, suddenly defensive. 'I know we lived miles apart . . .'

'But she had commitments; children, didn't she?' said Maggie. 'You weren't quite ready for that, and I doubt she'd have given them up for you.'

Doubts seeped into Mariner's mind. 'Wait a minute. Who did you think it was?'

'The girl from the jewellery stall.'

'Lesley? Even though she was twice my age?'

'She wasn't that much older than you,' Maggie corrected him. 'And you have to remember when this was. Things were more . . . free and easy back then. Especially among the fair people. And she was a lovely girl. You were very thick with her.'

'Well, it wasn't her,' Mariner said. But Rose and Maggie's misperception might account for why that letter had remained unopened.

'Then who . . . ?' Maggie began. But it didn't take her long. 'Robina Scanlon?'

'Yes.'

'But she wasn't with the fair, she was staying on the caravan site.'

'She came to the fair though. I met her at Lesley's stall.'

'Oh my. We assumed . . . Goodness, if we'd known the truth, it would have put a different complexion on things, wouldn't it? Why didn't you say?'

'I did, to the police.' Sort of.

'Were you a suspect?'

'Why would I be?' said Mariner. 'When we left she hadn't vanished yet. I could account for my movements after we got back to Leamington. There was nothing to suggest that I'd had any contact with Robina after the holiday.'

'And that was it?'

'They asked me about other people who had been around the campsite at the time, and the kids we hung around with. They asked me about Robina's family too; how she got on with them.'

'You remember all this?'

'The two officers who came to see me today brought my original statement. They asked me to read and verify it.'

'That young man who worked at the caravan park came under scrutiny, didn't he? The one who was a bit slow.'

'Peter?' said Mariner. *Don't mind him. He don't go no farther 'n Thursd'y.*

'That's right. He was sweet on the girl apparently.'

'Was he?' That was news to Mariner. He could imagine the press inventing the angle, though.

'And now I find out he wasn't the only one,' said Maggie. 'It's a shame. We had such a good summer that year, but then it all turned rather sour.'

'How do you mean?' said Mariner cautiously.

'Rose and I had a bit of a falling out.'

'Did you? I don't remember that.'

'Oh, it was something and nothing,' said Maggie. 'I had a fling with a man I met over there.'

'And Rose disapproved.'

'You sound as if you do, too. Don't forget it was our generation who invented free love.'

Mariner had never really thought about that side of Maggie's life. She'd never married, but now he realised there must have been men over the years.

'It wasn't so much the affair that upset Rose,' she went on. 'Your mum just didn't like him. She thought he was a pretentious waster.'

'Why?'

'Mainly because he'd given himself a mystical name and an exotic backstory.'

'Which was what?'

'He claimed he'd travelled to England as a stowaway, because there were some unsavoury types after him in the Netherlands and he'd had to leave in a hurry. He made it sound very romantic and clearly the itinerant life of the fair suited him, but Rose was sceptical. I can understand it in one way. He was into dope in a big way, and he did look a bit of a scarecrow. But I was flattered by the attentions of a foreign, younger man, and there was something about him; still is, as a matter of fact.'

'You've kept in touch?'

'On and off. No hanky-panky these days, we're both past that, thank you. But he lives in Lincolnshire now, so not very far. He still has a sister living in Eindhoven, so I'm a convenient stopping-off point on his way to the airport. It's strange, isn't it, how some quite fleeting friendships can endure? I wondered at the time if Rose was jealous. She wasn't used to sharing me with anyone else. But our disagreement soon blew over. After all, shortly after that she needed me more than ever.' She let that hang, perhaps deciding whether or not to say more. 'She fell apart when you left, you know.'

Mariner found himself suddenly unable to speak. He had never discussed that period of his life with his mother before she died, and up until now he and Maggie had skirted carefully around it too. 'You could have fooled me,' he said, eventually.

'Yes, well, what did you expect? By the time you deigned to come home, she'd put herself back together again, defences firmly in place.'

'Anger, mostly, as I recall.'

'And perfectly justified in my opinion,' said Maggie quietly. 'Rose spent most of her early life trying to do what was best for other people. And they deserted her; first your father and then you. She made genuine sacrifices, but look where it got her.'

It was the first time that Maggie had been anything other than supportive towards him. It was harsh, but he had no rejoinder. Not for the first time, he wished that he'd put in the effort to make things right with his mother.

CHAPTER EIGHT

Tuesday morning saw Bingley and Khatoon back at Briar Lane, along with two SOCOs to search the garage. Bingley tried the house next door again, but it still appeared empty and he wondered if the owners had gone away. He hoped it wasn't for a long trip.

They were working in the back living room this morning, but hadn't been in there for more than a few minutes when they heard the sound of wheels on the gravel. Moments later there was a rap on the door. Bingley was nearest, and went to find a man on the doorstep. Shorter than Bingley's average height, he was an older man, neatly turned out in a windcheater and pullover over collar and tie, his white hair trimmed short; what Bingley's mum would have called dapper. He leaned on a stick.

'Hello,' he said, looking down the hall. 'Is Viktor around?'

'I'm sorry, he's not,' said Bingley. 'And you are . . . ?'

'Eric Dillon. Friend of his. I hope everything's all right?'

'Not exactly,' said Bingley. 'I'm afraid Mr Paszek was in a nasty car accident on Sunday night. He didn't survive.'

'What? Oh no . . .' Eric leaned hard on his stick, which swayed alarmingly.

Bingley stepped forward and took his arm. 'Easy,' he said. 'Sorry, I can't ask you in. Let's get you back to your car for a minute.'

'It's just the shock,' said Eric. 'It'll pass. No point in asking me in anyway. There's never anywhere to sit.'

'That's right enough,' said Bingley. He opened the driver's door of the little hatchback and helped Eric into the seat, his feet still planted on the gravel. 'Can I get you a glass of water or something?'

'No, you're all right, son. Just give me a moment.' Eric caught his breath for a moment, then squinted up at Bingley. 'So, who are you?'

Bingley had his warrant card at the ready and introduced himself. 'How long have you known Viktor?' he asked.

Eric smiled faintly. 'Lord, we go back years. I met him on platform 9 at New Street. We were both there to see *King George V*.'

'That's going back a bit,' said Bingley, trying to visualise the dates of the monarchs.

'It would have been the mid-eighties, I suppose.'

'But . . .'

'I'm talking about a steam locomotive, son,' Eric chuckled, recognising Bingley's confusion. 'We collect train numbers.'

'Ah that explains the layout upstairs.'

'Vik's pride and joy, that is,' said Eric. 'I never got into that side of it myself.' Some of the colour was returning to his face, Bingley noticed, with some relief.

'When did you last see Viktor?' he asked, getting out his notebook. He had an idea this conversation would be fruitful.

'Sunday night,' said Eric. 'He came to my place for a few games of chess. We do it regular, like; once a week or so. He wasn't keen on me coming here. Well, you've seen the state of it.'

'We have.'

'It wasn't always like this,' said Eric, in defence of his friend. 'Irma kept the house spotless. But after she died it was like Vik couldn't bring himself to do it. I couldn't persuade him to part with most of her things and then it got so that he struggled to throw anything away.'

'And where do you live, Eric?' asked Bingley.

'I've got a flat in Brookfield Gardens; you know, the retirement place on the Bristol Road where the college used to be.' The complex was almost directly opposite Granville Lane, and would account for Viktor's sudden disappearance from Glover's radar.

'How did he seem on Sunday?'

'He wasn't playing well,' said Eric. 'He usually has the edge on me, but I whipped him — three times in a row.'

'Something on his mind?' asked Bingley.

'I asked him if he was feeling all right. He said he was fine. Just something he had to sort out.'

'He didn't say what?'

'I'm guessing it was one of the houses. He's got a couple of buy-to-lets in Selly Oak. He used to have more,' said Eric. 'But he sold some of them on a while back, when he started winding down. If you ask me, they're more trouble than they're worth.'

'Oh?'

'The tenants were always giving him grief. The students are usually the worst; damaging things or causing problems with the neighbours. And leaving the places in a mess when they move out at the end of the year. The other lot are all right though.'

'The other lot?'

'Foreigners, you know, immigrants and the like. They're good as gold, according to Viktor. On their best behaviour, I suppose, so that they can stay here. Good luck to 'em, I say.'

'If the houses were so much trouble, why keep them on? Viktor was well past retirement age.'

Eric hesitated. 'I think it's the money.' he said, reluctantly. 'He hardly ever talked about it, but Vik grew up poor. His parents came here from Poland before the war and they brought nothing with them. Vik always had a fear of going back to that, and the houses were his insurance.'

'He didn't have a family?'

'Not as such. Irma, his wife's been passed ten years or more. I think there's a nephew on her side. But I don't know that Vik's seen him for years, if ever.'

'What time did he leave your flat on Sunday?' asked Bingley.

'Late. He didn't seem in any hurry to go, which was strange, because he didn't like driving in the dark. His eyes were going, so the lights of the oncoming traffic bothered him. I'm the same. Never drive at night if I can help it.'

'From what we can tell, he didn't go straight home either,' said Bingley. 'We've caught him on camera around Cotteridge, Kingsmead. Any idea why he might have been there?'

'He's got a lock-up on the business park,' said Eric doubtfully. 'But that time of night? I can't imagine why he'd have been going there then.'

'What was the lock-up for?' asked Bingley, anticipating added mountains of junk. 'More of his "collections"?'

'No, it was for the cleaning. He had his own company; contract cleaning, offices and the like. Ironic now, given how he lives. But he gave all that up when Irma got sick. That was when he sold off the other properties too.'

'What about Viktor's other friends?'

'I don't know that he had any, aside from me. He and Irma were very self-contained as a couple so they didn't need anyone else. It hit him hard when she died. He was always very protective of her, almost obsessive. Had traditional ideas about how a husband should care for his wife and thought that women should be shielded from the harsh realities of life. I don't think he's ever really got over losing her. Since then, he keeps to himself. There is this Asian chap though; Indian, I think. He does Vic's accounts. Got a funny name. Agadoo or something.'

'Like the song?' said Bingley.

'Oh, I don't know about that.' It did seem unlikely, so Bingley put a question mark beside it.

Bingley looked up as Khatoon emerged from the house, pulling off her gloves.

'I wondered where you'd got to,' she said.

'I'm just finding out a bit more about Viktor,' said Bingley, and made the introductions.

'That's great,' said Khatoon, appreciatively. 'He's been a man of mystery. I thought I'd go and try the neighbours again,' she said to Bingley. 'Stretch my legs a bit.' But she was back in a matter of minutes, shaking her head.

'I should go,' said Eric. 'Leave you to get on with your work.'

'It's been really helpful to talk to you,' said Bingley, 'and I'm sorry for your loss.'

'Thank you, son.'

'You must have known Viktor well,' said Khatoon.

'As well as anyone, I suppose,' said Eric.

'Would you consider coming in to formally identify him?'

'Oh, I don't know about that.' It was a common reaction.

'Trouble is,' said Bingley, picking up the theme, 'we've got no one else, and until we do it, he can't be laid to rest.'

'I see that,' said Eric uncertainly. 'Well, all right then.'

'When would be a good time?' asked Khatoon. 'It would help to do it as soon as possible.'

Eric thought for a minute. 'I've got nothing on this afternoon.'

'Just wait a minute while I speak to my colleague.' Khatoon phoned through to Vicky Jesson.

'Two o'clock?' she asked Eric, who seemed happy with that.

'Great,' said Khatoon, relaying it to Jesson. 'If you'd like to give DC Bingley your address, we'll arrange for someone to pick you up.'

As he was dictating his details to Bingley, Eric's eyes filled up, and he had to search his pockets for a handkerchief. When he found one, he blew his nose loudly. 'I'm going to miss him,' he said. He looked up at the house. 'What will happen to all this now, I wonder?'

CHAPTER NINE

Waking early after a fitful night, Mariner decided for once to take the guvnor's advice, and go for a walk along the canal to clear his mind before heading in to work. There were few people about this morning, which suited him just fine. He felt a degree of apprehension about the IOPC investigation. It was natural and probably healthy, he concluded. If he was relaxed about the process, it would seem that he didn't care. And he did. Since Sunday, a family had been keeping vigil for a son, brother, grandson and they were entitled to know exactly how the catastrophic accident had happened.

He got in to Granville Lane in good time to meet Simon Bell — a consummate professional with the short, compact physique of a rugby player. Having read Mariner's written statement, Bell seemed cautious in his response to it.

'I thought it might help to have some additional context, so I spoke to someone I know at Belgravia,' he said. 'Clifford's backpack contained heroin, crack cocaine and a large amount of cash, along with another burner phone.'

'He's a runner?'

'Looks like it. And the family are well known to officers at Belgravia,' Bell went on. 'They're not happy, and looking for someone to blame.'

'Understandable,' said Mariner. 'Is that going to be problem?'

'Ordinarily, I'd say not,' said Bell. 'But the IOPC have come in for criticism of late that too many inquiries into West Mids have cleared the officers involved. My concern is that they might be looking to set an example.'

'Terrific.'

'All you can do is tell it like it happened, and trust them to do their jobs properly.'

At first meeting, the two IOPC officials — Martin Nawaz and Karen Osborne — were professional and objective, with no agenda that Mariner could detect.

'Given your exemplary career, we'd have been happy to allow a local inquiry,' said Nawaz, who was leading the questioning. 'But the young man's parents have made a complaint, and have presented evidence to support the request, so we have little choice; I hope you'll bear with us.'

'Of course.' Mariner exchanged a glance with Bell. What was this evidence?

'We've read your account of the incident, which is detailed and clear, as we'd expect,' Nawaz continued. 'We just have a few questions arising from it.'

These were primarily to verify Mariner's version of events, while he was travelling on the bus and afterwards. They circled around, gradually moving in on the crux of their investigation.

'Did you at any point during the pursuit make physical contact with the suspect?' asked Nawaz.

'None at all,' said Mariner. He held up his hand to show them the wound. 'His knife made contact, but that was it.'

'And you're sure about that?'

'Absolutely.'

'Just to be clear,' said Nawaz, 'you were about two metres away from the boy when he climbed up onto the garage roofs.'

'That's right — except I wouldn't say he climbed. That makes it sound laborious.'

Nawaz consulted the document before him. 'Yes, I see from your statement you say he "sprang" on to the skip and then the roof.'

'That's right,' said Mariner. 'He used the skip for leverage.'

'How long would you say it took him to complete that manoeuvre?'

Mariner bit back the urge to point out that he didn't have sight of a stopwatch. 'It was a matter of seconds; five or six, if that. I was impressed with his agility, to be honest, and I was sure the game was up. I knew I couldn't replicate the move.'

'So, those few seconds were your last chance to catch him,' concluded Nawaz. 'Where exactly were you, as he hit the skip and the roof?'

'I was closing in, covering the last metre or so, as he pushed off the skip.'

'Pretty close then,' said Osborne.

'Yes.' Mariner refrained from adding that all this was in his statement. He reminded himself that they were not being pedantic but thorough.

'How did you feel, knowing that, as you put it "the game was up"?' asked Nawaz.

'The same way I always do when I fail to apprehend a perpetrator,' said Mariner. 'Frustrated; annoyed that I couldn't have run faster. I'd just seen him commit a serious crime. As far as I knew at that moment, he could have killed someone, and he was getting away.'

'You must have been tempted then to make a last-ditch attempt to grab at him,' said Osborne.

'I did,' said Mariner. 'But I wasn't anywhere near close enough to make contact.'

'Are you sure about that?' asked Nawaz.

'Absolutely,' said Mariner, suppressing the first rumble of unease. Why was he pressing this?

The two officials exchanged a look. 'You see, the family have a witness who saw that you did make contact,' said Osborne.

'Well, they can't have, because I didn't.'

Nawaz shuffled through his papers until he found the pertinent quote.

"'I saw him grab the boy's foot and pull him off the roof. He fell and his head hit the skip,'" he read. So that was it.

'Didn't happen,' said Mariner. 'Dean Clifford fell because he dropped his rucksack and tried to catch it before it rolled off the roof. Anyway, there were no witnesses. It was peeing down with rain and it was at the back of the flats; all they have on that side is a high, narrow window. They couldn't have got an easy or decent angle. How could they possibly be sure of what they saw?'

'We have yet to visit the location to judge for ourselves,' said Nawaz. 'But the witness is in no doubt.'

'Perhaps that's so,' said Mariner. 'But they're mistaken.'

'If that's the case then you have nothing to worry about,' said Osborne, with a tight smile. 'I think that's as much as we can do today. It may be necessary to speak to you again, but for the moment we'll continue our enquiries. When we're satisfied that we have all the evidence, we'll notify all interested parties of our findings.'

Mariner walked with Bell down to the car park; he needed some air.

'Well at least we know now what's driving this,' said Bell.

'Doesn't help, though, does it?' said Mariner. 'It could boil down to my word against that of this witness. If the IOPC are intent on getting a result, it could go all the way. I'll lose my job and my pension.'

'We're a long way off that,' said Bell. 'I'll do what I can to find out about this witness.'

'Thanks for your help, Simon, I appreciate it.'

The two men shook hands and Mariner returned to his office. The guvnor must have been listening out for him. She appeared in his doorway the moment he sat down behind his desk.

'So?'

Mariner shrugged. 'Apparently there's a witness who saw me drag Clifford off the roof, which is impressive, considering it didn't happen. Simon's going to follow up on it, but there's little I can do now except let them do their worst.'

Sharp didn't make any reassuring noises. Neither of them could predict which way it would go. Instead she asked, 'How's the Paszek investigation going?'

'Early days,' said Mariner. 'I'll check in with Vicky, and then, if it's OK with you, I'll head over to Norfolk.'

'You'll have an interesting time over there.'

'And hopefully be of some help too.'

He found Vicky Jesson at her desk in CID.

'I heard that your meeting had finished,' she said. 'How was it?'

'Hard to say,' said Mariner, leaning on a nearby unoccupied desk. 'But it's out of my hands now. And parents' evening?'

'It went astonishingly well,' said Jesson, as though she still couldn't quite believe it. 'My older daughter might just turn out to have a sensible head on her shoulders.'

'I never doubted it,' said Mariner. 'What's happening here?'

'Millie and Kevin have found a useful witness at Briar Lane. A close friend of Viktor's — an Eric Dillon — turned up, so we've got some good background intel and he's prepared to do the formal ID for us this afternoon. I've just fixed up transport for him. We know now that Viktor rented a lock-up on the Kingsmead business park that he ran a cleaning company out of, and according to Eric, he still has *two* buy-to-lets in Selly Oak. We're looking for further evidence.'

'Any one of those locations could give us our crime scene,' said Mariner. 'Productive morning. And how's Charlie getting on?' asked Mariner. Unusually, Glover wasn't at his desk.

'He's still interrogating the CCTV,' said Jesson. 'Rather him than me.'

'Anything from Stuart Croghan?'

'Good news, yes. He can start work on John Doe this afternoon, so should have something for me when I go in for the ID.'

'See, you're a natural,' said Mariner. 'All over it already.'

Jesson drew a breath. 'So, why do I feel like a charlatan?'

'That'll pass,' said Mariner. 'Trust your instincts — they're sound — and don't be afraid to go to the guvnor if there's anything you're unsure of, especially around the budget. She'll have to authorise any extra resources you might need, but if you make a good case, you'll find her sympathetic. Use her as a sounding board, too.'

'It's going to take some getting used to, staying here instead of getting out and about,' she said.

'Oh, yes, on that, feel free to use my office any time,' said Mariner. 'You might want to put some distance between you and the others, or just have some space to think.'

'Thanks, I might do that.'

'Just don't get too comfortable, eh?'

'As if.'

* * *

It felt odd to be walking away from Granville Lane in the middle of the day. Mariner had already packed a bag, so after fuelling the car he went home and picked it up, before checking and locking the house. The drive over to East Norfolk was changed beyond recognition, mostly thanks to the A14, built in the early nineties, which circumvented the many tiny rural villages through Northamptonshire and Cambridgeshire. It was an opportunity too to give his new car a good run. He was still enjoying the comparative comfort of it after finally giving up his old Volvo — even if, technically speaking, it was the Volvo that had given up on him.

As the landscape turned greener, almost as a reflex, Mariner could feel the tension in his shoulders easing, and he passed any number of places where it would have been a pleasure to walk. With increasing frequency of late, he kept thinking about what it would be like if he didn't have a job to do any more. Perhaps the hassle of the IOPC had brought it to the fore, but he'd already passed the age at which he was eligible to retire and the idea of moving to somewhere completely different had been close to the surface for a while now. He wondered what Suzy would think of that. If he knew her at all, she'd embrace the opportunity.

From the Norwich bypass he saw the signs to Carrow Road football stadium and the one that would mystify any American tourists: *To Wroxham and the Broads*. From there he decided to take the slower, back route to the coast, the last leg of the journey taking him through sparsely populated rolling countryside, before he came to the flat open plains of the marshes. From here, a weird kind of familiarity made the hairs stand up on the back of his neck. Though the perspective was different — somehow smaller and quainter — landmarks that he imagined would be long gone were still in existence. A bowstring bridge over the river took him into the hamlet of St Ansgar, with its riverside pub across from what had been the village shop, but was now a boat hire office. A little further on, the old filling station had swapped selling fuel for car sales. Immediately in front of this, he turned right off the main road and into Sandy Lane.

From this point there were more changes. Where, years ago, he felt sure, the right-hand side of the road had been coniferous woodland, this had been cleared to make way for two rows of so-called 'affordable housing'. A fenced children's playground park rubbed shoulders with these, before another, slightly more upmarket housing development gave way to increasingly exclusive and secluded luxury homes set among the trees, which were eventually entirely concealed by banks of rhododendrons.

Mariner drove on slowly, scouring the land right and left for another familiar landmark, including a public footpath that dissected the road. On the right, the rhododendrons gave way to deciduous woodland, mature to begin with but thinning to a plantation of younger saplings, after which came two ploughed fields. These ended with heavy-duty steel railings enclosing more trees, before the rhododendrons appeared again. And then he arrived at a T-junction, of which he had no memory at all. Since turning into the lane at the garage, he had covered nearly three miles, so surely must have driven past the point where the campsite had been. The blare of a horn alerted him to a car right behind, so, waving an apology, he signalled and pulled over to the verge, to let it pass. Then he found a safe place to turn and drove back in the other direction, with a growing unease that bordered on mild panic. The land could have been re-purposed many times over since he was last here. If he couldn't even recognise this, he was going to be bugger all help to Reid, and he'd driven the width of the country to find out as much.

He drove on carefully, and, to his relief, saw that behind the steel fence and trees rose a steep grassy bank. A board, barely visible under a leafy branch confirmed it. This was the water-treatment facility that had been close to the camp-site. Checking his rear-view mirror frequently, he slowed to a crawl again, alongside the newer plantation of trees, until finally he spied the public footpath sign, which cut down off the road. Yes, this was it, he was sure of it. Thank God. Pulling as far into the verge as he dared at the head of the path, he went to investigate.

* * *

THEN

It was a freakishly hot summer and he was nearly seventeen years old. Already he was beginning to disappoint his mother, mainly by not doing as well as she thought he should be doing at the all-boys grammar school he attended. The reality was that he'd switched off from lessons long ago, unable to see the point of exams, when the prospect of working in any kind of office for the rest of his life held no interest for him. He felt instead as if he was waiting, biding his time, though for what, he didn't know.

When the school term ended, a group of the other lads were going off on their own, down to the south west, to Newquay in Cornwall. To begin with he played along, saying that he'd go too, though he knew deep down it wouldn't happen. The talk about surfing and getting a tan didn't interest him, but the talk about girls and getting laid was a different story. Robinson was obsessed with the Beach Boys and sang 'Surfin' USA' on a never-ending loop. Never mind that none of them had even seen a real surfboard. Mariner couldn't get into the spirit of it. The other boys' parents would be glad to get rid of them for the month of August, but not his. He'd be stuck with his mother as usual. He plucked up the courage to put it to her, eventually. He thought she was going to cry.

'I know you'll want to spread your wings soon, but this could be our last summer together,' she said. 'I thought we'd go away in the van. What will I do if it breaks down?' The camper van; not a proper one but one his grandad had helped her to convert. Then came the dire warnings about drugs, alcohol and the 'foolishness that young men get up to' whatever that was. After that, she said no more, but adopted a pained expression to demonstrate the depth of hurt she felt, and finally the guilt wore him down. When he agreed not to go, she announced that she'd got him a holiday job in the storeroom at Woodward's, where he'd be wearing a brown overall and working with men three times his age.

His mates were full of it. One Saturday morning a gang of them went into the town centre, for the sole purpose of buying condoms. Mariner still hadn't told them he wasn't going, so he went too and came home with a pack he'd probably never use, which he stashed under his mattress.

'Where are we going?' he asked his mother, as the holiday approached.
'Marsham Fair,' she said.

He couldn't be bothered to ask what it was, or why they were going there. On the appointed day, he and Rose set off in the camper van not long after dawn broke, and drove east, joining queues of traffic doing the same, many of the cars with caravans in tow. Norfolk had its share of holiday attractions from the seaside resorts and beaches to the waterways of the Norfolk Broads, but they were heading for neither.

After four hours they hit suburbia: 'Welcome to Norwich. A fine city' the sign proclaimed. They came to a halt on a residential city street beside what looked like an expanse of playing fields.

'First stop,' announced his mother.
'What is it?' he asked. It looked to him like a chunk of the Bullring had been transplanted into a field alongside a construction site.

'It's the University of East Anglia,' she said triumphantly. 'Impressive, isn't it?' Closing her eyes, she inhaled deeply, a soppy smile on her face. 'You can just smell the learning going on. Of course, you wouldn't have to come here, though it's a good one. Plenty more that you can choose from.'

'Why would I want to?'

'Because you're clever; all your teachers say so. You could study, oh, I don't know, law or something.'

'Law? Why on earth would I want to do that?'

'Because you can!' She was starting to get exasperated now, as she always did. That conversation had made no sense at all to him until thirty years later, when his mother had died and his father's identity was finally revealed.

'Anyway,' she said. 'I'm going to get out and have a nosy round; stretch my legs and get some air. Are you coming?'

'No thanks.' Even though the truth was he was desperate for a break from the stifling van. She returned after about half an hour, bursting with how wonderful it all looked. Then out of the city and back on the road again. Less than an hour later they pulled into the campsite; a field with a few cars and tents dotted around its circumference. Why the hell had they driven nearly two hundred miles for this? The so-called 'fair' was nothing more than a straggling line of hippy stalls spreading into adjacent woodland; all very New Age and Rose's style. They bumped over the grass of the meadow and she brought them to a halt in a space between a Vauxhall Viva and a trailer tent. Smoky with incense, the air caught in his throat as he got out of the van.

* * *

Retrieving his boots from the car, Mariner put them on and walked to the gate. The footpath marked a dividing line between the old and new woodland, now additionally separated by wildlife fencing. This newer plantation was the field where the campsite had been. The fair with its stalls and entertainment had for some reason been set among the trees of the more established woods. He walked down the path that sloped gently towards the furthest corner, where the plantation ended and was separated from what lay beyond by a thicket of hawthorn, the green tips of the leaves just beginning to emerge, amongst which was, as he'd hoped, a stile, so dilapidated that it had to be the original. Climbing it with care, he emerged from the hawthorn onto an incline of open ground covered with grass and brambles. This led down to acres of reed beds and marshland, which bordered the meandering river, and gave a panoramic view over miles of flat wetlands.

As the ground levelled off, he could see where the path picked up duckboards that cut through the reed beds and extended into the water as a wooden jetty. Close to where he stood, a smart new sign pointed off to the right and the 'Roman fort' — what they'd simply called 'the wall'. Back in the day some wag had added a simple downstroke to the old sign, turning it into a Roman fart. But apart from that, the familiarity of what he could see here was uncanny. Even the pale afternoon sun formed part of the memory. Something, or someone, walked over his grave and he shivered, despite his warm fleece.

Mariner wondered where Robina had been found. There was no indication of police activity round here that he could see, though they must surely still be searching the surrounding area. He would no doubt be returning here in the next day or two, but, for now, he should check in with Ginny Reid.

CHAPTER TEN

Jesson had arranged for a uniform to pick Eric up and take him to the mortuary, so she drove there alone. It was far from the first time she'd been through this routine, but nonetheless she felt a new weight of responsibility. She went first to the public waiting room, where she found an older man sitting, staring at the walls. He jumped up as soon as she entered the room, eager to get it over with. She could feel his apprehension.

'Hello, you must be Eric,' she said, taking his outstretched hand. 'We're so grateful to you for helping us with this.'

'Am I allowed to ask what kind of state he's in?' He held a cap in his hands and was turning it round and round, doing his best to conceal his nerves. Jesson felt a wave of sympathy for him. The majority of people never had to do this, but she knew from personal experience what it was like. It was often the moment when brutal reality struck.

'He looks fine,' she reassured him. 'A bit of bruising to his forehead, but peaceful.' That seemed to calm him.

When he saw the body, Eric confirmed, without hesitation, that the dead man was his friend, and though Jesson didn't turn to look, she could hear from the jagged breaths the emotion he was experiencing for this final parting of the ways. She slipped an arm round his shoulders. 'I understand it was quick,' she said. 'Viktor wouldn't have known any-thing about the accident.'

Fetching Eric another cup of tea afterwards in the wait-ing room, she asked, 'What was Viktor like?'

'He was a good man,' he replied, without hesitation. 'Kind, and loyal. He had a temper on him sometimes, espe-cially if he thought something wasn't fair. Us trainspotters get to know one another, you know? You see the same faces on the platforms. One lad — only a youngster — he wasn't quite right, if you know what I mean. This one day these two thugs started tormenting him. I thought Vic was going to throw them on the rails, he was so angry. But I probably saw it three times in all the years I knew him.'

When Eric had gone, Jesson put on protective clothing and joined Stuart Croghan in the examination suite for the latest on their unknown male.

'Just you today?' said Croghan.

'The boss has got other fish to fry,' said Jesson.

'Ah, I see. Well, nothing much new to report on Mr Paszek,' said Croghan. 'Toxicology is back and there were no drugs in his system, though there was a low level of alco-hol. The last meal he ate was steak and kidney pudding and potatoes.'

'Lovely,' said Jesson.

'So, to our mystery man.'

Croghan took hold of one corner of the sheet that cov-ered the body. 'Just to warn you, he's not a pretty sight, what's left of him.' He wasn't wrong, and as he removed the sheet Jesson drew the smallest involuntary breath.

To her, it would be miraculous if the pathologist could determine anything from a face so disfigured by damaged and swollen flesh. One side of the body was similarly man-gled from head to toe and grotesquely discoloured. His lower right leg sat at an improbable angle and his right foot was entirely crushed and misshapen.

'I'd put him in his mid-to-late thirties,' began Croghan. 'Though not particularly well-nourished. Slight nicotine stains on the first two fingers of the right hand, which would seem to confirm that the cigarette packet was his. He's five foot six and, as you can see, slight in stature.'

'And he died from his injuries?'

'I've found nothing yet to the contrary,' said Croghan. 'He's sustained considerable impact injuries: fractures, bruising and abrasions. I'd say that the most likely cause of death was being struck at high speed by a large vehicle; an HGV going at motorway speed or a train would do it. His left leg probably went under at some point too, it's badly fractured, which is why it's at that angle. And, as you can see—' Croghan walked around to the end of the gurney — 'his left foot is badly crushed.'

'Could it have been a car?' asked Jesson. 'They've found blood on the front bumper of the Passat.'

'It's highly unlikely that any car — even the biggest SUVs — could inflict this amount of damage over such an extensive area. There is another alternative,' said Croghan. 'Though it doesn't explain all his injuries, so I think it less likely. He could have fallen, from a considerable height.'

'How high?'

'I once examined a woman who fell from the ninth floor, maybe even higher. And a fall such as that wouldn't explain the crushed foot.'

'What about a combination of the two?' asked Jesson. 'Could he have fallen from a motorway bridge, say, and been hit by a vehicle?'

'If the timing was right, yes. The side of his body has taken the brunt of the impact; his left shoulder has almost entirely disintegrated. The contact could have thrown him to the side and his trailing left foot gone under the wheels. Could have been when he lost the shoe.'

'In which case, we'd have no way of telling if he did it voluntarily, or with help,' said Jesson, thinking aloud.

'Another thing to note is the livor mortis, here and here.' Croghan rolled the body to show Jesson areas down the right side, under the hip and shoulder, where the blood had pooled into barely discernible areas of purple lividity. 'It indicates that he landed more or less on his right side, and he remained in that position for up to two hours after death. The pooling faded as he was moved around. The other find that might help you is these.' Croghan walked Jesson over to the exhibits, where there was a dish containing a dozen or so pellets, about a half centimetre cubed, and what looked like blades of green organic matter.

'Gravel and leaves of some kind,' said Croghan. 'They were embedded in his face, again on the right side, so I would say were on the surface where he landed. I'll send them for analysis.'

'Let's hope they turn out to be something rare,' said Jesson. 'Preferably something that only exists in one tiny geographical area. If we're talking about a motorway, we're going to need a lot of help to narrow it down.'

'Some of his front teeth are missing and broken,' Croghan continued. 'But the back teeth are intact and though it doesn't look as if they've been properly brushed for a while, they are in good condition, as if they were once taken care of. That's about all I can tell you about him at present, but his clothing presents some additional clues.'

Croghan switched his attention to the dozen or so evidence bags. These contained a lightweight jacket, sweatshirt, jeans, underwear and socks, all spread out in their protective coverings to prevent cross-contamination. 'As you can see, there's minimal labelling on the clothing,' said Croghan. 'It's basic quality stuff, mostly manufactured in the Far East, and insofar as one can tell, none of it looks as if it's seen the inside of a washing machine lately. Heavy bloodstaining as we'd expect, but there are also traces of some other kind of dark residue on his socks and on the lower trouser legs of his jeans. It's some kind of purple dye, with a distinctive smell.' Croghan opened up the bag containing the socks and held it under Jesson's nose. 'Are you getting that?'

'It's chemical,' she said. 'Some kind of cleaning fluid? Viktor Paszek ran a contract cleaning outfit at one time and there was a large canister of cleaning fluid in the boot of the car.'

'Could be,' said Croghan. 'We'll need to wait for a full analysis. But this prompted me to have another look at his body. They're masked by his other injuries, but on the skin of his lower legs you can see some random red patches, like a developing rash. Could be a reaction to that residue, whatever it is.'

They moved on to the other bagged exhibits: a cheap digital watch, a plain gold wedding band, and a wallet containing six banknotes for five hundred thousand Vietnamese dong each.

'That looks a lot of money,' said Jesson.

'Hm, but best of all is this.'

The package Croghan passed her contained a small plastic wallet holding a family photograph: a young mother and father with a boy of about eight years old. The image quality suggested the photograph was recent.

'Thanks to the damage to his face, it's impossible to be absolutely certain, but the approximate age and build and what bone structure's left are all consistent. I think it's reasonable to conclude that it is him,' said Croghan.

That really was a breakthrough. But Jesson's gaze lingered on the woman and child in the photo. A wife and son? Where were they now, and did they have any idea about what had happened to their husband and father?

CHAPTER ELEVEN

It was late afternoon as Mariner completed his journey. He had to rely on the satnav for the last leg, which took him across the River Yare to Great Yarmouth police station. Although he'd made the journey into the town twice before, on both occasions it was as a passenger, long before he'd developed a driver's observational skills. He'd have been far more interested in what was going on inside the car back then. Driving through now, out of season, the town had the air of down-at-heel neglect common to many of England's old-fashioned seaside resorts, and everything seemed so *small*. He drove past the docks and into the centre of the town, crossing the river by a low, ornate bridge, which provoked a distant memory of watching it being raised to let a sailing boat through.

The police station was a wide two-storey 1960s building, of a similar generation and design to Granville Lane, and was situated next to a NatWest branch on the corner of a street intriguingly named 'The Conge'. Ginny Reid came down to meet Mariner at reception and furnished him with temporary ID before taking him straight to an interview room. 'We've just got a few questions, arising from the statement. Is it all right with you if we get all that on the record first?' she said. 'Then tomorrow morning we'll head out to the deposition site.'

'Whatever you think,' said Mariner. They would want to finish questioning before exposing him to any of the material they had, to try to get as objective and untarnished a version of events from him as possible. Through necessity, the formal interview was conducted in a room set up for the purpose, but there was a plate of pastries to go with the coffee Sinclair brought. Mariner was hungry so he dived in. They spent a large part of the interview revisiting the ground already covered at Granville Lane, before getting to the nitty-gritty.

'What exactly was your relationship with Robina?' asked Reid.

'I suppose you'd call it a holiday romance,' said Mariner.

'Can you give us a bit more detail?'

'What kind of detail?' asked Mariner, though he was pretty sure what she was getting at.

'Robina was almost nineteen. How old were you?'

'Sixteen, though I'm sure she thought I was older.' *What do you do, for a job and that?*

'You looked older,' said Reid. She saw Mariner's quizzical expression. 'You're in a couple of the family's holiday snaps in Robina's file. The two of you look close. Physically, I mean.'

'That was down to her,' said Mariner. 'She was very . . . tactile.'

'You said you met her at the fair?' said Sinclair.

'That's right. It was adjacent to the campsite. It was like nothing I'd experienced before, but just the sort of place my mother would take us to.'

* * *

THEN

He wasn't sure what he'd expected, but it wasn't this. To him, a fair meant the annual Warwick Mop with its gaudy lights, dodgems and irresistible undercurrent of violence; the tough-looking ride operators and the brassy girls. There were no leather jackets here, but instead lots of tie-dye and flowing cotton and stalls selling beaded jewellery, leather belts and wristbands and garments made from pungent-smelling Indian cotton. Most of this stuff could be bought off the market in Leamington, he thought, so why the hell had they come all the way over here for it?

The stallholders were hardcore hippies: men in linen trousers and collarless shirts, or vests, their feet dusty in open sandals. Many had long hair and straggling beards; some smoked roll-ups that hinted at more than just tobacco. He felt awkward and overdressed in his button-down Ben Sherman and new, stiff Levis that still needed wearing in, and the woodsmoke and incense made his skin itch.

Rose was in her element. She had reconnected with what she referred to as 'the sisterhood' and seemed to have some history with a couple of them. Her friend Maggie, who came to the house in Leamington, was here too. There were what he thought of as normal people too, but they were the ones who visited briefly — families come for an afternoon out, to gawp at the New Age spectacle and to buy some 'genuine' cultural artefacts.

After half an hour of wandering around the stalls, he was bored and already wondering how long Rose was going to make them stay here. He sat down on an upturned tree stump intended for the purpose and had picked up a piece of twine, twisting it idly in his fingers as he observed. Observation was what he did; as an only child he often found himself on the outside looking in, and most of the time he didn't mind that. There were little kids running around, the toddlers naked from the waist down, which he found vaguely distasteful, though he didn't really know why. And they were filthy. Why didn't these people wash?

Just up from where he sat, a youngish couple were working on a jewellery stall, although right now they were having sharp words. They were too far away to hear and he could only see the man's back, but the woman's frown signalled tension in the exchange. After a moment, the man stomped off. The woman was pretty, with long raven-black hair and — now the man had gone — a ready smile. She wore denim cut-offs and a loose cotton singlet with no bra so that her nipples were clearly visible. She laughed a lot with the customers and perhaps because of this — or maybe because of the nipples — she was doing a brisk trade. It was full on. When she wasn't serving customers, she was replenishing stock from half a dozen cardboard boxes on the floor at the back of the stall. Each time she turned and reached down into a box, he could see her bare breasts dangling. It was making him hard and he couldn't stop watching her, though he was sure she hadn't noticed. He found himself willing the punters to buy something from her, just so she'd have to do it again. Then suddenly she looked up and straight at him. 'You've sat there long enough, watching me do all the work,' she said, cheerfully. 'Do something useful like go and get me a cup of tea.'

The heat rushed to his face. He felt like walking away, but instead he obediently shuffled over to the stall, where she gave him 10p and sent him off to the refreshment van.

'Thanks, I really need this,' she said, when he got back with the tea. 'I'm Lesley.'

'Thomas,' he said in reply.

'Nice to meet you, Thomas. As you can see, I've been abandoned and left to cope,' she said, cheerfully. 'Story of my life. But I could use some help. You can see how much things are. People are allowed to try on rings, but watch them. Bags are here, and any questions, just ask me.'

The prices were on tiny cards, neatly written. Most of the merchandise was cheap ubiquitous stuff, but towards the back were some more expensive items, pinned to velvet-covered boards, like in a proper jeweller's.

'Solid silver,' she said. 'If you can sell one of them, you get a bonus.'

By the time she'd given him a run-down of some other dos and don'ts, there were customers waiting, so then they just got on with it. After that, the time passed quickly and it was only when the crowds began to dwindle and a small girl turned up whining that she was hungry, that Lesley called it a day. He helped her carry the boxes back to her tent across the field from where his own was pitched.

'See you tomorrow, maybe,' Lesley called after him as he left.

As he approached Rose's van, he saw that his mother was sitting outside on a deckchair surrounded by seven or eight other people, all deep in discussion. Someone was strumming a guitar. He tried to make it to his tent on the other side without Rose seeing him, but should have known he'd never manage that.

'Hello, my love,' she beamed at him. 'What have you been up to? This is my Thomas.' Oh God, did she realise what that sounded like? 'Can't you find anyone to hang out with?'

'They're all little kids,' he said.

'Don't be silly, darling. There must be some young people your age.'

'Well, there aren't.'

'Don't worry about it, Thomas,' said the man nearest to him, whose lank blond hair trailed from underneath his bush hat. 'Come and join us. Let's hear what you have to say about things.' Exhaling lazily as he spoke. He leaned over to proffer the cigarette he was smoking; probably a spliff. Tom knew that he should take it; that the man was only being friendly and trying to include him. But it felt patronising, so just to be awkward really (his speciality), he said no. The man was unfazed, and raised his hand in the open palmed two-finger salute and said, in pure cliché, 'No problem, man, good karma.'

Cringing, he retreated into his tent. By mid-evening, his mother's friends had disbanded and people were back at their own pitches cooking dinner. His tent was hot, so he tied back the flaps and lay watching the ebb and flow of campers. His mother heated up a stew she'd brought with them (vegetarian, of course), which seemed entirely inappropriate for the weather, but he ate it anyway. Later, he was outside brushing his teeth over a bowl of water when his attention was snagged by a noise. Then he saw them: girls and boys, tumbling up into the field from the lower corner, laughing and shouting. Some of the boys wore swimming shorts, towels draped around their necks, and a girl was carrying a bag and blanket as if they'd had a picnic. He felt a stab of jealousy. Where had they come from? As they crossed the field they spread out into single file, in a line that looked like the evolution of man. The younger ones at the front didn't look old enough to have started at secondary school yet, but the older ones lagging behind were almost adults. Rose came out just at that moment and saw them too. 'There,' she said. 'There are youngsters your age. Go on, go and say hello. Introduce yourself.'

But he couldn't. It was too late. Toothbrush poised in the corner of his mouth, he just stood and watched from the cover of the awning. Another club that he didn't belong to. He finished cleaning his teeth and crawled into his tent. That night he thought about Lesley's breasts and masturbated furiously until his cock was sore; angry with Rose and her

*stupid hippy friends, angry with those kids for turning up when they did,
but mostly angry with himself for being such a pathetic loser.*

*He woke hours later, desperate for a pee. Outside the sky was
starting to shift from indigo to blue, he could smell the dew on the grass
and a single blackbird was cueing in the dawn chorus. But as he walked
back to the tent, he thought he heard another sound — voices and
laughter wafting across the morning air. And music. Not folk songs
and guitars this time but the heavy beat of rock music. It seemed to be
coming from beyond the trees on the far side of the campsite. Someone
was having a good time. It felt as if they were mocking him.*

* * *

There was a knock on the door and a duty sergeant peered
in. 'You asked me to give you the heads-up for the press
conference,' he said to Reid. 'Ten minutes.'

'Thanks.' Reid gathered up the paperwork. 'Sorry, we'll
have to leave it there for today. We'll go out to the deposition
site first thing in the morning, if that's all right with you?'

'Sounds good,' said Mariner. 'Good luck.'

CHAPTER TWELVE

Vicky Jesson was feeling more of an imposter than ever. To fully prepare for the afternoon briefing, she needed to catch up on entries in the policy log and refresh her memory on where they were up to with the various lines of enquiry. To do all this in peace, she'd taken up Mariner's proposal and moved into his office, along the corridor from CID. But sitting here now, she felt like a child dressing up in her mum's high heels, everything a bit too big and grown-up for her. It felt plain weird. She shook herself out of it. There was a job to do. How good would it be to get this all sewn up before he got back?

Mariner had made sure she was copied into everything sent to him from the Forensic Science Service and she found her inbox pleasingly populated. At least she'd have something to say. More intel had been entered into the policy log since her last read-through, too, so she took the boss's other advice and made notes. All the same, she couldn't stop the nerves nibbling at her as she left his office and closed the door. She half-expected some smart-arse comments when she joined the team, but none were forthcoming. *See, you underestimate them*, she heard Mariner saying. Instead, as she walked across the room, the chat diminished and by the time she'd taken up a position beside the incident board, she found herself the centre of silent attention, everyone waiting for her to begin.

'Right,' she said, clearing her throat. 'Let's crack on, shall we?'

'Ready when you are, boss,' said Bingley. Jesson shot him a look. 'Too soon?' he said.

'Let's start with the easy stuff,' she said. 'Viktor Paszek's identity has now been confirmed — thanks for helping set that up, Millie. We've also had results back from FSS, confirming that fingerprints on the polythene sheet and the can of cleaning fluid belong to Paszek, and his DNA has also been found on the inside of the rubber gloves. Blood on those, and on the overalls, is from our John Doe. It's therefore reasonable to assume that whatever part Paszek did or didn't play in his death, it was him who dealt with — was dealing with — the aftermath. Nothing we've got so far suggests that anyone else was involved, though that doesn't necessarily make it true.' Jesson looked around. Even Bingley had abandoned his usual repertoire of irritating habits: bending paperclips, clicking pens, snapping elastic bands. It was unnerving, but also gave her a surprising feeling of power. 'Apart from what was in it, the Passat hasn't given us much,' she went on, detailing what the FSS technician had told them. 'What else have we got from his home? Are we starting to get a clearer sense of the man?'

Khatoon stepped up. 'SOCOs didn't find anything untoward in the garage,' she said. 'Even with the luminol out. I asked them to have a good look around the garden, but nothing out of place there either.'

'So, we still don't have a crime scene,' Jesson said.

'I've just had confirmation that the prints on the old woodchip sack were Paszek's,' Khatoon continued. 'But there was nothing else on it; no blood or anything. Inside the house, all the paperwork we've found so far — and there's a lot of it — is pretty old, with some exceptions. He was one of these people who kept all the bank statements, bills and correspondence he's ever received — and his wife's.'

'What fun,' said Charlie Glover, a nod to the fact that much of the material would be coming his way.

'The most useful thing today was meeting Viktor's friend Eric,' said Khatoon. 'And not just because of the ID. Do you want to . . . ?' She looked over at Bingley.

'Yeah. We had quite a chat,' said Bingley. 'And I learned a fair bit from him. Eric speaks highly of Viktor. We now know Viktor spent some of Sunday evening at Eric's place on the Brookfield Gardens development, but he was as surprised as us that Viktor would have still been on the road in the middle of the night. The only place he could think Viktor would have gone afterwards was the Kingsmead business park, to his lock-up.'

'Do we have a specific address?' asked Jesson.

'Not from Eric, and we haven't found any reference to it at the house yet,' said Bingley. 'Paszek used to run a cleaning business out of there, but doesn't seem to be registered at Companies House, so I thought I'd go out there in the morning, see if I can find it. Oh, and Eric mentioned a friend of Viktor's; an Indian guy called — and this was his take on it — Agadoo. Possibly Viktor's accountant.'

'Agadoo? Are you serious?' said Glover.

'I know. That's what Eric said, though he didn't seem a hundred per cent sure.'

'I'll google him,' said Glover. 'Can't be that many accountants with a name like that.'

'Have we had anything back from Max on Paszek's mobile?' asked Jesson.

'Not much,' said Glover. 'It's a basic pay-as-you-go with only a handful of contacts, and not often used. Max is tracing the numbers.'

'Well, we might not be seeing much for it yet, but this is all good,' said Jesson, cringing inwardly at how patronising that sounded. 'Now on to our mystery man.' But before she could go further, Glover raised a hand.

'I've come up with a name,' he said, getting up from his workstation and coming over to the whiteboard. Above the boxed question mark that represented their John Doe, he wrote the word HIEN. 'It means quiet and gentle.'

There were murmurs of approval from the others.

'Hien, it is,' said Jesson, marvelling at what a difference that made. 'And now we also have a picture.' She pinned two enlarged photographs underneath the name: the original one with the family, and a cropped one of Hien alone. 'As Croghan thought, we wouldn't get a useful post-mortem photo of his face, but this was in one of his pockets. Charlie, we should add it to the social media posts. Someone out there might recognise him.'

'It's definitely him?' said Khatoon.

'Looking at the physical characteristics he can assess, Croghan's satisfied that it is,' said Jesson. 'So, we'll run with it. DNA analysis so far confirms Hien's ethnicity as Southeast Asian, and a wallet found on him contained six banknotes for five hundred thousand Vietnamese dong each, which supports our theory of his nationality.'

'That sounds like a lot of money,' said Khatoon.

'Not as much as you'd think,' said Jesson. 'Each of the notes is only worth about sixteen quid, so we're looking at a value of less than fifty, all told. We have no matches on either his prints or his DNA profile,' she went on. 'Where are we up to with other efforts to ID?'

'Now that we've got more to go on, I'll post an appeal on the website and social media platforms,' said Glover. 'I'll start trawling through missing persons too, starting locally and regionally.'

'There's no doubt now that Hien died an unnatural death,' said Jesson. 'His injuries are more considerable than even Croghan predicted.' There were murmurs of disgust as she pinned up images of Hien's wounds. 'He'd initially posited a beating, but the injuries don't reflect that. The pattern of Paszek's blood on the overalls found in the car is also inconsistent with him having administered one; the blood is patchy rather than spattered.'

'So, what then?' asked Bingley.

'We're looking at something substantial slamming into Hien with extreme force. The most likely scenario is an HGV or a train, but Croghan did also say it could be the ground. He's seen this level of impact injuries on a woman who fell from a height.'

'What do you think, bo— er, ma—' began Khatoon.

'How about we just stick to Vicky?' Jesson smiled. 'The only inconsistency with a fall is the state of his foot, which was crushed. What seems most likely to me, is that he fell — or was pushed — from a motorway bridge, which still falls some distance short of explaining the circumstances. If he fell and then was hit by a vehicle, or even if he was run over by an HGV or similar, why didn't the driver stop? And how did Paszek get involved?'

'It could have been hit at night and the driver didn't know what had happened. Paszek, driving along behind, sees him, or even hits him again,' said Khatoon. 'Wasn't there blood on his car?'

'The blood is from a muntjac deer,' said Jesson, reporting what had come through via email.

'And if Paszek did hit Hien, why didn't *he* call the emergency services, or take him to a hospital?' countered Glover.

'Too many unanswered questions,' said Jesson. 'Let's stay open-minded about it until we have more evidence. If, however, Hien did come to grief on a motorway, then it's a huge task.' Jesson tapped the photograph of the trainer. 'This missing shoe remains a key piece of evidence. Obviously, searching the whole West Midlands motorway network isn't feasible, but it should be added to the search appeal, Charlie. Someone out there might recognise it, or, if we're really lucky, come up with the other one in the pair. There's also an unknown chemical substance on Hien's clothing. It's been sent for analysis, but again, it may give us a clue to his movements immediately before — or after — he died. We also have these.' She pinned the close-ups of the watch and a wedding band onto the board.

'His poor wife,' said Khatoon.

Jesson brought the briefing to a close by going over actions for the following day. 'Our priorities are to find and search this lock-up Paszek's supposed to have, and locate the other properties. And we need to talk to this "Agadoo", if that's really his name.'

First one's the worst one, she said to herself as she walked back to Mariner's office afterwards. It was something she always said to the kids when they were worried about something new. Not a bad mantra to have.

CHAPTER THIRTEEN

The hotel Reid had booked Mariner into was on the seafront. It would have been imposing once, and in its heyday would have been at the centre of the holiday trade. But even when he was last here, decades ago, the British seaside holiday was suffering from the increased range and affordability of foreign travel. The original Victorian facade had been retained, but when he stepped inside the lobby, it was all abruptly modern, and could have passed for a city-centre hotel in Birmingham. The number of conference and break-out rooms listed on the board beside the reception desk suggested that it was no longer much of a destination for holidaying families either. The receptionist who checked him in, a man in his thirties, did not have a Norfolk accent but an unidentifiable European one.

Mariner's check-in seemed to take for ever, mainly because a new member of staff was being trained at the same time. While it was in progress, he became aware of low voices behind him and as he turned away with his key, he found a queue had formed of a younger sharp-suited man and an elderly couple, all waiting patiently at a discreet distance. It was a snapshot of the hotel's main clientele, Mariner supposed: retired couples and business people. He flashed an

104

apologetic smile as he made for the stairs and the young man stepped forward to take his place.

Up on the second floor, the room was comfortable, if soulless, but its redeeming features were the two picture windows that looked out across the road and promenade towards the wide beach of pale, yellow sand, and beyond that, a band of hazy grey that was the North Sea, interrupted only by the rows and rows of wind turbines on the horizon.

Stiff from hours of driving, Mariner wanted to stretch his legs before eating, so went for a walk south along the promenade, which took him past the piers, restaurants and entertainment venues of the resort. Most of the attractions were closed up for the winter, but the doors of the amusement arcades remained open, the cacophony of machines and flashing lights making a dismal attempt to entice the punters inside. Beyond the tourist traps it was blissfully deserted, the only noise from the screaming gulls and the wind as it whipped across the sands.

Back at the hotel, he was pleasantly surprised to find that the bar had also kept its traditional look, and offered several local craft beers. After some deliberation, he bought a pint of a ruby ale and sat in the bar looking out over the promenade, as the dusk gathered. He considered whether to give Jesson a call to see how her first afternoon in charge had gone, but realised it was way too soon. She'd think he didn't trust her.

* * *

Mariner awoke to a misty and murky Wednesday, with fine drizzle blowing against the window. The promenade was deserted, the beach drab and there was little visibility beyond that. He also had a text on his phone from Sinclair, asking him to delay his arrival at the police station until ten thirty, which meant he could take his time going down to breakfast. The room was stuffy and the windows opened only a few centimetres, so, in spite of the weather, he put on his waterproof jacket and boots and ventured out. This time he walked directly down to the sea shore, and along the damp sand away from the town. Here there were just one or two other hardy souls out with their dogs and the top of the beach with its shaggy green dunes had a wilder, untamed feel.

By the time he returned and went into the dining room he had it to himself. The couple he'd seen checking in passed him on their way out. The husband walked slowly, supported by sticks; the woman fussing over him. Anywhere else in the world they would probably have exchanged pleasantries, but this was England, so except for a smile of acknowledgement, they kept to themselves.

After breakfast, taking Robina's letter and the envelope containing the photos with him, Mariner started out along the seafront again, but this time walked into the town. Shortly before he turned away from the beach to make his way towards the police station, he saw the old couple from the hotel walking slowly along the prom. Mariner nodded in recognition as they walked by. Only now Mariner wasn't so sure they were a couple. He skirted the top of the town passing through residential streets of Edwardian villas, many of which were formerly guest houses.

'Sorry for the delay,' Ginny Reid said when she and Sinclair appeared to meet Mariner in reception. 'A constable from the original investigation got in touch. He had time constraints so we had to prioritise getting him in for an interview.'

'Was he helpful?'

'He was a wet-behind-the-ears PC at the time, so not party to all the discussion. But he did recall that one of the detectives in charge had suspicions about a Ludovic Rothbury. Minor aristocracy, apparently. Did you come across him?'

'I did,' said Mariner. 'But before I tell you about him, you might be interested in these.' He held up the envelope.

'What's in there?' asked Reid.

'The photographs I mentioned, among other things.'

'That's great,' said Reid. 'Scott, would you mind?'

Scott looked as if actually he did mind being asked to haul his bulk back up the stairs again, but he took the package from Mariner anyway.

'We'll see you out at the car,' said Reid.

'Was Rothbury a serious suspect?' asked Mariner.

'It doesn't sound like it. Our constable thought that the officer concerned had a chip on his shoulder about the upper classes.' She had her coat on. 'Shall we go?'

* * *

They took a different route out of the town to the one Mariner had used, over a more modern viaduct, between the river and a wide expense of water, then through retail and low-level industrial complexes.

'What happened to Robina's family?' Mariner asked, as they drove. 'How did they cope?'

'Not well in the long term,' said Reid. 'Several years after Robina went missing, her parents split up. Her mum moved down here, to be closer to where Robina disappeared, I suppose. She died seven years ago, never knowing what had happened to her daughter.'

'Poor woman. And her brothers and sister?'

'One brother emigrated to Canada, and the other lives down south, but her sister still lives in Yorkshire, close to her dad. She keeps an eye out for him and broke the news about what had been found. They're expected down here any day.'

By now, Sinclair had picked up the road Mariner had come in on, which took them out into the countryside, and eventually to St Ansgar. They drove past what had been the caravan site and campsite, and the water-treatment plant, eventually turning off between wooden gates that bisected a high yew hedge, where they came to a stop. Mariner realised he must have driven past here yesterday, as he struggled to orientate himself. The board a little way down the drive said *Herringfleet House, Residential Care.* The uniformed constable at the gates recognised Sinclair and Reid and waved them through.

'We've had a lot of press interest, as you can imagine,' said Reid. The driveway cut through a dozen or so acres of lush grass dotted with trees, and brought them to a rambling brick-and-flint building with two giant monkey puzzle trees standing guard in front. It was immediately obvious that this was where the investigation was centred. Crime-scene tape cordoned off a large area some distance from the right-hand side of the main house, where trees had been felled and the enormous roots were being excavated. A JCB stood idle amid the ploughed-up earth, with more tape strung limply around it; symbolic rather than an effective deterrent. Reid would only have a small team, and nowhere near the level of resources that would be thrown at a live investigation. And she'd already indicated that they were time-limited, the nursing home eager to recommence construction as soon as possible. Leaving the car next to half a dozen others parked in front of the house, they walked down the damp grass to the scarred ground where Robina's remains had been discovered. Apart from the exposed soil and some numbered forensic markers, the area looked, to Mariner, like little more than another patch of uneven ground.

'This strip of land had public access but belonged to the water company until the nursing home acquired it eighteen months ago,' said Reid. 'They started excavating these foundations for an additional dementia facility and found Robina. You don't know this place?'

'No, but there was somewhere people referred to as "the big house",' Mariner said. 'Long before I knew about the euphemism. Could have been here.'

'Who used that phrase?'

'Ludo — Ludovic Rothbury — seemed to know more about it than anyone, but then he only lived up the road; ironically in a much bigger house.'

'At the time Robina died, most of the land around here was owned by the Rothbury family,' said Reid. 'In fact, this house belonged to them too. They sold it off some years ago, as part of a larger parcel that included woodland on the edge of the village. They never lived here — they rented it out. But we haven't got very far yet in finding out who was in residence when Robina died.'

'The name that comes into my head is Jimmy Finnegan.'

'The comedian?'

'Didn't he come under scrutiny during those historic sexual abuse investigations?' said Sinclair.

'Mainly because of the company he kept,' said Mariner. 'I don't know if he was ever charged with anything.'

'Why would he have been here?' asked Reid.

'He'd have been at the height of his popularity in the mid-seventies,' said Sinclair. 'He was mainstream, so I'd guess he was doing a summer season on one of the piers in Yarmouth.'

'That's right,' said Mariner. 'This was where he hung out when he wasn't on stage.'

'How did you know that?' asked Sinclair.

'Someone must have said as much, though it could have just been speculation. There was talk of parties, and there might have been something in that. Even before I'd met the other kids, I remember hearing music from this direction in the early hours of the morning, on at least one occasion.'

'We must look into that.' Reid gazed around her. 'So, we now know where Robina ended up, but what we don't know is how, or why, she got here from the campsite where she was last sighted. We're not even too clear on where exactly that was.'

'Shall I show you?' said Mariner.

They returned to the car and he instructed Sinclair to turn left out of the gates, and they drove on up the road to where Mariner had parked the previous day.

'This was the campsite,' he said, as they leaned on the gate looking out over the plantation of young saplings. 'Picture it as just a big grassy meadow. There was no fencing down the right-hand side then, so it merged into this woodland, which was where the fair stalls and entertainments were, in among the trees.'

'That's unusual,' said Reid.

'The place was run by hippies. It was more mystical, I suppose, and it was a hot summer, so maybe the shade helped. Here, look.' He pulled out the old OS map along with his own hand-drawn effort, which marked out the key features. 'The woods went on for about half a mile beyond that, and on the far side was the caravan site where Robina and her family were staying.'

'That works,' said Sinclair, who was studying their map. 'It's the area that's been developed into those posh houses.'

Reid nodded, beginning to understand.

'And in the other direction, you've got the water plant and Herringfleet House,' said Mariner. 'You said Robina was last seen on the campsite?'

'That's right. Walking away from the fair, the witnesses said,' confirmed Reid. 'Where would she have been going?'

'The Roman wall probably, or down to the river,' said Mariner. 'Us kids used to spend a lot of time down there.'

'Can you show us?'

Opening the gate, they walked down the path to the far corner and climbed the rickety stile. Reid was nimbly over it but the bulky Sinclair took longer. They arrived at the point where the vista opened up, and a chilly wind blew at them across the open landscape. 'This was a perfect playground for us,' said Mariner. 'We had the woods, the wall and the river.'

'This is where the search was centred, when Robina disappeared,' said Reid. 'They dredged the river and searched the marsh.'

'Did the original team consider the possibility of her having left the caravan site altogether?' Mariner asked.

'They seem to have dismissed the idea. She took nothing with her, not even a handbag.'

'She always had her handbag.'

As they scanned the surrounding area, Mariner took out a compass and checked their direction.

'Do you always carry one of those?' said Reid, not quite succeeding in suppressing a smile.

'When I think it might be needed,' said Mariner. 'I do a lot of walking.'

'Clearly,' said Sinclair.

'I'm just wondering how Robina ended up at Herringfleet House if she was last seen coming down here,' said Mariner. 'To get to it from here you'd have to cross the water company compound, which would have been impossible. Yet if Robina had gone back via the campsite again, someone would surely have seen her.'

'If it was late at night, people would have been asleep,' suggested Sinclair.

'It was the height of summer,' said Mariner. 'And hot. People were up and about till all hours.'

'And it doesn't explain why,' said Reid.

'What about those parties?' asked Sinclair. 'If they existed.'

'I was thinking that,' said Mariner. 'Robina was insatiably curious; wanted to experience everything.'

'Sex?'

'She was a teenager,' said Mariner, quickly turning away to study the view again. 'And the kind of girl she was, I think if the opportunity arose to go — if the parties even existed — she'd have jumped at it.'

'She still had to get there,' said Reid. 'Without anyone seeing her.'

* * *

THEN

On Sunday, as he and his mother were having breakfast at their little camping table, he saw Lesley appear from her tent and start out towards the woods, carrying a big box. She released one hand to give him a cheery wave.

'Who's that?' his mother wanted to know.

He shrugged. 'Just someone I met.'

When he wandered back to the stalls, Lesley called out to him. 'What are you up to? I'll pay you if you give me a hand here for a couple of hours.' Today she was wearing a long flowing dress, with less flesh on display and he wondered guiltily if it was because of him.

111

He didn't even need to think about her offer. There was bugger all else to do. He was sure he'd seen a pub back in the village they'd passed through on the way here. He was tall and looked mature for his age. If he had some more money, he could go and try his luck there.

'OK. Where's your husband?' he asked.

'Still in bed, I expect. He's a law unto himself,' she said, with a smile that wasn't entirely convincing. 'And we're not married. An outmoded convention, don't you think?'

She had him getting stuff out of boxes and setting up the stall and they were only just ready for when the customers began to roll in. It was hectic for an hour or more, until the food stalls got going and the numbers began to thin a little.

'Right,' she said. 'I'm going to grab a cup of tea while I can. Want one?'

'No thanks.' He hoped she wouldn't be long.

He heard the girl, before he saw her, a huge sigh followed by: 'Oh my God, this is so boring.' She had a northern accent and her voice cut through the gentle politeness of the hippy commune like a razorblade through butter. There was a short altercation with a man who looked as if he must be her dad, then she wandered over to the stall alone.

She looked different from the other women around here. Her dirty blonde hair was tied back in a ponytail and scarlet lipstick accentuated her full lips. Her short, sleeveless dress was tight around her hips and breasts, and she carried a white patent leather bag slung over one arm.

'I bet you're not here with your parents,' she said sulkily.

He considered lying, but something stopped him. 'My mum, yes.'

'What about your old man?'

Mariner gave his head the slightest shake.

'Too busy with the rat race?' she concluded, and it suited him that she thought that. 'Are you one of these hippies then?' she asked, picking over some of the cheaper bracelets.

'No, I'm just helping out.'

'What is all this crap?' She affected an upper-class accent. 'I mean, young man, do tell me more about these fascinating artefacts.'

He indicated a tray of rings. 'Well, here we have some useless tat.' He swept his hand across the display of pendants. 'And here, some further worthless cr—'

'Hey you. Behave yourself!' He hadn't noticed Lesley come back with her mug of tea, but she was grinning. 'And not so much of the "worthless". Some of these pieces are valuable.'

She weighed the two of them up for a moment, then dug into the money belt she carried and produced a pound note. 'Go on,' she said, proffering it at him. 'Go and conduct your love life somewhere else.'

Mariner blushed.

'Great,' said the girl. 'You can get me an ice cream. Then you can take me on a tour of your kingdom.'

He bought her a ninety-nine but didn't get one for himself. He didn't want to look a sissy. They walked around the stalls as she ate it. She didn't seem to mind that her high-heeled sandals, once the colour of her bag, were now covered in the dusty soil.

'What's your name, then?'

'Mariner,' he said, out of habit. It was surnames only at school. 'I mean . . . Thomas.' He was trying not to notice her lips and tongue working on the ice cream.

'Thomas? That's a bit old-fashioned, isn't it?'

'Is it?' He knew it was. The only Tommy he and his mates had heard of was the kid from the Who song. She was the kind of girl his grandad would have said 'calls a spade a bloody shovel'. He liked that.

'What about you?'

'Robina.'

'Ribena? Like the drink?' He was being deliberately obtuse.

'Ha,' she said. 'A comedian, are you? It's Robina. As in "Batman and". That's what it should've been, anyway. We're stopping at the caravan site over that way.' She gestured with the ice cream to the other end of the woods. 'How about you?'

'Camping, in the field.'

She'd finished her ice cream and rummaged in her bag for a lipstick which she applied carefully, pouting at him when she'd finished. He imagined how it would feel if he leaned in and kissed her.

CHAPTER FOURTEEN

Soon after Jesson got in to Granville Lane on Wednesday morning, Superintendent Sharp stopped by Mariner's office.

'It suits you,' she said, 'sitting behind that desk. How's it going?'

'So far, so good,' said Jesson. She summarised the highlights of the previous day's briefing and where they were going from there.

'All under control then,' said Sharp. 'And what do the family think of the new SIO?'

'They're teenagers, so utterly unimpressed,' said Jesson. 'My mum's doing a great job of keeping things going there.'

'Good,' said Sharp. 'I'm going to be tied up at Lloyd House for much of today, but don't forget, you're not fancy-free Tom Mariner. If the family needs you, there are people here to cover.'

'I won't,' said Jesson, grateful to have a guvnor who also had family obligations.

Shortly after Sharp left, Khatoon tapped on the door and looked in. 'I'm just off to Briar Lane, and Kevin's going to Kingsmead to try to locate the lock-up,' she said.

'Great,' said Jesson, thinking at that moment she'd quite like to be heading out somewhere instead of stuck behind a desk reading about it. It was common knowledge that the boss struggled with the desk-bound aspect of being a DCI. She wondered if she was going to be the same. She lasted until the middle of the morning, until she felt drawn to CID to check in with Charlie Glover.

'I've tried googling Agadoo accountants,' he told her. 'But the closest I could find was an *Agarwal*.' He spelled it out for her.

'That sounds close enough,' said Jesson. 'We should talk to him, if only to rule him out.'

'He's not answering his phone,' said Glover. 'And I've tried a few times now.'

'Have you got an address?' asked Jesson, sensing an excursion coming on. 'He might need a personal visit.'

* * *

Khatoon and Bingley parted company in the car park, after separating Paszek's house keys from the rest. 'I'll catch up with you later,' Bingley called. Khatoon stopped herself short of asking if he'd be all right. It was a while now since her partner had gone into a diabetic coma while following a lead solo, but she still couldn't get it out of her head that it might happen again; in the same way that every time Suli drove away from the house in the morning to go to work, she imagined him in a car crash. She needed to get a grip. All the same, she watched Bingley safely leave the car park before starting the ignition.

* * *

The problem with the warren of roads that made up what was locally known as Kingsmead 'factory centre', was that they all looked the same, so Bingley soon realised he had to take a systematic approach, crossing off each road as he went. Some of the units had shop-front signage advertising their trade, suggesting some sort of customer interface, and making them easy to eliminate. But many had nothing so obvious, so the only way he could check them out properly was on foot. He'd got to the end of Sovereign Road, and was about to give it up as a bad job, when he spied a small, handprinted sign in the window of the unit he was approaching, for ViP CLEANING. ViP — Viktor Paszek? Had to be it. The unit had a garage-sized steel shutter next to the windows and a glass-panelled door, both of which had the blinds pulled down — a sensible enough security precaution.

Putting on gloves, Bingley tried each of Paszek's keys in the lock of the glass door, and found success on the third attempt. It opened into a narrow office space, which ran along the outer wall towards the shuttered door and was partitioned from the main area by windows that enabled whoever was sitting at the desk to see what was going on out there. Bingley located the light switches just inside the door, and turned them all on, flooding the whole unit with light. Ignoring the office for the moment, he walked through it and into the compact warehouse, where the faint chemical odour grew stronger.

The unit was essentially a small hangar, about the size of two double garages with a concrete floor and a high ceiling supported by steel beams. Here, things were ordered without being excessively clean or tidy. Most of the space was given over to heavy-duty shelving, but immediately in front of Bingley, positioned in readiness to be driven out when the shutter was raised, was a nine-year-old dark-blue Ford Galaxy people carrier. So pungent was the chemical smell in here that after only a few minutes, Bingley could feel the beginnings of a headache coming on.

He found the button for the electric shutter and raised it to just above waist height, to let in some air. Then he took out his phone and began a more thorough search of the room, photographing what he saw and checking every nook and cranny for Hien's missing shoe.

A quick scan of the shelves identified the source of the heady smell: gallon canisters — variations on the one found in the back of the Passat — containing different types of cleaning fluid with some spillage in places. They'd need samples of these for comparison with Hien's clothes. Alongside these, cardboard boxes contained protective gloves, cloths and dusters bought in bulk, along with other odd items of cleaning paraphernalia. At the very end was a collection of empty boxes and a roll of unused heavy-duty plastic. Standing sentry in front of the shelves were two industrial floor polishers, side by side. So far, so unremarkable, though compared with Paszek's house, there was a notable absence of dust here, and it struck Bingley that this didn't look like a place that had been entirely mothballed.

The people carrier looked its age and hadn't been cleaned — at least not on the outside — for a while. There were cracks and scuffs to the front bumper that spoke of a collision at some point. It was locked. Stepping outside to clear his head, Bingley phoned Vicky Jesson to report what he'd found. He couldn't give her an obvious crime scene, but even if this wasn't where Hien had met his demise, it would help to know if he'd been here at all.

'I think we should get SOCOs out here and impound the people carrier,' he said. He wasn't sure if she'd go along with it. She'd be worrying about the budget. But she agreed to put it to Superintendent Sharp. While he waited for the outcome, Bingley turned his attention to the office.

Running the length of the space below the windows was a worktop, which served as a basic desk. It was preternaturally tidy, with pots of pens, Sellotape dispenser and assorted stationery items lined up along the back. A stack of paper trays held a few items of correspondence and a shelf at one end supported a row of folders and hardback notebooks. Tucked under the desk was a substantial office chair that had seen better days, which was back-to-back with a small safe with a tray of mugs and a kettle on top. Beside this was a filing cabinet against which leaned a small set of step ladders. Coat hooks had been attached to the wall nearest the door, a set of overalls hanging from one of them. While Bingley was assessing all this, a movement on his peripheral vision caused

117

him to glance up, and he saw that a man had ducked under the shutter and was loitering in front of the Ford. He wore a donkey jacket over jeans and a washed-out jumper. He stooped low to throw his cigarette butt outside, and when he straightened again, he saw Bingley.

'Hello,' said Bingley, coming out of the office to meet him. The man craned his neck to peer past him. 'Looking for someone?'

Closer to, the man was unshaven and had a pale, under-nourished look. He turned something over in his fingers. 'Mr Paszek,' he said and gestured towards the Ford.

'What do you want him for?' asked Bingley.

But the man was too preoccupied now with the possibility of Paszek appearing, to even hear the question, let alone understand it. He scanned the warehouse as if willing him to appear.

'Mr Paszek's not here,' said Bingley, somewhat dramatically drawing a finger across his throat. 'Accident.' He took a pace nearer the man and stuck out his hand. 'I'm Kevin,' he said.

But it was a step too far. In one swift movement the man dropped to the floor, and scrambled under the shutter. Something jangled to the ground, as he went.

'Shit!' Bingley's nearest route out was via the office and he lost valuable seconds running back through it and out of the other door. By the time he got outside the man was disappearing down the road at speed. Bingley ran after him, but after a few paces realised the man had too much of a head start. Bingley's last sighting was of the jeans and donkey jacket disappearing round a corner in the distance. He went to retrieve what had dropped on to the concourse. It was a ring with two more keys on it, one bearing the Ford logo. The first key fit the padlock on the shutter. Checking that the van was in neutral, Bingley reached inside and inserted the Ford ignition key. The engine gunned into life straightaway, like a vehicle that was still in use.

* * *

Khatoon made another foray to Viktor Paszek's next-door neighbour without much hope, but today it looked more promising, with a middle-range SUV parked alongside a compact hatchback. As she waited for someone to come to the door, she was struck again by the contrast with Paszek's house. This one was well-maintained, with a smart York stone drive around raised flower beds that left plenty of space for more vehicles. The door opened, and Khatoon turned to face a woman perhaps in her late forties, with blonde high-lighted hair. She was elegantly dressed in jeans and cashmere, a matching scarf draped round her neck.

'Can I help you?'

Khatoon held out her warrant card. 'I'm here about your neighbour Viktor Paszek,' she said. 'Do you know him?'

'I do,' said the woman, folding her arms. 'But he's not my neighbour — thankfully. This is my mother's house, I'm just visiting.'

'And you are?'

'Louisa Douglas.'

'Could I speak to your mother, please, Mrs Douglas?' asked Khatoon.

'I'm afraid she's not quite up and about yet. I'm helping her to get dressed. What's he done?' There was something about her tone implying that she wasn't a fan of Viktor's. It made Khatoon speak more brusquely than she might other-wise have done.

'He had a car accident,' she said. 'He was killed.'

'Oh God. Oh God, that's . . . that's terrible. When?'

Louisa Douglas seemed genuinely shocked and now Khatoon regretted being so blunt.

'The early hours of Monday morning.'

'Monday? Really?'

'Yes,' said Khatoon. 'We're trying to find out a bit more about him. Would you and your mother be able to help?'

'I'm not sure,' said Louisa, uncertainly. 'What did you want to know?'

Khatoon had seen this kind of discomfort a hundred times; the sudden backing away of someone who didn't want to get involved.

'Just some general background,' she persisted. 'How long have your mother and Viktor been neighbours?'

'A while,' she admitted. 'He must have moved in about ten years or so ago.'

'There you are, then. They must have known each other quite well.' Khatoon looked past her into the house. 'Could I speak to her? I don't mind waiting.'

'I'm not sure that's a good idea,' Louisa said, her guard well and truly up now. 'Mum is beginning to get confused about things. It's very stressful. She gets upset and unsettled by anything new or sudden. Perhaps if I speak to her on your behalf. . .'

'Best that I do it in person,' said Khatoon. 'Sometimes important details can be missed.' She wouldn't normally have been so pushy in this situation, but something about Louisa Douglas had put her back up. 'You met Viktor, presumably?'

'Oh yes.' Her eyes narrowed.

Now we're getting to it, thought Khatoon. 'You didn't like him?'

'I didn't like what he was up to — none of us did.'

'Who's "us"?'

'My sister and I, and the rest of the family.'

'And what was Viktor "up to"?'

'Oh, it was all right to start with. He could be a real charmer, and his wife was sweet. It all seemed very nice for Mum when they moved in and became . . . friendly.'

'What changed?'

'His wife died. And not long after that, Viktor began to take rather more of an interest in Mum. She's on her own too, you see.'

'So maybe they were just two lonely people who enjoyed each other's company,' said Khatoon. She had no idea why she felt the need to defend him. Perhaps it was Louisa's apparent prejudice against a man she claimed she barely knew.

'And the rest,' she said. 'Look, I don't like to speak ill of the dead . . .'

That was always an interesting start to a sentence.

'But he put all kinds of ridiculous notions into Mum's head.'

'Like what?'

'Mum's eighty-four now and this house is far too big her. We've been trying for years to get her to sell up and move to somewhere smaller and more manageable, now she needs more support; somewhere with a warden, so that there's someone keeping an eye on her. I have to come over from Bromsgrove, and my sister Samantha's in Tamworth. Anyway, we'd just about persuaded Mum to put the house on the market when Viktor stuck his oar in. I understand he's some kind of jumped-up landlord. Suddenly Mum was talking about renting out the house to generate an income to cover her living costs. She and Dad had good careers in the civil service, which had left them very comfortably off, so she could just about afford to do that. And no prizes for guessing who was planning to manage it all for her, and no doubt take a hefty slice of commission for himself. And if it all goes wrong, we'll be the ones left to pick up the pieces.'

'But she's going ahead with the sale?' said Khatoon, glancing pointedly at the For Sale signs.

'Only after a battle. Even now Mum has her doubts, which mysteriously, always seem to surface after a conversation with Viktor.'

'Well,' said Khatoon, tartly, 'that won't happen any-more, will it? I will be mindful of your mum's difficulties,' she went on. 'And tread very carefully. I'll pop back in about an hour, shall I? Perhaps you could prepare the way by telling her what has happened to Mr Paszek.' She said it with the sort of cheery determination that would brook no refusal.

'All right,' said Louisa, reluctantly. 'But I can't promise anything. Mum has good days and bad. I don't quite under-stand why this is necessary, anyway. You said Viktor died in a road accident.'

'He did,' said Khatoon, 'But there are some loose ends that we need to follow up on. I'm sorry, I can't tell you any more than that.'

* * *

Still chuntering to himself with frustration, Bingley jotted down a description of the man who'd run off, before continuing his search of the office. He started by taking the various ring binders off the shelf. Accounts, he discovered; columns of figures, with coded headings, dates and what added up to some hefty sums below. But the pages were tinged yellow with age, and the most up-to-date folder had had no new entries for five years. The hardback books were rent books and easier to decipher: monthly payments and outgoings for utilities and repairs, with each property address given inside the front cover. There were five in all and again, most of these were obsolete, but there were two that weren't; one for Hillfield Road and another for an address on Culloden Street, both in Selly Oak, which was consistent with their being student accommodation. Flicking back through the pages, Bingley could see where there had been changes of tenancy corresponding to the beginning and end of the academic year. But it would take time to go through all the names. A third book mirrored the contents of the first two, but with a much-simplified format; income and expenditure up until a week ago, but there was no address label on the front, and there were no names inside.

Finally, Bingley came to two big lever-arch folders, labelled ViP Cleaning. His fingers left marks in the frosting of dust they'd gathered, and the pages in these had discoloured with age. Correspondence inside indicated a number of local companies ViP Cleaning had served, including Partington's, a well-known local engineering company whose offices occupied the only high-rise office block in the area. That would take a big team. Evidently the cleaning operation was significant at one time. But much of the book-keeping looked archaic. The contents of each folder were divided into sections identified by the letters A to H. Within each of these were pages and pages of complex diagrams, almost like time-tables, with dates and initials, which to Bingley appeared meaningless. One section contained employee details going back years, but there were none more recent than five years ago. In fact, nothing here indicated that the business was anything more than defunct. So why had Viktor Paszek retained the lock-up and where did the Ford Galaxy and the man he'd just met fit in? It was too much for Bingley to get his head around immediately, so commandeering a couple of old boxes off the warehouse shelves, he packed up the most relevant material to take back to Granville Lane. If anyone could make sense of it, Charlie Glover could.

The only other potential source of information was the filing cabinet. It was locked, which was encouraging, but none of the keys on Paszek's keyring was the right size. A hunt around the desk turned up a pot of paperclips, at the bottom of which was the key. But when Bingley opened it up, it became clear that the filing cabinet was not used for its intended purpose. Instead, it seemed to be more of a secure storage cupboard. The top drawer held only a few empty suspension files, but as he went to slide it shut, Bingley saw a flash of colour. He reached down in between the swinging files and brought out a bundle of coloured booklets, eight in all, held together with an elastic band. Passports. They all belonged to foreign nationals, mostly from Eastern Europe. None of the photos was a match for Hien, but there was a Latvian one, for a Matejs Skrīvulis; he had less beard growth here, but staring back at Bingley from the inside cover was the man who had just bolted. Bingley felt a tickle of apprehension. This was starting to add up to something. He tried the bottom drawer, and here hit the potential jackpot — a new and expensive laptop. Hopefully it meant that Paszek's record-keeping had gone electronic and would tell them what he'd been up to more recently. Bingley bagged it up for Max, their IT expert, and tucked it in with the folders and record books. Not a bad morning's work.

* * *

Khatoon was running out of places to look in Viktor Paszek's house, or at least, places she was prepared to look. The understairs cupboard, for example, was stuffed to the gunnels with more magazines and old newspapers, with so much dust on them it had blackened to dirt. If Kev wanted to give it a go he was welcome, but she couldn't imagine there being anything worthwhile underneath. Taking off her gloves, she washed her hands, yet again, and went back to Louisa Douglas. This time there was, quite literally, a warmer welcome. She was invited into a house that, after Viktor's, felt like the tropics. But Louisa had a further word of warning before she met Gwen Franklin.

'If Mum says anything odd, it's best to just go along with it,' she told Khatoon. 'I have tried to explain what's happened to Viktor, but I'm not sure how much she's taken in.'

'I will try to make this as easy as I can for her,' Khatoon reassured her.

Louisa took her through a grand hallway, with its polished wood floor and antique furniture, into a spacious lounge. The sun streamed through the French windows, compounding the already stifling heat. Khatoon had come dressed for Viktor Paszek's house and began to sweat in her thick jumper. Gwen sat on a wide floral-covered sofa. Her hair was coloured a subtle auburn, a little lighter than her daughter's, and she wore glasses with modern frames, which made her look younger than her eighty-four years.

'Mum, this is the police officer I told you about,' said Louisa, sitting down beside her mother. 'Detective . . .'

'Khatoon.'

'Sorry, yes, Khatoon.'

The old lady smiled. 'Yes, yes dear, I know who she is. She was here before.'

'I see,' said Louisa, casting a sideways glance at Khatoon. 'Anyway, she'd like to talk to you about Viktor.'

'Where *is* he?' Gwen demanded, with some irritation. 'He hasn't brought my newspaper yet. I'll have to ask Samantha to fetch one up from the newsagent's for me.'

Louisa took her mother's hand. 'Listen, Mum. Do you remember me telling you that Viktor had an accident? He won't be . . .'

'Oh.' The old lady shook her head briskly, as if trying to shake her thoughts back into some semblance of order. 'Yes, of course. Poor Viktor. I don't know what I'm going to do without him.' Her voice faltered and Louisa stroked her hand, soothingly.

Khatoon was perspiring and perhaps Gwen noticed.

'Why don't we go out and sit on the terrace, darling, or at least open the windows?' she said to her daughter. 'This room feels stuffy.'

'No, Mum, we're fine in here,' said Louisa, firmly. 'It's much colder outside than it looks. Detective Khatoon needs to ask you some questions about Viktor.'

'Oh, yes.'

'Hello, Gwen,' said Khatoon, taking a seat in one of the armchairs. 'I'll try not to keep you too long.'

'Oh, that's all right, my dear,' said Gwen. 'Are they kind to you, in the police? I expect it can be difficult sometimes.'

'I'm fine.' Khatoon wondered if Gwen was alluding to her age, gender or skin colour. 'When did you last see Viktor?' she asked.

'Sunday teatime, I expect.'

'No, Mum,' said Louisa gently. 'You were at Sam's house for the weekend, remember? She collected you on Thursday.'

'Of course I remember,' Gwen snapped, suddenly irritable.

'It would have been sometime last week, I expect,' encouraged Louisa.

'Yes, I suppose it would,' her mother agreed.

'How did he seem, last time you saw him?' asked Khatoon.

Gwen smiled. 'Same as always,' she said. 'Such a kind man.'

'You've known him a few years.'

'Yes, he moved here with his wife, but she wasn't at all well, even then. She passed away not long after. It was a shame. I never really got to know her. Viktor always said we would have hit it off. The girls are very busy, so Viktor helps me out with odd jobs, that sort of thing. He's very practical. And he feeds Macavity for me.'

'The cat,' said Louisa.

Gwen blinked at her daughter. 'Did Viktor finish what he was doing on the terrace?'

'He did, but that was weeks ago, wasn't it?'

'Oh yes . . . It's infuriating,' she said to Khatoon. 'I do get so muddled.'

'Happens to all of us sometimes.' Khatoon took out the photograph of Hien and handed it to her. 'Do you know this man, Gwen? We think he might be a friend of Viktor's.'

'Of course I do,' said Gwen, without hesitation. 'It's Charles.'

Khatoon started. This could be a breakthrough . . . But then Louisa caught her eye again and with the slightest shake of the head, quashed her hopes.

'It looks a bit like him, but it isn't Charles. He was her gardener for a time,' Louisa explained. 'He was an interesting chap. I think he'd been in the Gurkhas.'

'Who is he then?' Gwen asked Khatoon.

'We don't know, but he was in Viktor's car when it crashed.'

'I expect Viktor was giving him a lift. He was considerate like that.' A frown creased Gwen's brow. 'When's Viktor coming back?' she asked her daughter. 'I want my newspaper.'

They'd come full circle and it seemed to Khatoon to be a good time to leave.

Louisa showed her out, and as she was doing so, another car pulled into the drive and parked behind the SUV. A woman got out. Ignoring Khatoon, she said, 'Why is Mum's car out?'

Louisa sighed. 'She wants to go to Morrison's.'

The other woman was appalled. 'But she can't. You know what she's like now!'

'You try telling her,' said Louisa, exasperated. 'It's the only place she drives to, and it's not far. She takes her phone with her in case she gets into any trouble. My sister, Samantha,' said Louisa, to Khatoon. 'Sam, this is Detective Khatoon. Viktor is dead; car accident, ironically.'

'Oh my God. Poor man.'

Louisa bridled. 'Poor man? You've changed your tune.'

'What's that supposed to mean?'

'Oh, come on. He could be a pain in the neck.'

'It's still awful that he's been killed,' said Samantha, reprovingly. 'He kept an eye on the house for Mum when she was away.'

'He also had Mum storing his roadkill in her freezer,' Louisa reminded her. 'He was weird.'

'It wasn't roadkill,' Samantha corrected her, sharply. 'He used to buy rabbits from the markets in town sometimes, that's all. He was just . . . different from us.'

'I won't argue with that,' said Louisa, then seemed suddenly to remember that DS Khatoon was standing beside her. 'I hope you got all you needed,' she said, ingratiatingly.

'I did, thank you,' said Khatoon. She had brought up the photograph of Hien and now showed it to Samantha. 'Do you know this man?' she asked. But Samantha was adamant that she didn't.

'Who is he?'

Offering the same explanation she'd given Gwen, she thanked them again and made her exit.

CHAPTER FIFTEEN

The incident room assigned to Reid and Sinclair was at the back of beyond and they seemed to walk down endless corridors to get there. It wasn't overly large either, meaning that the few desks furnishing it were almost back-to-back, a situation not improved by having a third of the room taken up by archive boxes of material. Two uniformed officers were systematically working through and meticulously recording the contents of each box, and another was seated at one of the desks reading, a stack of files beside him. Reid made brief introductions, and Sinclair went off to get coffees.

'You've got your work cut out,' said Mariner, eyeing the cartons.

'Most of it's from the original investigation,' said Reid. 'And we can't even be confident that it's complete. The archive has been moved a couple of times and unfortunately, no inventory was made at the time, so we're having to create one as we go along. We're more than a week in now and have hardly made a dent in it.'

'I'm not surprised,' said Mariner.

'Thanks to the number of people staying at the caravan and campsites,' continued Reid, 'we've got witness statements coming out of our ears. Lots of them will be worthless, but we have to go through them all just in case something was missed.'

'What about visitors to the fair?' asked Mariner.

'Some came forward, but there weren't that many apparently. On the day that Robina went missing, it rained heavily until the middle of the afternoon, so a lot of the stallholders packed up early. Getting an appeal out to the media should help, but we have to accept that some witnesses may no longer be around. So far we've had to confine ourselves to those we have been able to trace.'

'Like me.'

'Like you. If we manage to get any DNA from Robina's remains we can start requesting samples for comparison but if that doesn't work out, it'll come down to analysing that lot.'

'I'm probably going to be at a loose end at times, while I'm here,' said Mariner. 'It's a shame I can't help.'

'It is,' said Reid. 'But that could get complicated.'

Aside from the sheer scale of their task, the other thing that caught Mariner's attention was the incident board, which ran across one wall. He went over to take a closer look. What set it apart from those he was used to working with was the quality of some of the images, and the nature of the exhibits photographed. Robina's decayed remains were pictured in situ, alongside worn and rotten rags of fabric, itemised as her dress, underwear and bra. He was used to such sights and had steeled himself against this moment, but the poignancy of seeing her once-white patent leather sandals, blackened by the years of lying buried in the earth, made the breath catch in his chest. Next to these were a pair of hoop earrings and the soil-encrusted bangle he'd bought her.

'It's not much, is it?' said Reid. 'Though forensics have picked up some stray fibres from what's left of the dress. We're waiting on analysis.'

Robina's smiling face dominated the other side of the board, a blown-up print of the school photograph, surrounded by images of her family and other witnesses. He was there too, with collar-length hair as it had been then; a blurry snapshot cropped from a larger one. He barely recognised himself. Dividing the two halves of the board was a timeline.

'For the Thursday Robina went missing, such as it is,' Reid explained, seeing Mariner's interest. 'It was a wet morning so the family was cooped up in the caravan. There was a row between Robina and her dad, the usual teenager thing, then the rest of them went out in the car. Robina stayed behind because she was "feeling unwell". Her mum says in her statement that she was sulking.'

'Hard to imagine that,' said Mariner. 'It's not like the Robina I knew.'

'The family didn't return until late that evening, so we're reliant on sightings by people who hardly knew her, if at all. She wasn't reported missing until the next day.'

'Why?'

'It was dark when the family got back to the caravan, and her sister, who was sharing a room, thought she was in bed asleep. It wasn't until the following morning when they realised her bed was unslept in, that they called the police. By then the crucial golden hour was already a distant memory.'

'They were trying to get used to the idea of her being independent,' said Mariner. 'Her mum was struggling to cope with the notion of Robina going off to university a few weeks later. There was a conversation about it. Did any of the family come under suspicion?' They both knew that close relatives were the first to be considered in homicides.

'They were all alibied,' said Reid. 'You spent time with them, didn't you? That picture of you is from one of their holiday snaps.'

'I wasn't with them much, and my attention was very much on Robina. You know what it's like at that age; grown-ups are boring and to be avoided, if at all possible.'

Reid came to stand beside him and indicated a second creased and faded map, on which an irregular geometric shape had been drawn in red. 'These were her movements, as far as police were able to ascertain at the time. She wasn't sighted until the middle of the day when she went into the shop on the caravan site. And when the weather had cleared she helped for a short time on one of the stalls that was still going — jewellery, I think — and had a conversation with a couple of the other youngsters. The sightings late afternoon dry up a bit, but there were a couple at around 4 p.m. Then three separate witnesses saw her walking down the camping field, between seven thirty and eight that evening, with a man in scruffy clothes and, one said, "in need of a haircut".'

Mariner snorted. 'That describes practically everyone from the fair. Not many of them were big on personal care that I could see.'

'Robina, on the other hand, was reported to look "dolled-up".'

'She was always dolled-up,' said Mariner.

Sinclair appeared with a tray of drinks, and once they'd been distributed, Reid led Mariner over to a corner table, and they sat.

'Who were the persons of interest in the original investigation?' Mariner asked, taking a sip of scalding hot coffee.

'Only one, from what we can tell from the case notes,' said Reid. 'Peter Church. Son of the caravan site owner.

'That figures,' said Mariner. 'He hung around the site and shop, helping out a bit and doing odd jobs; a big lumbering bloke. Robina was good with him, but not in a condescending way. What did they have on him?'

'The shirt he wore that day was consistent with the description of the man last seen with Robina, and there seemed to be a consensus that he was scruffy.'

'His clothes might not have seen an iron, but this was a caravan site in the middle of the summer holidays. Nobody ironed clothes. And like I said, the fair people were hardly the epitome of sartorial elegance. It's a flimsy connection.'

'In itself, yes, but he was also one of the few who didn't have much of an alibi for around that time. According to his father, Church got home at about eight that evening, but the sighting was "around seven thirty to eight", so it wasn't enough to put him in the clear. On the other hand, none of the witnesses were able to pick Church out in a line-up and there doesn't seem to have been any strong physical evidence; this was before DNA profiling, of course. With no body either, there was insufficient evidence to charge him. But you get a sense from what was in the press at the time that lots of the locals thought if something had happened to Robina, Peter Church could well have been responsible.'

'I could see it being some sort of accident,' said Mariner. 'Peter was clumsy, heavy-handed. One of the kids had a pencil shaped like a corkscrew. It was being passed around. When it got to Peter, he just snapped it in two. He got into trouble for that, because the kid's parents said it was deliberate. But he didn't mean to break it; it looked bendy, so he thought it would bend.'

'His father described him at the time as "a man in a child's body",' said Sinclair. 'So, I'm guessing he would have a man's desires and impulses. People seemed to think it was him.'

'Because he was different, I expect,' said Mariner. 'People jump to conclusions. They would have been less enlightened back then.' It was the kind of thing that could have happened to Jamie, he thought. He was reminded of their first encounter, when he was the one who was clueless. 'And Peter wouldn't have done well in interviews.'

'I agree,' said Reid. 'He was an easy scapegoat. And sadly mud sticks. He and his father were targeted for a long time afterwards; vandalism and abuse. In the end, Church senior sold up the caravan site and they moved away.'

Mariner shook his head in disgust. 'Hounded out, even then.' As they considered this, Mariner caught sight of his envelope on the side of one of the vacant desks. 'May I? There are things in here that might be of interest to you.' Reaching over to pick it up, he tipped its contents on to the table in front of them. 'This is the crowd of us Robina spent most of her time with,' he said. 'I found them among my mother's things.'

As he spread the pictures out on the table, the detectives fell on them.

'These are terrific,' said Reid. 'All we've got at the moment are the family's photos and Robina hardly features in them at all. Here she is.' She picked out Robina on one of the group photos.

'And this is Ludo Rothbury.' Mariner pointed to the young man beside her.

'Did you know at the time he was aristocracy?' asked Reid.

'We knew he was a toff as soon as he opened his mouth. And there were other things that marked him out: the easy confidence of the public-school educated. And it was common knowledge that he lived in a mansion. The family stately home was a few miles away and the gardens were open to the public. My mother dragged me there one tortuous afternoon. But he wore it lightly. He still felt like part of the gang, one of us. His mate was altogether different.'

'His mate?'

'Yeah, this one.' Mariner pointed to a taller, heavy-set boy standing next to Rothbury. 'He was staying with Ludo for the holidays. They were at school together. God, what was his name? It was something out of the ordinary, although a lot of the kids had weird names, for different reasons. Chrysanthemum and Beeswax, you know the sort of thing.'

He tapped the photo impatiently, trying to summon the memory. 'Kit,' he said, the name finally coming back to him. 'That was it. What a pair; one named after a game and the other a chocolate bar. Ludo took it in his stride, but if any of us wanted to wind Kit up — and that was most of the time — we used to call him Kit-Kat or Kit-e-Kat. He really didn't like it. Now he *did* think he was better than the rest of us. He had a spiteful streak, too. There was a rope swing in the woods, and on one occasion he offered to give one of the smaller kids a push. He did it so hard he made her fall off. He found it hilarious, seemed to relish making her cry.

'He boasted about tormenting his kid sister too. Some of the stuff sounded plain cruel. Robina called him out on it at least once, and obviously didn't like him. He tried to take her on, making fun of her accent and the way she dressed.' Even after all this time, Mariner could recall the tone and volume of the bully's voice, entitled and secure in the knowledge that others would listen and respond. He had no desire to come face to face with the boorish Kit again.

'Did it upset her?' asked Reid.

'On the contrary, she absolutely wiped the floor with him. Pretentious prick. She wasn't the least bit intimidated by him. Had to get used to it, she said. Plenty more like him out there.'

'She sounds self-assured,' said Reid.

'I'm not so certain,' said Mariner. 'She came across as confident, but I think she was quite afraid of university and how she might be judged.'

'And the others?' asked Reid, turning back to the photo.

'These two were sisters, or cousins or something.' He indicated two girls, about twelve and fourteen, each with a cloud of dark curly hair and broad smiles, who stood with their arms linked. 'They were the ones with the freaky names; the older one was Solstice and the younger one was Juniper. I wonder how they've got on through life saddled with names like that? But they were nice kids. This smaller girl, standing just behind them, is Violet — an old-fashioned name back then. Her mum was Lesley, a stallholder at the fair.'

'I know her,' said Sinclair. He pulled a folder towards him off a nearby desk and started rifling through the papers. 'Gary Prosser and Lesley Eden,' he said, when he'd found what he was looking for. 'We've got their statements: spent time with Robina on the afternoon of the day she went missing.'

'Violet used to tag along sometimes, but she was much younger. Only about seven or eight,' said Mariner.

'And what about him?' Reid asked. Another teenage boy with a blonde crew cut stood a little apart, his arms folded.

'Smudge,' said Mariner. 'That was all anyone called him. I suppose his name must have been Smith — isn't that usually how it goes? He was OK too. My memory of him is always with a big grin on his face, cheerful and easy-going.

And strong. He used to carry the younger ones on his shoulders. He and the two girls were from the fair too. That is, their parents were part of that — running stalls, musicians or storytellers. The initial investigation must have included interviews with them, if only to eliminate them.'

'These kids were either among the last to see Robina alive, or were sighted with her the day before she disappeared,' said Reid. 'How did she get on with them?'

'It's a cliché, but Robina was friends with everyone. Including Peter Church.'

'And Rothbury?' asked Sinclair.

'He was all right,' said Mariner. 'I think he quite fancied Robina too.'

'He's agreed to be interviewed,' said Reid. 'As long as we go to him. We'd like his cooperation, so we're having to dance to his tune. But he's making us wait; he's out of the country on business. Gets back at the end of this week. Are there any pictures here of Peter Church?'

'I don't think so.' Mariner scanned the photos but it was as he'd thought. 'Like I said, he didn't spend much time with us. I don't think he was meant to leave the caravan park. We'd usually only see him if we used the site shop. It was nearer than the one in the village and better stocked. Do you know what became of him?'

'He's no longer alive,' said Reid. 'When his father passed away, he went into some kind of residential home, where he lived out his years. He died of natural causes. If he did have anything to do with Robina's death, we may never find out what happened.'

Mariner could hear the disappointment in her voice.

'What's this?' asked Sinclair. He'd found the letter, now wrapped in an evidence bag.

'It was in amongst the cuttings and photographs,' Mariner told him. 'It was still sealed, so must have arrived after I'd left home, and my mother kept it intact.'

Sinclair read it first. 'Blimey, if I'd had a girl send me that kind of letter when I was sixteen . . . .' He passed it to

Reid, whose eyebrows rose a little. Mariner probably should have felt embarrassed, but he didn't.

'There's something not right about it,' he said. 'I mean, we were just kids and the reality was we barely knew each other, but I'm not convinced that Robina wrote it. Something about it doesn't ring true.'

'In what way?'

'Robina didn't mince her words. I think she'd have used stronger language; more colloquial and less biology class.'

'Lots of people write differently to how they speak,' Sinclair pointed out.

'It's more than that, though. Look at the handwriting. It seems to me that there's a change to the shape of it after the first couple of sentences. Here.' He pointed to where he thought the change occurred. 'The letters aren't quite so rounded and uniform after this point, and more pressure is applied. It's more laboured.'

'It could be,' said Reid. 'Robina started it and someone else finished it?'

'I think the last bit is written by someone guessing at how a young girl would write it. Look at the postmark too.'

'Posted two days after she went missing,' said Reid. 'Perhaps by someone who wanted to give the impression she was still alive when she wasn't? Robina's killer could have sent it.'

'I'm just speculating,' said Mariner. He opened the evidence bag. 'Does it smell of anything to you?'

Reid sniffed it, then passed it to Sinclair.

'It's cigarette smoke,' he said, giving Mariner a questioning look.

'That's what I thought,' agreed Mariner. 'Robina abhorred smoking. It could be worth seeing if there's any DNA material on the seal. It's one of those lick-and-stick jobs.'

'Thank you, we will.'

'Why didn't your mum hand this over to the police at the time?' Sinclair wanted to know. 'She must have guessed who it was from.'

'Actually, she didn't,' said Mariner. 'My mother's friend Maggie Devlin was there with us that week. I spoke to her on Monday night. According to Maggie, they thought I was seeing Lesley, the stallholder. I'd spent a bit of time helping her out and she was, well, an attractive woman. I doubt my mother thought the letter was of any consequence.'

One of the uniforms had stood up and was hovering.

'Ma'am, I've just found this,' he said. 'It was stuffed down the side of one of the boxes.' He handed Reid a palm-sized box.

'It's a cassette tape,' she said, staring at it. 'Interview: Peter Church, 12 September 1976.'

'This was way before PACE came in,' said Sinclair. 'Why would they have done that?'

'It looks as if it was informal,' said Reid. 'The label's in biro.'

'Perhaps they recorded it because of Church's learning difficulties,' suggested Mariner. 'His speech wasn't always clear. A recording meant they could listen back to it.'

'Well, whatever the reason, this we have to hear,' said Reid. 'See if you can find us a machine, Scott.'

CHAPTER SIXTEEN

'I bring gifts,' said Bingley, depositing a box of paperwork in the only bit of free space on Charlie Glover's desk.

'Thanks a bunch,' said Glover, with a marked lack of sincerity.

'From Paszek's lock-up. And these might be the most interesting things.' Bingley fished the hardback notebooks out of the box. 'I couldn't make head or tail of them, but you might. And you might want to have a quick shufty at his laptop before it goes to Max.'

'You up for a working lunch?' said Glover, reaching over to his sandwich box. 'Mine's tea with one sugar.'

By the time Bingley returned with the drinks, the laptop was open on Glover's desk. 'Paszek was trusting,' was the first thing he observed. 'No password protection, though in fairness, there's not much on here to protect. His intention might have been to digitise his paperwork, but he'd hardly started.'

'Nothing, then?' said Bingley, disappointed.

'Not unless it's very well concealed.' Glover closed the machine down again and unplugged it. 'Let's hope these books tell us more.'

'This looks fun,' said Khatoon, coming back into CID with her own takeaway lunch and more evidence bags of paperwork.

'Viktor's stuff from the lock-up,' said Bingley. 'How did it go at Briar Lane?'

'I've met Viktor's neighbour now,' said Khatoon. 'But I think the main thing I learned is that he wasn't popular with her daughters. Where's the boss?'

'Gone to see Paszek's mate Eric,' said Glover. 'To show him the picture of Hien. Then I think she's going to see the accountant, Agarwal.'

'Did you get anywhere with Paszek's rented houses?'

'We've got addresses,' said Bingley. 'Want to go check them out?'

Khatoon held up the sandwich bag. 'Just as soon as I've finished this.'

Their first stop was a house on Hillfield Road, a long, steep street of terraces in the heart of student land, where cars were parked nose-to-tail from one end to the other. After ten minutes driving back and forth, and a couple of abortive attempts, Bingley eventually managed to manoeuvre the car into the only available space.

'They'd better bloody not all be at lectures now,' he said as they walked up the short pathway to the door. There was no bell so he knocked hard, and it was quite a wait until the door was opened by a lanky, unshaven youth in shorts and T-shirt.

'Yeah?' He squinted at them as if he was unaccustomed to daylight. A cliché on legs.

'You live here?' asked Bingley, holding up his warrant card.

More squinting. 'Yeah.'

'Who's your landlord?'

The sudden need for a response other than the affirmative seemed to throw him. 'Um. Aw, Vic, I think his name is. I don't have much to do with him. Baz sorts all that.'

'Is Baz here?' asked Khatoon.

'Yeah.'

'Can we come in then? We'd like to speak to him.'

'If you like.'

They stepped into the narrow hallway where they had to negotiate two mountain bikes propped against the wall, along with cycling helmets and assorted footwear littering the floor and a pile of coats thrown over the banister. Their host yelled up the stairs for Baz, at the same time leading them through to a small lounge, newly carpeted and furnished with a three-piece suite in wipe clean vinyl and a giant flatscreen TV. A table next to the window was stacked with books, and had an open laptop in front of the only high-backed chair. The smell throughout was predominantly of fried food. Having done his bit, the boy who'd let them in wandered on into the kitchen and was clattering about, so Bingley and Khatoon sat on the sofa and waited.

After a couple of minutes Baz bounded in, as high energy as his housemate was low. 'What is it?' he called, before sight of the two police officers stopped him in his tracks.

'It's us,' said Bingley, and showed his ID again. 'We just wanted to talk to you about your landlord, Viktor Paszek.'

Baz bounced on to one of the armchairs. 'Why? Has he reported us or something?'

Bingley and Khatoon traded glances. 'Have you done something that he might want to report?' asked Bingley.

'No! We're cool,' Baz said easily. 'It's just you hear stuff about other landlords, you know?'

'When did you last see Viktor?' asked Khatoon.

'Dunno. Couple of weeks ago? The boiler was playing up, so he came over to check it.' He looked at each of them in turn. 'What's going on, then?'

'Mr Paszek's had an accident,' said Khatoon. 'Last Monday. He was killed.'

'No way,' said Baz, stunned. 'That's savage.'

'What's going on?' His housemate's head appeared round the kitchen door.

'Viktor — he's been killed. What sort of accident?' he asked Khatoon.

'A road accident, early on Monday morning.'

Baz shook his head. 'Poor old Vic. He was all right. So, what happens now, with us, with the house?'

'I'm sure someone will be in touch,' said Khatoon, though in truth, she hadn't a clue. 'How many of you live here?' she asked.

'There's four of us. The other two are at lectures and that.'

'And you all get on all right with Viktor?'

'We don't see him that often, but yeah, he's cool. Doesn't — didn't — give us the grief that some of our mates get with their landlords.'

Khatoon showed them the photo on her phone. 'Have you ever seen the man in this picture, possibly with Viktor?'

Baz shook his head and his friend came to have a look and drew a blank too. 'Who is he?'

'That's what we don't know. He was in the car with Viktor when the accident happened.'

'What about those postgrads, Ed?' Baz turned to his housemate. 'They're Chinese or something, aren't they? Could it be one of them?'

Ed shrugged.

'Who do you mean?' Khatoon asked.

'Viktor's got another couple of houses he rents out, but one of them's strictly postgrads only. I get the idea it's more upmarket than this one; more expensive. Mostly Chinese students, from what he said.'

'He's got *two* more houses?' said Bingley. 'We know about the property on Culloden Street.'

'Yeah, and there's a place on Bennetts Road too,' said Baz authoritatively.

'Are you sure?'

'Certain. We used to chat, me and Viktor. He was a nice bloke, and I'm interested in how things work so when he was fixing anything, he'd talk me through it. I learned some useful stuff from him.' Unexpectedly, Baz turned away from them, wiping a hand irritably across his face. 'Anyway, I thanked him for coming out to the boiler and he said something like, "At least you lads pay your rent on time and aren't always complaining." I asked him who was, and he said, "Those mature students." He said, "You and the Bennetts Road tenants are good as gold, but those mature students are always whingeing." So, I said, "How many houses have you got, Viktor? Sounds like an empire," and he said he used to have a lot more, but now he's just got the three.'

'So, a third house,' said Bingley, as they went back to the car. 'I didn't find any reference to Bennetts Road in his papers.'

'If there are any more, Charlie will find them,' said Khatoon. 'Meanwhile, we have got the Culloden Street tenants to check out. If Baz is in the right ballpark about their ethnicity, we might have more chance of a lead with them. And it doesn't sound as if they and Paszek were on the best of terms.'

Although in the same district, the second house was modern and detached. A young Chinese woman came to the door, giving her name as Florence Wan in response to their own introductions. This time, though, she politely refused to admit the two officers.

'I would prefer to wait until all the other tenants are here,' Florence said, in precise, accented English. They had insufficient reason to press the issue, so conducted the conversation on the doorstep of what looked from their vantage point to be an immaculately kept house.

'How many tenants live here?' asked Khatoon.

'Three, all postgraduates. There used to be four, but the man on the top floor moved out two weeks ago.'

'Why was that?'

'I'm not really sure. The landlord came to see him, so perhaps he couldn't make the rent.'

But when they showed her the photograph of Hien, she confirmed that he was not the former tenant, nor one of her other housemates. She didn't know any of the other tenants very well, she explained. 'We say hi in the hall, maybe, but that's all.'

Although saddened to learn of her landlord's death, she was rather less moved than Baz had been, and was keen to end the conversation and get back to her work.

'What about this third house?' said Bingley as he and Khatoon walked back to the car.

'What about it?' said Khatoon. 'We don't have an address for it, do we? We'll have to wait for Charlie to do his stuff.'

'We know it's on Bennetts Road. We could drive along, see what it's like. We might be able to guess at the student properties — if it's like Baz and Ed's place, the garden might look a bit messier.'

'That Culloden Street house was pristine,' Khatoon pointed out, but she turned the car in that direction.

Bennetts Road was a carbon copy of Hillfield, with cars lining the kerb on either side. Negotiating the oncoming traffic was like a slow and tedious version of the dodgems.

'Well, we've established that there are plenty of scruffy gardens on this road, but there isn't a sign in any of them saying, "Viktor Paszek owned this",' said Khatoon. 'We're not going to achieve anything here. Let's head back to base and see what Charlie's got.'

CHAPTER SEVENTEEN

Scott Sinclair had managed to acquire a cassette player and found a free interview room where they could listen to the tape away from background noise.

'Do you want me to—?'

'It's fine,' Reid cut Mariner off. 'You met Peter Church, so you might be more attuned to his speech.'

Closing the door, Sinclair slipped the cassette into the machine and they settled down to listen. Although it pre-dated PACE protocols, the two detectives conducting the interview gave their names as DI Goodrum and DS Rallison, the latter going on to confirm that they were interviewing Peter Church. There was apparently no legal representative in the room.

The detectives weren't accustomed to recording interviews, it seemed, and in the early part of the interview they sounded self-conscious. It quickly became clear that their understanding of learning disabilities was non-existent and they made no allowance for Peter Church's limited mental capacity. They spoke to him in the same way they would any suspect, using complex language and long, rambling sentences. Nor did they allow Church sufficient time to process what they were asking of him. Frustrated by his apparent lack of cooperation, their tone became increasingly confrontational and aggressive, making Mariner cringe.

The line of questioning began with Church's movements on the afternoon and evening of the day Robina went missing, and his relationship with Robina. But about twenty minutes into the interview the focus suddenly changed. It began with a rustle and clatter; something being thrown on the table?

> GOODRUM: *Tell us about this.*
> RALLISON *[sotto voce]: The recording, boss . . .*
> GOODRUM: *Right, yes. It's a necklace that was found in Mr Church's possession.*

Mariner saw Reid and Sinclair exchange a puzzled glance. What necklace?

> GOODRUM: *Who does it belong to, Peter?*
> CHURCH: *'Bina.*
> GOODRUM: *That's right. It's Robina's. We found her fingerprints on it. So how come you had it? Did you take it off her?*
> CHURCH: *'Bina gev it to me.*
> GOODRUM: *Now why would she do that? It's a pretty necklace. Men don't wear necklaces. What would you want with it?*
> *[No response.]*
> GOODRUM: *Tell me, Peter, why did Robina give you the necklace? Look at me, Peter — I'm talking to you!*
> *[There was the swish of movement and then a whimper.]*
> GOODRUM: *Why did she give it to you?*
> CHURCH: *I liked it. But Mork'n munt find out or he be hoolly raw.*
> GOODRUM: *What? Who's Morken?*
> CHURCH: *MORK'N!*

'Blimey,' said Sinclair, pausing the tape. 'I haven't heard dialect like that for donkeys'.'

'Can we wind that bit back?' requested Reid. 'I didn't get exactly what he said.' Sinclair did as she asked, and Mariner was glad of it too. But even after two more repeats, they were none the wiser. They let the recording run on. Reid had written *Morken?* on the pad in front of her.

> GOODRUM: *I don't know what you're on about. I think you took this off Robina when you'd had your way with her and killed her. Did you touch her, Peter? Is that what got you going? Did you try to kiss her?*
> CHURCH: *No. I never.*
> GOODRUM: *Where is she, Peter? Where's Robina?*
> CHURCH: *I dunt know! I want my dad now. I wanta go hoom.*
> GOODRUM: *Your dad can't help you, Peter. And you're not going anywhere. We're the only ones who can get you out of this. But if we're going to do that, you have to tell us the truth about what you did to Robina and where she is.*
> *[Chair legs scraped on the floor.]*
> GOODRUM: *Sit down, Peter.*

Were things about to get physical? It was hard to tell from the tape exactly what was going on in the room but there followed more scuffling and a muffled cry, presumably from Peter. Despite this, the questioning continued in the same circles with no significant outcome.

The recording ended with Goodrum, his voice low:

> *Where's Robina, Peter? If you don't tell us, things could get unpleasant for you.*

'Christ,' said Sinclair, shuddering. 'That takes you back to the bad old days, doesn't it?'

'At least they didn't go as far as beating a confession out of him,' said Mariner. 'Is it any help?'

'We haven't come across a necklace,' said Sinclair. 'Nor any mention of one. Though there are boxes we haven't been through yet.'

'Well, we need to find it,' said Reid. 'It was obviously deemed important. And Peter Church was clearly afraid of this Morken, whoever he or she is.'

'That name doesn't ring any bells with me,' said Sinclair. He raised an eyebrow at Mariner.

'No, can't help you there.'

Reid sat back in her chair and stifled a yawn.

'I should leave you to it,' said Mariner.

'Thanks for your help today,' said Reid. 'It's filled in some of the gaps.' But they all knew there were plenty more. 'Do you mind if we hang on to the photographs for now, to make copies?'

'No problem,' said Mariner. 'If there's anything else, you know where I am.'

And picking up his jacket, he set off along the warren of corridors.

* * *

THEN

The day after he met Robina his mother asked him to go down to the village shop to get a loaf of bread. Her friend Maggie overheard.

'He doesn't need to go into the village,' she said. 'There's a little supermarket on the caravan site, the other side of the woods.'

He wouldn't have minded the longer walk, but if he went to the caravan park he might see Robina, and see where she was staying. He took the path through the trees, past all the fair stalls, already doing a brisk trade. Lesley was on her own again, he noticed, and felt bad that he wasn't going to help her. Further on, he came to the kids' area: storytelling and craft activities and the musicians with their weird and wonderful instruments. 'Surfin' USA' wouldn't be in their repertoire. He wondered how his mates were getting on down in Cornwall, but on balance he was beginning to feel glad he'd come here. At the far edge of the woods, he came to a chain-link fence with double gates opening on to the caravan site. Immediately inside the compound was a modern shower block that looked far preferable to the basic wash tents provided on the campsite. A tarmac road began here and wound through the rows of static caravans, which were just a few metres apart, and all exactly the same. There must have been a hundred or more. One or two seemed unoccupied, but most had the doors open, with deckchairs and tables set up outside, some with additional awnings and tents. Children and dogs played ball games or chased each other about in the sun.

He followed the track round as it curved through the middle, sweeping his gaze from side to side in the hope that he'd catch sight of her. At the main entrance to the site there was a children's playground and paddling pool and a collection of low buildings, which included a licensed social club and the shop. It was bigger than he'd expected and stocked everything from groceries and medicines to toys and games, to cheeky postcards. The only loaves were white sliced, wrapped in the orange and white waxed paper of a local bakery. His mother wouldn't be very happy with that — she favoured wholemeal or granary — but clearly most people were less particular.

A group of teens were hanging round the magazines at the end of an aisle, sniggering about something. He felt suddenly awkward, until he realised they weren't laughing at him, but at a hulk of a boy — or man? — with a mop of unruly hair, who was taking tins of soup from a box and putting them on the shelves one at a time, painfully slowly, chuntering nasally. The teenagers were mimicking it. He hesitated, knowing that he should challenge them for being mean but there were three of them, so it was easier to do nothing. Instead, he just picked up a loaf and went round in the opposite direction to the counter.

Then a familiar voice rang out: 'Did you just pinch something?'

'No.'

'I'm sure you did. Hey, mister!' Robina called to the shop's proprietor, 'there's three lads thieving here.'

The man serving behind the counter left his post and hastened round the shelves to where she was. An altercation ensued, which resulted in the boys being ejected from the shop.

'Got nothing better to do?' Robina called after them. 'You're pathetic.' He heard her speak to the shelf-stacker. 'All right, Peter?' then suddenly she was standing behind him in the queue. Today she was wearing pink shorts and a top that tied behind her neck, leaving her shoulders bare.

'Hello again,' she said. 'Not flogging jewellery today?' A small boy stood beside her clutching an ice lolly in its wrapper and looking on with interest.

'Not sure I'm much of a salesman.'

'Aw, and I thought you were a natural,' she said. 'I'm going down the wall with the others, when I've done this,' she said. 'Want to come?'

'All right.' He drove his mother up the wall on occasion but he had no idea what 'down the wall' meant. It was his turn at the counter, so he handed over the cash for the loaf.

'Just follow the sign in the bottom corner of your field,' she called as he left the shop. 'See you down there.'

* * *

As Mariner was about to leave the police station, the heavens opened. He was studying the sky trying to assess how long it would last, when he saw a woman hurrying across the car park, holding a briefcase over her head against the downpour. Pushing open the door, he stepped back to let her in and she rushed over the threshold, shaking the rain from her coat and bag.

'Thank you,' she gasped. 'What a day! It'll be wet letters and everything!'

She caught Mariner's baffled expression. 'Sorry, force of habit. *Postman Pat* circa 1994.' In those seconds Mariner decided she was probably a duty solicitor rushing to get to a client before he said something he'd regret. Flashing Mariner a brief smile, she went to the reception hatch. 'Hello, I'm Lesley Eden — I'm here to see Inspector Reid.'

'Right madam,' said the sergeant. 'If you'd like to take a seat, I'll let the inspector know that you're here.'

'Lesley?' said Mariner, as she made for the row of visitor chairs. She turned to look at him. 'You wouldn't remember me,' he said.

'I'm sorry . . . have we met before?' she asked, warily.

'We have,' said Mariner. 'A long time ago. You gave me my first paid work — on your jewellery stall at Marsham Fair.'

She studied his face some more, then her expression softened. 'You're that boy. Tom, wasn't it?' She laughed, shaking her head in disbelief. 'Oh my goodness, this is extraordinary. I want to say how much you've changed, but that's a ludicrous thing to say. Of course you have. I'd never have known it was you.'

'It helped that I overheard your name,' said Mariner. 'You've had something of a transformation too, in a good way,' he added hastily. 'How are you?'

'Well. And you?'

'The same. Are you staying here, in Yarmouth?'

'No,' she said. 'I'm travelling back to Suffolk this evening.' She saw what he meant. 'But I will need to get something to eat afterwards, before I drive. I don't know how long I'll be here, but . . . if you're still around later?'

Mariner took out his wallet and one of his business cards, borrowed a pen from the desk sergeant and wrote his personal number on the back. 'Text me when you're finished here and we can get a drink and something to eat.'

'I'd like that.'

'It might be as well to clear it with DCI Reid,' said Mariner. 'Though I'm sure she'll have no objection to us meeting after she's spoken to you.'

Lesley turned the card over and took in some of the details. 'Oh,' she said, trying to make sense of it. 'You work here?'

'No,' he said. 'I'm here for the same reason you are. See? I'm on the West Midlands force.'

'Goodness. This must be strange for you, then.'

'That's one word for it.'

And at that moment Sinclair appeared to take Lesley upstairs. He eyed Mariner with suspicion.

'Don't worry — no conferring,' said Mariner, holding up his hands in mock defence. Sinclair remained po-faced.

CHAPTER EIGHTEEN

Similar to many developments like it, the colourful billboard on the railings outside Brookfield Gardens featured a model-perfect, late-middle-aged couple, glowing with health and beaming at their good fortune to be living in such a place. Great if you could afford it, thought Jesson, wondering if her mum would ever consider somewhere like this. Somehow, she thought not. Swishing through the curved automatic doors of the main apartment block, she came into a lobby that could have graced a smart hotel. Five floors of balconies above overlooked the circular cavern, giving an impression of the Rotunda turned inside out. At ground level, through plate-glass windows, she passed a busy shop, gym and hairdresser's, as she made her way to the lifts and to Eric Dillon's third-floor flat. She had called ahead to let him know she'd be stopping by, and he was waiting for her.

'Come in, come in,' he said, arriving at the door only seconds after she'd knocked. 'I was just going to make a cup of tea. Will you have one?'

Jesson hadn't intended staying, but as she followed him into the kitchen/living room, she saw that he'd already set out a tray with two cups and saucers and a plate of chocolate digestives.

'I'd love one,' she said, and took a seat in one of the cottage armchairs. 'I wanted to make sure that you're all right after yesterday,' she went on, as Eric pottered around the little kitchenette. 'Identifications can be an ordeal. And we're very grateful to you for helping.'

'I can't say I enjoyed it very much,' he said, bringing across a large teapot. 'But I was glad to do it, for Viktor. Help yourself to biscuits, my dear.'

'I wanted to show you this, too,' said Jesson, when he had sat down. She took out the photograph of Hien. 'This man was in the car when Mr Paszek had his accident. Do you know him?'

Eric took it from her and, adjusting his glasses, studied it carefully. He shook his head. 'No, I've never seen him before, I'm sure,' he said, eventually.

'You don't remember seeing him with Viktor at all? A friend or business associate maybe?'

But Eric was adamant. 'Only place I see people like him is at the takeaway,' he quipped.

Jesson forced a weak smile and drank her tea, while they chatted about his life in the retirement home.

From Eric's flat, she went to the Harborne address Glover had given her for Mr Agarwal, but the only Richmond Road she could find in Harborne was strictly residential, when she'd expected to find offices. She hoped they'd got the name right. Number fourteen was a 1990s detached house with an elaborate pillared portico. A small saloon car was parked on the drive, which suggested someone at home, but anticipating redirection, Jesson rang the video bell. She was being watched. When nothing happened, she rang the bell again, then took a couple of steps back and looked up at the house. Was it the right place? Accountancy was the sort of job that could easily be done from home. But apparently there was no one doing it today. She tried the bell one last time, but no one came, so that was that. No choice but to return to Granville Lane and get ready for the afternoon briefing.

Today she felt more confident already and looked forward to the interaction. Charlie Glover's record-keeping was faultless, but the discussion always spawned new ideas. They'd all been productive in the last twenty-four hours. Jesson invited Khatoon to start things off.

'I've pretty much finished going through anything of interest at the house,' she said. 'What's left is ancient history, though I've made an inventory for reference, just in case. Anything I thought might be even vaguely relevant, I've brought back here.'

'I'm going through it bit by bit,' said Glover.

'More importantly, I have finally met Viktor's next-door neighbour,' Khatoon went on. 'An older lady called Gwen Franklin. Has lived there all the time Viktor did. She seems to have been fond of Viktor and it sounds as if he was a good neighbour, helping her out sometimes. She's away with the fairies a bit, so her daughter, Louisa Douglas, sat in, and Samantha, the other daughter, turned up as I was leaving. Their reaction was more illuminating. They didn't have a very high opinion of Viktor.'

'Any special reason?' asked Jesson.

'They claim he was interfering with their plans to sell Gwen's house.'

'In what way?'

'Apparently, Viktor suggested to Gwen that she could keep the house on and rent it out instead. Louisa and Samantha were pretty opposed to it, and plainly got their way because the place is up for sale.'

'It's registered with three different agents, so can't be going all that smoothly,' added Bingley.

'Any other reason for their hostility towards Viktor?' asked Jesson.

'Louisa said he was "weird", though Samantha modified that to "different". Kev and I also visited Paszek's rental properties, at least, two of them,' said Khatoon, and described their experiences.

'Do you think Florence Wan was stalling?' Jesson asked.

'Not necessarily,' said Khatoon. 'There could be a cultural reticence towards us.'

'But there may be another property, too,' said Bingley.

'There is,' said Glover, looking smug.

'OK, we'll come to that,' said Jesson. 'How did you get on at the factory centre?' she asked Bingley.

'Viktor's cleaning business went under the banner "ViP Cleaning",' he said. 'The lock-up is mostly storage space for the materials and a little office. And there's a people carrier that I'm guessing Paszek used to shift the stuff around in. Nothing I could see at the lock-up to indicate Hien came to harm there, and no obvious indication of what Paszek might have been up to on Sunday night, but SOCO are in there doing their thing as we speak. I brought back a bunch of more up-to-date paperwork, which Charlie's got, and a laptop's gone to Max.'

'Good,' said Jesson. 'If there's anything dubious on there, Max will find it.'

'I had a visitor while I was there, too,' said Bingley. 'He was looking for Paszek, when I told him about the RTC, he scarpered.'

'Your natural charm, Kev,' said Khatoon.

'He dropped these.' Bingley picked up an evidence bag from his desk. 'They're keys for the lock-up and the people carrier.'

'He was working with Paszek?'

'I'd say *for* him,' said Bingley. 'He was pretty shabbily dressed.'

'I thought Paszek had retired from the contract cleaning?' said Jesson.

'I don't think he had,' said Bingley. 'The lock-up didn't feel abandoned, and the people carrier started easily enough when I tried it.'

'What spooked him?' asked Jesson. 'Did you tell him you were police?'

'I didn't get that far. We just exchanged a few words. He had a strong accent and I don't think his English was that great. He's Latvian.'

'And you got that from just a few words?' said Jesson.

'And some help from these.' Bingley held up the bag of passports. 'They were locked in the filing cabinet. The picture's rubbish as they usually are, but I'm sure the guy who ran off is Matejs Skrīvulis.'

Everyone was staring at the passports.

'Any of those belong to Hien?' asked Glover.

'No. But I can think of only one reason Viktor might be holding a bunch of random passports.'

'Let's come back to the passports in a minute,' said Jesson. 'Charlie? Your turn. Just the edited highlights, please.'

'Well,' Glover began, 'luckily for us, Viktor Paszek hadn't exactly embraced modern technology, and believed in keeping everything, so we've got a solid hard-copy footprint for him. His income appears to be made up of a couple of private pensions, state pension, and income from savings and ISAs. His regular outgoings are all fairly obvious too — council tax, utilities, insurance, rent for the lock-up, MOT and servicing for both vehicles — which would confirm like Kevin said, that the Galaxy's still being used. And he paid his taxes. He supported a few charities too, with monthly standing orders, and he made modest cash withdrawals: rarely more than a couple of hundred a month. No credit cards that I've found yet. The only outgoing I can't readily identify is regular substantial payments to something called Tasuta,' said Glover. 'I'm trying to get hold of the bank.'

'Nice to have one mystery,' said Jesson.

'It's not the only one,' said Glover. 'Most of the hard-copy paperwork from the lock-up is old, really old. It looks as if at one time Paszek was running ten different teams of cleaners, all made up of between six and eight people.'

'That's a substantial operation,' Khatoon remarked.

'And he had some big clients,' said Glover. 'Including the city council and Partington's. That was up until about five years ago when he started closing the contracts.'

'That's when Eric said he retired,' Bingley reminded them.

'He didn't, though, not fully,' said Glover. 'Paszek was receiving a regular payment from Partington's right up until the end of last month that equates to what was being paid per team before, if you factor in inflation. So, I rang Partington's. They still have a contract with ViP and their offices are being cleaned overnight on Mondays, Wednesdays and Fridays, as they put it, "to Mr Paszek's usual high standard". As far as the lady I spoke to was aware, the team turned up as usual on Monday night.'

'One team? That block must be ten floors,' said Khatoon.

'It's eight floors, and ViP don't clean the whole block,' said Glover. 'Partington's has shrunk too and they only occupy the top three floors now. The bottom two are rented by different outfits, who arrange their own cleaning, and the remaining three floors are vacant.

'But this where I found a major anomaly. With the old teams, the paper trail is crystal clear. Each team of six to eight workers was paid via BACS; national insurance, payroll details, all kept bang up to date until the contracts ceased; personal details — names, addresses, present and presumably correct. For this current team? Zilch. No paperwork at all. I thought that perhaps Paszek had gone electronic, so I contacted Max about the laptop. But there's nothing on that either. Max reckons it's as if he bought it but then didn't know how to use it. All I could find that directly refers to ViP Cleaning in its current form are what look like some basic time sheets. But there are no personal details for any of the workers, or any payroll records. It doesn't look, on the face of it, as if he pays them.'

'Could it be cash in hand?' suggested Jesson.

'If it is, I don't know where Paszek was getting the cash, unless the pay's pitiful. Most weeks he was drawing out between thirty and seventy quid, which he had to live off too. And it doesn't sit right with his previous employees who were paid above minimum wage. If I hadn't spoken to the woman at Partington's, I would say these cleaners didn't exist.'

'Looks as if Gwen's daughters were right to be suspicious of Viktor,' said Khatoon.

'Then there are the houses,' said Glover. 'For Hillfield Road and Culloden Street the income from rent is again pretty obvious, along with everything else — buildings insurance and so on. The mortgages are paid off. But, as Kev said, there's a third property too.'

'Baz seemed pretty certain about it,' said Khatoon. 'He said Paszek talked about a house on Bennetts Road.'

'That's consistent with what I found,' said Glover. 'But it's a bit like the cleaning team,' he went on. 'It's there, but it's not there. The only place I can find reference to it is in the maintenance folder, where there's an occasional item of expenditure attributed for work that's been done there, as recently as four months ago.'

'What kind of work?' said Jesson. 'Could he have been doing it up to sell?'

'That's possible,' said Glover. 'If Paszek's accountant, Agarwal, was doing his job properly, he should be able to shed some light on all this.'

'If we ever get hold of him,' said Jesson and described her abortive visit.

'Unfortunately, we don't have a full address for the third house,' said Glover. 'We have a street but there's no record of the number. It's as if it's being deliberately hidden.'

'Bear with me on this,' said Jesson. 'But from where I'm sitting, we have Viktor Paszek running a cleaning team he doesn't apparently pay, along with a house for which he receives no rent. Seems to me we're building up a picture. And not a very pretty one.'

'We know slavery is on the rise,' said Khatoon.

'And office cleaning is the perfect cover,' said Glover. 'It's managed by the contractor, not the host employer. It goes on outside normal working hours, out of sight of the client firm's workforce, so the workers are kept isolated and dependent. They work in exchange for their board and lodgings, and their passports are confiscated, so they have no resources or means to escape.'

'Don't forget the possible intimidation too,' said Bingley.

'Paszek's set-up is the definition of modern-day slavery,' Glover concluded.

Khatoon was sceptical. 'It's a leap,' she said. 'And hardly consistent with what Eric's told us about his friend.'

'How well did he really know him though?' said Bingley. 'Perhaps it's a side of Paszek Eric knew nothing about. Jekyll and Hyde. Eric said he was a private person and clearly he was someone who compartmentalised his life — a cleaning business alongside a squalid house. It wouldn't be hard for him to conceal it.'

'And it would explain Hien,' said Jesson. 'Perhaps he worked for Paszek and tried to escape. Paszek hunted him down and, at best, there was some kind of accident. The passport isn't there because Paszek ditched it.'

'Didn't Croghan say Hien could have fallen?' said Khatoon. 'Do you think eight floors would do it?'

'Any volunteers?' said Bingley.

'I'll happily sacrifice the neighbours' cat,' said Glover. 'That'd teach the little git not to crap in our garden.'

'I'll talk to Stuart Croghan again,' said Jesson. 'But Partington's is surrounded by other commercial buildings. It's a pretty public place for it to happen, and to clean up afterwards. The crime scene would have been messy, remember. I doubt it could be done without alerting other people, or without leaving traces.'

'The cleaners are there in the middle of the night,' said Glover. 'Wouldn't be many people about then.'

'True,' said Jesson. 'But at the moment we still have no evidence linking Hien to any of Viktor's known or hypothetical activities. Finding that connection has to be a priority, along with locating this third house. If this is about slavery and the current workers have gone to ground, I'd lay odds on them being there.'

'We have a road name, so Land Registry might have a record of a property on Bennetts Road owned by Paszek,' said Glover.

'They're notoriously slow to respond,' said Jesson. 'If we think this is a slavery situation, we need to act fast.'

'Could we get uniform to go door to door?' Bingley suggested.

Khatoon was incredulous. 'We drove along Bennetts Road,' she said. 'Remember how long it took? There must be six hundred houses. Add into that that a lot are student lets, finding anyone at home could well take several attempts. Ralph Solomon would hang us out to dry.'

After a moment Bingley said, 'Charlie, you mentioned some big maintenance bills. Any way of knowing what they were for?'

They waited while Glover shuffled through papers on his desk. 'Only the ones whose company names specify: electricals, plumbing and heating . . .'

'Anything structural?'

The wait seemed to stretch for ever, before Glover finally said, 'There's a big payment to a roofer, six thousand. Less than twelve months ago.'

'That's something,' said Bingley. 'We could go to Bennetts Road and see who's got a new roof?'

Jesson was doubtful. 'Give it a go but don't waste too much time on it,' she said. 'And make it your first task of the morning. If we're right about this, Paszek can't have been operating alone. Sooner or later, whoever he worked with will get wind of the fact that he's dead, and won't want trafficked individuals on the loose.'

'Belt and braces,' said Glover. 'I'll contact Land Registry as well.'

'We need to get hold of this bloody accountant urgently,' said Jesson. 'It seems to me that he could hold the key to all this. Keep trying his number, Charlie.'

'Partington's said the cleaning team were there on Monday, didn't they?' said Bingley. 'And they're due again tonight. It'd be worth staking it out.'

'Will you be all right on your own?' said Khatoon.

'I only plan on talking to them.'

'They might have a minder,' warned Jesson.

'Want me to come?' offered Glover. 'I haven't got anything else going on tonight.'

'You're on,' said Bingley.

'OK that's good work everyone,' said Jesson. 'It feels as if we're making progress.'

* * *

Having established with Partington's that the cleaning team started work around 7 p.m., Bingley and Glover left Granville Lane just after five, and drove to the industrial estate that had grown up around Partington House. They were relying on the majority of employees working nine to five, which would allow time to do a search around the outside of the building before the cleaners showed up.

Situated behind the Kingsmead railway station, the block stood in its own compound, surrounded by chain-link fencing, with a handful of executive parking spaces on the front forecourt and waste skips at the back. Bingley settled kerbside on the approach road, amongst other parked cars, but still allowing a clear view of the main office block entrance.

The first arrival, not long after they got there, was a canine security patrol van, which parked on the forecourt. Bingley's guess had been accurate and most of the activity occurred between five twenty and six fifteen, as the Partington's workforce, and presumably those on the other three floors, departed, and the offices emptied. As six o'clock ticked by, the numbers dwindled and the cars on the forecourt went. Those parked around Bingley's car also thinned out, though not so much as to leave him and Glover conspicuous.

Just after six-twenty the security guard got out of his van and, letting out a long-haired German shepherd, took it, straining at the leash, to make a circuit of the grounds. He repeated the same exercise at six forty-five. Twilight turned to darkness.

'They're not coming, are they?' said Bingley to Glover, finally.

CHAPTER NINETEEN

To kill a bit of time while he was waiting for Lesley, Mariner walked into the town centre to search out somewhere to eat. The rain had stopped and the marketplace echoed to the clang of steel tubing as the stalls were dismantled at the close of the day's trading. Racks of cheap clothing and boxes of hardware were being loaded into vans and crates of leftover fruit and veg were being stowed away. Only the chip stalls remained open for business and the smell of cooking fat and vinegar was sharp in the air.

Even in the centre of town, restaurants were few and far between. Mariner guessed that most would be in out-of-town retail parks, leaving only a few snack outlets here, so in the end, he settled on a cosy-looking pub that had a decent menu. It was busy enough to have atmosphere without being uncomfortably full. He'd just started his second pint when the text came through from Lesley. He sent her details of how to find him, and by the time he was paying for her chilled Chablis, she was walking through the door.

'We're over here,' he said, leading her to the table he'd chosen, away from the TV screen and fruit machine. Mariner waited for her to take off her coat and sit down before raising his glass. 'Cheers.'

'Cheers.' She smiled. 'To old times.'

Looking at her now, Mariner realised Maggie was right — Lesley wasn't much older than him; maybe a decade or so, which would put her at around seventy. She wore the years with grace, her silver-grey hair cut into a short bob and glowing skin that had need for little make-up. He thought of her as she was then, and an image of her breasts flashed into his head, bringing a sudden heat flush to his neck. He hoped she hadn't noticed.

'How did it go?' he asked.

'Fine, I think, though I'm ready for this.' She took another sip of her wine. 'I can't imagine I was much help.'

'You told Ginny Reid we were meeting?'

'Yes. Did you think she might object?'

'Normally in an investigation you'd discourage witnesses from talking to each other,' said Mariner. 'But this one's a bit different. And I get the impression that she's a pragmatist. Best that she knows, though. She might even think that, between us, we'll come up with something useful. Shall we order some food?'

'Good idea. I'm famished.'

They made their choices and Mariner went up to the bar to place the order.

'I was astonished to get the call,' Lesley said, when he returned to his seat. 'I haven't thought about it — her, Robina — in years. It's an awful business, isn't it? I mean, it was at the time, of course, but I lived in hope that whatever had happened, she was still alive.'

'Me too,' said Mariner. 'You got to know her after I left.'

'A bit. She started coming to help on the stall, like you did. She hinted that she was getting some unwelcome male attention, so I think we were a kind of refuge.'

'Which male?'

'I wish I knew. Given how things turned out, I assumed it was Peter Church, but I never actually saw them together, so can't be sure. She was a lovely girl, and very easy company, though she did go on about you quite a lot. I feel so sad about what happened to her, to think that so soon after that . . . It must have been tough on you at that age too.'

'Perhaps not as tough as it should have been,' said Mariner.

The food arrived and for a few minutes they ate in companionable silence, thinking about the young woman they'd known.

'DCI Reid was asking about the necklace again,' said Lesley, resting her cutlery for a moment. 'The one Peter Church had.'

'Have they found it?' asked Mariner.

'Not yet. They asked me to draw it for them. I remember the police being obsessed with it at the time. I suppose they kept asking us because we had them on the stall — pendants on leather thongs. They were solid silver, and one of our more expensive items.'

'One of those on the boards?'

'That's right. They were popular, we sold quite a few, but too many to remember who'd bought them. The pendant was a silver ring — some pseudo-religious karma thing.'

'Do you think the police were right about Church; that he would have been capable of doing Robina harm?' asked Mariner.

'I didn't know him well enough to judge,' she said, straight away. 'I only saw him once or twice. There seemed to be an innocence about him though. What do you think?'

'The same, though I'm not sure if my judgement is clouded these days because I've got guardianship of a man with learning difficulties — my late fiancée's brother.'

'Gosh, that sounds like a challenge.'

'He's in residential care, so other people do all the hard work these days, but Jamie has made me more aware of how people that are different can be misunderstood. And this is now, when we're more enlightened. It would have been far worse for Peter Church.'

'You said "late" fiancée,' said Lesley.

'She died some years ago now.'

'I'm sorry.'

'Just one of those things,' he said. 'Life goes on. How about you? Are you still with Gary?'

'Oh God, no. I was already starting to realise what a liability he was. It was a toss-up what I would ditch him for — the laziness or the serial shagging. I'm sure he had someone else on the go at the fair. Came back filthy in the early hours of one morning having fallen in the reed beds. Free love, he called it — the word "love" used very loosely.'

'And now?' said Mariner. 'Are you with someone?'

'Would you believe, I went all traditional and got married after all. The whole white-wedding shebang. What about you?'

'I never made it as far as the altar, no. But I have got a partner. She's on sabbatical at the moment in Beijing, but coming back soon. How's Violet?'

'She's doing well; got three children of her own now. And you're a police officer yourself? I often thought about you after that time; wondered what you'd got up to. You were an interesting young man.'

'That's a generous way of putting it,' said Mariner. 'I liked to think that I was silent and mysterious, but I suspect I was just an idiot. Are you still selling jewellery?'

'Sadly not. It was fun, but not much of a living to be made out of the sort of stuff we sold. When Violet was older, I trained to be a teacher.'

'I bet you're good at that. You'd be one of the cool ones,' said Mariner.

'Not any more, if I ever was. Technically I'm retired, but they wheel me in to do the occasional Ofsted inspection when they're desperate. Not futures either of us could have predicted, eh?'

She was right about that, thought Mariner. 'How are you finding retirement?'

'Liberating. You must be coming up for it soon?'

'Oh, I've done my service,' said Mariner, 'and for the first time I'm seriously thinking about it.'

'You should do more than think,' she advised. 'Time to enjoy yourself.' She glanced at her phone. 'This has been lovely, but I ought to go. I've got an hour and a half's drive, if the roads are clear.'

'To where?'

'Just outside Ipswich. But I need to find my way back to the police station first. I left my car there.'

'I'll walk you,' said Mariner. 'It's on the way to my hotel.'

They parted company in the station car park. 'I've enjoyed seeing you again, Tom,' said Lesley. 'You've turned out well.'

'As have you.' Mariner smiled. 'Good to see you, too. Something positive to come out of all this.'

'Indeed.' And with a peck on the cheek, she was gone.

Mariner realised, walking back to the hotel, that it was probable he'd never see her again.

It was still only mid-evening, and getting back to the hotel, Mariner was ready for a last pint. Going into the bar, he saw that the old man had beaten him to it and was sitting in a corner reading the paper, the dregs of his ale on the table in front of him.

'Can I get you another?' Mariner asked.

He looked up from his paper. 'Aye, thanks lad, that's very kind. Pint of Tetley's will do nicely.'

'You should get some sun cream on, Tommy lad, or you'll burn.'

'I'll do it.'

'You bloody won't. He'll do it himself.'

The voice was gruff with age, but there was no mistaking it. Suddenly Mariner knew for sure that the woman he'd seen with the old man wasn't his wife. The pint poured, Mariner took it over to the table. The first glass was empty now and the old man immediately raised the fresh one. Had he recognised Mariner? If he did, he was keeping it well disguised.

'Cheers.' He swallowed big mouthfuls. No, he was just grateful to be bought a drink. With another nod of thanks, the old boy returned to his paper, happily resolving the dilemma of whether Mariner should encourage conversation. He'd got the old OS map in his coat pocket, and there was something he wanted to look for. By the time he was draining his glass, he thought he might have found it. Bidding the old man a good night, he went up to his room, when he noticed he had a missed call from Jesson.

* * *

Vicky Jesson was in Mariner's office, munching on a Twix and catching up on things when the call came through from him.

'You've got me bang to rights,' she said, guiltily. 'I found the stash of goodies in your drawer.'

'You're welcome to them,' said Mariner. 'I'd forgotten they were there.'

'So, how are things in the far east?' she asked.

'Quiet,' he said, realising at that moment how true that was. He was standing looking out over the coast road, and it was some minutes since the last set of headlights had swooped past.

'That's a coincidence,' said Jesson. 'Quiet and gentle — it's the meaning of the name Charlie has come up with for our unidentified man. Hien.' She spelled it out for him.

'Good old Charlie,' said Mariner. 'He has a knack for it. And are we any closer to knowing who he really is?'

Jesson brought him up to date with what had been learned since his departure. 'I think we're all of a mind that this could all point to Paszek being involved in slavery.'

'Christ.'

'I know. Who'd have thought?' said Jesson. 'But he's got a cleaning operation that's a perfect fit.'

'I thought he'd retired from that,' said Mariner.

'So did we,' said Jesson. 'Till we found a ghost team, along with a ghost house. The thing I can't quite get my head round, is why. Viktor Paszek obviously had a successful, legitimate and lucrative operation. So why do it? Why take the risk?'

'The usual motivation is greed,' said Mariner. 'Perhaps an opportunity presented itself that was too hard to resist.

Have you found anything that would indicate he might have contacts in that line of business?'

'Not yet,' said Jesson. 'We're struggling to get hold of the accountant and Eric, the only friend we've come across, gives us the impression that Paszek was a bit of a loner.'

'You should talk to Tony Knox,' said Mariner. 'He's with Regional Organised Crime. He might have come across Paszek's name. I'll text you his number.'

'Thanks.'

'If Hien was trafficked into the country, unless he's actually been reported missing by his family — which is unlikely — he's going to be near to impossible to identify,' said Mariner.

'That's what I've been thinking,' said Jesson. 'But I haven't voiced it yet, for the sake of morale.'

'Good call,' said Mariner. 'Everyone OK?'

She chuckled. 'Bingley and Khatoon bickering like an old married couple, so no change there.'

'Sounds as if you're on top of things,' said Mariner. 'I might stay away a bit longer — extend my holiday while I'm here.'

'Oh no you don't!' said Jesson, not sure if he was joking. 'I'm holding the fort in your absence, but only because I have to.'

'Ah, admit it, you're loving it — especially not having me looking over your shoulder. Is it working out with the family?'

'Yes, all good thanks.' Jesson had her fingers crossed as she spoke.

CHAPTER TWENTY

Signing off, Jesson fought off a wave of exhaustion. Shit, and this was only the second day of flying solo. Nice to hear the boss was pleased with things so far, but could she sustain the pace?

The drive home revived her and she had switched to full mum mode by the time she walked in through the front door. All was calm and quiet, as she'd known it would be. Maisie was in front of the TV in the lounge, though in deep conversation with someone on the phone at the same time. Mum was in the kitchen, already filling the kettle at the sound of her entrance.

'How's it been?' Doris asked.

'OK, I think. It's weird knowing that Tom isn't around, and it's still a bit daunting seeing all those expectant faces in briefings, but they're a good bunch. Aaron not home?' she asked, noting the absence of her son's shoes in the hall.

'He was in for his tea,' said Doris. 'He's gone over to Mo's.'

As Jesson sat down to have her tea, Maisie drifted into the kitchen. 'Hi, sweetheart. Who were you talking to?'

'Callie and Lexa. They've been to Nando's in town.' Maisie gave her mother a hard stare, just in case she hadn't picked up the full meaning of the statement.

'As you will be able to at the weekend,' said Jesson firmly, not wanting to get into this argument again.

'Hm.' Unsatisfied with the reply, Maisie floated out again.

'And Emily?' Jesson asked, unable to stop herself sighing.

'In her room,' said Doris, failing in her attempt to sound nonchalant.

'And?'

'She's got something to tell you.'

Gravity asserted itself in Jesson's stomach, but though she waited, Doris wasn't about to elaborate.

'Best if you talk to her,' was all she would say, before putting a steaming casserole on the table. 'Hot pot,' she said. 'I hope that's OK.'

It was delicious as always, and after she'd eaten and seen her mum off home, Jesson went up to her older daughter's bedroom. The climb up the stairs was more than enough time for trepidation to set in. Emily always had the power to do this to her and usually it was when she was feeling complacent. After such a good parents' evening, she'd hoped that they'd turned a corner, but should have known it was too good to last. What would it be this time? Jesson took a breath and tapped on the bedroom door.

The response was surprisingly meek. 'You can come in, Mum.' Emily was lying on the bed, laptop propped up on her raised knees. It didn't look comfortable.

'No Jayden tonight?' said Jesson. 'Have the two of you fallen out?' She hoped not. Emily needed her friends.

'Nah. He's been grounded.'

'Why?'

Emily shrugged. 'He won't say.'

'Embarrassed, probably,' said Jesson. 'Gran says you've got something to tell me.'

'Promise you won't shout? I'm really sorry.'

'Please tell me you're not pregnant.' Jesson said it as a joke but Emily was horrified.

'What? No!'

'What then?'

'I've lost my phone.'

Jesson fought down the sharp bite of anger. 'That would be the brand-new iPhone that cost me a month's wages,' she said, with forced calm.

Emily held her gaze, until the tears forming in the corners of her eyes threatened to erupt and she turned to wipe them away. 'I'm really sorry, Mum.'

The contrition was unexpected and so genuine that Jesson's anger receded a little. She sat down beside her daughter on the bed with a sigh. 'It's all right,' she said, even though it was anything but. 'It's only a phone. I'm sure we can sort something out.'

'I thought you'd go ballistic.'

'That's not going to help anyone, is it? Where did you lose it?'

'I don't know.'

'Well, when did you last have it? Was it at school, or after school?' Jesson persisted.

'It might have been.'

'It might have been which?'

'At school.'

'Did you retrace your steps, see if you could find it?'

'Duh. Course I did.' Emily's natural defensiveness began to kick in.

'You reported it?'

'What's the point?'

'Someone may have found it and handed it in.'

'Who would do that? Like you said, it's a brand-new iPhone.'

'You'd hand it in if you found it.' Jesson suddenly hoped that her confidence was justified. 'Wouldn't you?'

'Yeah, I suppose.'

'Well then. That's something you can do first thing in the morning. Have you tried ringing the number?' Jesson realised Emily probably wouldn't have wanted to borrow her sister's phone. 'Here, use mine.'

'I already tried that. Kirsten let me borrow hers.'

'And?'

'Nothing.'

'What kind of nothing? Did it ring out, or go to voice-mail or what?' Jesson did her best to temper her growing annoyance.

'I can't remember.'

'Surely you can—'

'Mum! Will you stop interrogating me. You're not at work. I'll try again tomorrow, OK?' Dumping the lap-top on the bed beside her, Emily turned to face the wall. Conversation over.

There were so many things Jesson wanted to say. She wanted to rail at her daughter for her carelessness, and her lack of appreciation and consideration, but she realised it would get her nowhere. She got up to go.

'Mum?' Emily's voice was small. Jesson paused in the doorway. 'It means I haven't got a phone. . .'

'Think of it as a learning experience,' Jesson said tightly, her anger threatening to surface.

CHAPTER TWENTY-ONE

Thursday morning was Mariner's first free time in Norfolk and he planned to take a longer walk. Until he had an unexpected call from Ginny Reid.

'Viscount Rothbury has very reluctantly deigned to give us an audience this morning,' she said, her opinion of him obvious from the tone of her voice.

'That's good of him,' said Mariner.

'Isn't it? I wondered if you'd like to come along.'

'I would,' said Mariner. 'All right if I meet you there? I'll need my car afterwards.'

'Of course. I'll be at Flintmore Hall at about eleven. Come to the service entrance, otherwise we'll be fleeced for the entrance fee.'

'I'll be there,' said Mariner.

The drive out to Flintmore Hall was a pleasant one, through gently undulating farmland. Mariner drove past the ornate gates of the hall, and found the service entrance, which took him round to the back of the house and to a yard with outbuildings and assorted maintenance vehicles. From this angle, the hall was a jumble of mismatched roofs all at different levels, and rather less imposing than he remembered the front facade to be. Reid was already there. She got out of her car as he pulled into a parking space.

'Thanks for doing this,' she said. 'It's moral support really. Scott's had a family emergency, so he's working from home today.' She looked up at the building. 'Not quite so grand from this side, is it? I looked Rothbury up. Inherited peerage. Some ancestor made money from farm machinery in the nineteenth century and was made a viscount.'

'We came here during that holiday,' said Mariner. 'I hated it.'

'Sixteen-year-old boy?' said Reid. 'Can't imagine why.'

'It was so inconsistent of my mother, too. The last thing she'd have wanted was to be seen to be pandering to the upper classes, let alone putting money in their coffers. I hadn't dared tell her I was hanging out with Kit and Ludo. Her friend Maggie was meant to have come with her. They probably intended to dig up the croquet lawn or something. But at the last minute Maggie had a better offer — a man, I think — so I ended up here instead.'

They were met at the side entrance by one of Rothbury's staff, a young man, who took them upstairs and along a corridor to a small and functional seating area where a middle-aged woman, smartly turned out, looked up from her computer screen. Reid introduced herself.

'Lord Rothbury's busy on a call at present,' the woman said, getting to her feet. She led them into the room next door, empty but for a row of four chairs along one wall. 'If you could wait here, please, I will fetch you when he's free. Can I get you anything?'

'Just an audience with your boss as soon as possible, please,' said Reid, with a smile. 'We're all busy people. Sorry, was that rude?' she added, when the PA had gone. 'I have a natural aversion to this kind of situation.'

'Not at all,' said Mariner. 'It was the perfect response.'

And perhaps it had the desired effect, because just a few moments later the PA returned to usher them through to Rothbury's office. It was plain and workmanlike, and not at all as sumptuous as Mariner had imagined it would be. And while he had aged like they all had, Mariner would have had no trouble picking Ludo out in a crowd. The looks were still there, but mostly, it was his posture: upright and confident, just as he'd been as a young man.

Reid introduced Mariner as 'my colleague DI Mariner', as they had agreed, and Rothbury gave him a cursory glance. Reid opened her mouth to form the first question but he cut her off. 'I realise why you're here,' he said, seating himself behind the desk, and gesturing for them to take the chairs before him. 'But really, I've nothing to add to my original statement.'

Mariner took out a notebook and pen, and Rothbury hesitated for a second, before continuing.

'If anything, after such a long time the events are rather less clear in my mind than they would have been at the time.'

'I understand that,' said Reid. 'But we're talking to as many of the original witnesses as we can. It's surprising what can emerge, especially as some of you were young at the time, and now have the benefit of a more worldly and mature perspective.'

'Perhaps,' said Rothbury dismissively. 'But I barely remember the girl; yes, I suppose we met on a number of occasions, but it was in a much larger group of young people. I hardly recall any of them. I really can't see that anything has changed.' He was finding it hard to make eye contact. The papers on his desk were apparently more interesting.

'What has changed', said Reid, quietly, 'is that we have found Robina's remains. We know now that she died an unnatural death, and we know where—'

'Yes, yes . . . in the woods close to the big house. I know all that. But as I said at the time, in my statement, on the night that she went missing, I was here.'

'With your friend,' said Reid.

'What?' That threw him, but only for a moment. 'Oh, yes, I think I did have a friend staying.'

'That would be Kit,' said Reid.

'Ha! Oh yes, him. Bland; by name and by nature. Lord, I haven't thought about him in a long time,' he said. 'But we were here, and not anywhere near the big house or Herringfleet or whatever it's called now.'

'Which your family owned.'

'My family owns, or has owned, much of the land hereabouts. It doesn't make us responsible for everything that happens on it. As I remember it, the big house was always rented out during the summer. You'd be better off talking to whoever was the tenant at that time.'

'I understand the comedian Jimmy Finnegan was staying there at the time of Robina's disappearance.'

'Was he? I really have no idea. It was often rented out to showbiz types in the summer, but that would all have been managed by my father.' He gave an impatient sigh. 'Stella, who you just met, may be able to help.'

'Why was the land sold?' asked Reid.

'Have you ever tried running an estate this size?' said Rothbury, sitting back and regarding them both properly for the first time. Mariner assumed the question was rhetorical. 'It's enormously expensive, and there's the constant need for renovation. I don't remember when exactly my father sold the land, but that's why he'd have done it. I'm sorry but there really is nothing more I can say.'

'Well, thank you for your time,' said Reid tightly, and they got up to leave.

'I hope you catch whoever killed the girl,' said Rothbury, but when Mariner looked back, his nose was already in his accounts.

'Ever felt you've been had?' said Reid as they descended the stairs. 'I'll stand you lunch. It's the least I can do. Do you know where the Three Bells is?'

'I do,' said Mariner. It was the riverside pub in Ansgar.

'I'll meet you there in a few minutes.'

* * *

'Some things don't change,' said Mariner, when they walked in. The interior looked as if it hadn't been touched for decades.

'I wonder if the Rothburys owned this place at one time too.'

'God, he's become an arrogant bastard,' said Mariner. 'Did you notice he didn't once use Robina's name?'

'I suppose that's what a life of privilege does to a man,' said Reid.

'Not to everyone, I'm sure. I'm disappointed in him.'

Reid insisted on paying for lunch. Mariner had a half-pint but she had coffee. As she came back from ordering their sandwiches at the bar, she was checking her phone.

'Scott,' she said.

'Everything OK?'

'His young son had a high temperature and a very suspect rash this morning, but it sounds as if it's just a regular virus.' She put her phone away. 'Scott's a real family man — devoted to his kids. He's not the most dynamic, but he really cares.'

'I've got a DC like that,' said Mariner. 'We couldn't manage without him. We've just got our second John Doe in recent times. Charlie's the one who comes up with a name, to make them real for us.' He noticed that she wore wedding and engagement rings. 'What about you? Do you have kids?'

'Two teenagers. You?'

Mariner shook his head. 'Never worked out. Probably just as well.'

'So, what name has Charlie given him, your John Doe?'

'Hien. It means "quiet and gentle" in Vietnamese — we're pretty certain he had links to Vietnam.'

'And are you likely to find out his real identity?'

'Hard to say. He's got severe injuries, so there's not much left of his face. But he had a cigarette pack on him, and currency, and a photo of a man with a woman and young kid, which we're assuming is him.'

'Injuries from what?' asked Reid.

'Something else we don't know. The likelihood is he was struck by an HGV or something going at speed. He was found in the boot of a car, probably on the way to being dumped.'

'That's gruesome.'

'Yeah, as cases go, it's not one of the best,' Mariner agreed.

'The worst I ever saw was years ago; a skydiver whose parachute didn't open.' She shuddered. 'That stayed with me a long time.'

'An accident?'

'Not as it turned out. His mate had packed both the chutes and sabotaged it deliberately. He was having an affair with the victim's wife.'

'Jesus, the things people do to each other.'

'It shouldn't surprise us any more, should it?'

Their sandwiches arrived and for a while they focused on eating.

'Was Lesley any help yesterday?' asked Mariner eventually, coming up for air.

'Maybe, in terms of corroborating what we already know.'

'And you're still looking at Peter Church as the most likely perpetrator?' asked Mariner.

'Not necessarily,' said Reid. 'We've had the results back on the fibres on Robina's dress. They're not a match for the samples of Peter's clothing. They're Indian cotton and the colour analysis suggests pale green or blue. Peter was wearing a mid-blue polycotton shirt and dark grey trousers in a man-made fabric. So, the fibres could be from anywhere; anyone. Obviously that doesn't categorically rule him out. And we're woefully short of other lines of enquiry.'

'Frustrating.'

'Mm. Especially as we're seeing Robina's father and sister tomorrow, to update them on so-called progress.'

'Talking to them might open something up,' said Mariner.

'Maybe. They've asked to see Robina and her belongings, but I'm hoping to dissuade them. I'm not sure they appreciate how upsetting that could be.'

'Did you know they're staying in the same hotel as me?'

'Yes. We suggested a couple to them and they chose,' said Reid, wiping her mouth with the napkin. 'We're footing the bill, but I wanted them to be comfortable. Have you spoken to them?'

'Briefly, to him, but I don't think he's recognised me. She's not said anything, but then I remember her being like that as a kid — shy. She was a funny one, Dawn. Very different to Robina. The first time I saw her I thought she was a boy. She had her hair cut short and was wearing jeans and one of those budgie jackets.'

'Oh God, budgie jackets! That's a blast from the past.'

'Robina was very feminine, sexy, gregarious. Her sister was the opposite. And she didn't hang out with the rest of us but stayed at the caravan site with the younger kids. She seemed younger than Robina though I'm sure someone said she was older.'

'She was, but not by much. Just a few months,' said Reid.

It took a moment for Mariner to digest that, then he looked quizzically at Reid.

'They were step-sisters,' she said. 'You didn't know?'

'No. But that explains a lot.'

'Robina was Trish's daughter. Dawn is Trevor's.'

'I don't know how I didn't see that,' said Mariner. 'And Mikey and Paul?'

'They're their half-brothers, Trish and Trevor's sons.'

'That explains the different surnames in the news reports I saw. I thought Trish must have reverted to her maiden name. What about Robina's biological father?'

'He hadn't had contact with her for some years. He was interviewed as part of the investigation but was never a POI. I've spoken to Dawn several times now, on the phone, from the point at which the remains were found. I've found her guarded, reluctant even, but perhaps, as you say, that's her natural disposition.'

'Or it could be a protection strategy,' said Mariner. 'It's a highly emotional time for them, isn't it?'

'I do feel as if she's holding back,' said Reid. 'But we'll see.'

'I should probably head back to Birmingham tomorrow,' Mariner said. 'I can't think that I'll be of much more use to your investigation. What I've told you is just a tiny piece of the puzzle you're tasked with assembling.'

'But crucial,' said Reid. 'I really appreciate that you came across. We've made copies of everything you brought with you, if you want to stop by and pick up the originals before you go.'

'I'll do that.'

'I should probably get back to the station now.'

'Thanks for lunch.'

CHAPTER TWENTY-TWO

Jesson had got into Granville Lane early on Thursday morning. She went over the briefing notes again, then picked up the phone to call Tony Knox. He and Mariner went way back, and Knox had a reputation as a bit of a rascal. Jesson had met him a couple of times, but wasn't sure how well he'd remember her, so went into a lengthy introduction, reminding him who she was, which proved to be entirely unnecessary.

'What can I do for you, Vicky?' he said.

She sketched out the case as it had progressed so far, and the direction of their thinking.

'Interesting,' was Knox's response. 'Tell me the guy's name again.'

'Viktor Paszek,' said Jesson, spelling it out. 'He was in his seventies.'

'That's quite an age to be involved in that kind of stuff,' said Knox. 'Would suggest he'd been in it for a while. If he was, there'll be history with ROC. I'll talk to people and do some sniffing around, see if I can find anything out. Is Tom in on this?'

'He would be, but he's not here,' Jesson explained. 'He's been asked to help out on a cold case in Norfolk. He said he had links with it. Something from your day?'

'Norfolk? Not that I can remember. Must be something from way back, before my time. Good to talk to you, Vicky, I'll get back to you with anything I find.'

'Cheers, Tony, I appreciate it.'

* * *

Millie Khatoon arrived in CID with the first coffee of the morning when Bingley came in, yawning expansively, with Charlie Glover just behind him.

'Nice tonsils,' said Khatoon. 'How did you get on last night?'

'It was a no show,' said Bingley. 'Skrīvulis seeing me at the lock-up must have been enough to scare them off. I'm about to phone Partington's to make sure that no cleaning was done last night.'

'They also have a night security patrol,' said Glover. 'So, I don't think there's any chance Paszek could have pushed Hien out of the window and got away with it.'

'We thought it was improbable, didn't we?' said Khatoon, and to Bingley: 'Talking of poor odds, we'd best get out to Bennetts Road.'

* * *

Once they were there, it was nigh on impossible to see which, if any, of the houses on Bennetts Road had recently had a new roof. Khatoon and Bingley narrowed it down to about a dozen likely possibilities, and despondently started knocking on those doors. Just as they were about to give it up as a bad job, Glover phoned Khatoon.

'Miracles do happen,' he said. 'Land Registry got back to me practically straight away. You want number 292.'

'That one isn't even on our list,' said Bingley. 'Good old Charlie.'

When they found it, near the opposite end of the street, naturally, number 292 was indistinguishable from any of the houses around it.

'We'd never have found this in a million years,' said Bingley, and climbed the three steps to ring the doorbell. Khatoon held back, watching the windows for any sign of movement, though with heavy net curtains at all of them, it would be a tough one. Bingley's persistent ringing raised no response, so he hopped over the low wall in between, and rapped the knocker on the door at 290, eliciting a fusillade of barking from within. This time an older man appeared, with a small terrier tucked under his arm. It struggled frantically to get at Bingley.

'Calm down, Billy!' he ordered, which had no effect at all.

'Hello,' said Bingley, showing his warrant card. 'This your house Mr . . . ?'

'Stan Avery. Has been for the last forty years, son.' Avery had a weathered face and sparse white hair sticking out at all angles. His Brummy accent was strong.

'Do you know who lives next door there?' asked Bingley.

'Hardly,' said Avery. 'They come and go so fast I can't keep track of them. What they been up to?'

'Probably nothing,' said Bingley. 'Are they students?'

'Used to be, but not anymore. This lot's older, different.'

'In what way?'

'Quieter, for one thing,' he said. 'No loud music or parties. If Billy didn't bark now and then, I'd swear there was no one lived there. Not that I'm complaining. Makes a pleasant change.'

'How many of them are there?' Bingley asked.

'I dunno, about five or six maybe. Must be cramped; these are only two-up, two-down.'

'Have you seen them go out today?' asked Khatoon, from the pavement.

'Too early,' Avery told them. 'They generally go out of an evening, about six. I think they must do shift work, because Billy starts barking again early hours of the morning. I sleep in the back room.'

'Any other activity you're aware of?' asked Bingley.

'A couple of times there's been a van in the middle of the night dropping one of them off. There's no parking spaces round here after seven, so they just have to stop in the road and leave the engine running. Sets the dog off again. What is it then? One of them cannabis factories?'

'I don't think so,' said Bingley. 'Thanks for your help, Mr Avery.'

'Happy to oblige, son.'

Just a few metres from the houses, Bingley suddenly turned on his heel and looked back at 292. Khatoon, just ahead of him, stopped too.

'Anything?'

'Top-right window?' he said. 'Some movement?'

'Could be,' said Khatoon. They watched and waited, but it didn't happen again.

Back at the car Khatoon put a call through to Vicky Jesson and explained their situation. 'What would you like us to do—?' She just stopped herself from adding 'boss'.

'Do you think there's anyone inside?' asked Jesson.

'Hard to tell,' she said. 'If they're in there lying low, they're making a good job of it. The bloke next door seems to know a bit about the comings and goings, and they'd fit our theory.'

'I don't think we've got enough yet to force entry,' said Jesson. 'What've you got next?'

'Agarwal,' said Khatoon.

'Carry on and see him,' said Jesson. 'You'll find it's just a suburban house, so I'm not entirely convinced we've got the right person, but if we have, with luck he'll enlighten us about what's going on with Bennetts Road. If our suspicions are confirmed, that's when we go in.'

* * *

'You getting a sense of déjà vu too?' asked Bingley. He and Khatoon had been standing on the doorstep of the Agarwal residence, ringing the doorbell, but without any kind of outcome.

'There's someone in there,' said Khatoon, from where she was peering in through the windows. 'I saw her. She just appeared for a second and then vanished again. A middle-aged woman.'

Bingley rang the bells again. 'Hello,' he said loudly to the front door. 'Police. We'd just like to talk to you.' But still the door wasn't answered, and the woman wasn't seen again.

'Why would she be afraid to come to the door?' wondered Bingley.

'Makes you wonder if Agarwal's at the same game,' said Khatoon. 'He's using forced labour to get his housework done.'

CHAPTER TWENTY-THREE

When Reid left to return to the station, Mariner drove back to Herringfleet House. The uniform on duty today looked bored out of his skull and was eager to have someone to interact with, if only for a minute or two.

'I'm assisting the police investigation into the remains found here,' Mariner said, which was technically true. 'I'm just going to take another quick look round the grounds.'

'Yes, sir.'

Mariner drove down and parked in front of the building, then taking out the old OS map, he walked across to the deposition site, which was a good hundred metres away from the house. He was intrigued as to what Robina could have been doing out here — so far from the building and in what, at the time, was dense woodland. Coming this way, however, would have taken her in the general direction of the caravan site, which made him wonder if there was a way through after all — one which might be clearer from this side.

Guided by his compass and the map, he set off from the burial site, keeping to the same line from the house, and climbed over the new perimeter fence. Bracken and brambles had not yet taken over, so he moved through the trees easily, only occasionally deviating from his path. And in less than ten minutes, he came to the robust steel fencing of the water-treatment compound. Turning left, he followed the fence down, in the general direction of the river. As he'd expected, he soon came to the bottom corner of the enclosure. Here he had hoped to turn right and follow the bottom fencing along, maintaining a course towards the Roman wall and the caravan site, but it wasn't to be. Instead, the compound rubbed up against the reeds, so to do that he'd have to wade in thigh-depth water through the reeds. Mariner wasn't up for that. The only direction remaining to him was to the left and back towards the big house, along the narrow space between the woods and the reed beds. For the sake of completeness, he chose to take this route to see where it ended up, and was surprised to find that instead of taking him back to the big house, it veered off suddenly down through the reeds — a firm path that brought him down to a clearing on the riverbank with a couple of old mooring posts. Effectively a dead end. A breeze ruffled the reeds. It was a beautiful spot. Even though it was still low season, a pleasure craft glided by on the water. It was modern, built out of some kind of plastic composite, but apart from that, nothing would have changed here for years.

* * *

THEN

He didn't have to look for the sign. By the time he'd delivered the bread to his mother they were congregating on the far end of the field — the group of kids that had walked past him that first evening, so he went down to join them. She was there already. Beside her was an older boy, who exuded confidence and looked like a film star: blond hair, piercing blue eyes and perfect teeth.

'This is Tommy,' she told them as he approached, shortening his name for the first time he could remember. 'He's all right.'

'Ludo,' said the good-looking one, raising a hand in greeting, and one by one the other kids said their names.

'Are you in a caravan too?' he asked Ludo, which set everyone else off laughing. 'What did I say?'

'I live here,' said Ludo. 'Well, not here exactly, but down the road.' As soon as he heard the accent, he realised his mistake.

'In a bloody massive house,' said Robina. 'We have to doff us caps to him.'

'Why?'

'His dad owns all this.'

'She's kidding,' said Ludo.

'It's true about the land,' she corrected him.

Ludo had everything going for him; he was handsome, clever and funny. The other kids hung on his every word. Robina would lose interest in Mariner now. Another boy the same age joined them.

'This is Kit,' said Ludo.

'Kit-Kat,' said one of the younger girls, with a giggle she shared with her friend.

'Moron,' growled Kit, and the girl flushed.

'Right, then,' said Ludo, taking charge. 'What are we waiting for?'

Climbing over the stile, they followed a meandering footpath through, overgrown grasses and brush. It emerged at the end of a rough-hewn flint wall four-and-a-half metres high and three metres thick that ran along the edge of a furrowed field.

On the other side, long grass gave way to a sharp slope down to rough pasture, which in turn ran down to mud flats and finally a river. The perfectly level marshland went on as far as the horizon, where they could see a village and a church tower amid trees. The land in between was dotted with broken windmills.

'The Romans built this,' said the kid called Smudge, starting to scramble up the wall. One of the younger girls followed him.

Getting to a ledge, Smudge launched himself off with a cry of 'Geronimo!', laughing as he landed and rolled over on the soft hay. It looked like fun, but clearly Ludo and Kit thought it below their dignity, so he stood watching too, while Robina topped up her lipstick.

Ludo took a pack of cigarettes from his shorts pocket and offered it to him. Mariner turned him down.

'Quite right,' said Robina. 'Filthy habit.' But Ludo smiled and lit up anyway, and Kit followed suit, like they'd been doing it for years.

They whiled away the afternoon sitting on the grass, talking about anything and nothing. Ludo and Kit were schoolfriends, dominating the conversation, Robina asking most of the questions. She was fascinated by their public-school lives. The two younger girls claimed that their school had no classrooms and they called the teachers by their first names. Instead of set timetables they were allowed to choose what activities they did every day. Kit said, unkindly, that it explained why they were so thick, but they just laughed.

After a while Mariner got tired of the squabbling and broke away from the group. The others started off towards the campsite, but he wanted to stay a bit longer in the peace and quiet, so he made for the river, where the sinking sun was lighting the ripples on the surface. A rowing boat, complete with oars, was tied to the jetty. It looked sound enough, although there was a puddle of water in the bottom. He wondered who it belonged to. He'd done a bit of canoeing at school, so he knew he could handle the boat. He stepped down into it and it rocked violently from side to side before stabilising again.

A voice called out, 'What are you doing?' It surprised him. He'd assumed Robina would go with the crowd, but she'd followed him down to the jetty.

'Going for a row,' he said, making the decision in that instant.

'You know what to do with that?'

'I've canoed before. It's all the same thing. Want to come?'

'All right, then,' she said, uncertainly.

He held her hand as she stepped off the jetty and she shrieked as the boat bobbed precariously. 'Sit down', he said, 'and it'll settle. The lower you are in the boat the more stable it will be.'

Doing as instructed, the first thing she did was take out her lipstick.

'We won't be seeing anyone,' he teased.

'How do you know?' she said. 'There might be swans.' She glanced down with distaste to where a handful of dog-ends lay in the slop of water at the bottom.

The water was flat calm, with no river traffic at all. He'd heard that cruisers and sailing boats had to moor before sunset, and they were far away from pubs and boatyards.

'It's dead peaceful here, isn't it?' Robina looked back up towards the wall. ''Specially without that lot.'

That was unexpected. He thought she'd miss them, especially Ludo. She sat in the stern of the boat, directly in front of him and when she was admiring the view, he stole glances at her. The halter-neck top had come a bit loose and was showing more of her cleavage. He could barely take his eyes off her. The only sound was the rhythmic dipping of the oars. Suddenly he was having to work harder and realised they had left the shelter of the river and were coming into open water. A breeze had got up, turning the water choppy, and he could feel the resistance of the current against the oars. It was time to turn back.

He helped her back onto the jetty before stepping out of the boat himself. By the time he'd tied up the boat she was sitting down, her feet dangling over the edge. He went to sit beside her. The cooling air smelled damp and peaty and crane flies danced over the gently rippling water.

She'd kicked off her sandals, and now she wriggled her toes, stretching them out until her painted nails broke the surface of the water. His heart was thumping hard. He badly wanted to kiss her but didn't know if he should say it. She might just laugh at him.

'What is it you do?' she asked, turning to him. 'For a job, like?'

He didn't know how to answer that, so instead he moved his face towards hers. She didn't pull away, so he let his lips touch hers and was taken aback by their softness and the sweet taste of her lipstick. He held back a moment, then sensing no resistance, kissed her again, harder this time, trying to replicate what he'd seen people do in films and on TV. It was remarkably easy. Before he knew it his tongue and hers were seeking each other out and his hand was on her back, drawing her closer so that he could feel the cushions of her breasts against him, and they were really snogging. Her breath came in gulps, which turned him on even more so that he felt he'd burst through his jeans. When they broke the kiss, he waited for the smart remark, but instead she gave a contented sigh and leaned into him, drawing his arm round her like it was the most natural thing in the world.

'You take your time, don't you,' she said, and his heart sang with a joy that he'd never felt before. They sat gazing out over the darkening water, inhaling the dank dusky air. A grebe a little way out ducked under the surface and disappeared.

'Oh God! What happened to that duck? Something under the water just grabbed it!'

He laughed. 'Like this, you mean?'

After a moment she draped her other hand across his stomach. He wished she'd go lower but didn't want to spoil it by pushing his luck. Instead, he nudged the top of her head gently with his chin and then they were kissing again.

'What about you?' he asked, when they surfaced. 'What do you do?'

'You being funny? I've only just finished school, so now I'm off to university; first one in my family to go. I think my mum and dad are more excited about it than I am.'

'Which one are you going to?' Probably not the UEA, he thought.

'Birmingham. My parents aren't quite so happy about that bit.'

Birmingham? His heart jumped. 'Aren't they worried about bombs?' It wasn't so long since the IRA had exploded bombs in the city centre, killing and maiming dozens of people.

'That could happen in London or anywhere, couldn't it? Dad's more worried about all the coloureds. Not that we don't have plenty of them in Yorkshire.'

Coloureds? His mum wouldn't have liked that word. 'What are you going to study?' Art, he'd decided; something creative and unconventional.

'Theology,' she said.

'Theology? I didn't have you down as the religious type.'

'It's not just about religion,' she said, in a weary tone that suggested she'd said all this before, numerous times. 'It's about ethics and philosophy. The meaning of life.'

'The easy stuff then,' he said.

'I should get back,' she said. 'It's getting dark.'

As he helped her up, he noticed they were being watched; a lean figure lurking up by the wall, drawing on a cigarette. But by the time they got up there he had gone.

He walked her back to the caravan site. Now dusk was falling, most people had retreated to their vans, but the murmur of conversation and the clatter of domestic chores could still be heard behind the flimsy fibreglass walls.

'I'd best go on my own now,' she said, turning to him. 'My dad.' She pulled a face. Mariner let go of her hand and put his arms around

191

her. This time when they kissed, she pressed her whole body against his and when they broke apart, she let her hand drop, deliberately or not, brushing his crotch. As she turned away, out came the lipstick again.

'See you tomorrow, then,' she said, with a cheeky grin, and walked off down the campsite, hips swaying.

* * *

Mariner was disappointed. He'd thought he'd found a possible route from the campsite to the big house, but it wasn't to be. And it still begged the question of why she'd gone there. Knowing Robina, Mariner felt sure that a party would have been a draw. Yet no one had come forward to say they'd seen her at the house, and clearly the police at the time had never considered it a possibility. Getting no further insight here, he turned and retraced his steps back to Herringfleet House.

CHAPTER TWENTY-FOUR

Jesson returned to Mariner's office at the end of that day to find Superintendent Sharp hovering outside. 'How are things going?' Sharp asked.

'It's been a disappointing day,' Jesson told her, as they went in and sat down. 'All we've actually got is some under-the-radar cleaners and what appears to be an empty house. I hope I haven't been too quick to embrace the slavery theory to the exclusion of other possibilities. Forensically, we've got barely anything to back it up. The lock-up that Paszek rented, and the Galaxy parked there were promising, but the SOCOs have found no trace of Hien in either. The fingerprints are mainly Paszek's and the others don't match anyone on the database. The few numbers on Viktor's mobile are legit, and Max has found nothing untoward on the laptop. So the only part we can be certain Paszek played in Hien's death, was to move the body.'

'You're still waiting on test results,' said Sharp. 'All you need is for one of them to come good.'

It was true enough, but didn't make Jesson feel much better.

'You look tired,' said Sharp. 'Go home and get some rest. Make a fresh start in the morning. It's what Tom would do. How's it going with your team?'

'Well, I think,' said Jesson, glad to have something positive to say. 'In fact, it doesn't feel all that different from when the boss is around.'

'Hold on to that,' said Sharp, throwing her a meaningful look. 'You're doing a good job. And believe me, I'd be first in the queue to tell you if you weren't.'

When Sharp had gone, Jesson allowed herself a moment of satisfaction. *Yes,* she thought. *I* am *doing an OK job.* All right, much of it was down to having a tight team of competent, reliable and supportive colleagues. But investigations usually progressed in fits and starts, and she was confident they were covering all the bases.

The phone on her desk was blinking to signal a recorded message. It was from Stuart Croghan, asking her to call him back. It could be just the break they were looking for, but bearing in mind what the superintendent had just said, it would keep till the morning. She made a note on the desk notepad to follow it up as the next priority. When the phone rang again, she debated for a second whether to pick it up. It was late, and time to go home; surely whatever it was could also wait until tomorrow. As she was putting on her coat, she had one ear on the answer machine as it kicked in. It was a shock then to hear her mum's voice, hesitant and shaky.

'Hello, I was hoping to speak to Sergeant . . . no, no, *Acting Inspector* Jesson—'

Jesson snatched up the phone. 'Mum?'

'Oh, Vicky, thank goodness. I mean, I tried your mobile but it just went to voicemail.' Doris sounded stressed. And that was a rare thing indeed.

'What is it?'

'Probably nothing. I wasn't even sure if I should call, but I wanted to catch you before you left in case there were any friends you could call in on, on your way home.'

'Why? What friends?' Was her mum finally losing the plot? All the feelings of being in control evaporated, quicker than a puddle on a hot day.

'It's just that Maisie hasn't come home from school yet.'

Jesson quashed a hot surge of panic. It was nearly seven. Why hadn't Doris phoned her before?

'I was trying to remember if she was going to a friend's for tea tonight,' said Doris. 'Something I'd forgotten . . .'

What day was it? She'd lost track. Thursday. No there was nothing. 'Is there anything on the calendar?'

'No. I've tried her phone too,' Doris went on. 'But it just goes straight to the recorded thing.'

'They're discouraged from having them on in school,' Jesson reminded her. 'She may not have turned it back on. It's OK, Mum, you've done the right thing. I'll call round a few of her friends. Just drop me a text if she turns up, will you?'

Ending the call Jesson took a few moments to think it through, trying desperately not to let panic take over. This could just be Maisie reacting to the city centre ban. Had she defied Jesson and gone anyway? If so, Jesson would be furious with her for causing all this worry. She tried Maisie's phone, but, as her mum had said, it went straight to voicemail. Superintendent Sharp had gone back to her office. Should she go and tell her?

In the end she didn't have to. As she was staring, undecided, out of the doorway, Sharp appeared, coat slung over her arm. 'I'm done in,' she said. 'And don't you go developing Tom's late-night habits either.' Then she read Jesson's face, and her smile faded. 'What is it?'

'Nothing, I'm sure,' said Jesson working hard to convince herself. 'Maisie, my youngest, hasn't got home from school yet, and we're not sure where she is.'

Sharp dropped her coat and bag on the nearest chair, her tiredness instantly swept aside.

'She's only in year seven, isn't she? Does she have a phone?'

'I've just tried; it seems to be switched off. Don't worry, you get off. The chances are that she'll arrive home any minute and it'll have been a big fuss over nothing.'

'How long has she been off the radar?' asked Sharp, ignoring the advice.

'Since leaving school; so, coming up to three hours.'

'Has she done anything like this before?'

'No, but . . .'

Sharp raised her eyebrows.

'A couple of her friends go into the city on a regular basis after school. Maisie's been nagging me to let her go with them.'

'And you said no?'

'I said at weekends it's fine, as long as I know who she's going with and when she'll be back. But not on a school night. And, naturally, I'm the worst mum in the world for putting my foot down.'

'Could she have gone anyway?'

'That's what I'm thinking,' said Jesson.

'Have you got contact details of these friends?'

'Only Saira, and I don't think she goes with them. Honestly, boss, I'm sure it'll be fine. You should go home.'

'Is that what you'd say to a mum who came to the front desk to report her eleven-year-old daughter missing?'

Jesson knew that it wasn't. Maisie was young and vulnerable and a high risk. The conversation would go something like:

When was the last time you saw her?

Breakfast time this morning.

How did she seem? That was the one that would trip her up. How many times had she been frustrated by a lack of basic information? But her contact with Maisie this morning was so fleeting that she could think of barely anything to say. Now everyone would find out what a terrible mother she was. Too focused on her career.

Most young people that go missing turn up safe and well, blah de blah . . .

Sharp was still waiting for an answer but it was there in Jesson's silence.

'Right, well, I'll make the usual checks,' said Sharp, decisively. She meant calling round the local hospitals and checking accident reports. 'And you are going to start contacting Maisie's friends.'

'Easier said than done,' said Jesson, scrolling through her phone contacts. 'At her previous school I knew almost everyone in her class, but since we moved, I've had to start all over again.' As she spoke, Saira's name slid on to the screen. Saira often walked home with Maisie, and was one of the few who had been for tea, and when the invitation was reciprocated, Jesson had collected her afterwards, so had met Saira's parents. Other names had been mentioned, of course, including Callie and Lexa, and Jesson was counting on them being Saira's friends too, so she could get their numbers. Short of that, it would be a call to the head teacher on the emergency number. She'd had to do it once before, not long ago, when a little girl's mum went missing. Jesson shuddered. That hadn't ended well.

'I'll go and speak to Ralph Solomon and get the ball rolling downstairs with uniform,' said Sharp quietly. 'We'll need a photo.'

Jesson found one on her phone. She didn't linger on it, but just forwarded it to Sharp.

'Follow me down when you've made your calls,' said Sharp. 'Ralph'll want to talk to you.'

Jesson nodded, numbly. 'There's something else,' she said.

'What?'

'Michael Corbett.'

'Sorry, what does he—?'

'I was the arresting officer,' said Jesson. 'I charged him and gave evidence against him. And now he's out on parole.'

'I'll get someone to pay him a visit. Right away.'

As Sharp departed down to uniform, Jesson tried not to think of the first actions Solomon would take. As the ring tone for Saira's parents' number sounded in her ear, she put such thoughts out of her mind. In her head, Saira's mum answered the phone: *I'm so sorry, Maisie is here. She stopped by at our house and we completely lost track of time.*

But the reality went rather differently. Saira was hunkered down watching TV and hadn't walked home with Maisie today.

'Does Saira have contact details for any other friends who Maisie might have gone with?' asked Jesson. She got the numbers for Callie and Lexa, but both girls were accounted for too.

In a rush of hope, Jesson suddenly wondered if Maisie might have gone to meet friends from her old school; the ones she had known for years. Thank God she hadn't deleted them from her contacts. But with each fruitless call, her optimism dwindled.

CHAPTER TWENTY-FIVE

When Mariner collected his key from reception that evening, Robina's father and sister were getting into the lift. Trevor bid Mariner hello, but Dawn was finding it difficult to make eye contact. Just as shy as she used to be, or was the recognition mutual?

'That's the lad as bought me a pint,' Mariner overheard Trevor telling her, as the lift doors closed. Mariner wondered if he should have introduced himself. But his opportunity came later. When he went into the bar after dinner, Dawn appeared in the doorway, hovering on the threshold, as if undecided about coming in.

'Hello, Dawn,' he said.

She breathed a sigh. 'So it is you.'

Mariner hesitated a moment, unsure of whether a conversation was a good idea. But in the end his manners kicked in. Even in these enlightened times it wasn't always easy for a middle-aged woman to sit alone in a bar.

'Come and join me,' he said. 'Can I get you a drink?'

'Thanks.' As she came over to the table, she saw him glance over her shoulder. 'Dad's resting upstairs,' she said. 'He tires easily these days. Actually, he didn't want to come to Norfolk at all, but I couldn't leave him on his own at home, and I wanted to be here.'

'I'm sorry,' said Mariner. 'It must be incredibly difficult, all this. What can I get you?'

'You're the last person I expected to see,' she said, as he set her gin and tonic down on the table, a few moments later. Now that they were seated, he got a better look at her. The years hadn't been kind, but then, life must have been unbearable for her at times. 'How did they track you down?' she asked.

'Through my witness statement,' said Mariner.

'After all this time . . . ?'

'And this.' Mariner took out his warrant card.

'Well, that's a turn-up,' she said. But something in her demeanour subtly changed. Her eyes took on a new wariness. 'I suppose this is all routine to you then.' Though lower in tone, the inflection in her voice was uncannily close to Mariner's memory of her sister's.

'There's nothing routine about murder, ever,' said Mariner. 'It's always shocking and awful. But this is different, stirring up stuff I haven't thought about for years.'

'How much do the police know?' Dawn asked. 'Have you spoken to them? Are they on to someone?'

He'd seen that expression before. The painful, desperate need for some sort of resolution; feeding off any crumbs of information that might help make sense of the chaos. Time hadn't diminished that craving for this woman. But there was something else there too. Fear?

'I don't know what they're thinking,' said Mariner, being economical with the truth. 'I'm here like you, only as a witness.'

'Are we allowed to speak to each other like this?' she asked anxiously.

'There's nothing to say that we can't, though it's probably best to steer clear of talking too much about what happened back then.' He waited, taking a few mouthfuls of beer.

'It's just that Dad . . . his memory hasn't been right for a while now,' she added, candidly. 'He gets confused about things. It's the alcohol.' That was the likely cause of the unease, then. Her father. 'It got worse after Robina, but he always liked a drink and it was easy for him to use her as an excuse. That's why Trish left, although I don't know if she'd have stuck around for much longer anyway. It all got too much for them.'

'I can understand how it would,' said Mariner. 'It's not uncommon. And how are you doing?' he asked.

She seemed startled by the question. 'Me? Oh, you know. I just get on with it — stay busy and keep a low profile.'

Mariner smiled. 'That's how I remember you.'

'What do you mean?'

'Only that you seemed quiet back then, blended in. Nothing wrong with that.'

She gave a derisory laugh. 'I didn't have much choice,' she said. 'How could I possibly compete with Robina? She had everything — the brains, the looks and the personality. Everybody loved her. It was bad enough when she was alive, but after she went missing, she achieved sainthood overnight.' An edge of bitterness had crept into her voice.

'It can happen,' said Mariner.

'Friends, teachers . . . even dads were completely besotted by her.'

'The two of you seemed to get on all right.' But as he said it, Mariner could hardly think of a single exchange he'd seen between the two girls.

'We had our ups and downs. You know.'

'I don't, really,' Mariner admitted. 'I'm an only child, so don't have much to compare with. I've only just found out that you were step-sisters.'

'Hm. We were ten when Dad and Dawn got together. Maybe that's why we weren't close. So how will it work, with the police?' she asked. 'Will we have to go into one of those interview rooms like you see on TV?'

'Only because it means they'll have recording equipment to hand,' said Mariner. 'They'll want to be able to refer back to what you say.'

'That makes it sound so important.' She was staring at her glass, turning it round and round on the coaster. 'I'm scared I won't be able to remember.'

'It's all right — they won't expect you to recall every detail. They'll understand it was a long time ago, and that it was a very stressful time for your family. And they've got most of the original statements to hand.'

'It's just . . . I keep thinking, what if we mis-speak?'

'If you tell the truth, nothing you can say will be wrong,' Mariner reminded her, wondering what it really was that was bothering her.

'Will they let us go in together? If Dad says the wrong thing now, they might arrest him. He's nearly ninety, and you've seen him. It would kill him.' She was frantic now, and close to tears.

'Why would they arrest him?' Mariner felt a prickle of anticipation.

'If he lets on—' She stopped abruptly.

He waited a beat, and when she didn't continue, asked carefully, 'Lets on what?'

'I mean, if he gets in a muddle,' she corrected herself. She picked up her drink and took a hefty gulp.

'Dawn, if you tell me, I might be able to help,' said Mariner. 'I've had my interview, so they're finished with me now, and you might be worrying about nothing. What is it?'

Putting down her glass, she gazed down into her lap. 'Dad wasn't there,' she said.

'Wasn't where?'

'Dad wasn't in the caravan that night, when Robina disappeared. I didn't know it at the time, of course. Me and Paul and Mikey all went to bed as soon as we got back. But Trish told me, years after: "Your dad wasn't there. He says he went to the bar, for a lock-in, like he did every night." But she said he didn't roll in till the early hours and he looked like he'd been dragged through a hedge backwards.'

Christ. Mariner made himself breathe evenly. 'Have you ever asked your dad directly?'

'I tried to, once. I told him what Trish had said. He went ballistic, so I had to let it go. At the time . . . We didn't even know for sure that Robina was dead. But now . . .'

'You must be honest with DCI Reid,' said Mariner. 'It may not matter anyway. Robina could have been killed any time after she was seen that evening and it may have nothing to do with your dad. They might even be able to find someone from the bar who can give your dad an alibi. It would mean you can stop worrying.' It was unlikely in the extreme.

'But I keep thinking, if Dad had nothing to hide, why not just admit to it at the time?'

'Perhaps he was worried about the way it looked. Or it could just be that he didn't want to get the site owner into trouble for flouting licensing laws.' Or perhaps he *did* have something to hide. 'How are your brothers getting on?' he asked, to break the tension.

'Mikey's all right; he's the son and heir, gone to Canada to make something of himself.'

'And Paul?'

'Working as a chef, down in London. Comes to see us now and again; maybe three times a year. And then there's me; half a lifetime of looking after a drunken old man. We're not exactly what you'd call a close family.'

'You seemed like it to me, back then,' said Mariner and for a moment they were both lost in thought.

* * *

THEN

The next morning, he was up early and one of the first to the wash tent, where he showered carefully and washed his hair before putting on his cleanest shorts and T-shirt. He got out the OS map, with its magenta cover. As he'd thought, there were loads of footpaths that would take them to nice, secluded spots. Then . . . anything might happen. He searched out the condoms he'd never really expected to use — definitely not so soon — and stared at the packet, feeling nothing but gratitude to Brooks for insisting they buy them. Little had he known . . .

'You're up with the lark.' His mother's face appeared at the entrance to his tent and he shoved the condoms into his pocket. 'Scrambled eggs are ready if you want some.'

After brushing his teeth, and at what he thought was a respectable time, he walked back to the caravan park ready to intercept Robina as she headed for the shower block. Lesley called out a greeting as he went through the woods past the stalls. But today her old man was with her, so he just smiled and waved. He had a wait by the showers, but eventually she appeared, still in her pyjamas and carrying a towel and washbag. She was sleepy-eyed, with her hair in tangled disarray, and looked gorgeous.

'I thought we could go for a walk today,' he said (and have sex). *'We could take a picnic.'* (And have sex.)

She rolled her eyes. 'I can't. We're going to the beach at Yarmouth. And then we're going for chicken in a basket and to a show.'

No! *He wanted to wail.* You can't! We're going to have sex today, more than once, and then again, every day until we have to go back home!

'You could come with us,' Robina said, perking up a bit. 'Mum and Dad won't mind. They're always terrified I'll get bored and be "difficult". You'd have to tell your mum, though, I suppose.'

He was torn. Did he want to spend a day in the company of her whole family of complete strangers? But on the beach and in the sea . . . where she'd probably wear a swimsuit, or even a bikini . . . and they still might be able to get some time alone. 'It might be nice to meet your family,' he said.

'There are dunes,' she said, a glint in her eye.

'I'll go and tell her.' But he only told Rose he was going out with 'some of the others', letting her draw her own conclusions.

'Get your cozzie and come to our caravan. Number sixty-eight!' she called after him. 'Tell her you'll be back late!'

He was back in no time and caught her up before she got to the caravan after her shower. 'Play it cool,' she instructed him. 'We're just friends, OK?'

It was a squash getting six of them in the Morris Marina. 'I'll sit on Tommy's lap,' she said.

'Don't be daft,' said her mum. 'Our Michael can sit with me, in the front.'

Robina's mum was open and friendly, but deferred to Robina's dad all the time. He couldn't imagine his own mum doing that to any man. Her dad was harder to read. He didn't say much, and had a cigarette on the go for most of the drive, so that despite the open windows the car soon filled with smoke. The younger brothers, Paul and Mikey, seemed like nice kids. Dawn, her sister, was close to Robina's age but quiet and mousy. All combined, it was a loud and chaotic family, a direct contrast to his. But they accepted his presence with a cautious nonchalance.

When they got to the beach, they had so much stuff they needed him to help carry it. Windbreaker, buckets and spades for the younger ones, towels, swimsuits and a bag with the picnic lunch in it, bats and balls, books and sun hats. By the time they got there on such a warm sunny day, many of the best pitches, close to the promenade, had already been taken. They found a spot not far from one of the piers.

'That's where we're going tonight,' said Robina, tilting her head towards the building at the end of it.

As soon as they'd put down all the stuff, Robina's dad went off to get a newspaper, lighting up a cigarette as he went, so he was left to put up the windbreaker. They needed it too, against the cool offshore breeze. He'd never done it before but found it easy enough to hammer in the stakes with the wooden mallet. The kids all stripped off their outer clothes to swimsuits underneath. He was thrilled to see that Robina was wearing a bikini. The deep yellow accentuated her tan and made him wish he wasn't so pale.

'Last one in the water's a sissy!' she yelled, grabbing playfully at Mikey, and then they were all running down the sand and into the dull grey foaming waves. They played around for a while, ducking each other, and he put Mikey on his shoulders and tipped him into the sea, making him squeal. But Mikey just came back for more.

He wanted to put his arms round Robina in the water; press his body to hers. But she wouldn't let him near, and when he looked round, he saw that her mum had walked down to paddle on the shoreline, to keep a watchful eye, and not just on her young sons. By the time they came out of the water, her dad was back, sitting in the only deckchair, reading the paper.

'You should get some sun cream on, Tommy lad, or you'll burn,' her mum said.

'I'll do it,' Robina volunteered.

'You bloody won't,' said her dad, without looking up from his paper, cigarette clamped between his lips. 'He'll do it himself.' There was an edge to his voice and when he suddenly got to his feet, everything went quiet. 'I'm going for the tickets,' he said, tucking his newspaper under his arm.

'We're taking in a show,' Robina's mum told him. He wanted to ask what kind of show, but he'd find out soon enough.

Robina waited until her father had left the beach and her brothers were digging a trench with some other kids down by the water's edge, then she said, casually, 'Tommy's got some money, Mum. Can we go up to the arcades?'

Her mother looked off in the direction her husband had gone, assessing the situation. 'Cover yourself up then.' She threw across a T-shirt.

Robina picked up her flip-flops and started out towards the promenade. He pulled on his shorts, grabbed his sneakers and followed.

'Are we really going to the arcades?' Seeing how busy they were, he tried to keep the disappointment from his voice.

'What do you think?' she asked with a smile. But she didn't want to lie to her mum, so they walked in past the slot machines and out of the other side, where they doubled back along the promenade and headed towards the pale green expanse of the dunes. Away from the beach shops and amusements, the crowds gradually petered out, until all that was left were a couple of dog walkers down by the water's edge. She jumped off the edge of the promenade onto the sand and started towards the sea. After climbing several hillocks of tough, spiky marram grass, they found a dip that was out of sight of both the promenade and the shore.

'This'll do,' she said, peeling off her T-shirt and spreading it on the ground. 'But we'll have to be quick or Mum'll get suspicious.' He stripped to his trunks again and self-consciously took the condoms out of his pocket.

'You won't be needing them,' she said. 'Not this time.'

But she let him touch her, and she touched him.

As they wandered back later, a misty cloud had rolled in off the sea, covering the sun and lowering the temperature. People were packing up their things. They got back just before her dad and he felt that what they'd done must be written all over his face. But her dad seemed in better spirits, even making jokes.

'He's been in the pub,' Robina muttered under her breath.

Dumping all the beach stuff back in the car, they went to one of the seafront restaurants; not chicken but fish and chips which everyone except Paul and Mikey had with bread and butter and mugs of tea. Afterwards they went to the pier and joined the queue for the theatre, where a giant hand-painted sign announced that Jimmy Finnegan was topping the bill. They waited for Robina's dad to finish his cigarette standing beneath a huge caricature of the comedian's face winking down at them from above the entrance. 'Good thing I didn't tell my mum it's Jimmy Finnegan we're seeing,' he said. Rose didn't approve of 'light entertainers' with their racist and sexist jokes.

'Doesn't she like him?'

'He's on ITV,' said Mariner, as if it explained everything.

'He's stopping up at the big house, you know,' Robina said.

It meant nothing to him.

'You know, up by the campsite. They have these parties, so Ludo says.'

'I hear music sometimes in the middle of the night,' he said.

'Ludo said we might go to one.'

'Why? I mean, why would you want to go?'

She grinned up at him. 'Might be my big chance.' He never knew when she was sending herself up. 'Dad would probably kill me, though.'

When they took their seats in the theatre, he held her hand, drawing it on to his lap, but then he saw her sister murmur something to her dad and they all had to swap places, so that Robina sat at one end of the row, and him at the other. Dawn caught his eye and smirked. The show was loud and raucous, so-called family entertainment, with plenty of smutty asides thrown in for the adults, and her family seemed to lap it up. But he was distracted and hard, as he relived every moment of their time alone on the beach. A bunch of firsts for him; first time he'd touched a girl's breasts. First time he'd touched a girl intimately. First time someone else had brought him to climax. He wanted to do it again and more. Soon.

The drive to the caravan site was subdued. The two younger boys fell asleep and Dawn was planted firmly between Robina and Mariner

207

in the back seat. Remembering his manners, he thanked her parents and offered money for his dinner and the theatre but her dad wouldn't accept it.

'You were our guest, Tommy,' her mum said.

'Well, goodnight then.'

He wondered if Robina might walk with him, but she just whispered, 'Wait by the showers.' So he dawdled along the track. A few moments later, he heard the caravan door open and turned to see her dad emerge again, and walk away. Then the door went again and her voice cut across the still evening air: 'Going to brush me teeth, Mam!' Seconds later she was beside him, slipping her hand into his.

'Where's your dad going?'

'Where do you think? Same as every night.' She made a drinking gesture.

* * *

'Whoever took Robina ruined a lot of lives that day,' said Mariner. 'And I can't imagine how it's been for you since. In my line of work, I meet families — thankfully not many — who are going through something similar. But it can never be the same as experiencing something directly. Did you have any feeling at the time about what had happened to your sister?'

'To begin with I just thought she must have run away,' said Dawn. 'She and Dad argued sometimes and she'd threatened it before. But as the years went by, I started to realise something serious had happened. Trish was convinced of it.'

'Did you have any ideas about who might have harmed her?'

'That man from the caravan site, I suppose.'

'Peter Church?'

'Robina said he gave her goosebumps. He used to appear out of nowhere and follow her around.' She let out a little involuntary laugh. 'Gave her presents she didn't want. And he smelled funny.'

It sounded as if Church had become quite a nuisance to Robina after he'd left. Up until then, she had been so accepting.

CHAPTER TWENTY-SIX

Downstairs in uniform, familiar faces were a blur, though Jesson felt a reassuring squeeze to her arm a couple of times as she crossed the room to where Ralph Solomon sat. Jesson didn't know him well, but Mariner and Glover both rated him, and his sheer physical presence was reassuring. She was in safe hands.

'Describe Maisie to me,' said Solomon, as she dropped into the seat by his desk. He was trying to calm her down, but she did as he asked, in as much detail as she could. 'That's brilliant,' said Solomon, with a humourless smile. 'Anyone would think you'd done this before. We're gathering CCTV from around the school and your house,' he said. 'And linking up with other cameras in the area. I understand you've rung round her friends, but is there anywhere else you can think of that Maisie might have gone?'

'Did the superintendent tell you about the city centre?' said Jesson. A mug of tea had appeared beside her, as if by magic.

'Yes, we'll check buses and trains, and that Nando's branch you mentioned. Is there anywhere back where you used to live that she could have gone to? Any other family members?'

'I've tried her old friends,' said Jesson. 'Nothing.' She racked her brains. Where would she go? Oh God, her other grandparents. 'There's Thelma and Doug, Brian's parents. Maisie's always been close to Nana Thelma.' Jesson had been putting off going to see them; it was never easy. 'They live down near Worcester.'

'Would you like me to call them?'

'No, it's fine. I'll do it.' Her hands trembling, she brought the number up on her phone. But apart from giving two more people something to worry about, the call was fruitless.

'What kit has Maisie got?' asked Solomon.

'What?'

'Phone? Tablet?'

'Oh yes, both of those,' said Jesson. 'You'll need her number and passwords.' She hoped Maisie hadn't changed them in recent weeks. 'And she has access to a laptop for her homework.'

'What social media does she use?' Solomon asked.

'She's too young and I monitor what she's doing online.' Did she? As the words were spilling from her mouth, Jesson tried to remember the last time she'd checked any of Maisie's online activity. Would she actually know if her daughter had set up a profile?

'That's great,' said Solomon, reassuringly, taking her at her word.

'And there's a man you should know about.'

'The super's already told me about Michael Corbett,' said Solomon. 'I've got a couple of guys on their way to speak to him right now.'

A voice from behind Jesson said, 'Sir?'

Solomon looked up. 'Ah, good, Lorraine.' He got to his feet. 'Don't know if you two have met but Vicky, this is Constable Lorraine Wyatt, who's going to be your family liaison officer.'

'Oh there's no need . . .' Jesson began, before realising she was wrong. Someone had to keep her from haranguing Solomon and let him get on with his job. She turned to see a pretty girl with cropped fair hair framing an intelligent face, who looked not much older than Emily. Jesson had seen her around, but they had never been introduced.

'I think that's enough for now,' said Solomon. 'You should go home — the rest of the family needs you. Lorraine will go with you, and I'll keep in touch.' Another arm squeeze.

Jesson didn't want to go. She wanted to stay here, to be the first to hear any news. But Solomon was right. If it was someone else's child, she'd be telling the parents that the best thing they could do would be to go home and wait. She also knew that in a hostile abduction, it's generally about six hours before the victim is killed.

Throughout the painfully long drive home, Jesson was constantly risk-assessing in her head. The best outcome now — embarrassing as it may be — would be to open the front door and see her daughter safe, well and being cheeky. She hoped that, by sheer force of will, she could make it happen. But there had been nothing from Doris and when Jesson put her key in the door and walked into the hall, she knew instantly from her mum's stance that Maisie wasn't home. Doris let her daughter take off her coat and come into the kitchen, busying herself putting the kettle on to make Jesson a drink.

'Where are the other two?' Jesson asked, too wired to sit down.

'Emily's upstairs. Aaron's gone out on his bike looking for Maisie.'

'Oh great,' said Jesson. 'That's all we need, for him to have an accident!' It was the fear talking.

'He won't, and you know it,' soothed Doris. 'He's as frightened as we are. He wants to do his bit.' She was right. And Aaron would be sensible enough to stay in touch.

'Mum?' Emily appeared at the top of the stairs. She was as white as a sheet. This had hit her hard.

'It'll be OK, sweetheart.'

Ascending the stairs, Jesson hugged her older daughter tightly, fighting to stop herself from breaking down. She needed Doris and the kids to think that everything was under control.

'Are there any other girls at school that Maisie hangs around with who I don't know about?' she asked, but Emily couldn't think of any.

The doorbell rang and they all jumped. 'It'll be Lorraine, the family liaison officer,' said Jesson. 'She followed me back.' Letting Wyatt in, she made the introductions. The first thing Wyatt did was take Maisie's tablet and the laptop and give them to the uniform who was waiting outside to courier them back to Granville Lane. *Max's team will have had their evenings ruined,* Jesson thought idly. When she checked her phone, for the umpteenth time, she found messages from Khatoon and Glover: *Here if you need me* and *Helen and I are praying for Maisie's safe return.*

And all the time, hovering at Jesson's shoulder, was the thought of Michael Corbett.

CHAPTER TWENTY-SEVEN

When Mariner got up to his room and checked his phone, there were missed calls from Khatoon, Glover and Superintendent Sharp. He called Sharp back first.

'How's it going over there?' she asked.

'It's been interesting,' he said, neutrally.

'Not too interesting, I hope.' She cut to the chase. 'You know about Maisie?'

'Maisie? Vicky's Maisie? No, what about her?'

'I didn't know if anyone let you know. She's gone missing.'

Mariner's stomach turned leaden. 'Christ, poor Vicky — she must be beside herself. What's going on?'

'We're still ruling out the possibility that this is a protest against Mum's rules.'

'Is that likely?' asked Mariner.

'I really hope so,' said Sharp. 'The unsavoury alternative at present is Michael Corbett,' said Sharp. 'Vicky helped put him away on child sex offences, but he's out on parole.'

'Shit. You're watching him?'

'We will do, when we find him,' said Sharp. 'Uniform are at his house but last I heard he hadn't turned up there.' That wasn't good. 'I just wanted to put you in the picture.

But before you come charging back here, we've got search advisers involved and Ralph Solomon and his team are all over it.'

'I've no doubt about that,' said Mariner. 'If anyone can find her, Ralph will. But I'm coming back tomorrow anyway; had already planned to. I've done about all I can here.'

Immediately after the call, Mariner texted Jesson: *I just heard. You know where I am. Anytime.*

It took him a few minutes then to re-focus, but he needed to report to Reid on his conversation with Dawn, and he wanted to do it before they went in to the station tomorrow morning. Reid picked up on the first ring.

'Hope it's not too late to call,' he said. 'I've had a chat with Robina's sister.'

'How did it go?' asked Reid, sounding as alert as ever.

Mariner summed up the conversation as best he could. 'It might be useful to interview separately if you can, though Dawn might be resistant to that. I'd be tempted to push Trevor on where he was the night Robina disappeared. It's made me wonder about that letter, too. He was a chain smoker and a manual labourer, and if the late postmark was a crude attempt to muddy the waters . . . It might be interesting to see his reaction to it.'

'That gives us something to work with,' said Reid. 'I'll let you know how we get on. That child missing in Birmingham,' she added. 'I understand her mum's a police officer. Do you know her?'

'I've just found out,' said Mariner. 'Vicky's one of my sergeants. She's been covering for me while I'm off.'

'Oh God, poor woman. You'll want to get back.'

'Yes. I'll leave in the morning, but good people are looking for Maisie,' Mariner said.

'You'll call in here, before you go?'

'Of course. Good luck with Dawn and Trevor.'

'Thanks.'

Mariner was shattered. But when he got to bed, he lay awake, unable to tear his thoughts from what Jesson must be going through. And how would Aaron and Emily be coping with their little sister being out there and potentially in danger? In the time he'd worked with Jesson he'd got to know them a bit and they were good kids. He had a particular soft spot for Emily. She was gutsy and reminded him a lot of Anna, his late fiancée. When he eventually fell asleep, he dreamed of the campsite, overrun with children of all ages, running amok. He and Maggie Devlin seemed to be the only adults trying to get them all to sit and listen to a story. He awoke again before six, to the sound of footsteps scampering across the floor in the room above his.

Trevor and Dawn were nowhere to be seen for breakfast, but the room was livened up by a family with energetic and excitable children, toddlers through to young teens, several of whom seemed unable to sit still for more than a minute at a time. Mariner surmised that they were the family staying in the room above his. The kids were clearly enjoying the novelty of a hotel breakfast and were making as many incursions to the buffet table as they could. Their parents were taking the whole thing in their stride, doggedly ploughing on with their own meal amid the chaos, and batting away the constant, rapid-fire questions from their offspring with practiced ease.

When he could put it off no longer, Mariner went up to refill his coffee cup and had to wait while one of the children, aged about five, was precariously pouring juice from a heavy glass jug into a tumbler. It was a disaster waiting to happen and he had to resist an overwhelming urge to step in and help. After several nerve-wracking minutes, the child managed to complete the task and return the jug to the table and Mariner breathed again. Then the child picked up his glass, turned and ran headlong into him, dropping the tumbler and showering Mariner liberally with its contents.

'Oscar!' cried one of his older siblings.

The room went horribly quiet, and when the parents finally looked up to see what had happened, the father jumped to his feet.

'I'm most terribly sorry,' he said, then to the child: 'Oscar, you should look where you're going! What do you say to the man?'

Oscar had gone pink. 'Thank you?' he whispered, his lower lip trembling.

Oscar's father tutted in exasperation. 'No, Oscar—'

'It's fine,' said Mariner, wiping down his jeans with a napkin and trying hard not to smile. 'Really. It was an accident. No harm done.' He held out his hand. 'Tom Mariner,' he said.

The man was slightly nonplussed but responded in kind. 'Crispin Bland.'

'I know,' said Mariner. And for the first time in forty years, he looked into Kit's eyes. He'd filled out a bit and Mariner may well not have recognised him by sight, but the voice had given him away.

'How the devil . . . ?' He examined Mariner anew. A long minute passed. 'Good God, you're that boy from the campsite; the one who was . . . er, involved with Robina,' he said, eventually.

'Tommy, you all called me then,' said Mariner. Here they were, two middle-aged men, gone soft around the edges, but underneath that, still recognisable.

'You must be here for the same reason I am,' Bland concluded eagerly.

Mariner became aware of the increased cacophony coming from the family's table, and the mother was getting to her feet.

'Kit, I think we're finished here,' she called across to her husband. 'I'll take them upstairs.'

'Yes, of course, darling. This is Tommy . . . er, Tom, one of the other kids we hung around with that summer.' He turned to Mariner. 'My wife, Bella.'

'Hello,' Bella said. 'How fortunate to bump into you.' She was an attractive woman and considerably younger than Kit. 'Listen, Kit, darling, you stay and talk,' she said to her husband. 'I can sort the kids out. It was nice meeting you.' She pulled a face. 'Sorry about the juice.'

'It's no problem,' Mariner reassured her.

As the children left and the clamour faded away, Kit rescued his coffee cup from the ruin of his family's table and brought it over to sit with Mariner.

'This is a strange business, isn't it?' he said. 'Hearing Robina's name after all these years, and finally knowing what became of her. You must have come under scrutiny at the time.'

'Briefly,' said Mariner, deciding to keep things simple. 'But as I'd left the area before she disappeared, I was ruled out early on.' He was trying to make sense of this. 'Has DCI Reid been in touch with you?' If she had, he wondered why she had claimed not to know of Kit's existence.

'No, no. Is that the name of the chap running things?'

'She's a woman actually, but yes, she's heading the investigation. So, I don't understand—'

'I must see her, as soon as possible,' said Kit.

'I can tell you that she's occupied this morning. She's with Robina's father and sister.'

'Oh God,' said Kit. 'Her poor family. If it's strange for us, what on earth must it be like for them?'

Mariner was taken aback by the concern. The Kit he remembered wouldn't have cared less about them. He might even have revelled in their misery.

'It's *imperative* that I speak to someone,' he said, grabbing Mariner's arm. 'It's been a burden all these years. I'm ashamed to say it, but what I told the police at the time wasn't quite the truth.' Mariner felt the kind of frisson he got when getting a breakthrough on a case. He should have left it to Reid, but he couldn't help himself.

'About what?' he asked.

'I said that the last time I saw Robina was early on the afternoon that she went missing.' Kit gazed out of the window. 'But that wasn't true. Ludo and I saw her that night too.'

'Where?' This was a game-changer.

'At the big house.'

Mariner stared at him.

'What? What have I said?'

'That's where her remains were found. At least, in close proximity to the house.'

'Good God.'

'What happened?'

Kit shifted uncomfortably. 'I'm not sure I should . . .'

'No, you're right; you shouldn't,' said Mariner. 'But you certainly need to talk to DCI Reid.' He took out his warrant card. 'It's been an informal arrangement — I'm with another force — but I've been assisting her with the inquiry. I'm going in to see her shortly, to sign off. You can come with me. I think she'll be delighted to see you.'

CHAPTER TWENTY-EIGHT

'And then there were three,' said Bingley, drily. The atmosphere in CID was tense and subdued. Everyone was rooting for Maisie and Jesson; Glover and Khatoon, as parents, feeling it particularly keenly.

Superintendent Sharp had held a press conference first thing in the morning, which was televised soon after on the national breakfast news stations. For twenty minutes the Hien incident room was quiet while they watched. Often in this situation the tearful parents would appear, but for Jesson's own protection, on this occasion it was conducted by Ralph Solomon and Superintendent Sharp. They fielded questions admirably and remained upbeat throughout, but deciphering the coded language, it became patently obvious that there were no strong leads.

'Poor Vicky,' said Khatoon, voicing what they were all thinking.

At that moment, fresh from running the gauntlet of the press, Superintendent Sharp walked in. 'Yes indeed, poor Vicky,' she echoed.

'How's she bearing up?' asked Glover.

'Oh, you know Vicky,' said Sharp. 'She's strong.'

'Have you got anything?' asked Khatoon.

'I understand that following the appeal, we've already had calls about a car seen near the school. I don't know the details yet.'

'What about Corbett?'

'Eventually showed up at his home late last night,' said Sharp. 'His alibi is weak for the late afternoon, so we're keeping him under surveillance. Anyway,' she went on, 'what I came here to say was, regardless of how difficult it might be, the best thing you can do for Vicky now is to press on with finding Hien's killer. I'm sure I know the answer to this, but I've got to ask: do I need to draft someone in to take the lead, or can you keep the show on the road?'

'It's all under control, ma'am,' said Glover, with a new authority. 'I can coordinate from here, and we've got a number of actions to follow up on this morning.'

'Good,' said Sharp. 'I understand Tom's coming back later today but in the interim, I'm still available, should you need to run anything by me. Clearly, I have other demands on my time at present, but keep me in touch with what's going on down here too. Is there anything urgent I need to know?'

'We might need to force entry to one of Viktor Paszek's rental properties,' said Khatoon. 'We have reason to believe that there may be victims of slavery living there, and nobody's answering the door.'

'Any safety concerns about going in?'

'I don't think so. If we're right about what we think's going on, these people will be scared rather than hostile.'

'Might be helpful to have a couple of bodies as backup though, in case any of them makes a run for it,' said Bingley.

'And fear can make people aggressive, so don't get too complacent,' Sharp told them. 'I'll have a word with Ralph, but it goes without saying that resources are stretched.' No one was about to argue with that.

* * *

Two special constables were allocated to assist Bingley and Khatoon at Bennetts Road. Taking one of them with him, Bingley went round to the back of the property, leaving Khatoon and the other to take the front. After ringing the bell again and getting no response, they took a battering ram to the door. Once inside, the four of them fanned out and searched the two floors, but it was as if nobody had ever lived there. The bedrooms were stripped of all personal belongings; there was no clothing, no linen. The only room that indicated recent habitation was the kitchen, where dishes had been left in the drainer and there was a small quantity of food in the cupboards and fridge.

'Shit,' said Khatoon. 'We're too late — if they were ever here.'

'But where would they have gone?' said Bingley.

'The place has been cleaned out. The traffickers could have got wind of our investigation and moved them on.'

'That or they're so scared they've taken off on their own,' said Bingley. 'Do you think the superintendent would sanction forensics?'

'Right now? I'm not sure,' said Khatoon. 'And what would it achieve? The place has been emptied, but not cleaned. There's no sign of anyone taking a pasting here. At most, we might establish that Hien has been here, but not much else. And I'm not even sure where that would get us.'

'Let's see if Mr Avery heard or saw anything since yesterday,' said Bingley. 'We might get a hint of where they've gone.'

It was as if Avery was waiting for their knock; he answered the door in seconds, dog tucked under his arm.

'One of them minibuses came and took them away last night, about half nine,' he said.

Bingley got out his phone and scrolled through until he found the image of the Galaxy. 'A people carrier, like this?' he asked.

'Nah, bigger than that. Grey. I didn't get the number. Couldn't see from here.'

'Was it old or new?' asked Khatoon, just as her phone started to ring. She walked a little way off to answer it.

'Looked shiny and new to me,' Avery told Bingley. 'I don't think they're coming back, either. They took their bags and stuff with them.'

'Did you see who was driving the minibus?' asked Bingley.

'A big feller. Tall, but big muscles too. He did all the ordering around. He wasn't English, either, had an accent. And he was swarthy. Could've been Asian or half-caste.'

'Thanks,' said Bingley, cringing at the language. 'You've been really helpful. Could you do me another favour?'

'All right.'

Bingley took out his card. 'Keep an eye out in case anyone comes back and give me a call right away if they do.' It was an unlikely scenario, but worth a punt.

CHAPTER TWENTY-NINE

'Your wife will have her hands full,' said Mariner. He'd packed his bags and arranged to meet Bland in the hotel reception lobby just before 11 a.m., and now they were making their way on foot to Yarmouth police station. It was a sunny day, but a sharp sea breeze was blowing.

'She's a marvel,' said Bland, with obvious affection. 'At my age, I'd become resigned to missing out on ever having children. My first wife wasn't keen. But Bella loves them. They're exhausting, but so much fun too.'

* * *

At the station, Mariner got Kit signed in before taking him along to the incident room, and was glad to see Reid and Sinclair were already there. Trevor and Dawn must be either in an interview room somewhere, or on their way back to the hotel.

'Wait here,' he said to Bland. He knocked lightly on the door and went in. Reid and Sinclair were each sitting at a desk.

'Tom,' said Reid, looking up. She looked drained. 'You're off back to Birmingham now?'

'Shortly,' said Mariner. 'How did it go?'

Reid pulled a face. 'It was an emotional morning, for Dawn especially. I'm not sure with Trevor if it's really struck home yet. We offered to let them come back later today or tomorrow for the interviews, but Dawn wanted to get it over with. I think they both just want to go home. But we didn't get much from them,' she added. 'Trevor denied writing the letter, and his handwriting isn't a close match.'

'Do you believe him?'

'Yes,' she said. 'But mainly because we now know who *did* write it. The DNA results came back this morning.'

'Who was it?'

'It was Dawn.'

'Christ.'

'She found it after Robina went missing and decided to finish it for her and post it anyway. Apparently, she had quite a crush on you. Poor woman, she was so embarrassed.'

'She sounded resentful of Robina when she spoke about her. Do you think . . . ?'

'It crossed my mind too, but some of the questions she asked — I can't see it. She recognised the drawing of the necklace, remembered Robina offering it to her, because "that creep" had given it to her and she didn't want it.'

'Peter Church?'

'That's what we've concluded.'

'And Trevor?'

'We're satisfied that he was in the bar the night Robina disappeared. He broke down when he admitted to that. He'd convinced himself that she'd run away, and I think he felt guilty that to begin with, he and Trish didn't realise she was gone. I'm not sure if he's fully grasped that she's dead, even now. So that's that.' Reid shook her head. 'We're running out of live witnesses.'

'Not quite,' said Mariner. 'There's someone you'll want to meet.' He waved across to where Bland was lurking just outside the door.

'This is Ludo's friend, Kit. I'll leave you to get to know each other.'

Reid studied him for an explanation.

'He was on his way to see you anyway; he just didn't know where to look.'

As Sinclair showed Kit to an interview room, Reid smiled.

'Want to stay and observe?'

'I was hoping you'd ask that.'

* * *

'It was a last-minute, impulsive thing, going to the party,' Kit began. 'Ludo's idea. He thought we should gatecrash. I knew Ludo fancied Robina and he'd thought he was in with a chance until Tommy — Tom — came along. I suggested we could take her with us, but he laughed and said there'd be "much classier" girls there. So, we were astonished when we spotted her there anyway. It was fleeting, seconds at most. And she looked different.'

'In what way?'

'She looked — for want of a better word — cheap. She was wearing one of those short, tight dresses and had piled on the make-up. It was almost grotesque. There was this heaving mass of people, there must have been going on a hundred. She was standing by the wall on the other side of the room, watching, but sort of . . . glazed over. I said to Ludo, "Look who's over there!" We went to find her, to talk to her, but by the time we'd crossed the room, she was gone.'

'But you're certain it was her,' said Reid.

'Unquestionably.'

'Was she with anyone?'

'It was hard to tell. We talked about that afterwards, Ludo and me. We'd both noticed a man quite near her. He stood out because he didn't have the style of the other guests. At the time, I felt sure he was someone I'd seen before.'

'Someone you knew?'

'Or someone on TV. The host of the party was that godawful comedian Jimmy Finnegan, and there were a few other "faces" there. Isn't that what they call them? Peculiar to see them so up close and personal like that. After that we got rather caught up in it all, and didn't see Robina again, either at or after the party, I swear.'

'Why didn't you come forward with this information at the time?' Reid asked, reasonably.

'Believe me, I've been asking myself that question every day since the news broke,' said Kit. 'Ludo's father was a dominant force. The next day, when Robina was reported missing, Ludo told him we thought we'd seen her. He seemed less sure than I was. His father — and then his father's lawyer — decided that we were mistaken. And we started to believe it — that we'd simply seen someone who looked like her. We'd both indulged the night before; drink and drugs, so we were fragile, to say the least. Ludo rather more than me. So, we went along with it because it was easier to do that. I think Ludo's father was keen to avoid implicating anyone at the big house too. They told us to forget we were at the party and to tell no one we were there. To make matters worse, I then told the police that I'd seen that chap Peter following Robina around and touching himself. But it wasn't true, I made it up. At the time though they seized on it and it made me feel important. From that point on, Ludo and I were grounded — if you can call being limited to the vast acreage of the Flintmore estate grounded — for our own safety. And, the damage done, a week or so later, I went home to my parents.'

'Is there anything else you remember about the party?'

'It was hot and sweaty; lots of scantily clad women,' said Kit, grimly. 'People were jumping into the swimming pool. It all seemed unbelievably glamorous to me. There were drugs in circulation — that was the summer Ludo developed a taste for them. We both smoked cannabis that night. And what with that and the booze we were both pretty out of it early on. I started to feel seriously unwell. Ludo had disappeared. A couple of the women were quite taken with him, and afterwards he told me they'd taken him upstairs. When I couldn't find him, I set off back to Flintmore, along the road. I had to puke into a hedge more than once.'

'You left Ludo at the party?'

'Yes, I did.'

Reid glanced up at the two-way mirror, where she knew Mariner stood.

'The whole debacle has remained imprinted on my mind, and will be for ever,' said Kit. 'It had a profound impact.'

'In what way?'

'Up until that point, my life had been so predictable; so easy and comfortable. And frankly? I took it all for granted. Robina's disappearance was a shock. I'd never had to confront that kind of uncertainty before.'

'What did you think had happened to her?'

'To begin with? I was utterly naïve. Nothing bad had ever happened to me, and imagination's never been my strong point, so I thought she would turn up; having run away or got lost or something. It was only as the years went on and I began to wake up to the harsh realities of life, that it became obvious I was wrong. And I think about the other people at that party. We were only eighteen, but I'm sure there were kids — girls — there who were younger than us.'

'Did you ever think about who could have harmed Robina?'

'At first I believed what the papers had said — that it was Church. He was very keen on her, and a strange man-boy. It was a bad summer all round: I discovered the truth shortly after that about how my father really treated my mother. Worse, I recognised the same traits in myself; what a cruel bastard I could be at that age. Bullying Peter Church when I should have defended him. Taking the piss out of Robina's accent. Ludo did it too, but only in private, and I mainly did it to try to impress him. God I was a stuck-up little twat back then. Honestly? I think what needled me about Robina was how authentic she was; how true to herself. She was everything I was not.'

'As I got older and wiser, I knew it hadn't been right to lie about that night, but I tried to bury it. Told myself it was too late to do anything about it. I didn't even think about it for years apart from the odd twinge of guilt. But now . . . I gather from Tom Mariner that she was found at the big house?'

'The surrounding woods,' said Reid. 'Does Ludo know that you're coming clean?'

'Good God, no. Why would he? I haven't seen him for years. Not long after that, the following summer, I think, he and I hitch-hiked around Europe. We got into a bit of bother.'

'What kind of bother?'

'A girl. Ludo came on a bit strong with her and she accused him of assault. Ludo's father pulled some strings, got us home, and it went away. I didn't want to be around him after that.'

'You've been very helpful,' said Reid. 'Thank you for coming to find us.'

* * *

'What will you do now?' asked Mariner, as Kit left the interview room.

'Oh, I don't know,' said Kit. 'Spend a few days on the beach with the kids, if the weather holds, then we'll head back to Sussex.'

'It's been good to see you,' said Mariner, as the two men shook hands. He meant it. Kit was right; he had been an unpleasant youth all those years ago, but he'd changed.

'We'll have to go back to Rothbury,' said Reid, when Kit had left. 'Though I can't imagine he'll be any more cooperative.'

'You have grounds to challenge him directly on where he was that night,' said Mariner. 'And it opens up possibilities for anyone who was at that party. There might be something Jimmy Finnegan wants to get off his chest too.'

'I'll have to clear that with my super,' she said. 'And it's a tough call, isn't it? We're asking people to remember that one night, many years ago.'

'If something happened, he'll remember it,' said Mariner. 'Whatever you choose to do, I wish you the best of luck with it.'

'Thank you, and thanks for all your help. Keep in touch. And I hope your sergeant's daughter turns up safe and well.'

Mariner went back to the hotel and paid his bar bill, then went to find his car. It had been a surreal time, he thought, as he headed out west towards Birmingham. At times he'd felt removed from reality while he relived the past. He really hoped that Reid and Sinclair would find Robina's killer.

* * *

THEN

Her dad must have suspected something because after that they seemed determined to keep her away from him. Of the few days he had left, there were too many when she had to go out with her family, leaving him with only snatched hours in the evenings around the busy campsite. All too quickly, the end of his holiday was drawing near. His last day was the same. They were taking a boat out on the broads.

'It only takes six people,' she said, close to tears.

'But we'll make tonight special,' he promised.

The time passed painfully slowly. He helped for a while on Lesley's stall, then he went down to the wall, but on his own today. He didn't feel like company. At the end of the afternoon, he hung around the shower block, far too early, hoping to see her. Eventually, there she was.

'Good day?' he asked, slipping his arms around her.

'Crap,' she said. 'But it's going to get better, isn't it?' She reached down and gently squeezed his crotch.

Her family were going to the bar for the evening. 'I'll try to get away,' she said. 'Seven o'clock back here.'

When she went, he wandered back to the tent. His mother was starting to pack up the van, so he gave her a hand. 'We're all going to the pub later,' she said. 'You can come along if you like.'

'No, thanks. I think I'll go for a walk, take some final photos,' he said, not meeting her eye.

Tomorrow was changeover day at the caravan site too, so there was lots of activity this evening; people coming and going as he waited. And finally Robina was there. Walking back to the campsite, he really hoped they wouldn't bump into anyone they knew. They lingered at the edge of the field until they saw Rose going off down the lane with her friends. Then casually, so as not to draw attention to themselves, they strolled back to his tent. The ridge was only a metre high, so they had to crawl inside. The air was stagnant and smelled of warm canvas and cut grass. Once they were inside, he spent anxious moments ensuring that the flaps were firmly closed. When he turned, she was kneeling before him completely naked, her skin glowing orange from the evening sunlight filtering through the canvas. He thought his whole body would explode.

'Your turn now,' she said. 'Slowly.' And she watched as he undressed.

Naked, he shuffled towards her on his knees, so that they faced each other, inches apart. It was over before it started and he wanted to cry with frustration.

'We'll just lie together,' she said, and then just lying together turned into something more. It was her first time too, but while she was shy, she seemed to know what to do.

'I know where my dad hides his mucky magazines,' she said. She set the bar high. Not until she shushed him did he realise that he was making a noise.

Later, but much too soon, his whole body ached as he watched her walking away from him for the last time and back to her family; blissfully unaware of what was to follow.

* * *

A violent sob escaped Mariner's chest and the road ahead blurred. He pulled over to the next lay-by and let the tears fall, for Robina and all the other young lives needlessly lost. After a while, he pulled himself together. It was time to leave the past behind. He was about to crash back into the here and now, and in a big way. There had been no further news about Maisie, either on the news broadcasts or from anyone at Granville Lane. Poor Vicky. He'd go to her house first and hope to speak to her.

CHAPTER THIRTY

Mariner's arrival in the city coincided with the school run, which added maddening extra time to his journey, so it was late afternoon by the time he got to Jesson's home. A uniformed constable outside the house was doing his best to keep the press at bay. He didn't know if he'd be allowed access, but Jesson must have heard his voice, because she appeared at the shoulder of the FLO at the door to let him in. He hastened inside, shepherding her before him, before any pictures could be taken.

He didn't need to ask how she was. In other circumstances he'd have barely recognised her. She was dressed in a baggy black tracksuit and with no make-up. Her hair had been untidily tied back. Pale skin and sunken eyes said she hadn't slept last night. Although Mariner considered his work colleagues friends, it was always within strict professional parameters. Today was different. He took her in his arms and held her close, feeling the spasm of a sob pass through her; capable, pragmatic Vicky Jesson now no more than a frightened child. Mariner bit back anger. If Michael Corbett was behind this and his motive was revenge, then the bastard had got his wish.

'Ralph and his team are doing everything in their power,' he said, as she stepped away again, even though she already knew that. He stopped short of saying, *They'll find her.* Both he and Jesson knew it was a guarantee he couldn't make. Had Trevor and Trish been told that about Robina, he wondered?

In the lounge, Doris stood straight-backed, her arms folded across her chest as she stared sightlessly out of the window. The FLO — Mariner thought her name was Lorraine — was picking up used mugs from the coffee table and the TV was playing so low it was virtually inaudible. The room was stuffy, the atmosphere thick with tension and expectation. Mariner had been in this situation a handful of times, visiting families to update them on progress in finding their missing loved one, and, on more occasions than he wanted, to break the dreaded news. It was the worst place in the world to be. He sat down next to Jesson on the sofa and she hugged her cardigan around her.

'What happened?' he asked. She took him through the events of the previous evening. Sharp had already told him most of it, but it would help her to talk.

'How are Aaron and Emily doing?'

'Aaron's gone to school and is going to his mate's house afterwards,' said Jesson. 'He wanted to, and I thought the distraction would be good for him. They're letting him keep his phone switched on. Emily's up in her room, beside herself with worry. I've tried to tell her she'd be better down here, in company, but she won't come down. Lorraine has tried to talk to her, but she hasn't been very receptive.'

'Do you want me to have a go?'

'Would you? She might listen to you.'

Mariner wasn't so sure. Much as he liked Emily, he was hardly the expert on teenage girls. He climbed the stairs fully expecting to be rebuffed. Of the five doors off the landing, only one was firmly closed. The rooms he could see into were empty, leaving the one with 'Maisie' on the nameplate with the shut door. Mariner knocked gently. Nothing.

'Emily, it's Tom Mariner,' he said. 'Your mum's worried about you. Can I get you anything?' Listening hard, he just caught the wan 'no thanks' that came in reply. He wasn't going to force it, so he started back towards the stairs. As he reached the top step, the door opened and Emily's tear-stained, puffy face appeared.

'Can I talk to you?' she said.

'Course you can.' Following her back, he found her sitting on her sister's bed, holding a worn soft toy in her hands. He leaned on the door jamb and waited.

'I think it's all my fault,' Emily said, finally.

'Why?' He made a show of looking back on to the landing. 'We're on our own,' he said. 'I promise, no one else here.'

'I stopped Maisie from walking home with us after school.'

'OK,' said Mariner, sensing there was more.

'I lost my rag with her. She can be so annoying sometimes and—'

'Wait,' cut in Mariner. 'Just because your kid sister gets on your nerves . . . There are some nasty people out there and your mum crosses paths with them all the time. This has nothing to do with you.'

'No, no!' Exasperated, Emily shook her head. 'I've got this friend, Jayden. He's in some kind of trouble, I mean serious trouble. He owes money.'

'To someone at school?' said Mariner.

'It's much worse than that. And it's a lot of money.' As she spoke, the toy — a rabbit — was about to get its ears pulled off. 'I gave him my new phone so he could sell it or give it to them, but it wasn't enough. And now this has happened and Jayden's been grounded, and his mum and dad won't let me speak to him. I'm scared they've taken Maisie, the people he owes the money to.'

Shit. 'Do you have any idea who they are, or why he owes them this money?' asked Mariner, calmly.

'He wouldn't tell me. When I gave him the phone, he said he'd get it sorted.'

'And you haven't spoken to him since?'

'He's off social media and everything.'

'Where does Jayden live?' Mariner asked. The address she gave him was a couple of streets away. 'Right. I'm going to make some phone calls and pass this on to the people who are looking for Maisie.'

Emily's eyes welled up. 'Mum's going to kill me,' she wailed.

'No, she's not,' said Mariner. 'Chances are, this has nothing at all to do with what's happened to Maisie, and even if it does, you need to remember it's not your fault. Emily, look at me.' He waited until she raised her eyes to his. 'All you've done is try to help a friend who was in trouble. In the meantime, I need you to keep this to yourself a bit longer, while it's checked out. Can you do that for me?'

She nodded, miserably.

'I don't want to worry your mum, or get her hopes up unnecessarily. Do you understand? Emily, you've done a brave thing; you've done the right thing.' He squeezed her shoulder, then descended the stairs, his mind racing.

'How is she?' asked Jesson, when he looked in on her.

'She's fine in the circumstances,' said Mariner. 'Just anxious about Maisie.'

'Thanks,' said Jesson.

'I have to go now,' said Mariner. 'But I'll keep in touch.'

On his way out, Mariner gestured for Wyatt to follow him into the hall. There, in a low voice, he relayed his conversation with Emily.

'I'm going to contact Ralph Solomon about this, but it mustn't get back to Vicky or her mum.'

'Right, sir.'

He called Ralph Solomon from his car and explained. 'Emily's convinced that this has something to do with Maisie's disappearance, and we can't discount it. I know you're stretched, and I'm on the spot. Would you like me to go and talk to this Jayden? It could be that Emily's reading something into the situation that isn't there.'

'I'm not sure that she is,' said Solomon, grimly.

'What?'

'We've had a call from the abductor — if it's genuine. A male voice. He said: "The kid will be returned when we've got what's rightfully ours. You have until midnight tomorrow." At the end, he said, "*He* knows what to do." We've been trying to figure out what that means. If it was about Vicky, it would be "she". We even considered whether Aaron might be involved. But what you've said now might make sense of it.'

'I've told Lorraine,' said Mariner. 'But she and Emily have promised to keep it to themselves. I thought it was best until we know where we stand with it.'

'I'd appreciate you doing this,' said Solomon.

'I'll keep you informed,' said Mariner.

CHAPTER THIRTY-ONE

Mariner drove the short distance to Jayden's home, a typical pre-war suburban detached house in the same respectable neighbourhood as Jesson's. He walked up the paved drive, where a two-year-old hatchback sat. In a window of the porch hung a decorative sign heralding a welcome to visitors. When he rang the bell, a woman came to the door, unfastening an apron and bringing with her the smell of home baking. Mariner showed his warrant card and introduced himself, and immediately she seemed on her guard.

'I wondered if I could speak to Jayden, please, Mrs . . . ?'

'About what?' The guard inched up a little.

'I understand he's friends with Emily Riddell?' said Mariner 'You know that her sister has gone missing?'

'We heard that. It's terrible, I can't imagine what their mum must be going through. But what has that to do with Jayden?'

'Nothing, I hope,' said Mariner. 'But Emily's got it into her head that Maisie's abduction is her fault, and it would really help me to reassure her if I could have a quick word with Jayden. Is he at home?'

'Not yet. My husband has just gone to pick him and the others up from ju-jitsu.'

'Would you mind if I waited?' said Mariner. 'It is important. I can wait in the car if you'd prefer.'

'No, it's fine,' she said, her reluctance giving a lie to the words, and held the door wider for him to go into the house. 'I'm Carol, by the way.'

'Thank you, Carol.' Mariner was glad she'd let him in. There was something in her demeanour that made him want to be present when Jayden came home.

She showed Mariner into the lounge, which was unmistakably a room in a house where children lived, with toys stacked up in every available space. He'd barely sat down when he heard the sound of a vehicle pulling on to the drive. He stood and watched through the window as it disgorged a couple of pre-teens and a harassed-looking father. Mariner hoped it didn't mean Jayden had gone on somewhere else. Seconds later the key turned in the lock and as the door opened, Mariner heard the children directed upstairs. The mother was there instantly and there followed a muffled exchange, presumably while she explained Mariner's presence to her husband. Then they both appeared in the doorway, looking rather more panicked than he had anticipated. Nothing hidden about their feelings now.

'Chief Inspector Mariner? I'm Jim, Carol's husband. I'm afraid we have a problem,' said the father. 'You can't see Jayden. He didn't turn up for lessons this afternoon, and we don't know where he is. His mobile's off.'

'What about friends?' Mariner suggested. He had a sudden cold feeling that Emily had been right.

'He's new to the area,' said Carol. 'He hasn't really got any friends like that, except for Emily.'

'Could he have gone to see her?' asked Mariner. 'She wasn't at school today. He wasn't there when I left the house, but that was half an hour ago.'

'He might have, I suppose.' Jayden's mum exchanged a look with her husband; she didn't seem convinced of that either.

'Let me make a call.' Mariner phoned Lorraine Wyatt, but Jayden hadn't turned up there. 'Let me know if he does,' said Mariner.

He'd been aware of the couple speaking in low voices and now Jim said, 'I need to make a call too, and then there's something we must tell you.'

'Does this have anything to do with Maisie?'

'I really hope not.'

Mariner could tell from his tone that it wasn't going to be good.

Jayden's mum and Mariner sat in silence, she worrying at a thread on the sleeve of her sweatshirt, as her husband made a call to an unknown person informing them of Jayden's disappearance. When he'd finished, they came and sat down.

'Well?' Mariner said.

'That was Jayden's social worker,' Carol began, with an anxious glance towards her husband. 'We're not Jayden's biological parents. We're foster carers. Jayden came to live with us just a few months ago. He has a troubled background. He's been in and out of care for years now and where he was living before, he got involved with drugs in a big way — dealing and couriering. He came here for a fresh start, to get away from all that, and he's been doing really well, thanks in part to Emily.'

'But?' Mariner had a nasty a feeling about what was coming.

She looked to her husband for reassurance that she should continue.

'The last couple of weeks, he's been different, hasn't he?' Again a glance at her husband. 'He's been withdrawn, and, when you do get anything out of him, he's uncooperative and impatient with the younger ones. He's been late getting home from school and one night stayed out until nearly midnight and wouldn't say where he'd been. Then last weekend, he came home with some new, expensive trainers. He said his dad had sent him the money, though we thought that was unlikely. I mean, he's been doing some babysitting for us, but that wouldn't have earned him nearly enough to pay for them. So, we grounded him and contacted his social worker, but we've been waiting for her to get back to us.'

'Emily gave Jayden her brand-new iPhone,' said Mariner. 'She thinks he owes money to people. Could that be true?'

'Given his history, yes,' said Jim.

'Were the police ever involved in the past?'

'He's been cautioned before, but never been charged with anything. The view was that he was vulnerable, and being exploited.'

'Where did Jayden live before coming here?'

'Telford. They didn't want to move him too far from there because he still has some family in that area.'

'I'll need the details of his social worker,' said Mariner. 'And I'm going to get someone here to take full statements from you both. What you've told me is helpful, but I wish you had alerted us to Jayden's past sooner.'

'We did talk about it, didn't we?' said Carol. 'But we had no reason to think Jayden would have anything to do with the little girl's disappearance. It sounds harsh but our priority is to take care of Jayden. We were trying to give him a chance.'

Mariner softened a little. 'He's a lucky lad to have you on his side,' he said. 'Could I see his room?'

But the space was impersonal, with only a few belongings. 'I looked around while he was at school,' admitted Jim. 'Didn't find anything.'

Mariner had taken out his phone before the couple had closed the door on him. He rang Ralph Solomon and told him everything he'd just learned, including details of Jayden's social worker.

'I'll brief the team,' said Solomon. 'Then we'll take it from there.'

'She should be able to put you in touch with the other agencies Jayden's known to, including West Mercia. They'll have a sense of Jayden's contacts. Your resources are stretched,' said Mariner as they went out to the car. 'You want me to pick any of it up?'

'Thanks, but I've got people I can put on it,' said Solomon. 'What do you think about letting Emily and Vicky know?'

'It'd make both of them feel better to hear that you've got something tangible,' said Mariner.

'Yeah, that's what I was thinking too,' said Solomon. 'That's something you could usefully do, if you've got time?'

'Happy to,' said Mariner.

'I'll keep you in the loop.'

'Don't worry about it. I can pick up any developments on the intranet.'

'Cheers, mate.'

Jesson took the news better than Mariner expected, relieved perhaps for the moment that Michael Corbett might not be behind Maisie's abduction. 'But Jayden?' she said. 'I can't believe it. He's a lovely boy. I would never have guessed at his background. Why didn't Emily tell me?'

'She doesn't know much and she's terrified,' said Mariner. 'She's already blaming herself for Maisie's abduction, and she thinks you will too. You want me to . . . ?'

'No, it's fine. This is one for me.'

'This is a strong lead,' said Mariner. 'It could be the break they need.'

'Yes,' said Jesson, wanly. 'But you and I both know what these people are like. And Maisie's so young and so trusting.' She broke down then and Mariner just sat with her, an arm about her shoulders, until she'd recovered herself.

Before he left, Mariner went to speak to Lorraine Wyatt who was washing up more mugs in the kitchen.

'Tough job for you,' said Mariner.

He could do no more here, so giving Jesson a final hug, he headed for Granville Lane.

Despite the lateness of the hour, everywhere was hectic today. After a week of life in the slow lane, it was a shock to the system. Granville Lane was also under siege — from news and media crews waiting for the scoop on the little girl's disappearance. He managed to push through, largely unscathed, ignoring the barrage of questions, and went straight to the incident room set up for Maisie, where he found Ralph Solomon. It was buzzing with activity; lots of faces he recognised. Those he didn't were probably PolSA, the police search advisers. Solomon saw him and came over.

'You made it then,' he said. 'How did Vicky take it?'

'Mixed feelings, as you'd expect,' said Mariner. 'What about you?'

'This has galvanised us. West Mercia have passed on some solid intel. And we're following up some possible sightings arising from the press conference.'

'Anything promising?'

'A witness who saw Maisie with two young men, not far from the school. They got into a dark saloon, Mercedes or BMW. We got a partial number for it, but it's cloned, so has probably been changed since the abduction. I've got people interrogating CCTV but you know how long that takes.' He indicated three officers, their eyes glued to a bank of screens on the far side of the room.

'What about Corbett?'

'Hasn't put a foot wrong while we've been watching him.'

'Is there anything else I can do here?' asked Mariner.

Solomon shook his head. 'A hundred and one things, probably, but your team'll crucify me if I keep you away from them any longer. The super's had to take her hands off the wheel there too, and at a crucial time.'

'Is she around?'

'Yeah, think so,' said Solomon. 'She stopped by here not long ago. Listen, I'm grateful for your help, Tom. This feels like we're getting somewhere.'

CHAPTER THIRTY-TWO

In stark contrast to everywhere else Mariner had been since his return, away from the incident room, the first floor of the building seemed deserted. But as Mariner made his way to his office, he heard voices coming from CID. He found Charlie Glover and Kevin Bingley, sitting at their respective desks, chewing the end-of-the-day fat.

'What are you two doing still here?' he asked.

'Can't be bothered to get off our arses and go home,' said Bingley, swinging from side to side in his chair. 'And keeping half an ear on what's going on downstairs. Millie's gone, though.'

'We weren't sure if you'd make it back today,' said Glover.

'I might have got here earlier, but I got held up,' said Mariner, and told them about developments with Maisie. 'Vicky asked me to thank you for all the messages,' he said. 'She's doing OK. Just about.'

'I just wish there was more we could do,' said Glover.

'Me too. Just keep praying for her,' said Mariner. He wasn't a believer himself, but Glover's faith was central to his life. If there was anything to it, they could do with Glover's help right now.

'What about Norfolk, boss?' asked Bingley. 'Are we allowed to know what you were doing there now?'

'I don't see why not.' He explained about the discovery of Robina's remains.

'I saw something about that on the news last weekend,' said Glover. 'But surely it was before your time. You're not *that* old.'

'Thanks,' said Mariner, wryly. 'No, I was a school kid.'

'What, you weren't born a copper?' said Bingley with mock surprise.

'Are they going to crack it?' Glover asked.

'A bit of new evidence has turned up,' said Mariner. 'Another sighting. But I can't see that it will make much difference. The original suspect is still the favourite for it, and he died some time ago.'

'Disappointing.'

'Yeah. It's hard on the family. How about Hien?' asked Mariner, inclining his head towards the incident board. 'When I spoke to Vicky on Wednesday evening, it sounded as if there had been developments.'

Glover outlined what had happened since, concluding with the suspicions about Bennetts Road. 'But we think the workers must've been moved on,' he said.

'That would make sense,' said Mariner. 'Especially if it's known that we've been nosing around. No hope of tracing this minibus?'

'It's a challenge,' said Glover. All we have is that it's a grey minibus, and that it picked them up yesterday evening, somewhere between nine and ten.'

'What about CCTV?'

'There's not much in that area because it's mainly residential. The first time it's likely to be picked up is when it joined the Pershore Road or Bristol Road but that could be at any number of places. They might not have even been moved that far.'

'Paszek can't have been working alone,' said Mariner. 'Vicky said something about an accountant. Did we get anywhere with him?'

'We haven't got hold of him yet,' said Glover. 'And he doesn't answer his phone.'

'The boss— er, Vicky went round to his place, and we tried again yesterday,' said Bingley. No one came to the door, but there was definitely someone inside. A woman, we think, and she was keeping out of sight.'

'Another victim?'

'That's what we thought.'

'We'll persevere with it,' said Mariner. 'Out of hours, if necessary.' He stood up. 'But you two should go home now. Get some rest.'

* * *

It was dark beyond the windows by the time Mariner finally made it along the corridor to his office. He was gratified to see that Jesson had made herself at home while he'd been away, and wished she was sitting behind his desk right now, demonstrating how dispensable he was. Her mug was on the coaster amid a stormy sea of notes and Post-its. The answer machine was blinking: two new messages. The first was from Simon Bell. It was a long shot but Mariner called him back. His was evidently a quiet Friday night.

'I thought you'd want to know, ASAP,' Bell said. 'The IOPC have interviewed the witness. She insists that she saw the incident from her flat. I've been and had a look. Naturally I couldn't go inside, but I've a nasty feeling that it would be possible. The fact that she just happened to be looking out there when the incident occurred is debatable, but it'll be hard to prove otherwise.'

'Is she being leaned on?' asked Mariner.

'That's my take on it,' said Bell. 'My mate at Belgravia thinks it could be a stash flat, so therefore some association between Clifford's family and the witness. If we can establish that, we might have something to work on.'

'If not, it's basically my word against hers.'

'They might question her plausibility as a witness,' said Bell. 'And the good news is that there's no physical evidence of you having made contact with Clifford's foot, leg or shoe.'

'I knew there wouldn't be,' said Mariner. But it wouldn't help him much if the witness was believed.

The second message was for Jesson, from Stuart Croghan, asking her to call him back. Mariner tried, but wasn't remotely surprised to find the pathologist had left for the weekend. It would have to wait for Monday, but Hien wasn't going anywhere.

The call from Simon Bell prompted Mariner to make one final call — to the QE hospital. This time the ward staff were more guarded and would only speak to Clifford's family, so Mariner took a chance and asked to be put through to Dr Ellen Kingsley, a doctor he'd come to know professionally — and personally — working on a job a couple of years back.

'Hello, stranger,' she said, when he announced himself.

'Yes, sorry, you know how it is.'

'I do.'

'How are you?' Mariner asked.

'Well, thank you. You're lucky to catch me — I'm about to leave.'

'Yeah, sorry, I'll only keep you a minute.'

'No, I mean I'm leaving the hospital, and the city,' she said. 'Next week's my last here.'

'Wow, where are you going?'

'To Edinburgh, where I'm getting married.'

'Wow again,' said Mariner. 'Congratulations. And the lucky man?'

'Another doctor, of course; Robert Nutter, so do your worst.'

'I'm saying nothing. A man can't help his name. Anyway, I'm calling for a favour as I expect you've already guessed. You have a patient in critical care: Dean Clifford.'

'Yes, he's not one of mine, but I know who he is.'

'How's he doing?'

'He's stable but still in a coma. I don't think the prognosis is very good. There's likely to be permanent brain damage. What's the interest?'

'He fell and sustained his injuries while I was in pursuit,' said Mariner. 'He'd just assaulted someone.'

'Nasty.'

'Yes. Anyway, I appreciate the update, and all the best for your new life in Scotland.'

'Thanks. You take care too.'

'I will.'

Permanent brain damage. What would that mean for Dean Clifford, his young life irrevocably changed in just a few short seconds? What a waste.

CHAPTER THIRTY-THREE

First thing on Saturday morning, Mariner got out his laptop and logged into the PNC to see if there was any progress with Maisie, but except for an influx of intel from ROCU concerning Jayden Starr, there was little change. The news bulletins he heard on the radio bore it out. He felt helpless, and had to keep reminding himself that Ralph Solomon would call on him if he needed to. With Solomon's team and PolSA in the mix, he was mindful of not treading on anyone else's toes. He was about to embark on a round of domestic chores, when his landline rang.

'You're back!' said Maggie. 'I thought I'd get your answer machine. How was your sojourn in Norfolk?' Norfolk. It seemed astonishing to him that less than twenty-four hours earlier he had been there.

'It was interesting,' Mariner said. 'Dredged all kinds of stuff to the surface, as you can imagine.'

'You and me both,' said Maggie. 'I've been able to think of very little else since we spoke. So irritating that as you get older the short-term memory becomes ever more unreliable, while the smallest details from years ago come back to one so easily. I've found one or two snaps, and didn't know if you'd like to come and have a look.'

Mariner remembered then that, as well as her painting, Maggie had been quite the amateur photographer, and used a decent SLR camera; a great big thing that she carried slung around her neck.

'Will you be around tomorrow morning?' he asked.

'Anytime. I've got a friend coming to stay, so I'll be trying to tidy up the place.'

'I'll see you about ten then.'

He was popular today, his next caller Millie Khatoon, who was also finding it impossible to focus on anything other than what might be happening with Maisie. It was a good opportunity for a catch-up and got Mariner thinking about Hien again. He should read through the policy log in preparation for Monday morning. There was no question that Glover would have thoroughly and conscientiously kept it up to date, and sometimes a fresh pair of eyes picked up something that had been missed. But Mariner's Wi-Fi wasn't in the mood for cooperation, so after two hours of slow or interrupted connection he gave up, in favour of watching *Final Score* with an accompanying bottle of Spitfire. He'd started to nod off a bit when he suddenly realised that the background noise he could hear was his work mobile.

'We've got her!' said Sharp, the tremor in her voice audible.

'Got . . . ?' Then he understood and relief swamped him. 'Thank God,' he said. 'How is she?'

'She's fine,' said Sharp. 'Scared. And worried about her mum, of all things, but they'd looked after her.'

'It was quick,' said Mariner. 'How did they . . . ?' He stopped himself. 'No, sorry, this isn't the time. Congratulations, guv, it's a fantastic result.'

'Thanks. It is, isn't it? Ralph Solomon's been brilliant.'

The first thing Mariner did when he rang off, was to text Jesson: *So happy for you. Don't come into work until you're ready. Spend some time with the family.* Her reply came as a string of celebratory emojis. It was probably the most she could manage right now.

* * *

On Sunday morning, Mariner drove over to Berkswell, the outlying Warwickshire village where Maggie now lived. For a while she'd been based in London, but had returned to the Midlands some years ago. Despite what she'd told him yesterday, he caught her working, and she came to the door in a faded and outsized man's collarless shirt over a paint-daubed T-shirt.

'Excuse the hand-me-downs,' she said, holding her arms out from her body. 'Woman at work.'

'Still knocking out the masterpieces, then,' said Mariner, feeling a pang of guilt as he thought of those pictures gathering dust in his cellar.

'Keeps me out of trouble.' She smiled. She seemed delighted to see him, and if there was any residual resentment from their previous phone call, she'd put it behind her. She must be approaching eighty now, he realised, though seemed as energetic as ever, and despite her generous size, moved easily. All that yoga she did, he supposed.

The cottage where she lived was very much in her style, with tiny rooms crammed with old furniture and interesting artefacts gathered on her travels on every continent. A PC and scanner/printer sat incongruously amongst it all, but Maggie would need those for her political activism. The sofas were covered in colourful throws and any number of scatter cushions, which Mariner put to one side so that he could sit down, while Maggie brought tea and homemade shortbread.

'Are they going to find whoever killed Robina?' she asked, when she had at last settled into the worn armchair facing him.

'I don't know,' said Mariner, truthfully. He told her about the changes of witness testimony from Trevor and Kit. 'But it's not enough. They only lead to a different angle on the speculation. In cold cases you're always hoping to capitalise on advances in forensic analysis technology, like DNA profiling. But that's dependent on having available physical evidence and nothing new had come to light on that score when I left on Friday.'

'Let me show you what I found,' said Maggie. She had her own Kodak envelopes and passed the photos across to him, one by one. 'From the days when I fancied myself as a bit of a David Bailey.'

Not without cause, thought Mariner. They were terrific pictures, artistic and well composed; candid shots, catching their subjects unawares and therefore entirely naturally.

'This one's lovely of Rose, isn't it?' Maggie said, as Mariner took the next one from her.

She was right; glass of wine in hand, sharing a joke with two women, as a man looked on. Rose was laughing, her head tipped back, and she was completely lost in the moment. It saddened him that in his mind's eye he never pictured his mother like that, but instead as the belligerent woman she'd become in later life.

'That was taken on your last night,' said Maggie.

'He offered me a spliff,' said Mariner, pointing to the onlooker.

'I'm not at all surprised,' said Maggie. 'That's him,' she added.

'Who?'

'You're rather slow for a policeman, aren't you?' she teased. 'He's the man your mother and I fell out about — Elued. Real name Johannes Visser, though I didn't find that out for a long time. The Elued was because of some druid thing relating to his birthday, as I recall. It's him who's coming to stay.' She brightened. 'Why don't you come over too? You could get reacquainted.'

'Thanks, but I've got a busy week ahead of me,' said Mariner. And from what Maggie had told him, he rather suspected he might share his mother's view of Elued. He turned back to the photographs. There were none of Robina, but he spotted himself in one or two and there were some good ones of the fair people. They might be of no help at all, but on the other hand . . .

'Would you mind if I borrowed these?' he asked Maggie. 'I can scan them across to Ginny Reid, who's conducting the investigation.'

'Of course, be my guest.'

* * *

After leaving Maggie's house, Mariner decided to head in to Granville Lane. At least there he could be sure of reliable Wi-Fi and he should get up to speed for the following day. On his way to CID, he had to pass by the incident room for Maisie, and stopped off to see if anyone was around. The room looked as if a hurricane had hit, leaving just a handful of survivors picking over the detritus. Computers were being dismantled, a couple of officers were clearing up bottles and cans left over from the celebrations, and in the far corner, Ralph Solomon still sat at his desk.

'Someone welded your backside to that chair?' said Mariner, leaning across to shake Solomon's beefy hand. 'Congratulations, mate. Brilliant result.'

'Thanks.' Solomon was in a post-investigation stupor; the combined effects of lack of sleep and the comedown from a sustained adrenalin high.

'You're allowed to go home now, you know.'

Solomon grinned. 'That's a bit rich coming from you,' he said. 'I will soon, but I just want to tie up some loose ends while it's all still in here.' He tapped his head.

Mariner knew exactly what he meant. 'How did you find her, in the end?'

'It was ROCU and West Mercia, really,' said Ralph, with typical modesty. 'Between them, they were able to identify the county lines network Jayden Starr was involved with, and that gave us a number of associated addresses in the city. CCTV had picked up the car Maisie was taken in, which was traced to the Highgate area. Then it was just a question of cross-referencing and elimination. We carried out a series of raids in the early hours of yesterday morning, but Maisie wasn't at any of the properties. We were gutted. I really thought we'd screwed up.

'But then one of our guys turned up two phones, including a brand-new iPhone. He'd remembered about Emily's phone, so he knew it could be significant. There was a text on it, purportedly sent by Emily to Maisie, on the afternoon she went missing. It said to meet her and Starr at a spot near to where that car was seen. There were subsequent calls to an unknown number, because whoever had it had stupidly gone on using it, and there were prints on it too. Long story short, the prints and number gave us a few more options, which led us to where she was being held, along with Starr; a cuckoo flat in Highgate.' Mariner had come across the term before: a drug dealer forcibly moving in with a vulnerable person. 'It all happened really fast in the end — we were bloody lucky.'

'So, who'd got her?'

'We're still getting to the bottom of it, but what it looks like is that the OCG Starr was running for in Telford didn't like it that he left. They managed to track him down here, and a couple of local lads further down the food chain were assigned to persuade him to re-join their little enterprise. They met him outside school a couple of weeks back and claimed that when he'd left a consignment had gone missing, and he owed them the money for it. Threatened dire consequences if he didn't do one last job for them.'

'Debt-bondage blackmail,' said Mariner.

'Exactly,' said Solomon. 'Starr tried to pay them off instead, but was naïve in the extreme. Emily's phone was never going to be enough, and by now they'd been watching him. They decided Maisie was the leverage they needed to bring him back on to the operation.'

'Jesus,' Mariner closed his eyes, imagining how it all could have ended.

'Fortunately for us, these kids were in way over their heads. They'd seen *Taken* too many times. Once they'd got Maisie, they hadn't a clue what they were going to do next.

I think they were relieved that our lads showed. It was crazy. I'm still trying to get my head around it.'

'Sounds as if that might take a few days.'

'I can live with it.'

On his way out, Mariner passed the corner where the CCTV viewers had been working and were beginning to pack up their equipment. On two of the machines, the screens were still frozen in shot. One of the views looked vaguely familiar.

'Where's that?' Mariner asked the constable closest to it. She leaned over and called up the data.

'Belgravia, sir. Ludlow Grove.'

'Have you got anything else in that area?'

'I expect so; the disks and USBs are all in there.' She indicated the box on an adjacent desk.

'Thanks, do you mind if I . . . ?'

'Not at all, sir. I'm just off anyway.' Closing her machine, she got to her feet.

Mariner checked what was on the particular USB in the machine. There were files of recorded material from the Thursday when Maisie was abducted and going back seven days.

What he needed was the locations of all the other CCTV cameras in the area. And there it was, a map on the wall beside another of the desks. Each of the cameras marked had a number, and those he was interested in were attributed to Sphere Housing Association, same as the memory stick that showed the Ludlow Grove footage. It didn't take him long to find the other Sphere USBs, tagged with the company logo and the camera numbers. He narrowed it down to four possible cameras that might give him what he wanted.

'I know there's not much on telly at the moment, but isn't this a bit desperate, Tom?' Ralph Solomon came up from behind him, jacket now on, messenger bag slung over his shoulder.

'I'm just checking something out,' said Mariner. 'Do you mind?'

'Knock yourself out,' said Solomon amiably. 'You can't do any damage in here.'

'Thanks,' said Mariner. 'Go home and get some rest. You deserve it, big man.'

Solomon waved without a backward glance.

Mariner's heart was thudding as he put in the first of the memory sticks and went to the first clip. Just a few seconds in, he froze the footage and studied the screen. But it wasn't what he wanted. He repeated the process with the second, with the same outcome. But when he froze the third, he paused. The view was of the entrance and parking space outside a block of flats, but to the right and incidental in the foreground was a high wall topped with broken glass, the bottom corner of a roof, and just beyond that a view into a skip. Closing the clip, he sought out the MP4 for the day he was interested in and fast-forwarded through to the approximate time, when he slowed to normal playback. He had to wait an agonising few minutes before suddenly a blob, which turned out to be a person, bobbed into view approaching the skip and vaulted up and on to the roof. Something big and bulky fell away, rolling down the slates behind him. In slow motion, the figure turned, grabbed and missed and tumbled backwards, his head bouncing off the skip, just as, a spilt second later, another figure lumbered onto the screen. It was tight. To be conclusive it would need to be enhanced, but it was better than nothing. Mariner emailed Simon Bell right away, and attached a copy of the footage. His message was brief: 'I think this might help.'

CHAPTER THIRTY-FOUR

On Monday morning at Granville Lane, everything seemed refreshingly normal, apart from the absence of Vicky Jesson. Superintendent Sharp sought Mariner out, early on.

'Sorry I didn't catch you on Friday,' she said.

'You had your hands full,' said Mariner. 'And what a result.'

'Yes, thank God. You heard what happened?'

'I saw Ralph yesterday. Have you spoken to Vicky?'

'We had a chat yesterday afternoon, though I'm not sure how present she was. I reiterated what you told her: to take a few days off. And how was Norfolk?'

'Interesting,' said Mariner. 'Some new evidence turned up, in the shape of revised witness statements. And there was a curiosity. They found an audio interview recorded with the main person of interest.'

'From that long ago?'

'I know,' said Mariner. 'It's thrown up a possible name, "Morken", but it's not one that was known to me.'

'Dare I ask about the IOPC?' asked Sharp.

Mariner's gut contracted. 'Nothing yet,' he said. He resisted the urge to tell her about the video file, until he knew if it'd be any use.

'And you're up to speed with the Hien investigation?'

'More or less,' said Mariner. 'I can understand the direction the thinking's going in, and we've got a couple of live leads to follow.'

As if to illustrate the point, Charlie Glover knocked lightly on the open door. 'Sorry to interrupt, boss,' he said. 'I've finally got hold of the elusive Mr Agarwal. He can see someone at ten o'clock.'

'I'll let you get on,' said Sharp, leaving them to it.

* * *

Mariner took Khatoon with him to Agarwal's and this time the door was answered promptly by a slight man with gunmetal hair and dark brown skin. He wore an open-necked shirt and cardigan. On the face of it, he didn't look like your typical gangland criminal, but that didn't necessarily mean anything.

'Mr Agarwal?' Mariner held out his warrant card. Agarwal barely gave it a glance.

'Yes, yes. Come in and, please, call me Rai.' He spoke precisely, with the slightest trace of an accent, and seemed perfectly relaxed about inviting them in.

'You're a hard man to get hold of,' Mariner said. 'My colleagues came here last week on two separate occasions. They saw a woman inside, but no one came to the door.'

'I must apologise,' said Agarwal. 'My wife is unwell. She never answers the door if I am not here.'

'I see,' said Mariner. 'And you don't have business premises?'

'Once upon a time, but no more. I all but retired several years ago, so although I have kept one or two of my oldest clients, I dispensed with the office.'

The house was as neat and trim as Agarwal himself. Windows to the back looked out over an expansive garden, and they could see a woman of Agarwal's age kneeling to pull weeds from a flower bed against a backdrop of lush greenery.

'Your wife?' said Mariner.

'Yes, she loves her garden.' Agarwal smiled.

He led them through to a home office, at the centre of which stood an impressive, highly polished hardwood desk. Agarwal picked up a velvet upholstered chair and placed it in front of the desk for Khatoon, and Mariner grabbed another.

'Can I get you some refreshment?' Agarwal asked, and when they declined, he took the captain's chair behind the desk. 'So, Detective Mariner,' he said, 'how can I help you?'

'Would one of your oldest clients happen to be Viktor Paszek?' asked Mariner.

'Ah, yes.' Agarwal smiled. 'I have known Viktor for many years, as a client and a friend. We have a mutual enthusiasm for the games of chess and cricket, so we usually find time for a game — chess, that is — when we meet.'

He doesn't know, thought Mariner. 'I'm afraid I have bad news, sir,' he said. 'I'm sorry to have to tell you that Mr Paszek died in an accident, in the early hours of last Monday morning.'

For a moment Agarwal looked stricken, and his grip on the arms of the chair tightened. 'Oh no, no . . . poor Viktor. What kind of accident?'

Mariner studied him for signs of anxiety or fear, and knew that Khatoon would be doing the same. But he couldn't see it. Only sadness.

'It was a road traffic collision,' said Mariner. 'When was the last time you saw him?'

'Some weeks ago. Let me see, back in early February, I think. We spoke on the phone quite often.'

'How was he, the last time you spoke?'

'Cheerful. Busy. The same as always.'

'You did the accounting for his businesses.'

'For more than thirty years.'

'And recently?'

'He gave me little to do. Like me, Viktor had retired from most. He sold some of his properties — retaining only those that were not too demanding of his time and energy.'

'Exactly how many properties did he keep on?'

When Agarwal didn't respond, Mariner held the man's gaze, where, for the first time, he saw an inner conflict at play.

'Why does this concern you?' said Agarwal. 'I don't understand.'

'Then let me explain,' said Mariner. 'At the time of the road accident there was another man in Mr Paszek's car.' Taking out Hien's picture, Mariner placed it on the desk in front of Agarwal. 'Do you know him?'

Agarwal shook his head.

'He was dead too, but it wasn't the accident that killed him. He had suffered severe injuries and his body had been unceremoniously stuffed into a sack and further concealed with bark chippings. Our evidence so far suggests that Mr Paszek may well have killed him.'

'No!' Agarwal was appalled. 'Viktor would never do such a thing. It's impossible.'

'Our belief is that when he had the accident, Mr Paszek was on his way to dispose of the body. Our problem is that we don't know the identity of this man. We have been trying, so far without success, to find out who he was and what he might have been doing in Mr Paszek's car.

'Maybe you can understand now why we've taken an interest in Mr Paszek's businesses. And what we've found is a cleaning operation that does an excellent job for the client, but which has no paid employees, and a house for which Mr Paszek apparently receives no rent. Logic dictates that the death of this man—' Mariner tapped a forefinger on the image of Hien — 'is in some way connected with those dubious enterprises. The sort of world we inhabit, it can't help but lead us to conclude that something illegal is going on; in fact, both illegal and immoral.'

'You are wrong, so very wrong,' said Agarwal, wringing his hands. 'Viktor was not that kind of man.'

'So we've been told,' said Mariner, sceptically. 'But can you explain how an unidentifiable dead man came to be in his car?'

'I don't know anything about that.'

'But you know something,' said Mariner. 'What is it that you *do* know, Mr Agarwal?'

For the first time they saw something like anguish cross Agarwal's features. Then he got up and went over to a cupboard that concealed a filing cabinet. Pulling open a drawer, he flicked through the folders until he found what he was looking for. Returning to the desk, he tore a sheet from the jotter beside him and wrote something down. He handed it to Mariner. It was a name, 'Kaspa', and a mobile phone number.

'You need to speak to this man,' Agarwal said.

'Who is he?'

'He is the person who can explain everything to you. I can't tell you anything else, but I know Viktor. It's not what you think.' He glanced into the garden. 'And now I must go to my wife. Please. I have left her alone for long enough.'

Outside, Mariner phoned the number Agarwal had given him from the car, but it rang out then went to voicemail. Khatoon continued to try it, on and off, throughout the drive to the station. Still, no one picked up.

'We can get Max to try to trace it for us, but I don't hold out too much hope,' he said, when they were back at the station.

'Shall I give it a go, boss?' asked Glover.

'Knock yourself out,' said Mariner, passing him the number. 'But I think we'll be making a return visit to Mr Agarwal very soon.'

* * *

Mariner hadn't even got as far as his office, when Glover, hand over the handset, called out, 'Boss, we're on!' And in the few steps back to CID he'd put the call on speaker. Mariner had the forethought to introduce himself as just Tom Mariner.

'I'd like to speak to Kaspa,' he said.

'What do you want?' asked the voice, accented and cagey.

'We need to talk,' said Mariner. 'Rai Agarwal gave me your number.'

'Who?'

'Rai Agarwal. He's Viktor Paszek's accountant.' He let that information sink in. 'I need to speak to you urgently. Can we meet?'

'One moment.'

There followed a pause, while an inaudible conversation ensued at the other end of the line. Eventually the same man came back on the line.

'I can meet you in one hour. You know Hazelwell Lane?' He pronounced it 'Hazzelwell'.

'I do,' said Mariner.

'Meet me at the corner Hazelwell and Ripple Road. Come alone.' The call ended.

'You know it?' asked Glover.

'It's a bit of wasteland in Stirchley — the site where Tesco's were going to build a store, then pulled out,' said Mariner, going over to the wall map and pointing it out. 'It's exposed, so I'll have no choice but to go alone. Millie, you and Kevin can be there as backup. Follow me down and park here, on Hunts Road. It's the nearest you can get without being spotted.'

'What about firearms officers?'

Mariner drew breath and exhaled. 'We don't know who this man is, but there's no reason to think that he'll be armed. We're just going to talk. I'll wear a Kevlar. I think the worst he'll do is run. And you two are there to pursue if necessary.'

'Your call, boss.'

CHAPTER THIRTY-FIVE

Mariner drove his car to the specified junction. The rough ground was, as he'd expected, deserted. It was a grey day and a bitter wind sliced across the open space. He'd been there half a minute when the radio came to life.

'We're in position,' said Bingley.

Mariner phoned through to them on his mobile, and leaving the call open, slipped his phone into his pocket. He wasn't gathering evidence, just ensuring that Khatoon and Bingley would know what was going on. He'd sat for a few minutes when he saw a tall figure approaching across the wasteland, braced against the wind, his hands shoved into his coat pockets. 'Single male approaching on foot from the direction of the Pershore Road,' he said.

'We have eyes on,' said Bingley.

As the figure got nearer, Mariner climbed out of the car and the two men stood face to face.

'Kaspa?' called Mariner. The man nodded and stopped a couple of metres away. Mariner had already decided to play it straight, and had his warrant card at the ready. He held it up.

'Detective Chief Inspector Tom Mariner,' he said. 'We spoke a short time ago.' Mariner was primed and ready to run if the man took off, but it didn't happen. Instead, he simply looked curious.

'You're police? But I don't know you. What do you want?'

'To talk to you about Viktor Paszek.'

'What about him?'

'Did you know that he's dead?'

Kaspa's eyes widened. 'No.' He turned and took a couple of paces away. After a moment he turned back to Mariner and stepped closer, his hand extended. 'Now I understand. Kaspa Kostabi. It's cold,' he said, as they shook hands. 'There's a café.' He waved back in the direction of the main road.

'Good idea,' said Mariner. He took his phone out of his pocket. 'Did you get that?' he asked.

'Yes, boss.'

'Millie, why don't you come and join us? Kevin, you can head back to base.'

Then he relieved himself of the cumbersome stab vest and locked it in the car. The café Kostabi took them to was a greasy spoon on the main road. It was warm and steamy inside, with just a handful of other customers. They bought hot drinks and took a table by the window.

'So Viktor is dead,' said Kostabi, sadly.

'He had a fatal heart attack, while he was driving,' said Mariner. 'His car went off the road.'

'Poor Viktor.' He looked up at them. 'It's why you came to Bennetts Road.'

'You had people living there, didn't you?' said Mariner. 'Did they work for Viktor?'

'Yes.'

'I don't understand,' said Khatoon. But Mariner had guessed.

'Viktor wasn't exploiting his employees; he was helping to rescue them from exploitation,' he said. 'Is that right?'

Kostabi nodded. 'I run a small charity — Tasuta. It means "free". We have a hostel near here. When we first pick people up, they come to stay at the hostel. But it takes time for the process of recovery and repatriation. Some people don't want to go back to their country, and may be eligible to seek asylum or get refugee status. Our accommodation is limited, and they want to work, so Viktor takes people to work for him and gives them somewhere to live, until their status is resolved or they can return to their home country.'

'Like you did for Katarina,' Khatoon said to Mariner, referring to the Albanian girl he had freed on a dawn raid some years before. Thanks to her English, she had acted as interpreter during the investigation. She had found work and accommodation locally afterwards, but had since returned to Tirana.

'How did Viktor get involved?' Mariner asked.

'Trafficking is a big problem in Estonia. I was rescued myself, from a farm. I was brought to Birmingham and helped to find proper work. I went to do cleaning for Viktor. He was a good man. We talked. He was interested in what had happened to me and he wanted to do something. Tasuta is a small charity. His help has a been vital for us. And he was planning to do more.'

But Mariner was still puzzled. 'I understand that Viktor would treat these workers well, but still they were not paid?'

'They were paid, but by Tasuta. Viktor made a donation each month to cover the wages. It was more simple for Viktor. He was an old man.'

'Why was he holding their passports?'

'It was a safe place. A little while back we had people in the hostel who were not good people. Some papers were stolen. What will happen now that Viktor is gone? We had people living in his house who are very afraid.'

'Where are they now?' asked Mariner.

'They are at the hostel, but it is very cramped, we have no space. They want to do their jobs.'

'I really don't know,' said Mariner. 'I see no reason why they couldn't go back and live in the house, if you think it's safe. We understand that Viktor has a nephew somewhere, but that's all. You need to speak to Rai Agarwal,' he continued, feeling like a go-between. 'He may know what arrangements Viktor made, if any.' He wrote down Agarwal's name and phone number. 'Are all the workers accounted for? They are all at the hostel?'

'Yes.' Understandably, he was puzzled by the question.

'I'm afraid Viktor's death is not the only reason we're here,' Mariner told him, adding his now customary explanation. He pulled out the photo of Hien. Beside him, Khatoon stiffened in anticipation. 'The dead man was carrying this photo, so we think this must be him — he was too disfigured to be absolutely certain. Do you know him? We thought he might be one of the workers.' Were they at last on the verge of identifying Hien?

Kostabi studied the photo carefully, but to no avail. 'I have never seen this man.'

'Did Viktor help any other organisations like yours?'

Kostabi shrugged. 'I don't know.' And they had no evidence to suggest that he did.

'If I send you the image, could you circulate it amongst your colleagues and any other organisations you work with?' asked Mariner.

'Of course.'

* * *

'Crap!' said Mariner as they got back to the car. Khatoon, beside him, was similarly deflated. 'Where do we go now?'

* * *

Back at Granville Lane, Mariner and Khatoon briefed Glover and Bingley.

'We got this wrong from every angle,' said Khatoon. 'Viktor really was the good guy Eric said he was.'

'That still doesn't explain why he was driving out of the city with a dead man in his car, and his prints and DNA all

264

over the scene,' pointed out Bingley. 'If he was that good a bloke, why didn't he report it and allow Hien a proper burial?'

After all the work it felt as if they were back where they'd started. And now with no clear indications about where to go next.

*　*　*

Mariner returned to his office weary with it all. Maybe this was another sign that he should pack it in. In the short space of one week, he'd failed at everything he'd set out to achieve. He wondered now if Hien would be consigned to the catalogue of unsolved mysteries. After all, it was where Robina Scanlon had languished for decades. Perhaps it was a mystery that would be solved by someone else and not him.

For a moment, Mariner considered calling Simon Bell. He might know where the IOPC were up to with the inquiry. It occurred to him suddenly that a negative outcome might be a blessing in disguise. The integrity of the complaints procedure would be upheld, and after weathering some initial bad press, he would be able to quietly resign. The loss of his pension would be significant, but he'd never lived extravagantly and would be far from destitute. Suzy would be home soon, so it would be an opportunity for them both to think about what their future together might be.

The phone ringing brought him down to earth. It was Stuart Croghan. With all that had happened, Mariner hadn't yet found time to return his call.

'I'm so relieved for Vicky,' said the pathologist immediately. 'Give her my best, will you?'

'Of course,' said Mariner. 'What did you want to speak to her about?'

'I had some suspicions about your unknown fatality,' Croghan said. 'But I wanted to check the research before I threw it into the mix.'

'What is it?'

'I think your man has been frozen,' said Croghan. 'When human flesh freezes and then thaws, the slowing down of the metabolism causes subtle changes in the histology — the minute structures of the tissue. It's something commonly seen in high-altitude climbers or avalanche fatalities.'

Mariner's mind was running through the possibilities. 'You mean Hien could have been stored in a freezer, or something?'

'In these circumstances, I'd say it's the most likely scenario,' said Croghan.

'Can you tell how long he was frozen for?'

'I'm afraid not,' said Croghan. 'If he'd been repeatedly thawed and frozen it might show, but I can't give you a timescale.'

'So, it could be weeks or months?'

'Or only a matter of days or even hours. Sorry,' he added. 'I know this throws a spanner in the works for you.'

'We had to know,' said Mariner. 'And it's not as if you're blowing open a watertight theory. Did you get anything on that residue on his clothing?'

'Not yet,' said Croghan pensively. 'Those results are overdue. I'll chase them.'

* * *

On Monday evening, Mariner was pleasantly surprised to get a call from Ginny Reid, but she didn't have good news to share either.

'We've been back to see Rothbury,' she said. 'And we're reluctantly ruling him out. He eventually admitted to being at the party, and his account of the evening chimes more or less with what Crispin Bland told us. But unlike Bland, he stands by the assertion that it might not have been Robina they saw at the party.'

'It's enough to put him in the clear?' said Mariner. He didn't think Reid would let it go so easily.

'There's more,' she said. 'Scott went to see Jimmy Finnegan. By sheer fluke, he alibied Rothbury without even

266

knowing he was doing it. The main reason he remembered that night, apart from Robina, was because Ludo Rothbury collapsed *in flagrante* from a combination of drink and drugs. Rothbury's father had to come and get him, and paid off Finnegan to keep it quiet. Fortunately for them, none of the other guests knew who Ludo was. Finnegan claimed not to have seen Robina at the party until Scott showed him one of your snapshots of her. Then he wasn't so sure.'

'Did the necklace turn up?' asked Mariner.

'It hasn't, and we've been through all the archive boxes now. Must've been lost along the way. So we've hit a wall.'

'Tell me about it,' said Mariner.

CHAPTER THIRTY-SIX

As soon as the team was assembled on Tuesday morning, Mariner shared Stuart Croghan's findings.

'Gordon Bennett,' said Glover, who had a quaint line in non-blasphemous curses. 'If he's been in a freezer for weeks, we haven't got a hope in hell of solving it.'

'We have to,' said Khatoon. 'What about his wife and child?'

'But where do we start?'

'With the freezer,' said Mariner. Overnight, it was the only way forward he could think of. 'Let's start with the premise that he was stored in it recently. Given that he was still more or less in one piece, it'll have to be a chest freezer. If we can locate that, it might yield up more information.'

'There isn't one at Viktor's house,' said Khatoon. 'Me and Kevin and the SOCOs went all over it.'

'He could have had one and got rid of it,' said Bingley.

'Let's not go there yet,' said Mariner.

'What about the rental properties?'

'Would they have one?' asked Khatoon. 'And it'd be a bit tricky with the tenants, wouldn't it? "Do you mind if I just pop something in your freezer for a few days . . . ?" Shit,' she said, as something came to her. 'When I went to talk to the neighbour, Gwen, her younger daughter said something about Viktor storing roadkill in Gwen's freezer. They were talking about rabbits and the like, but what if it literally was . . . roadkill?'

'That's mental,' said Bingley. 'The family would have noticed, surely.'

'Depends on where the freezer is,' said Mariner. 'If it's in the garage . . .'

'And Gwen is starting to lose touch with things, so it wouldn't have been hard to pull the wool over her eyes,' added Khatoon. 'She trusted Viktor. He did odd jobs for her, and fed the cat when she was away.'

Bingley jumped up from his seat. 'I think Viktor's got a set of her keys,' he said, going to where the boxes of exhibits from the house were stored. After rummaging around for a bit, he held up the keys labelled with a 'G'.

'It wouldn't do any harm to look,' said Mariner. 'At the very least, it's something that can be easily ruled out. And I haven't been to Paszek's house yet. I'd like to get a sense of the place, and him. We'll take those keys with us, just in case.'

Mariner and Khatoon parked in the drive of Viktor's house, before walking around to Gwen's next door. It was one of the first really mild days of spring, the sun flitting between the clouds.

'That looks a bit desperate,' Mariner remarked, seeing the three For Sale signs.

'Yeah, I don't think Viktor was much help with that,' said Khatoon. She pointed at the SUV parked in front of the garage. 'Samantha must be here — one of Gwen's daughters.'

'Is that going to be a problem?' asked Mariner.

'Not necessarily. Of the two, she seemed more sympathetic to Viktor.' Khatoon rang the bell twice, but there was no answer.

Mariner was peering in through the window. 'I can see her,' he said. 'She's in the back garden.'

The layout of Gwen's property was similar to Viktor's, with the detached garage off to the left, but Gwen also had a two-metre-high wooden fence and side gate between that and the house, effectively dividing the front garden from the rear. Mariner lifted the latch and pushed it open, but as he did, a chunk of wood fell off the bottom.

'Hooligan,' said Khatoon.

'I didn't do that.' Squatting down, Mariner saw where the wood had broken away and further planks that were buckled and split.

'That's taken a bit of force,' he said, propping the wayward piece against the fence.

'Gwen probably,' said Khatoon. 'I got the impression she's a bit of a liability in the car.'

Passing through the gate brought them round the side of the house and into a garden that was smaller than Viktor's but still substantial. The lawn was in need of mowing and the plants in the borders had grown tall and rangy, with last year's dead weeds rotting in between. Up by the house, the French windows of the lounge were open on to a sunny terrace, and it was here that they found Samantha, pegging washing on a rotary clothes line.

'Hello again,' said Khatoon. 'Good drying day.'

'I thought I'd make the most of it,' said Samantha. She broke off what she was doing, a damp towel in her hands. 'Lou's taken Mum to a hospital appointment and they'll be out for most of the day. What can I do for you?'

Khatoon introduced Mariner, then said, 'When I was last here, you mentioned something about Viktor storing things in your mum's freezer. We wondered if we could take a quick look.'

'Yes, of course.' Samantha dropped the towel into a laundry basket on the ground. 'It's in the garage. I'll get you the keys. Though I'm not sure what you expect to find.'

'We're just crossing the ts,' said Khatoon.

Samantha was back in moments, handing Khatoon the keys. 'Did you need me to . . . ?'

'No, it's fine, we can manage,' said Khatoon, allowing Samantha to continue her task.

'Nowhere to hide here,' said Mariner, as he opened the door. The garage was scrupulously clean, and lit by a fluorescent tube. A long workbench ran the length of one side, with tools stored in boxes underneath or hanging on wall hooks above. The red Fiat took up the other side, and just past the bonnet was the chest freezer, humming away, its lights blinking at them. Putting on gloves, Mariner lifted the lid. It was about two thirds full of unidentifiable items crusted with ice. Mariner picked up a couple, and the first thing he saw was the brown fur of several rabbits, along with sealed packs of fish, chicken and vegetables. It all looked disappointingly normal.

'Is it worth getting the SOCOs to take a look?' asked Khatoon.

'It'd be tight, but not impossible, to get a body in here,' said Mariner. 'And it wouldn't take too much effort to rearrange stuff after it's been removed, and leave the lid open a fraction to create this build-up of ice. We'll need a warrant though.' But even if Hien had been stored here, it still didn't explain where he had come from, or how he had died.

Disappointed, they returned to the back garden, which was now empty but for the washing line swinging round in the breeze. Samantha had dropped a couple of pegs on the patio, so Mariner bent down to pick them up. Over on this side a tarpaulin had been laid on the flagstones, held down by a dozen or so large pots containing an assortment of plants.

'Pretty, aren't they?' said Khatoon. 'There to distract from the rest of the garden, do we think?'

As Mariner reached down, the wind caught the edge of the tarpaulin, and whipped it back, to reveal a dark stain. 'Either that, or from what's underneath,' he said. 'What do you think of this?'

Khatoon crouched down beside him. 'I don't know. It could just be spilled soil that's been swept away.' She was right; the red-brown clay soil of this area could stain the concrete slabs that colour, if only temporarily. 'But I'm not so sure about this.' Khatoon was digging into the grout between

271

the slabs with a gloved fingernail. She came up with something fibrous that definitely wasn't soil.

Mariner glanced up at the house. The French windows were closed now and Samantha was nowhere in sight. Squatting down, he moved a pot and peeled back the corner of the tarpaulin further.

'Question is,' said Mariner. 'Whose is it and how did it get here?' They both looked up. Wisteria covered the wall of the house, just coming into leaf. Embedded in the foliage was a window, directly above where they stood; a large pane with a smaller top window, which was open.

'Could Hien have fallen from there?' said Khatoon.

'Croghan's estimate was nine floors or more,' said Mariner, raising his voice, as, simultaneously, a plane flew low overhead, and a train rattled by, picking up speed as it headed away from Bromsgrove.

'What about that?' said Khatoon, gesturing down to the track. 'Being hit by a train would cause a lot of damage.'

The French door behind them opened. 'Sorry,' said Samantha. 'I didn't realise you'd finished. Was it any good; the garage?'

'Possibly,' said Mariner. 'Can I ask you about this tarpaulin, though? Do you know who put it down and when?'

Samantha looked at it as if she'd never seen it before. 'I don't know,' she said. 'Perhaps Charles put it down to protect the slabs from soil spillage?'

'Charles?'

'He used to do Mum's garden for her, but he hasn't been here in ages. Why?'

Mariner ignored the question. 'I understand Viktor Paszek would have had access to your mother's house and garden at times?' he said.

'He fed the cat when she was away and checked that everything was all right, that sort of thing.'

'How often is she away?' asked Mariner.

'Quite a lot these days. Since she began to be unwell, she's been staying with me or Lou most weekends.'

'What about the weekend before last?'

'Let me see. Oh, yes, she was staying with us.'

Mariner exchanged a look with Khatoon. 'I'm afraid we're going to need to do a more thorough search of your mother's garden,' he said. 'We have reason to suspect that a serious crime may have been committed here.'

Samantha gaped. 'What are you talking about?' she asked, when she found her voice.

'I'm sorry, that's all I can say,' said Mariner. 'I will arrange for a search warrant, but if you have no objection, we can start right away and will be finished sooner.'

'I don't know. Are you accusing my mother of something?'

'Not at all,' said Mariner.

'I should speak to my sister,' said Samantha.

While she was in the house contacting Louisa, Mariner put a call through to Glover and asked him to expedite the search warrant. He was just ringing off when Samantha appeared again. 'Her phone's off,' she said. 'I suppose because they're in the hospital. You're going to do this anyway, aren't you?'

'We will get a warrant, yes,' said Mariner.

She shrugged. 'Well, you might as well start, then.'

'It'll be quite disruptive,' said Khatoon. 'You may want to think about your mother staying somewhere else tonight.'

'Yes.' She was distracted now. 'I'll go and pack some things for her. How long will it take?'

'It's hard to say,' Mariner told her. 'Perhaps a day or two. But we'll try not to take longer than is absolutely necessary.'

As soon as he and Khatoon were alone again, Mariner called SOCO and arranged for a team of officers to come out immediately. 'So, what about this train?' he asked Khatoon, ending the call.

'Could be nothing,' she said. 'But it occurred to me; maybe we got the exploitation bit right, but not who was doing it,' she said. 'Hien could have been trying to escape from somewhere, got on to the railway track and was hit by a train. It might explain why we haven't found his shoe.'

'How did he get up here, to the terrace?' asked Mariner. 'The impact didn't kill him.'

'And he dragged himself up the garden? If he did, there will be evidence.' It was clutching at straws, but Mariner went along with it for now. The SOCOs would confirm it, but there appeared to be no other disturbance to the garden between the patio and railway track; what's more, the line was separated from the garden by a sturdy steel fence. It was compromised in two places but neither gap was large enough for a human.

While they were looking, there was a shout from up by the house; Carina Woodward and her team had arrived. Mariner briefed them, with a request to focus on the freezer, garage and patio, but to search everywhere else for trace evidence of Hien. 'The big thing to look out for is the missing shoe.'

Woodward was highly competent, and there was nothing more Mariner and Khatoon could do here, except get in the way, so they returned to Granville Lane. Mariner hadn't been long in his office, when there was a knock on the door.

'Hi, boss.'

'Vicky! You're back . . . obviously.'

'I'm fine,' she said, in reply to his expectant look. 'And so is Maisie. She wasn't badly treated and she wanted to go back to school. You don't need to get the kid gloves out.' She came and sat in front of his desk.

'What about Emily?' he asked.

Jesson waggled her head side-to-side in a so-so motion. 'It's going to be a long time before she forgives herself, despite all my reassurances,' she said. 'But she'll get there. I won't need to do much persuading to get her to keep an eye on her sister from now on, that's for sure. Thank you for what you did, boss. If you hadn't spoken to Emily, Maisie might still be out there.'

Mariner demurred. 'It was Emily who had to make the leap of faith. Anyway, it's good to see you. We can use your input.'

'I hear you're close to solving the mystery of Hien,' Jesson said.

'Hm, that might be a tad optimistic. We still haven't identified him. Charlie's been chasing up with Interpol, but with zero outcome so far. But we're due a break. We've put so many man hours and resources into this, and so far with bugger all to show for it; no murder weapon and no motive and still no actual link between Hien and Paszek. I don't think I've ever had such an utterly bewildering case. Nothing we discover has any traction.'

'Kevin says you've got a potential crime scene, though,' said Jesson. 'You really think it's Hien's blood on the slabs?'

'Who knows?'

'The shoe hasn't turned up?'

'Not yet. But if we've got a crime scene, it might not be so crucial now.' Mariner sighed. 'We really need Carina and her team to work their magic.'

* * *

But two days later, the outcomes of the search were far from what anyone had hoped. DNA from the blood and organic matter on the patio was confirmed to match with Hien, but there was nothing found in the house, the garage, or elsewhere in the garden.

'How confident are you?' Mariner asked Woodward, when she came to brief him.

'Close to a hundred per cent that the deceased was not in the house or the garage,' she said. 'The garden is trickier. It's been compromised by the elements and wildlife. Just because we haven't found anything, doesn't mean that there aren't minute traces in there, but it would take weeks to do a detailed forensic search of a garden that size.'

'Yeah, Sharp's not going to sanction that,' said Mariner, struggling to keep the bitter disappointment from his voice.

CHAPTER THIRTY-SEVEN

Disappointment was the sentiment Mariner saw reflected around the room when he reported back at the next briefing, on Thursday afternoon. 'The only thing we do have now is a possible timeframe. According to FSS, the tarp and the cold weather helped to slow any degradation of the samples from the patio. By their estimation the deposits had been there for no more than ten to fourteen days, which gives us the likely scenario that Hien was killed sometime over the weekend before Viktor's accident.'

'It takes Gwen and her daughters out of the frame — if they were ever there,' said Khatoon. 'Gwen was staying at Louisa's for the weekend.'

'And that got me thinking,' said Mariner. 'Have we been blinded by Hien's ethnicity? We may be right about him being an immigrant, and he might have been trafficked here in the first instance — after all, he had Vietnamese currency and cigarettes on him. Our inevitable conclusions were therefore that his death was related to organised crime, and that he was a victim of abuse. But what if it was simpler than that, and Hien was as much perpetrator as victim?'

'How do you mean, boss?' asked Bingley.

'Stuart Croghan offered up two alternatives for cause of death; that Hien had suffered a severe beating, or a catastrophic fall. What we haven't fully considered is a combination of the two.' Mariner pinned up one of the SOCO photographs: a view towards the back of Gwen Franklin's house. 'The strong evidence — heavy bloodstaining and organic matter — was found immediately below this first-floor window, which, we've been told, doesn't shut properly. Think about Hien's physique,' he continued. 'He was slight, wiry — the perfect build for a burglar. We know Gwen was away that weekend.' He pointed to the picture. 'And it would be easy to climb up the wisteria. But it's a narrow window, awkward,' Mariner went on. 'Not easy to get into. Supposing he slipped and fell. A fall from that height wouldn't necessarily be enough to kill him, but he would be incapacitated, even knock himself out.'

'But his injuries?' asked Khatoon.

'We know that Viktor Paszek kept an eye on Gwen's house when she was away,' said Mariner.

'You think he found Hien, on the patio,' said Jesson, warming to this idea.

'Eric told me that Viktor was obsessively protective towards women,' said Bingley. 'He'd be outraged that Hien was trying to get into Gwen's house, especially on his watch.'

'So,' said Mariner. 'Viktor finds Hien, realises what he was up to and loses it. We've been told that he had a temper on him, however rarely it manifested. He'd be driven by anger and fear of what could have happened if Hien had got in while Gwen was at home. Perhaps at this point, Hien even tries to get away, or fights back.'

'There was no blood spatter on the overalls,' Glover pointed out.

'Paszek must have destroyed the clothes he was wearing for the assault,' said Jesson. 'That was spontaneous. But he had the forethought to put on the overalls for the clean-up.'

'So,' said Mariner. 'Paszek beats Hien to a pulp. Perhaps he didn't mean to, perhaps he just got carried away. But now he has to clean up the mess. He brings his car round to Gwen's house, reverses into the gate — which is when it gets damaged. He manhandles Hien into the builders' bag and into the boot of his car.'

'What about the freezer?' asked Khatoon.

'I've checked back on the weather reports,' said Mariner. 'It was cold that weekend with hard, overnight frosts. Stuart Croghan couldn't say how long Hien was frozen, but it could have been only a matter of hours. Say this happened on the Saturday before the RTC. At most Hien is left in the car overnight and during the next day. Then on Sunday night, Paszek goes to Eric's.'

'And parks the car in plain sight?' Glover was sceptical.

'It would have been dark,' Bingley pointed out. 'And Hien was in the builders' bag. I don't think that would be a problem.'

'Paszek wouldn't have wanted to venture out too early to dispose of the body,' said Jesson. 'So, he whiled away a few hours at the factory centre after leaving Eric's.'

'Exactly,' said Mariner. 'If he'd left *home* in the early hours, the neighbours at the end might have noticed. Better to stay in the city, where people moving around at that time of night goes unremarked.'

'Managing that kind of stress could easily precipitate a heart attack, too,' said Jesson.

'And the rest, we know,' said Mariner.

'It makes sense,' said Glover, and the others seemed to agree.

'It's just a shame that it's all conjecture,' said Mariner. 'And we'll never know for sure.'

Which was entirely unsatisfactory. It felt like an anti-climax, and gazing around him, Mariner could see that everyone felt the same as he did. If they were right and Hien was simply one of those who had fallen through the cracks, then their chances of ever identifying him were slipping away.

His phone rang. It was Simon Bell. Mariner left CID to take it.

'Have you heard anything yet?' Bell asked, after the usual greetings.

'I haven't,' said Mariner. 'Is that good news or bad?'

'No idea,' said Bell. 'I'll see what I can find out.'

No hurry, Mariner wanted to say.

When Mariner got home, he was restless and couldn't settle. He'd offered a theory about Hien but it felt plucked from thin air and even to his own ears, hadn't sounded particularly convincing. If he thought hard enough, he could probably come up with half a dozen scenarios, all equally fanciful and unproveable. His mind was elsewhere when he put his beer bottle down on the living-room table — he caught the edge, and it slid out of his grip and tipped over. *Shit!* He snatched it up, but not before some of it had spilled onto the table and spread quickly to the packets of Maggie's photos that he hadn't yet scanned to Reid. Grabbing some kitchen towel, he rescued the wettest, hastily dabbing them dry.

Luckily, only three of the images had been affected, and the damage didn't look too bad. He should send them now, before he forgot. There were thirty-six in all — far too many to bombard Reid with, especially as some of them were duplicates — so he sat down to filter out the extraneous pictures. He wondered now if any of them would be of help. Reid hadn't indicated that anyone from the campsite was under suspicion at all.

The one of Rose and Elued caught his eye, and he studied it again. God, how did Maggie end up with that man, even for a short time? Her feelings for him were evident in the number of pictures in which he featured, but he was rough; a genuine hardcore hippy, right down to the jewellery. Mariner did a double-take. *Men don't wear necklaces.* In some of the pictures, but not all, Elued wore something around his neck: a silver ring on a leather thong.

Mariner pulled out all the photos in which Elued featured. There were fourteen in all. By looking at the people present and what they were wearing, he could group together those snaps taken on the same occasion. He could also apply a crude timeline, thanks to Rose. There were three sets of pictures in which she was absent, and looking at who else was there, he could deduce that they were taken after she and Mariner had left. In one set of these final pictures Elued's neck was bare. Was that significant? He needed to see Lesley's drawing of that necklace.

Mariner picked up his mobile and phoned DCI Reid. The call went to voicemail so he left a message. Then he realised he still had Lesley's number on his phone. He hesitated to call her but as it turned out, she was unfazed, both to hear from him again so soon, and by the request. While he was waiting, he jotted down some bullet points to clarify his thoughts. Elued, thought Mariner. The man who'd offered Mariner a spliff — *'Good karma, man'* — and who Rose had disliked because of his drugs habit. Did he supply as well? Had he sold at the big house, and taken Robina with him? If so, then at the very least he might have been one of the last people to see her alive.

Minutes later, Mariner's phone pinged, an incoming text with an image attached. He compared it with one of the photographs. As far as he could tell, the necklace was the same. Then he called Maggie.

'Those photographs you gave me,' he said. 'Is it possible to know when they were taken, I mean, which exact day?'

'If I can find the negatives.'

'Could you do that for me, please?'

'Not right now, I'm afraid; I'm entertaining. But I'll get on to it in the morning. Just a sec . . .' She broke off to address the other person in the room with her. 'It's Tom, you know, Rose's son. Now,' she said to Mariner, 'my supper's getting cold. Speak soon.'

Disappointed, Mariner paced the room, wondering if he was clinging on to this as compensation for the let-down of Hien. Robina had been seen walking down the field with a scruffy man. Elued certainly ticked that box. But Peter Church was worried about 'Morken' finding out, not Elued or Johannes Visser, Maggie had said. Nothing like it. What was Sinclair's remark, when they listened to the interview? '*I haven't heard dialect like that for donkeys*.' Mariner booted up his laptop. There were several sites devoted to regional dialects, and after a few minutes he found it: not morken but mawkin — Norfolk dialect for scarecrow. '*A bit of a scarecrow*,' was exactly how Maggie had described Elued.

But even if Robina had walked down the field with Elued, how did they both then end up at the big house without being seen? Then, something else dropped into his mind. Elued had offered him a spliff, not unlike those Robina had noticed lying in the bottom of the boat. Christ, he'd even found the mooring posts the other day. He had rowed Robina downstream to the open water of the broad, but the quickest route from the campsite to the big house was upstream, by boat.

Mariner tried Reid's number again, this time asking her to call him back urgently. Meanwhile he summarised his thoughts in an email, adding Maggie's phone number for good measure, and sent it through with the relevant images attached. It would have been good to include the dates when they were taken, but he could forward those tomorrow after Maggie's . . . Mariner's stomach dropped. When he'd seen Maggie on Sunday, she'd told him Elued was coming to stay. And this evening she had company. Holy shit, it must be him. They must have talked about Robina. Would Maggie tell Elued why Mariner had called, and that he was police? If she did, how long before Elued put two and two together? If he did that, Maggie could be in danger. He had to get over there.

Jumping in his car, Mariner set off at speed, dialling Maggie's number as he went. It rang on ominously, with no response. But as he drove, he started to talk himself down. The evidence he'd come up with against Elued was only circumstantial, and insubstantial at that. The man may have been a pretentious git, but that in itself wasn't illegal. Mariner had a sudden comedic vision of bursting in on a stunned Maggie and innocent Elued, and having to justify himself. Was he about to make a big mistake? For a moment, he considered turning back, but was nearly halfway there now, and it would do no harm. Maggie had invited him to meet Elued again, so he could just say that he'd changed his mind.

He made good time, until three-way roadworks just outside the village brought him to a halt. As he waited, the white, illuminated bulk of an A380 Airbus lumbered across the night sky, perilously low, the landing gear unfolding as it made its approach to Birmingham Airport. Nothing else moved. No other cars came through the lights, and if he'd been in a service vehicle, he'd have whacked on the blues and twos and taken his chance. In fact . . . He signalled to pull out, but then, out of nowhere, a red Golf came racing at him from the other direction. Just as well he'd stayed put. Finally, *finally*, the lights turned green.

* * *

The front door of Maggie's cottage was wide open. As he approached, Mariner heard a whimper from inside.

'Maggie?'

She was lying on the rug in the living room, her eyes closed, angry bruises already breaking out across her left cheek and eye. Calling an ambulance, Mariner knelt down beside her. 'Maggie?'

She opened her eyes.

'What has he done to you?'

'I'll live,' she said, with a wan smile. 'But I won't get up, if it's all the same to you.'

'What happened?'

'I was reminding him about you, and he flipped,' she sobbed. 'I don't know why. I thought he'd like to know about you.'

Shit.

'Why did he hurt me?'

'Where did he go?' asked Mariner.

'To the airport, I suppose. His flight isn't until the morning, but he just left. His car wouldn't start, though, I heard it. He only left a couple of minutes ago.'

'Christ, he must have passed me at the lights — the red Golf?'

'That's him. But why—?'

'I think he killed Robina.' Perhaps she'd worked it out herself by now.

'Go,' she said. 'Catch the bastard. I'll be all right.'

'The paramedics will be here soon.'

Hoping he was doing the right thing in leaving her, Mariner ran back to his car and hurtled away, phoning Warwickshire and then the airport police as he went and abandoning efforts to secure his seatbelt. Elued had to be stopped, but until they could get there, he had the best chance. This time the lights at the roadworks were on green, so he sailed through, but even so, he was astonished when, minutes later, he came up behind the red Golf.

On the narrow, gently winding country road, Elued was going dangerously fast, and put on an extra burst of speed as Mariner came up behind him, forcing him to accelerate too. In tandem, they veered into the oncoming carriageway, and back towards the verge, round one bend, then another. Amid the stress, an idea randomly pinged into Mariner's head and he couldn't believe he hadn't thought of it before. Taking his eyes off the road for a second, he speed-dialled Vicky Jesson. She didn't answer so he left a message: 'Can you get away? Meet me at the airport. This'll sound crazy, but I think Hien—'

Then on the edge of his vision, crimson brake lights flared. Mariner slammed on his brakes but it was too late, and as Elued's car went into a spin, Mariner smashed into the nearside wing and ricocheted up the bank, too fast, hurtling towards a massive tree. The airbag deployed, stunning him, and the world beyond the window turned over. Something huge rocketed towards him and he blacked out.

* * *

A fox came by, enticed by the smells of churned-up soil and shattered vegetation. Drawing nearer, it smelled the strong, unnatural odour of fuel, and beneath it, another, human scent. It stopped to watch, and waited, but nothing stirred.

* * *

Mariner forced his stinging eyes open a fraction, but could see only dark, fuzzy forms. Cold soil and grass pressed into his face, and he tasted blood, earth and grit. He gasped for breath, unbearable pain slicing through his chest with each wheeze, and warm liquid bubbled in his throat. When he tried to move an agonising pain seared through him, and every part of him felt pressed into the ground. The low pounding in his ears, kept time with the tick-tick-tick of cooling metal. Then the throbbing began to slow, and the beats got out of sync; slower, and slower. Closing his eyes, he let the darkness claim him.

CHAPTER THIRTY-EIGHT

Vicky Jesson strode into Birmingham Airport, face grim as she tried to concentrate on the here and now. Superintendent Sharp had called her first thing with the awful news and she was still in a state of shock; they all were.

'Is this a wild-goose chase, boss?' Kevin Bingley was trying to keep pace at her side.

'I don't know,' said Jesson. 'But it's all we've got, and we owe it to him to try.'

It was only later that she'd found the voicemail from him: *'Can you get away? Meet me at the airport. This'll sound crazy, but I think Hien—'* The impact of the collision must have cut him off. The thought made her feel sick. To begin with, she didn't know what the message meant. What was he about to say, and why the airport?

It only made sense when she got the call from Stuart Croghan. He'd finally identified the residue on Hien's clothing, the substance that had caused the skin reaction. 'It's a mineral hydraulic fluid,' he said. 'Commonly used in aircraft landing gears.'

'Shit,' she said. 'Hien was a stowaway.'

'He fucking was,' said Croghan, his professionalism slipping for once. 'Falling from a plane, even one making its approach, would be absolutely consistent with his injuries. And at altitude his body would have frozen.'

'It's why we couldn't find a link between him and Viktor Paszek,' said Jesson. 'There isn't one.'

She'd heard of stowaways dropping out of the sky. It was rare, but it happened. Stowing away in a landing gear was almost always fatal, and yet there were people desperate enough to try it. But could they prove the theory? And more importantly, would finding the aircraft get them any closer to Hien's real identity? As she and Bingley approached the low building from which the ground crew operated, Jesson steeled herself. She didn't know if they were about to be laughed off the site. But when she put her questions to the manager on duty, she didn't find it funny.

'Have you ever had experience of them here?' asked Jesson.

'We haven't ever found any stowaways, if that's what you mean. But you hear about bodies, or the remains of them being found in the landing gear. It's rare, but very occasionally our ground crews find indications that someone could have been in there.'

'Like what?' asked Bingley.

'Crushed drinks cans or bottles, the remains of foodstuffs that have got wedged in or just smeared on the metal work. It's more likely that it's just what the plane's picked up from the runway, though we found a sleeping bag once, rolled up and wedged into a gap in the housing.'

'Do you know if there's been anything like that found recently?' asked Jesson, her hopes falling through the floor.

'No one's reported anything to me, but let me go and ask around.' She left them sitting in the warm office, with two cups of tepid water in plastic cups. The clock ticked round ten minutes, then fifteen, twenty.

'You might have been right about the wild-goose chase,' said Jesson.

'Do you think she's been called away to something else?' Bingley conjectured. 'Forgotten we're here?'

'We'll give her half an hour. Then we'll . . .'

The door opened and the manager reappeared, followed by a young man dressed in ground-crew overalls.

'Sorry to keep you waiting,' the manager said. 'You're in luck. This is Amrit. He collects things.'

And in Amrit's right hand was a misshapen object made of black leather, with a white sole. Jesson wanted to kiss him.

* * *

'I can't believe it,' said Bingley, for about the tenth time, as they drove back along the M42.

'Me neither,' said Jesson, though she couldn't quite match his enthusiasm. It was beyond belief that Hien's shoe had been found squashed into the undercarriage of a flight diverted from Heathrow due to fog. They even had the number of the flight from Ho Chi Minh City. Though it wouldn't be easy, their chances of identifying Hien had increased considerably. But any elation she'd felt had quickly turned to wretchedness, when she'd remembered that one person who should know about this couldn't be told.

Her phone rang. It was Charlie Glover, sounding excited. 'Louisa Douglas has come in,' he said. 'There's something she wants to get off her chest.'

'We're on our way,' said Jesson. It was time to reward all Glover's hard work, she thought. She would observe, while he and Khatoon took the interview. As it turned out, they had little to do.

* * *

Louisa Douglas was jittery in the interview room. She repeatedly moved around her mug of coffee, but didn't drink.

'Since we found out what was — sorry *who* was — on the patio, I've been wrestling with whether I should come and tell you, or not,' she said, her eyes flicking between Khatoon and Glover. 'Then when you showed me the picture — that young man with his family . . . I can't bear it anymore. Out there is a woman who has no idea what has happened to her husband, and a boy who will grow up not knowing why his father isn't around. What we did might have prevented them from ever finding out. I keep thinking how I would feel if it was one of my sons.'

'We?' said Khatoon.

'Viktor and me. At least if you know everything there is to know, maybe there's some slim chance of identifying him.'

Glover and Khatoon exchanged a glance.

'What is there to know?' asked Khatoon.

Louisa cleared her throat and took a sip of water. 'On the Sunday before Viktor died, we had people coming to view Mum's house,' she began. 'We were getting desperate. Two sales have fallen through already and now they're building that eyesore of an estate down the way. There'd been no interest in Mum's house for months, then eventually this couple came to see it — a doctor and his wife and children moving up here. We knew they were looking at other properties too, so we bent over backwards to try to accommodate them. We'd arranged a second informal viewing specially on that Sunday, because it was more convenient to them. They were going to take the kids to Cadbury World afterwards and make a day of it.' She picked up the coffee mug, then put it down again. 'Mum went to stay with Samantha, so I came over that morning just to tidy up a bit. I thought the patio would look better if I swept some of the leaves and debris off it.' She was trying hard to make it all sound routine. 'Then when I came outside, I saw it: this mangled body, lying there, in a pool of blood.' Her voice dropped to a whisper and she screwed up her face against the memory. 'I just screamed. It was horrible and I couldn't understand how on earth it had got here. It crossed my mind that Viktor could be responsible, some kind of ploy to deter potential buyers so that Mum would stay, but then I realised how absurd that would be, even for him.

'Anyway, Viktor must have been in his garden too, and heard me. He came rushing round because he thought something had happened to Mum, so then he saw it. I was panicking. Our buyers were due in less than an hour. They were driving up from Bristol so it was too late to put them off, and now they'd arrive to find the emergency services and this dreadful thing on the patio. How could it do anything but put them off? I mean, there was obviously nothing we could do for the poor man.' She looked up at Khatoon and Glover, perhaps seeking reassurance. They each remained impassive, inviting her to continue.

'For once, I was so glad to see Viktor. He said he thought the man could have fallen from a plane. I didn't even know that could happen. He told me to go back in the house and keep watch for the buyers, and that he would take care of it. He completely understood why I just had to make it go away. Perhaps with what his family went through before coming to this country, you're more pragmatic. You learn to deal with crises and steer clear of the authorities as much as possible.'

'What happened next?' prompted Khatoon.

'Viktor had his faults but he was a very capable man, so I left him to it and got ready for the viewing,' said Louisa. 'I could hear noises outside; at one point I heard the pots being moved about, and he brought his car round. I think he hit the fence. By the time our buyers turned up, he'd gone. I was dreading them wanting to come into the garden, but when we got out there, it looked as if nothing had happened. Viktor had moved the body and put down a ground-sheet thing to cover the worst of the mess. He'd arranged the pots to make it look as if someone had been working there.

'Afterwards, I thought I should go and see if he was all right. He seemed shaken, and he didn't look well, but he'd worked out what he would do with the body. He said it'd be best to drop it onto the hard shoulder of the motorway, in the early hours, before daybreak, so that when it got light it would be seen and someone would take care of it. They might guess at what had really happened, or they might think he'd been hit by a truck. Either way it would be treated as an accident, which is what it was, and someone would try to trace the poor man's family and see that he got a proper burial. All we'd done was delay things. He made it sound so reasonable. He told me that the man was only wearing one shoe, and that if I found the other, I should throw it away, somewhere it couldn't be found. When you came round to tell me that Viktor was dead, I was scared, so I panicked. Then after that it seemed too late. Owning up later would only make things worse. And I reasoned that the outcome for the man would be the same.' She'd kept it together until now but finally her voice cracked and she began to weep.

'And what about Viktor?' asked Glover. 'What about his reputation? What about the hours we've spent on trying to work out what happened here?'

'I know, and I'm so sorry.' She broke down, sobbing.

* * *

Superintendent Davina Sharp was in the cafeteria of the Queen Elizabeth hospital, and she was on edge. She'd never liked hospitals, but then, who did? And today she was here for one of the worst reasons. She was thinking about Tom Mariner, how much she would miss him, and the gaping hole he would leave behind in the station and in the city. They had worked together for more than ten years and in that time, she had come to rely on him as a colleague and a friend.

'Superintendent Sharp?' A voice at her shoulder made her turn. At first she couldn't place the face.

'Ginny Reid,' Reid reminded her.

'Oh, I'm so sorry.'

'Don't be,' said Reid. 'We only met once, and in these circumstances . . .'

They'd met only once but they had spoken again, when Reid had contacted Sharp, yesterday. She had been trying to reach Tom Mariner. *'He sent me some superb new evidence, but I haven't been able to get hold of him since.'* Reid had hardly known Mariner, but still, there was a stunned silence at the other end of the phone when Sharp had broken the news.

'You're here to see Johannes Visser?' said Sharp, now.

'Yes. He'll be brought over to Norfolk when he's well enough, but I wanted to talk to him sooner. It's a gross injustice that he should have got off so lightly, when . . .'

'It is,' said Sharp. 'And he's definitely your man?'

'Thanks to Tom joining up the dots for us, I think we'll have enough evidence to charge him. Tom's friend Maggie is really smart. She realised that she still had an old shirt belonging to Visser. She'd kept it for sentimental reasons. He wore it a lot that summer and we're hoping that fibres from it will match with those found on Robina Scanlon's dress. Plus we have a fingerprint from a bangle Robina was wearing. We have high hopes for that.'

'And his motive?'

Reid scoffed. 'Nothing original about that. Maggie was also able to give us a date of birth for Visser, so once we had that we could contact colleagues in the Netherlands. Maggie thought a drug deal gone wrong had forced his escape to England, but he was, in fact, wanted by the police in connection with a number of sexual assaults on young women, some of them very young. By the time he wanted to get back into the country, he'd acquired a passport under his assumed name.'

'Sexual assault to murder then.'

'Not uncommon, is it? And knowing what I do about Robina, I think she'd have put up a fight, which might have been what tipped him over the edge, but we may never know.'

'I'm glad you've caught him. And I hope you make it stick. I wish you well.'

'And you too,' said Reid.

* * *

Sharp finally got the summons and made her way up to the critical care ward. There wasn't much to see of Tom Mariner beneath all the tubes, wires and dressings. The first time she'd met him he was in a hospital bed. He'd been in much better shape on that occasion.

'We've put him into an induced coma,' the consultant told her, coming to stand at her side. 'He's had a bleed on the brain, and has a punctured lung and multiple other serious injuries. It will be a few days until we know if he's out of danger and then, if all goes well, it will be a long, slow recovery process.'

* * *

A little later, Sharp was sitting at her desk gazing absently at her computer screen when Vicky Jesson knocked tentatively on the open door.

'Sorry, guv, am I interrupting?'

'Not at all,' said Sharp, with a sigh. 'Come in. Sit. I finished reading ages ago, and now all the unwanted thoughts are crowding in.'

'I know just what you mean,' said Jesson. 'What were you reading?'

'The IPOC's report on Dean Clifford.'

'Oh. Can I ask?'

'It exonerates Tom of any blame,' said Sharp. 'I never doubted that it would. All we need now is for him to pull through.'

THE END

ALSO BY CHRIS COLLETT

DI MARINER SERIES
Book 1: DEADLY LIES
Book 2: INNOCENT LIES
Book 3: KILLER LIES
Book 4: BABY LIES
Book 5: MARRIED LIES
Book 6: BURIED LIES
Book 7: MISSING LIES
Book 8: DARKEST LIES
Book 9: MIDNIGHT LIES

STANDALONE
THE TRUTH ABOUT MURDER

Thank you for reading this book.

If you enjoyed it please leave feedback on Amazon or Goodreads, and if there is anything we missed or you have a question about, then please get in touch. We appreciate you choosing our book.

Founded in 2014 in Shoreditch, London, we at Joffe Books pride ourselves on our history of innovative publishing. We were thrilled to be shortlisted for Independent Publisher of the Year at the British Book Awards.

www.joffebooks.com

We're very grateful to eagle-eyed readers who take the time to contact us. Please send any errors you find to corrections@joffebooks.com. We'll get them fixed ASAP.

www.ingramcontent.com/pod-product-compliance
Lightning Source LLC
Chambersburg PA
CBHW020301200626
46814CB00006BA/2023